Praise for Jon Gingerich's

The Appetite Factory

"*The Appetite Factory* is a brilliant satire that draws a bulls-eye on multiple targets—mindless consumption, outrage culture, corporate dystopia, the post-truth era—and then hits each one with deadly accuracy. The fact that it's so well-written on top of that elevates it to must-read status."

—Rob Hart,

author of *The Paradox Hotel*

"Cautionary tale? Satire? An unflinching look at the ways we manipulate each other? All of the above. If Chuck Palahniuk and Irvine Welsh had a baby—after watching *Mad Men*, *Swallow*, and *Secretary*—it might look something like this."

—Richard Thomas,

author of *Spontaneous Human Combustion*

"*The Appetite Factory* lays bare the cynicism of modern media damage control, where any disaster can be spun to someone's advantage, and Jon Gingerich does it all with scalpel-sharp prose and searing wit."

—Craig Clevenger,

author of *The Contortionist's Handbook*

THE APPETITE FACTORY

THE
APPETITE
FACTORY

A NOVEL

JON GINGERICH

KEYLIGHT
BOOKS
AN IMPRINT
OF TURNER
PUBLISHING

KEYLIGHT BOOKS
AN IMPRINT OF TURNER PUBLISHING COMPANY
Nashville, Tennessee
www.turnerpublishing.com

The Appetite Factory

Cover design by William Ruoto
Text design by William Ruoto

Library of Congress Cataloging-in-Publication Data
Names: Gingerich, Jon, author.
Title: The appetite factory / by Jon Gingerich.
Description: Nashville, Tennessee : Keylight Books, [2022]
Identifiers: LCCN 2021049435 (print) | LCCN 2021049436 (ebook) |
   ISBN 9781684428694 (hardcover) | ISBN 9781684428700 (paperback) |
   ISBN 9781684428717 (ebook)
Subjects: LCGFT: Novels.
Classification: LCC PS3607.I4575 A88 2022 (print) | LCC PS3607.I4575 (ebook) |
   DDC 813/.6—dc23
LC record available at https://lccn.loc.gov/2021049435
LC ebook record available at https://lccn.loc.gov/2021049436

Printed in the United States of America

FOR LISA
FOR AUDREY

"When the average citizen hears the phrase 'press agent,' his mind flies at once to the drama. He pictures to himself that mendacious and amusing individual, the only man in the world proud of being called a liar."

Will Irwin

"The Press Agent, His Rise and Decline"

Collier's

Vol. XLVIII, Dec. 2, 1911

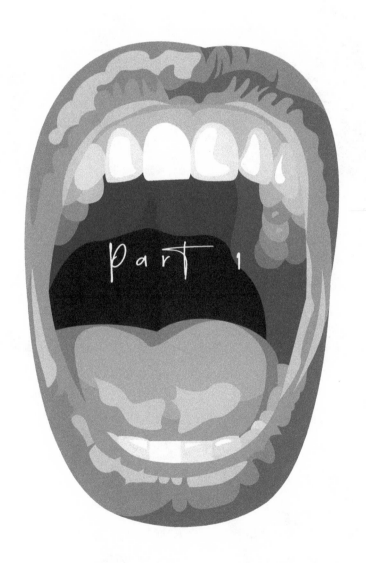

Part 1

Chapter 1

L eonard waited for the man to say something. It was easier to gauge the
dynamics that way, to let them talk it out. Sometimes they argued,
sometimes they cried. They'd go on about their careers or their kids or the
money they'd lost, how they'd contemplated suicide, attended rehab, found
God. Every job was different, and every job was the same.

"So, how do you feel?"

His client sat fidgeting in his bathrobe. He was several days unshaven,
and his face looked ruddy in the sour light, like a microwaved hot dog. Leonard recognized the movements, the wringing hands, the restive eyes. Animal distress, mechanical failure. Stricken with some newfound realization,
as though the ground was dipping beneath his feet. It was an unfortunate
requirement of his work that he saw people at their worst. His best guess
as to why he possessed a gift for fixing their problems was he recognized a
latent truth in them, that maybe, given enough money and opportunity,
we'd all eventually become what we hate.

"You had a rough night," Leonard said.

The hotel room was spare and sanitized, walls and textiles assigned muted
colors: taupe, sage, and slate. There was a low purling in the ducts and hints of
disinfectant in the air, laboratory interpretations of vanilla. A band of sunlight
crossed the floor from the window, motes of dust winnowing away from the sill.

"Are you sorry for what you did?"

His client pitched forward and barked a spume of bile into the gap between the bed and wall, pawed at the covers, and gasped for air as an ace-
tone stink of spirits filled the room.

"I don't know," the man said. "Why do I have to apologize?"

"Because that's how this works."

"But I'm not sorry. An apology wouldn't be real."

"Nobody likes reality," Leonard said. "That's why we tell stories."

Leonard crossed the room to open the window. He palmed the glass, shielding his eyes from the skyline's opalescent glow as he watched the street's swelling crowds. To the south a range of buildings poked through a yellow brume of fog. Beyond it pillars of smoke rose from jetties of Hudson shoreline.

"This wouldn't have been a big deal a couple years ago."

"We're more connected now. The whole thing was on video. It's trending online, on the social media network you created."

"That doesn't make what I did any worse."

"You assaulted a competitor in a bar," Leonard said. "You dropped your pants and tried to urinate on him. You referred to him with a homophobic epithet."

"Cocksucker is an epithet now? It's still a free country."

"That isn't the issue. You're a brand. If we don't push back against what they're saying, the public will resurrect this incident anytime your name is mentioned for the rest of your life."

"It just feels phony." The man stood and staggered to the bathroom.

The thing about drunks, they were already crisis experts in their own way. They'd been selling different versions of themselves to family and co-workers for years, and they were resistant to change because they believed their own fictions. Leonard noticed subtle incongruities in the room now, stray details that disrupted the four-star narrative. A dime-sized chip of particleboard was missing from a corner of the dresser. A framed print to the left of the television hung conspicuously lower than a print to the right. The wall clock's minute hand didn't line up with the dial markings.

"I won't deny there's a performance element," Leonard said as the man knelt on the tile and hugged the toilet. "We're a sentimental species. The only thing we like more than watching public figures self-immolate is a redemption narrative. That's why most people in my position advise the traditional route: own up to what you did so you can stir their sympathies. So, we send out these canned, corny statements acknowledging your new-found self-awareness in the hopes you'll get off the media's radar as quickly as possible. It's shortsighted. It fails to recognize the opportunity events like this present."

The man stifled a laugh as he returned to the bed. "What opportunity?"

"You keep a low profile. You never talk to the press."

"I'm a computer programmer, not a celebrity."

"You basically created social media. You should put yourself out there, own your authority. Facts and rumors are treated the same online, but we can use that to our advantage."

"I don't follow."

"You're launching a new software company."

"This summer. So, yeah, last night comes at a bad time."

"I want your team to dovetail the launch announcement with the apology statement we discussed over the phone."

"I can't. We're in beta. It's months away."

"The blogs have been speculating on it for a year. Push it forward. In the meantime, I want you to change your clothes. Start wearing jeans, don't shave."

"I see where this is going," the man said. "The populist image—"

"The founder of a cutting-edge software company gets into bar fights. It's Steve McQueen with a laptop. Just the image your industry needs."

"Why do you think it'll work?"

"Because people can't process new information without leaning on their prejudices. So, if you want to build a better brand, leverage the prejudice."

"And you make a living coming up with this stuff?"

"That and counseling adults who don't understand what constitutes good behavior."

The client consulted a muted television: B-roll footage of mobs at some cow-country political rally. A chyron on the bottom of the screen reported that Senator Barack Obama had been projected winner of the North Carolina primary. Leonard took further inventory of the room. A sweating rocks glass on the nightstand beside an empty pint of vodka. A scattering of pocket change and wadded receipts. A cellphone, and next to it a tear-shaped bottle of men's body soap. Leonard waited a beat and slipped the soap into his pocket.

"I'll be honest, I don't even want to go back home," the man said, eyes still on the screen. "You wouldn't believe the culture there nowadays. Fifty-year-old men riding longboards to work. Millionaire housewives who discovered the internet and refuse to vaccinate their kids." He paused, and his face seemed to darken. "People ask why I sold my shares last year, and I always say something about value propositions or slowdowns in social media ad spends, but I just wanted out. I swear, if they open that dog-yoga studio down the street from my apartment, I'm going to throw myself onto the CalTrain tracks."

"That sounds extreme," Leonard said.

"The life I had is over. This new venture, I don't know—"

"Please. You should hear some of my other clients' problems. You're young. Things are bad now, but they'll get better. You have to think positively."

Of all the prescripts Leonard brought to these sessions, only the last one was a lie. Optimism was the worst impulse a person could indulge. The doubts we entertain when we're alone, the anxieties that visit us in the small hours, those are the meditations worth holding on to. No matter how good things looked now, life always regressed to the mean.

"People externalize themselves in brands," Leonard said. "It doesn't matter if it's a beer or a sports team, they consign their identities to an artifact that will achieve greater fame and success than they can hope for. It's eternal life in a can."

"So what?"

"So, if you forge a strong enough bond with people, you can get away with anything. They won't criticize something they believe in, because that means they'd have to be critical of themselves. And that won't happen."

"Look," the man said. "I make software. These theories don't mean anything to me."

"I'm telling you. As long as you can avoid challenging their worldviews, as long as you can make them believe they're being represented in the marketplace, as long as you can feed their narcissistic obsessions enough to distract them from their shortcomings, the bullshit gets to walk."

The man kept his eyes to the floor. "Why?"

"Because all we're doing is tapping into their irrational behavior."

Leonard gathered his things, opened the door, and stood with a foot in the hallway peering into a roaring atrium, the descending spiral of floors to a panopticon lobby twenty-four stories below. He gripped the railing for a moment, considered the dizzying distance to the ground, spinning tourbillons of light that refracted from a bay of revolving glass doors and cast prismatic pinwheels along the lobby floors.

"What's the matter?"

"Old coworker of mine. Killed himself six months ago," Leonard said. "I just realized this was the hotel. He jumped off one of these ledges."

"Jesus. I'll take it as an omen. Meeting adjourned?"

"A crisis is like a wildfire," Leonard said. "You have, conservatively, five hours to get this story contained. If your apology isn't circulating on the news this evening, the public will take your silence as an admission of guilt. I'll have a press release ready within an hour. I want you to get a launch announcement prepared by the time I start booking satellite interviews this afternoon."

"Fine, whatever."

"There's a silver lining to this," Leonard said. "We learn more about ourselves in a crisis than any other situation. You find out what you're made of. In the meantime, lie low. Focus on the message, practice reading our prepared statement aloud. Don't get upset if someone asks what happened."

"I don't care what people think about me."

"Everybody says that. You're supposed to say that. It's not true," Leonard said. "It sounds strange, but the public is poised to love you. They hate you only when you begin reminding them of themselves."

"Anything else?"

"You drink too much," Leonard said. "Maybe take it easy."

LEONARD WALKED AGAINST THE CROWD. HIS FACE APPEARED MOST HON-est in the daylight, pale and porous like a lemon peel. He had a downturned mouth that sank into his chin with a permafrown, alert eyes that huddled close together, dull green, the color of tempered glass. His spine canted slightly, burdened under some obscure weight, a dogged nervousness in his gait, a look of repressed irritation as he negotiated his way up the swarming stretch of sidewalk, shoulders pitched forward, a mustache of sweat on his upper lip. It was an unseasonably warm spring morning, the first day that truly felt like summer, the air torrid and the avenue blanched with light, glass towers reflecting panels of unblemished sky. As the subway sent trem-ors through the pavement, he concentrated on the farrago of smells—vendor food, asphalt heat, piss—while his fellow commuters marched in various states of harmony and disarray up the conveyor belt of the concourse, a Whac-A-Mole of interlocking heads and shoulders filing into the revolv-ing glass mouths of buildings or wandering into the vexations of traffic. They avoided each other's eyes, appeared time-wary yet oblivious, wound on some mystery automation as though they were chasing after something just out of reach and trying to get away from it at the same time.

Just south of Fortieth, he entered a tired-looking building faced with windows that wept rust. A warren of delis and travel agencies, arterial, neon-lit passageways advertising locksmiths and massage parlors knotted around its perimeter. Leonard took the elevator, disembarked on the sixth floor, and entered the offices of Gurney Public Relations. The foyer smelled of dust and heated rubber, like the inside of a vacuum bag, walls yellowed and pocked with liver spots of mold and volutes of peeling paint, the heavily trafficked carpets, once maroon, now faded dull cerise. He grabbed a newspaper from the waiting area, nodded to a yawning receptionist, and entered an encampment of cream-colored cubicles that buzzed with keyboards and the cricket drone of phones. He reached the aisle along the back wall, passed the Travel and Hospitality division, Health and Wellness, Investor Relations. Silhouettes of Gurney lifers twisted behind the blinds of their respective offices: Ron Viola, Managing Director, Financial Communications, a garden-variety drunk for whom no company party was official until he broke down over his eternally failing marriage; Karen Clinkenbeard, Deputy Head, Technology, who insisted on printing every email she sent and received, erecting a paper fortress that encircled her desk; Bonnie Yoon, Practice Leader, Food and Nutrition, who crushed ephedrine hydrochloride tablets into her Diet Coke and rattled in her seat like a combine operator. After the photocopy machines stood the double oak doors to the office formerly belonging to Gibby Goodfriend, Senior Vice President and Chief Financial Officer, still vacant since his suicide. Then it was home, identified by the metal-rimmed nameplate: "Leonard Lundell, Managing Director, Crisis Communications."

The team was waiting inside: Todd Shillenburg, Todd Armitage, Todd Colton. Stiff, streamlined-looking men in identical slim-fit charcoal. Leonard's office was a stark contrast to the rumpus outside, the cherry bookshelves that lined the walls harboring Pantone scales of swaybacked industry journals and cloth-bound textbooks that gave off loamy, cellar smells. He acknowledged the men with a tired smile and settled behind his desk.

"All right," Leonard said. "Let's make the donuts."

For the next several hours, they worked on accounts. They made lists and lists of lists, devised slogans and strategies, identified data sets of cooperative behaviors. *Crisis:* A recent oil spill in the Gulf had caused a precipitous drop in foreign and domestic travel visits to a luxury resort in Florida. *Strategy:* Offer a special, inclusive vacation package—prospective title: "EcoCation"—wherein families can pay to be admitted to disaster areas to help clean up the spill. Pitch earned media spots in progressive markets such as *Mother Jones, Harper's,* and National Public Radio. *Crisis:* A beverage company expressed concerns over an upcoming article in a scientific journal regarding small levels of arsenic that had reportedly been found in apple juice. *Strategy:* Hire a research firm and publish a white paper detailing similar levels of arsenic found in rice, suggesting the chemical element, when ingested in small quantities, is safe. *Crisis:* A cosmetics brand, in a bid to connect with the Black American market, was accused of racism after it hired an advertising agency to manage a campaign in consumer magazines for its newest line of blemish concealer. The ad's caption, posted above a photo of a female model, read: "Unlike the man in your life, this actually works!" *Strategy:* Apologize. Invite prospective customers to visit the company website for complimentary haircare products.

THEY TOOK A BREAK SOMETIME THAT AFTERNOON. AN ASSISTANT DRIFTED into the office with coffee and bottled water as the team mulled over press releases overflowing with aggressively cheery marketing superlatives. Leonard turned on the television affixed to the wall and jogged through channels. A study found people who consume large amounts of margarine enjoy amusement parks. Click. A network news special recapped George Clooney's thoughts on child poverty. Groans, eye-rolling incredulity. A team of scientists had discovered a new way to make crispbread. On C-SPAN, crowds had convened on the National Mall in Washington, D.C. to protest the war in Iraq.

Leonard continued scanning channels as Todd Armitage read aloud a newswire release that had drifted out of the fax machine. "Our mission is to leverage impactful communications strategies that deliver game-changing solutions," he said. "Our team of information pollinators . . . information pollinators," he repeated, "offers a vertical acuity to bridge the gap between globally evolving brands and today's content curators."

"Content curators. Jesus," Todd Colton said.

"That last strategy is a loser's game," Todd Shillenburg said. "The client needs a media relations campaign, not a bunch of pissed-off moms."

"People love to be outraged," Todd Armitage said. "Pretending to be offended gives them an excuse to be self-righteous."

"Put it back on the news," Todd Colton said. "I want to hear about the protest."

"Those assholes aren't accomplishing anything," Todd Shillenburg said.

"Of course you would say that," Todd Armitage said. "At this point, your observations are a symposium on yourself."

"Standing in a park and shouting slogans at passersby who don't have any say in stopping the war is a narcissist's idea of dialogue," Todd Shillenburg said. "It's a performative stance against a problem they know they'll never be called on to actually fix."

It was the same thing every day. They talked and talked and talked, as though it relieved a welling pressure inside them, found gladiatorial entertainment providing color commentary against coworkers, clients, competitors, and, above all, the television, their animus a crude emotional reward for leading tractable, workaday lives. Leonard flipped open his cellphone and noticed he'd missed a call from his mother. He deleted her voicemail, stuck a ballpoint pen in his mouth, and looked over an earnings report riddled with industry koans. Zoning out, he considered his body for a moment. His stomach knotted with hunger. There was a twitch in his right eyelid, a slight pinch in his cervical spine. He consulted his reflexes, crossed his legs. Everything seemed to be in working order.

"Scuttlebutt has it Griffin Cruz is getting Goodfriend's Senior VP slot," Todd Colton said.

"The guy's a creep," Todd Armitage said. "Goldbricked every account he's had."

"Elephant in the room," Todd Colton said. "Leonard should be moving into Goodfriend's office. That's some bullshit, Leonard."

"Goodfriend, poor bastard," Todd Shillenburg said. "Should've known he was cashing in his chips once he started giving away his coffee mugs."

"I heard his wife is suing his doctor for putting him on those meds," Todd Armitage said.

"Sue the agency. They're the ones who worked him to death," Todd Colton said.

The television now captured the Illinois senator in a candid moment, eyes squinting in the sunlight, a high, unburdened smile as a headline anchored on the bottom of the screen read "Obama Wins North Carolina."

"How about this?" Leonard said.

"He'll never win," Todd Colton said.

The team left, and Leonard closed the door. He found a can of air freshener and hosed down the chairs, retrieved a handheld vacuum from his closet and voided the area of its human crumbs, discarded hairs and castaway threads and dermal detritus, before returning to his desk. Tobacco sunlight slanted through the window as he made a half attempt to organize piles of paperwork, brochures modeling condominiums he'd been researching for his mother. Then he reached into his pocket and removed the bottle of soap he'd lifted from the hotel that morning. He thumbed open the cap, held its plastic nipple under his nose, and drew in a warm profile. Citrus notes, bridle leather, the first breath of spring.

Sometimes he imagined what he'd say if they found out, if he was ever called to explain. The first taste made his tongue curl and resulted in a gag, because even after years of experience he couldn't help it; no one could. As he continued draining the syrup into his mouth, bitter proofs began to rile his senses, tasked his palate with sour plastics, distant flavors of dried apricot and aged wood. By the second taste he was used to it, and then a strange and evocative warmth arrived, as though someone had told him a secret. He tilted his head back and drank the entire bottle this way, and there was an exhilarating rush, a roaring in his ears as he was plunged under impossible waves, drunk and helpless but safe somehow, cradled in great arms at a time before he'd been apprised of the world's disappointments. He gagged again and grasped for water, which he threw down before surrendering in a grind of coughing and keening, as a single iridescent bubble that had traveled up from his gullet emerged at the gate of his mouth and popped on his bottom lip.

When he recovered, he found himself on the floor, licking a leg of his desk. He made his way back to the chair like this, combing through an archive of wood oil and aged newspapers and dust, before he transitioned to base pleasures and began gnawing at the colony of pencils stationed in a ceramic coffee mug, licked and bit them, emancipating a sawdust mesquite in the erasers, salines in their ringed aluminum housings, before mowing down on the meat, eviscerating each wooden soldier with his molars into a mash cornmeal where a sour hibiscus lingered in the grain, coughing when the slivers stabbed his gums or caught in the recesses of his esophagus.

He hung his head in the bone pile, feeling jilted and satisfied. Something else had moved in now, the crash, the embargoed dread, a guilt that loomed over him like an old lie. He stood and examined the mess, feeling incorrigibly ugly, and went to work hiding the evidence, swept wooden chips into the wastebasket with his palm and tied the trash bag before stuffing it into a larger bag, which he left by the door for the janitor. Then he retrieved the handheld vacuum and got on his knees, where he attacked the floor under his desk, scrutinizing the shadows like some pitiful creature forced to live below the surface, searching for any stray pieces that had gotten away.

Chapter 2

The thing about people's problems, they were almost never worth taking seriously. Listening to someone's problems for a living was an exploration into the banal. Ultimately, people wanted a state of shared perceptions, to have what others said about them align with what they thought about themselves. There was always this gap between what we expected and the reality of our experiences, between who we'd wanted to be and who we actually were. There was no greater reminder of our inelegance as a species than the practice of persuading others to adopt our narcissistic perceptions of ourselves. It was as though we possessed only enough awareness to imagine a world that complied with our self-interests.

"As a species, people possess two key advantages: an ability to see patterns, and an ability to tell stories based on those patterns." Leonard crossed the boardroom table, stopped at the windowsill, and eyed an abandoned bottle of glass cleaner that stood next to a waterlogged roll of paper towels. "And those are the only reasons we're no longer living in caves."

The executives sat in a triangle formation. The first was older, had a slack face with leathery skin artificially tanned to a tawny bronze. A younger man sat beside him, was square-shouldered and looked like he needed to shave once a week. A third executive blinked incessantly and jerked with manic pep, seemed vitalized by the lecture, and nodded with servile compliance, turning to her teammates with leering, wide-eyed excitement an~ Leonard said something that sounded vaguely aphoristic.

"The problem," Leonard continued, "is we aren't pa. distinguishing the meaningful patterns from the meaningle

---

image
"Becau
"Trust," Leo
brands exhibit four o
own religion. And anyth
ideology, it's because there's fa
sions and behaviors. Trust builds th
Now, how is that trust earned?" the older man srutte
"Great marketing?" the older man srutte
of mouth—"
"Number two, authority. Authority is an issue of e
tice of proposing that the illusion of the brand is as real a
sitting at. Authority is the company's history and success sto
that it's managed by capable, innovative leaders. Authority c
a brand's message be authentic and believable, that it reflec
unwavering awareness of identity."
His cellphone began ringing again.
"Number three, the mission. Successful brands always h
rience. Sometimes they petition a cause or align themselves
social issue. These aren't just slogans, they're a tribal argo
the reason for a brand's existence. These recognitionals hu
place it in the catalog of history—"
For the third time, the cellphone began to ring. The
Leonard crossed the room, fingers cra
their eyes.
"Excuse me." Leonard
pocket. "Leonard Lundell."
"Leonard, baby?"
"Mom," he whispered. "I can't talk. I'm in a meet

and grasped for water, which he threw down before surrendering in a grind of coughing and keening, as a single iridescent bubble that had traveled up from his gullet emerged at the gate of his mouth and popped on his bottom lip.

When he recovered, he found himself on the floor, licking a leg of his desk. He made his way back to the chair like this, combing through an archive of wood oil and aged newspapers and dust, before he transitioned to base pleasures and began gnawing at the colony of pencils stationed in a ceramic coffee mug, licked and bit them, emancipating a sawdust mesquite in the erasers, salines in their ringed aluminum housings, before mowing down on the meat, eviscerating each wooden soldier with his molars into a mash cornmeal where a sour hibiscus lingered in the grain, coughing when the slivers stabbed his gums or caught in the recesses of his esophagus.

He hung his head in the bone pile, feeling jilted and satisfied. Something else had moved in now, the crash, the embargoed dread, a guilt that loomed over him like an old lie. He stood and examined the mess, feeling incorrigibly ugly, and went to work hiding the evidence, swept wooden chips into the wastebasket with his palm and tied the trash bag before stuffing it into a larger bag, which he left by the door for the janitor. Then he retrieved the handheld vacuum and got on his knees, where he attacked the floor under his desk, scrutinizing the shadows like some pitiful creature forced to live below the surface, searching for any stray pieces that had gotten away.

Chapter 2

The thing about people's problems, they were almost never worth taking seriously. Listening to someone's problems for a living was an exploration into the banal. Ultimately, people wanted a state of shared perceptions, to have what others said about them align with what they thought about themselves. There was always this gap between what we expected and the reality of our experiences, between who we'd wanted to be and who we actually were. There was no greater reminder of our inelegance as a species than the practice of persuading others to adopt our narcissistic perceptions of ourselves. It was as though we possessed only enough awareness to imagine a world that complied with our self-interests.

"As a species, people possess two key advantages: an ability to see patterns, and an ability to tell stories based on those patterns." Leonard crossed the boardroom table, stopped at the windowsill, and eyed an abandoned bottle of glass cleaner that stood next to a waterlogged roll of paper towels. "And those are the only reasons we're no longer living in caves."

The executives sat in a triangle formation. The first was older, had a slack face with leathery skin artificially tanned to a tawny bronze. A younger man sat beside him, was square-shouldered and looked like he needed to shave once a week. A third executive blinked incessantly and jerked with manic pep, seemed vitalized by the lecture, and nodded with servile compliance, turning to her teammates with leering, wide-eyed excitement anytime Leonard said something that sounded vaguely aphoristic.

"The problem," Leonard continued, "is we aren't particularly good at distinguishing the meaningful patterns from the meaningless. We confuse correlation with causation, gossip as gospel. Many of the ideas we share are, essentially, well-articulated nonsense."

The woman bounced in her seat. Leonard's thoughts returned to the glass cleaner on the sill. He wanted to be alone with it, draw in its astringent colognes, imagined soaking a square of towel and dabbing its electric-blue tonics over his tongue. He wondered what it tasted like. Abrasively sharp, he decided, metallic but with a fatty brine finish. Glacial waters and berry vinaigrettes.

"Brands touch upon human truths," he said. "They satisfy emotional and social needs. Products simply express a brand's tenets, and for the sake of this conversation are immaterial. Products mean nothing. There are only stories, minds connecting with other minds."

The cellphone in his pocket began to ring.

"Close your eyes," Leonard said. "And pick up your spokescreatures."

In their laps, each executive held a primitive puppet fashioned out of mauve-colored cloth. They were gingerbread genderless, naked, and devoid of distinguishing attributes, a stitched line of embroidery thread establishing an expressionless mouth, two googly, saucer-shaped eyes.

"Tell me," Leonard said as the executives gloved their hands with the puppets. "What did your company do wrong?"

"We inflated our assets." The older man coughed as he set his eyes on a felt nib of nose. He held a distant, drained expression, the look of someone recently deposed. "We failed to disclose debts on our balance sheets."

"It worked for a while," Leonard said. "Please, keep your eyes closed."

"We got lucky."

"Luck isn't a business model. What changed?"

"We got caught."

"Tyco, Union Carbide, Enron. They got caught too."

"We fired our CFO, were transparent with the SEC. We knew if we rebranded—"

"Let me stop you there," Leonard said. " 'The pride connected with knowing and sensing lies like a blinding fog over the eyes and senses of men, thus deceiving them concerning the value of existence.' You know who said that?"

"Lee Iacocca?" the man said.

"Friedrich Nietzsche," Leonard said. "Why do you think your public image hasn't recovered?"

"Because they don't trust us." The man's voice was strained.

"Trust," Leonard repeated. "As we discussed this morning, all successful brands exhibit four essential traits. Number one is trust. Every brand is its own religion. And anytime someone believes in something, adheres to an ideology, it's because there's faith, an assurance that reinforces their decisions and behaviors. Trust builds the ecosystem where brand loyalty thrives. Now, how is that trust earned?"

"Great marketing?" the older man stuttered. "Favorable reviews, word of mouth—"

"Number two, authority. Authority is an issue of expertise; it's the practice of proposing that the illusion of the brand is as real as the table we're sitting at. Authority is the company's history and success story, the idea that it's managed by capable, innovative leaders. Authority demands that a brand's message be authentic and believable, that it reflect a consistent, unwavering awareness of identity."

His cellphone began ringing again.

"Number three, the mission. Successful brands always provide an experience. Sometimes they petition a cause or align themselves with an existing social issue. These aren't just slogans, they're a tribal argot that crystallizes the reason for a brand's existence. These recognitionals humanize the brand, place it in the catalog of history—"

For the third time, the cellphone began to ring. The executives opened their eyes.

"Excuse me." Leonard crossed the room, fingers crawling into his jacket pocket. "Leonard Lundell."

"Leonard, baby?"

"Mom," he whispered. "I can't talk. I'm in a meeting."

"I've been calling for a week—"

"I'll email you or something," he said and stuffed the phone into his pocket.

"Number four remains the most misunderstood, and it's the reason ninety percent of brands fail," Leonard said. "The people who pursue your brand aren't consumers; they're loyalists who take up arms for your movement. Brands turn buyers into believers, audiences into advocates, and the followers who heed this call form a heterogeneous tribe, a cult driven by the most vital component your brand must possess."

Leonard paused for effect.

"The appetite. People like what's familiar to them. Given time, once trust has been earned, once devotees have been submersed in its language and culture, they begin not only to identify with the brand, but they adopt it into the milieu of their personal traditions. It's the reason we patronize fast-food restaurants we loved as children, why we buy the same brand of beer our grandfather kept in the garage. Brands offer a subscription to the past. They satisfy a nostalgia for simpler times, like a song that lets us revisit our most carefree years. Brands exist because they're a source of eternal comfort. They're the idea of going home, which is the reward offered by every religion that has survived, from Christianity to Coke."

A muddle of coughs and clearing throats. Leonard surveyed the executives, their deferential smiles, and thought about those illusory interpretations we cultivate of ourselves that never quite define who we are. The older one, he'd made peace with his shortcomings years ago, convinced himself he'd achieved everything he'd wanted. What choice did he have at this point? The younger two, though, Leonard wondered what went on in there, what maladaptive daydreams they indulged in of futures that aligned with their aggrieved expectations, imaginary worlds they inhabited as their idealized selves as opposed to the people they actually were. They'd played this game of quiet resentments their entire adult lives, as though they'd started with their futures and worked their way backward, emulating the types of people they thought they were supposed to be until settling in defeat somewhere amid the necessary adaptation. The world never gave enough to allow the illusion to hold, but it was remarkably adept at reminding us of our failures.

"This is a positioning session to uncover your brand's identity," Leonard said. "Given everything we've discussed, I want you to imagine the puppet on your hand is a living, breathing thing, a flesh-and-blood person formed by the confluence of ideas your company has put into this rebrand. I want you to think about the community it belongs to, its history, its habits, its wants and needs. I want you to envision its face, the color of its eyes. I want you to imagine the words it speaks, the voice it uses to say them."

They would be thinking now, and they would each be thinking the same thing, the same cutout tropes, the canned concepts already developed by their in-house marketing team. Leonard had been doing this long enough to know that when called upon, the barons of the private sector were incapable of expressing an idea without resorting to clichés. That's why lying to them was easy. You simply told them what they wanted to hear and let them sit with their assumption that the world worked in accordance with their views of it.

"The brand isn't something you can create in a laboratory," Leonard continued. "When the four conditions are in place, it reveals itself organically, perhaps at first only to the shrewdest practitioners . . . but if your message is clear, if it's consistent and strong and true, the brand will manifest as a specific shattering the abstract, a bold, compelling concept—"

"I—I can see it!" the woman shrieked. The other executives opened their eyes and turned to Leonard. She shook in nodding tremors, rattled in her chair, seemed possessed by tics. She turned to her coworkers, her eyes swimming with tears. "I can see the brand! I can see the brand!"

AFTER THE MEETING WAS OVER, LEONARD RAN BACK TO HIS OFFICE, locked the door, and removed the glass cleaner from his jacket. He huddled behind the desk, unscrewed the bottle's spray nozzle, and held its handlebar shaft under his nose before pillaging its nectars: burning, assertive flavors humming with mints and chalks. Biting winds, downy clouds, whirling eddies of snow. Dizzy and sated, he knelt there for a moment, spitting into the wastebasket as he felt the tension release in his shoulders. Then he wiped his mouth on his shirt cuff, unlocked the door, and staggered to the bathroom.

The afternoon was wasted on paperwork. Leonard wrote reports and answered phone calls and stuffed envelopes addressed to his mother with condominium brochures. On the television, an investigative report showed algorithms dictate fifty percent of all stock market trades. A study found that people this year were smiling, on average, thirty percent less than usual. On C-SPAN, Senator Clinton spoke to a blue-collar assembly gathered in a cornfield. Then the Todds arrived for the day's crisis meeting.

Crisis: After his latest venture was blasted in a newspaper's restaurant review, a chef responded by sending an irate, profanity-laden email to the publication, wherein he made veiled threats against the journalist's life. The newspaper printed the email, and the internet dog-piling began, with the public excoriating the restaurant and its chef on review forums and social media pages. *Strategy:* Issue a press release claiming the chef's email had been hacked. Drop the release on a Friday so the public has the weekend to mull over the development without an active news cycle to decode potential believability issues. *Crisis:* An airline's standby ticket policy came under fire after a mother found herself stranded at an airport hundreds of miles from home. Once her flight landed in Phoenix, the woman had raced her sick child to the bathroom, and by the time she arrived at the connecting flight's gate, discovered the airline had sold her ticket. She later created a blog detailing her experience, which went viral. *Strategy:* Apologize. Give the victim a lifetime of free flier miles, then contact an SEO specialist and have the blog buried in internet search results. *Crisis:* A soft-drink company defended itself in civil court after a Wisconsin man claimed he'd discovered a dead mouse in his soda can. The story took a turn during a press conference, when the company's spokesperson carelessly noted the plaintiff's accusations were baseless, because high citric acid content in the drink would've effectively "dissolved the mouse into jelly." The case was dismissed—and the plaintiff later admitted he had, in fact, fabricated the incident—but the spokesperson's candor ignited a barrage of criticisms from health advocates who derided the effects of sugary beverages. *Strategy:* Launch a national ad campaign aimed at younger audiences with the following tagline: "Extreme enough to dissolve your fears!"

LEONARD TOOK A LATE LUNCH, WALKED TO A DEPARTMENT STORE IN Herald Square, and bought several pairs of slacks, which he refrained from trying on for fear of confronting the changing room's conditions. The sun was setting, and amber curtains of light draped over Madison Avenue by the time he returned to his office, where he slipped on the pants and discovered they were too large. An aborted attempt at work followed, and soon he found himself under the desk, where he dug up a squeeze bottle of lemon-scented dish soap he'd lifted from the janitor's cart. The label was in Spanish, and its logo—*Sabroso!*—and accompanying text were delightfully strange. The liquid was electric yellow, with a heady scent and an alkaline taste that stung his tongue and caused his face to seize up before leaving ribbons of drool over the chair legs. He was chewing on a handful of antacids when something punched the glass with such force it caused him to jump backward. He approached the window on his knees and listened to a chorus of horns before he noticed the bull's-eye of blood centering a webbed impact pattern in the pane. Outside, a bird carcass lay on the sill. It had empty obsidian eyes, russet-colored wings folded as though sleeping. Leonard grabbed a newspaper from his desk, winched up the rusted frame, clawed for the bird with the sports section, and stuffed it into a trash bag. He opened his door to discover an empty office, the cubicles vacant, a hallway columned with shafts of crepuscule shadow. He cradled the bird under his arm as he walked the corridors and stopped before the bezel of light that ran around the doorframe of the office of Jack Gurney, President and CEO.

"A bird," Leonard began. "It hit my window."

He peered into the doorway and found the old man asleep in the chair, chin folded into his neck. His shoes were off, and a pair of black nylon socks trailed from his feet over the carpet like molting snakeskins. Under the jade light of the banker's lamp, a fly inched its way across his forehead.

IT WAS DARK WHEN LEONARD GRABBED HIS BRIEFCASE, LOCKED THE door, and walked corridors illuminated by the carmine glow of an emergency exit. He paused near the printers and thought about the men and women who'd occupied these halls alongside him, many spending their best years in this place, working, laughing, buzzing through time. Somewhere before the foyer he heard shuffling and spotted a secretary, illuminated by the emerald light of a computer monitor as she hoisted a stack of manila folders into a filing cabinet. She looked him over and slammed the cabinet door before disappearing into the darkness.

He returned to the department store that evening and exchanged the slacks for two identical pairs in a smaller size. Foreseeing another miscalculation, he'd packed a bottle of disinfectant spray in his briefcase this time, along with an assortment of swabs, and forced himself into the changing room. As he'd expected, the facilities were filthy: Graffiti riddled the walls and snowdrifts of lint blanketed the carpets, so he got on his knees and began to clean, which was interrupted by a visit from the store's security team, and there was a showing of receipts, and his cleaning supplies were confiscated before he was eventually allowed to exchange the slacks for two pairs that fit and was then escorted outside.

The offices along the avenue were mostly empty now, windows haunted by the mannequin silhouettes of cleaning crews. The street thrummed with cabs as the accordion steel gates of shops shuttered for the night. A defeated man sat on the curb, straddling a sign that read: "No way home! Need help!" and soon Leonard came upon a row of buzzing restaurants, where behind cataracts of fog on the glass he made out the shapes of well-dressed men and women inside. He stood there in the shadows as a young couple passed, busying themselves with nervous chatter. Leonard wondered if they ever felt like impostors in their lives, if they'd had hopes and plans at one point, ideas of the people they'd wanted to become, and if all of that had since been overwritten, attenuated by an unstated reminder that the people they'd always been were the people they'd always be.

He resurfaced from the subway and entered a narrow street bracketed by brownstones. His building was a double-take in the neighborhood's trademark West End charm, a sea-green glass silo that looked like rows of shower stalls bolted into place with a trusswork of tubular plastics. The eggshell interior of his apartment was defined by a negative space, by the things that were missing, walls bare and managed by clean lines, curtained with a scrim of shadow from the ribs of vaulted ceiling beams. A bone-colored sofa and chaise longue, still wrapped in factory plastics, divided the living room; the only other clues of occupancy were a television anchored to the far wall and a titanic fish tank whose halogen shroud cast a pale glow along the floors. The kitchen revealed ad hoc arrangements of anality: doorknobs and cabinet handles wrapped with medical dressings of cling film, emergency stations of paper towels and latex gloves beside alabaster appliances. He loved the sight of things neatly lined up, every item in its proper place. It reminded him that his corner of the universe, however small, still abided by a system of order.

He checked his messages, noticing his mother had called, then approached the aquarium and tapped on the glass. Several figures scattered behind an outcrop of algae-speckled slates before a lemon-colored fish emerged from the murk. It had an oblong head patterned with tangerine dots that shimmered under the pale bulbs, fins that wept like fronds in a breeze as it followed Leonard's tracing finger. He opened a canister of flakes, and the fish bobbed its head, arched the tip of its nose until its mouth breached the surface agape as Leonard lifted the lid and crushed a pinch of flakes over the water, which the fish sucked down before disappearing.

That night, Leonard opened a can of corn and ate it cold as he watched television. CNN predicted Hillary Clinton would win the West Virginia primary. A sports channel profiled American athletes slated to compete in the Beijing Olympics. A study found consumers who used coupons were more likely to suffer from joint pain. The corn's flavor was one-note and underwhelming, and its rubber textures began to irritate him, so he foraged in the kitchen and returned with a box of detergent for texture. He scooped turquoise grounds into the can, gave it a stir, and watched the slurry thicken into an iridescent gravy. The corn was studded with life now, sang with anise and dill, tones so dizzyingly complex he imagined them lying dormant for a millennium, waiting to be uncovered. He sucked on the kernels, then abandoned the can and went straight for the box. Alone, the detergent harbored a simpler composition, an effervescence of cilantro and lime that teased his tongue with earthy chars.

He swallowed a stack of antacid tablets in the bathroom, washed his mouth out, and scrubbed his tongue with a toothbrush before returning to the kitchen in search of a scouring pad. That was the problem with detergent: A film lingered after the thrill was gone. Soon he was on his knees, picking through the graveyard of cleaning supplies under the sink. He found a tumbler of wood soap, unscrewed the cap, and sniffed. Behind a soft spruce exterior, he was surprised to discover an ambrosia warmth of varietal grapes, and within minutes he retrieved an aluminum mixing bowl from the cupboard, poured the soap, emptied an ice-cube tray into it, and soaked a wad of paper towels. He brought it to his nose and inhaled cedar oil perfumes, felt like he'd stuck his head inside a lawn mower catch bag. He grew lightheaded and, when he opened his eyes, saw rain squalls, alpine vistas, a blue ridge of mountains.

He was vomiting in the sink when the telephone rang. He faltered into the living room, and his stomach wound when *MOM* flashed in an alarm-clock typeface on the caller ID. He set the mixing bowl on the floor when something winked at him from the far side of the room, turned in a sort of marionette dance in the shadows that nested in an alcove corner. He retrieved the paper towels, returned to the living room, and picked up the receiver on the sixth ring, bracing himself for the long haul.

"Mom," he began, but the call had gone to voicemail.

Leonard crossed the room and inspected the corner. It was nothing, a residual hallucination or a trick played on him by crosshatches of light and shade. But with his face to the floor, he was apprised of another imperfection, a gray beard of dust that had grown over the baseboards. He dipped a wedge of towel into the bowl and huffed it, then scrubbed the offending area. A cuticle of white paint made itself known, which he peeled from the slat, sniffed, and slipped into his mouth. Hints of aspirin and banana peel.

He retreated to the icebox conditions of his bedroom and dialed the noise generator to the setting labeled "arboreal forest." Lying in the diaper contours of his down comforter, his eyelids fluttered, but now the phone was ringing again, and he was up, pacing. He walked to the window and listened to the sighs of traffic, studied darkened mylar window panels of the condo tower across the street. Somewhere a light went on, and Leonard watched as a man in a bathrobe lumbered across his living room and turned on the television. How strange, he thought, that a city brimming with life could be so lonely.

Chapter 3

He liked to tell his clients that their value was determined by how they lived and not a label others assigned them. He repeated oven-ready statements like that because they sounded nice and played well in the office, but in reality this was counterintuitive advice. In a crisis, how we're perceived meant everything. We'd convinced ourselves that being coolly detached, as outlandishly individualistic as possible, was a precondition for a meaningful life, but when our reputations were under attack, anything we could do to present a relatable, shared experience, to convince others we were normal, was a step toward improving our public image. Given the choice, if the circumstances were bad enough, we always choose to express how we're just like everyone else.

There was a lightness to the air as Leonard walked to the office. People had dressed optimistically that morning, shed layers of clothing in anticipation of summer. He crossed Park Avenue and headed west by way of Fortieth, where traffic was at a standstill. There was a cry of sirens, and approaching the next intersection he noticed a police barricade erected in the middle of the street. Three fire trucks blocked off Madison, flanked by a convoy of cruisers lining the bus lane. A crowd swelled on the sidewalk, heads drawn skyward, eyes on the building just before the corner. Leonard scanned windows and chamfered ledges, instinctively looking for smoke. There was just the silver ridge of rooftops, a livid blue sky, a cloud in the shape of Greenland.

A crush of bodies spilled out of the building's entrance like a labour of moles forced to the surface. A garrison of police officers attempted to corral them, but the crowd broke loose and patched out over the sidewalk.

Rattled, trenchant voices. Several people were crying. Leonard recalled an adage he'd heard regarding dispatching protocols: two trucks, a mess; three trucks, a disaster; four trucks, hell on earth. When the fourth fire truck skied into the bus lane, Leonard crossed the street and wended through the sprawling crowd that wheeled around the barricade. Employee shooting? Men staggered past him, faces riddled with shock. Another terrorist attack? Someone was screaming.

Leonard knelt under the barricade and navigated through the crowd, cut past a cluster of suits on the corner, their eyes ranging toward the building in dumb wonder. More bodies swarmed out of the entrance. A man guided a sobbing woman down the sidewalk. Firemen interviewed doormen who equivocated in Brooklynese, hands flapping at the sky and back to the ground. A police officer told bystanders to vacate the area, as a procession of paramedics wound out of the building with industrial-grade trash bags. A man in a janitor's uniform sat on a siamese connector and wept.

Leonard reached his building and took the elevator to the sixth floor. He was crossing the cubicles when Jack Gurney's door swung open, and Roger Lawton, Partner, Director of Strategy and Research, stumbled into the hall. He was red-faced and had a thinning hairline that resembled refuse in a shower drain.

"About time you got here," Roger said.

"What's going on?"

"Something terrible happened. You'd better come to Jack's office."

CONTRARY TO WHAT THE ADDRESS IMPLIED, 274 MADISON AVENUE—colloquially referred to as the Pinnacle Building—was located on Fortieth Street. Constructed during the skyscraper boom that enveloped parcels of the Grand Central District in the twenties, the building's spare, pinstriped exterior was graphed with sterling columns, its vertical assembly shouldering every ten floors so the highest tiers were set recessed from the street. Its three-story granite base bore a triptych of vaulted windows, each accented with floral spandrels as well as a wide proscenium arch that ran above a trio of revolving doors. Probably owing to its lack of exterior flair, 274 Madison rarely provoked more than a glance from passersby, but historians and those specializing in architecture from the period had long cited the building for its significance as a transitional work between the Beaux Arts style and Deco designs that would become synonymous with Americans' veneration of mass production. Nowhere was this more apparent than in the Pinnacle Building's vestibule, where an unlikely juxtaposition of Grecian and modernist ornamentation suggested a fusion of classicalism and assembly-line efficiency. Standing in its windswept lobby, the first thing visitors noticed were the expansive floors, lacquered sheets of black marble that rivered into east and west corridors. Walls were rose-colored marble, transported from a Tennessee quarry and framed by bronze columns that dually served as light fixtures. Against its far wall stood a bay of six elevators, each decorated with bronze relief art: radial lines suggesting the rays of the rising sun, and, below it, rolling fields of country bisected by twin locomotive rails.

For decades, 274 Madison had served as worldwide headquarters for advertising and marketing conglomerate Pinnacle International. As recently as a quarterly earnings meeting a year prior, shareholders had voiced their desires to relocate to a more contemporary facility, Columbus Circle or Varick Street among the commercial hubs that better reflected the company's upward mobility in a global marketplace. The building was old, they said. The elevators stalled, the stairwells were rashed with mold, and, in the spring of 2006, a seventy-year-old water pipe had burst between the fourth and fifth floors, destroying much of the creative department and sidelining several important projects. Board members balked at the idea, claiming Pinnacle's brand benefited from its Mad Ave association, even if the building wasn't located on Madison per se.

One of the building's elevators—the fourth left from the lobby desk—had been acting up for some time. Work logs later subpoenaed from maintenance company Easel Elevator Inc. surmised an electrical short in the elevator's call bank was causing its cab to make intermittent mystery stops on the ninth floor, where the bank would clear itself of data and leave riders to reenter their intended destination. After months of complaints, inspectors were dispatched to the building on the afternoon of Thursday, May 8, 2008, to repair the problem. Court documents revealed the inspectors had disabled the elevator door's safety circuit using a jumper wire to bypass a flow of electricity to the cab as they recalibrated its tripping speed. At 4:45 p.m., inspectors logged that they'd found the culprit—a corroded control circuit—and replaced it, then reactivated the door's safety brake and left the premises.

Though few were in the building that evening, a janitor later testified the elevator continued to malfunction into the night, making unprovoked ghost jogs to the ninth floor. Elevator specialists would tell investigators a bad chip in the cab's control panel—EPROM, erasable programmable read-only memory—was likely responsible for sending the elevator on the false calls. Further investigation revealed it was also possible one of the inspectors had failed to re-enable the door safety circuit after the work had been completed.

At 8:48 a.m. on Friday, May 9, Arthur Goldstein, a Pinnacle Senior Account Manager, entered the building. Witness testimony alleged Goldstein, apparently noticing the closing door, ran across the lobby and threw his shoulders into the elevator, which under normal circumstances would've activated the motion sensor to disengage the door's arm mechanism. Goldstein apparently failed to notice the car had already lurched several inches by the time he placed his right foot inside. Elevators accelerate at an average rate of four feet per second; Goldstein's body would've been halfway inside as the car, its door still open, continued to climb, and was probably several feet off the ground when he noticed the narrowing space closing in on his shoulders. Witnesses inside the elevator told investigators they only remembered hearing a gasp as he seemed to realize the impossible was upon him. By that time, it was too late.

"He was crushed to death," Roger said. "Sucked into the shaft between the elevator and the wall."

The Gurney PR Principals looked Leonard over from high-back

chairs: Roger Lawton, Partner, Director of Strategy and Research; Wanda Markowski, Partner, COO, Director of Branding; and Jack Gurney, Partner, President, and CEO. They sat in a conspiratorial huddle behind Jack's desk, with Wanda in the middle and the men flanking both sides. The room smelled like a cigar box, and the air held a somber quality, a weight of accusation. The door was closed, which was normally a bad sign.

"Apparently, he was cut in half," Roger continued. Roger was short and shaped like an avocado. He spoke with the drawn lilt of a cattle rancher and smiled constantly. Leonard realized this wasn't because he was kind or because he sought to avoid confrontation. Roger simply had a natural predisposition to look stupid. "I heard one guy say the paramedics are scraping his remains from the walls—"

"Enough," Wanda said. "How are you, Leonard?"

This was one of Leonard's pet peeves, establishing good faith through small talk. Wanda smiled with forced gravity, like it was something she needed to practice. She had a small face and a strained, sour look about her, lips crimped together as though she'd been weaned on onions and bar olives.

"Fine," Leonard said.

She stabbed her legal pad with a pencil and kept her eyes on him, awaiting elaboration. Another one of her habits, using silence as a peremptory means of extracting information. The room grew hot, and he felt itchy.

"I was just telling Jack—" She turned to the old man, who had fallen asleep in his chair. "Wake up," she said and tugged his lapel.

The old man stirred. He was usually lucid once the meds kicked in, had a gray face lined with cracks like an old painting, and a penchant for Yale Club casual: navy jacket, burgundy tie, penny loafers. He reached into his ear, and a hearing aid chirped with feedback.

"We've got a job for you," Jack said.

"Care to be more specific?" Leonard said.

"The CEO is here," Roger whispered. "Graydon Trotwood, the goddamn CEO of Pinnacle, is in our boardroom."

"I don't get it," Leonard said.

"We were at a dopey New York Press Club breakfast panel this morning. Trotwood was presented with some honorary award because he gives the place ten grand a year. We were having a convo with the CMO on our way back to the office when we heard sirens. We told them they could use our boardroom to decompress until they're allowed back in the building."

"Don't you and that Pinnacle guy have a history?" Leonard said.

"We were staff writers together at the *Journal-American* in the sixties," Jack said. "He's a snake."

"Do you have any idea what this means?" Roger said.

"I know what it doesn't mean," Leonard said. "Pinnacle is a Fortune 500 company. They have an agency of record. A good one, I'm sure."

"Here's where it gets tasty," Roger said. "Trotwood's on the phone. He's frantic, screaming at his yes-men, and before long we start asking questions: when they're doing a press conference, who their PR firm is—"

"Congratulations," Leonard said. "The PR industry doesn't have enough of an image problem. Now we're on par with sidewalk injury attorneys."

Roger smiled. Jack yawned. Wanda resumed tapping her pencil.

"Come to find out, their crisis counselor is at a family reunion in D.C.," Roger continued. "He's getting a flight back home. They don't have a prepared statement. They don't have a plan of attack. The senior management of a company with every mega-cap client you can think of is sitting in our boardroom, and the only barrier between them and us is standing at a gate in Dulles Airport with his dick in his hand."

Leonard went to the window. A fleet of mobile news units was parked at the curb. Men were dropping vines of cable in the gutter, mounting klieg lights, adjusting boom microphones. Reporters with pocket notebooks intercepted the crowd.

"They don't have that kind of time," Leonard said. "When it bleeds, it leads."

"Exactly," Roger said. "Let's say we go to the boardroom and make donuts."

"You're wasting your time," Leonard said. "I can't lead a crisis campaign that big on such short notice."

"Todd Armenburg can help you," Wanda said.

"Todd Armitage," Leonard said. "Todd Shillenburg."

"Whatever."

Bosses lived with a confabulation of reality. They had a habit of adopting a collective identity that obscured their individual flaws. They did this because they were expertly attuned to the idea that no one sells themselves on talent alone. That's why they took it personally when you rocked the applecart; they'd been drinking the Kool-Aid so long they conflated the company's capabilities with their own, and this was probably why he'd harbored contempt for every superior he'd had.

"Why don't you get Griffin Cruz to handle it?" Leonard said. "I hear he's getting Goodfriend's Senior VP slot."

The room grew quiet, and the group looked him over with faces suggesting equal parts concern and bemusement.

"Cruz heads the travel division. You handle crisis," Wanda said. "Jealousy isn't a good look, Leonard."

"Jack promised me that title six months ago."

The old man sat with his shoulders stooped, hands crossed like a child caught in some act.

"I don't know what to tell you," Wanda said. "But any chance you could come down from the cross so we can discuss the problem at hand?"

"Do you have any idea how many clients I've been getting?" Leonard said. "I just had a meeting with the founder of Mumblr two days ago."

Wanda rolled her eyes. "The drunk? At least get us Tom from Myspace."

"All we're asking for is thirty minutes of your time," Roger said. "These are the kinds of relationships we need to build. If we can snag Pinnacle as a crisis client, that's billing for the year."

"Yeah, I just don't know." Leonard watched their expressions change, the proprietary confidence in their faces slip into a tentative glowering, and instantly he felt better. Bosses bore the power of guilt; the only remaining weapon in his cache was insubordination. "Fine. Give me a minute to round up my team."

LEONARD FOUND TODD SHILLENBURG, TODD ARMITAGE, AND TODD Colton in his office. A lifestyle report on the television claimed smelling like certain foods could help women attract a mate. The segment ended, and the feed cut to an anchorman wading through a Midtown crowd.

"Shit, that's right on the corner," Todd Armitage said.

"Brain trust," Leonard said from the doorway. "Conference room in five."

"Why's there tape all over your window?" Todd Colton said.

"A bird hit it," Leonard said. He heard chatter from the hall and watched as a band of suits crossed the cubicle aisle. "Let's get to work."

The Gurney conference room was claustrophobically narrow and capped with low-hanging drop-ceiling tiles. A walnut desk ran the room's length, elbow-worn and checked with scars. A discarded computer monitor lay under a silt of dust in a corner, and, below it, snaking coils of wire disappeared into a slit that had been cut in the carpet. Reflections of Madison Avenue traffic spilled in from a single picture window and cast auroras of light against the back wall.

Leonard entered and gave a nod to Wanda, Roger, and Jack, then exchanged hands with the three men who'd settled in at the far side of the table. The first introduced himself as Bernie Feinblum, Chief Marketing Officer. He had a wide face with pink undertones and looked like he was made of ham. Next to him was an older man who looked as though he'd been assembled by committee: tan, track-runner thin, eyebrows that suggested he'd been in the shop a few times. Graydon Trotwood, Chief Executive Officer. A third man stood in the shadows. He was small, and his features held the mystical simplicity of a golem: shaved head, a hard face crossed with stern lines, eyes that judged everything. The lawyer.

"Didn't get your name," Leonard said.

"It doesn't matter," the man said.

The guests positioned themselves away from the table, establishing a sort of linear allegiance with one another. They offered vacant expressions, to which Roger responded with a compulsory smile.

"Well, Jack, here we are," Trotwood said behind a flash of teeth. "PR and advertising, the two hands of the corporate conscience meet at last."

"You sell products, we manage conversations," Jack said. "What's the connection?"

Wanda's hand disappeared under the table, and the old man jerked.

"You consider yourselves a small agency?" Trotwood said.

"Midsized," Roger said. "I like to say we offer boutique services with a value price point."

Leonard cringed, as he did every time Roger repeated that line.

"We own several PR firms," Trotwood said. "Got a healthcare shop up the block."

"Healthcare, smart," Roger said. "Recession-proof."

The Todds entered the room single-file and slid into a corner. Leonard took the break in chatter as his cue. "I'm sorry to hear what happened," he said as he closed the door. "It's awful."

"His name was Arthur Goldstein," Feinblum said. "He managed consumer accounts, worked for us twenty-three years. He had a family. I can't believe it."

The Todds scribbled notes. Jack crossed his legs and looked at his watch.

"I understand he was religious," Trotwood said. "I mean, I didn't know him."

"Of course," Leonard said. "Gentlemen, when it comes to reputation, you can't let rumors write the headlines. When the press comes knocking—"

"I'm sure you're a fine company," Feinblum said. "But we already have a crisis agency. Frazer Rae and Associates has been our counsel for years."

"Frazer's a good man to have in your corner," Leonard said.

"You know him?"

"Frazer's washed up," Jack muttered.

"He's a legend," Leonard said. "But I understand he's . . . unaccounted for?"

"He's in Washington, waiting on a flight."

"Doesn't he have a cellphone?"

"He didn't take it with him."

The Todds exchanged glances. There was a language of uncomfortable fidgeting in the room, crosstalk of asses in squeaking chairs.

"Sounds bad, I know," Feinblum said. "What can I say, Frazer's old-school."

"Doesn't he have staff?" Leonard said.

"Assistants," Feinblum said. "But he won't let anyone handle press."

"It's embarrassing," Trotwood said.

"I hope you recognize the urgency this situation demands," Leonard said. "First, you'll need to prepare a statement. We can have a press release, with your approval and quotes, written within an hour."

"Frazer said he's working on it," Feinblum said.

"You should also host a press conference to show Pinnacle is prepared to confront this crisis. Every detail should be plotted and rehearsed: the announcement, the setting, answers to potential questions. We can lay the groundwork, get things rolling with the media—"

"Frazer's handling it," Feinblum said. "He wants to have the conference in our lobby after the police let us back in."

"That's . . . not a good idea," Leonard said. "But I'll respect the decisions your counsel makes." He paused, let the silence accrue weight. "There's still the issue of the witnesses, your two employees who were in the elevator when the accident happened."

"They're in the basement of our building," Trotwood said. "Giving the police their statements."

"Gentlemen, I hope you'll consider your vulnerabilities here. This morning, one of your employees was killed in a horrific manner on your property, and the two witnesses who saw everything are currently a half block away, in a building surrounded by press. Meanwhile, your crisis coun-selor can't coach them or draft a strategy because he's unaccounted for."

The men nodded, said nothing. Whether they were contemplating what he'd said or ignoring it, he wasn't sure.

"First," Leonard said, "I suggest Frazer's office contact the victim's fam-ily as soon as possible. I give it a few hours until the press starts knocking on doors."

"God, the family," Trotwood said. "Will they sue? That's what I'd like to know."

"Right now, those witnesses are your greatest liability," Leonard said. "You can knock out the best press conference in the world, but if one of them goes public, our narrative goes off-script, and the entire dynamic of this story changes. We'll need to sequester them and make sure they don't say a word, at least until you've released your statement. They'll need emer-gency media training. I can keep them on lockdown, offer the basics, make sure they're prepared before the press figures out who they are."

"They haven't spoken to anyone yet, aside from the police," Feinblum said.

"Let's keep it that way. Give me thirty minutes with each witness, and I can brief them on how to handle the media until Frazer's staff arrives, at which time they'll be handed over to your agency of record."

"Fine," Trotwood said. "They're yours. Do it."

And there it was, the account win, wild game in his grip. The air in the room lifted. Roger and Wanda couldn't contain their smiles; it was as though twin sparrows had alighted on their shoulders.

"We're in for media training, but there's still a problem," Feinblum said. "The building's been evacuated except for the cops and the witnesses. How do we get them here without getting the press's attention?"

"We could ask for a police escort," Roger said.

"Bring in the cops and we may as well stamp 'witness' on their fore-heads," Jack said.

"How far do you think the building is from here?" Leonard said.

"Hundred feet as the crow flies," Todd Shillenburg said.

"Let's send some people down as security and make a run for it," Wanda said.

"The press knows anyone who comes out of that building is part of the story," Jack said. "All it takes is one photo, and they'll have names within an hour."

Leonard walked to the window and looked to the thrumming crowds below. Onlookers clustered around the building like insects in the bottom of a chandelier.

"I have an idea," he said. "It'll take a phone call."

"Just do it," Trotwood said and stood. His functionaries followed. "Draw up a contract, will you? I want my guy to see it while I have him here. How much will this cost us, anyway?"

"We can stretch a dollar until it screams," Roger said.

The room rose and the meeting concluded with a flock of shaking hands, Wanda patting backs and making forced laughter.

"I still don't know how you're going to get those witnesses up here without the press noticing," Feinblum said.

"There's something else I wanted to bring up," Leonard said. "Those witnesses are traumatized. They've seen something that's going to haunt them for the rest of their lives. At the least, you'll need to offer them psychological counseling. Forget what's in-network, get them specialists."

"Fine," Feinblum said.

"We'll also need to let them know how valuable they are to the company. They're the only element of this narrative we can control, but if they realize the ball's in their court, they may want to know what's in it for them. I'll need collateral, something compensatory. Could they be up for a promotion in several months?"

"I don't know," Feinblum said. "We could ask HR."

"I'll ask again. Could these exemplary employees who have bright futures with Pinnacle possibly be up for a promotion?"

"Sure," Feinblum said. "If it comes to that."

"I'd like to have their personnel files."

"We don't have access to that stuff. We can't get into the building."

"At the least, I'll need to know their names and titles. Maybe how long they've been with the company." Leonard closed his eyes. "And I'm sure your counsel knows this, but I can't stress enough that you use the press conference as an opportunity to make the victim's name public. This compels the media to share your side of the story—"

"One step at a time," Wanda said and placed a hand on Leonard's shoulder. She laughed as though she was being graded for performance, then escorted the men to the door. When Feinblum's back was turned, she leaned over and whispered into Leonard's ear: "Don't fuck this up."

LEONARD RAN TO HIS OFFICE, PICKED UP THE PHONE, AND CALLED SAUL Borovitz, who ran a video production company agencies hired for broadcast services.

"Saul, this is Leonard."

"Leonard, you son of a bitch. I'm still editing that VNR. You have to give me another week."

"I'm not calling about the segment. I have to cash in a favor. It's a big one." He drew a breath, sought a rhetorical strategy, and demurred. "I need to borrow two cameras for an hour or so."

"I don't have two extra cameras. I've got a crew covering Hillary Clinton's speech uptown right now."

"This is an emergency. I've been to your shop. You've got dozens of cameras in the back."

"Those are spare parts, Leonard. They're busted."

"Broken cameras are fine. But the newer-looking, the better."

"What the hell do you want broken cameras for?"

"Just get two ready for me. I'm sending someone down."

Leonard hung up, picked up the receiver again, and dialed Todd Armitage. "I need you and one of the boys to take a cab ride downtown for a pickup. I'm emailing you the address now. Also, I need the art department to design some laminates, and I want them to look like press passes. I'm emailing you the details for that too. Third, round up some people to escort the witnesses to our building. Get me the biggest guys we have."

"Viola's big," Armitage said.

"Viola's in his fifties. I need someone young."

"What about Hector, the janitor? He's shithouse big and has all those tattoos."

"Perfect. Give him fifty bucks and get some of the interns to go with him."

Leonard swiveled in his chair and surveyed the room. A single frayed cord bladed above the lawn of carpet. He knelt and picked at it with his fingers, then retrieved a pair of scissors from the drawer, got on his knees, clipped the knot, and slipped it under his tongue. It was rough and fibrous and had an earthy bite, a homespun heat that surprised him, a subtle rub of dust in the fibers, traps of mesquite. A crumble of dirt brushed his lip as his teeth discovered a bulb of carpet glue, which he chewed as an unfamiliar warmth took over.

AN HOUR LATER, LEONARD STOOD AT HIS WINDOW AND SURVEYED THE sidewalk. A cab pulled up to the curb, and a pair of suits carting cardboard boxes leaped out and jogged through the crowd. They crossed under the barricade, cut through the cohort of reporters, then disappeared behind the corner. Leonard paced. Within minutes he spotted the Todds again, this time accompanied by four new additions, two of whom Leonard presumed were his witnesses. Both held television cameras at their shoulders, and the laminated press passes Leonard had asked the art department to design—belonging to an imaginary German television station—glimmered off their chests in the midday sun. Leonard held his breath as the group passed photographers and anchors and reporters before entering the building. Then his phone rang, and he spit the nugget of carpet into the trash.

"We're in the lobby," Todd Armitage said. "We have our witnesses."

Leonard sprinted to the elevators. He checked his watch, paced from the reception desk to the restrooms. Five minutes later, Armitage jogged up the aisle. He was sweating and clutched a manila folder.

"Where did you come from?" Leonard said.

"We had to take the stairs," Armitage said, panting. "One of the witnesses, he refused to take the elevator."

"Where are they now?"

"In the break room, with Shillenburg and Colton. The other witness is getting something to eat."

"Eating," Leonard said. "Okay."

"Here, Colton got their info," Armitage said and slapped the folder into Leonard's hands.

"Get the first witness and bring him to my office when he's ready."

"Sure, but fair warning," Armitage said. "He's not doing well."

Leonard returned to his office and turned off the TV. His cellphone buzzed. He saw his mother's number and stuffed the phone in his pocket. A light knock sounded on his door before a small man entered. He had a wan pallor, and his torso appeared misshapen, like he'd been assembled from mismatched parts. Leonard noticed he was shaking.

"Hugh Sneery?" Leonard read from the folder. "Have a seat."

The man sat and began to weep. After letting him go on for what seemed like an appropriate amount of time, Leonard decided to begin.

"You're in shock," he said. "You saw something no one should see. I'm terribly sorry."

"It's not shock," he said. "I'm just sad. That man, he was cut in half."

"His name was Arthur Goldstein."

"It's such a simple thing, you know? An elevator. I swear to God, I'll never ride one again." The man looked outside, as if the rows of glass offered something, an answer that could assuage him.

"The world's an uncertain place, that's the problem with it," Leonard said. "Our brains are wired to look for patterns. When the patterns stop making sense, when we realize there's no certainty, our worldviews collapse."

"You're a psychologist, aren't you? Figures. They sent me to a shrink."

"Aside from the police, have you spoken with anyone about what you've seen? Called a family member or a friend?"

"I haven't talked to anyone." The man looked around the room. "Why would a shrink have an office like this?"

"Here's the deal," Leonard said. "I'm here to tell you Pinnacle is with you all the way. First, management is offering you free counseling services with a reputable professional. You're in good hands."

"Okay."

"They're also willing to compensate you for sticking by them through this difficult time." Leonard picked up the folder and flipped through it. "I see you're up for review in several months."

"I am?"

"I understand you're a graphic designer." Leonard looked at a blank page. "How does Senior Project Manager sound?"

"I work in production. Why would they offer me a management position?"

"Just telling you what the file says." Leonard slapped the folder shut, stood, and moved around his desk. "Here's the important part. The press is going to contact you sooner or later. They'll want to know who the victim was, what he was like around the office, his habits—"

"I didn't know him," Hugh said.

"That doesn't matter. Right now, you're a key detail in an unraveling narrative that's going to be national news by five o'clock. The press might get your number. They might get your address."

"I'll tell them to fuck off," Sneery said.

"You say that now, but have you been on TV? Cameras lobotomize people. You become a deer in headlights. That's why there's only one thing you say in these moments, and it's a statement comprised of two words: 'No comment.'"

"No comment," the man repeated.

"I want to try an exercise," Leonard said. "I'm going to ask you a series of questions, and I want you to respond by repeating exactly what you just said. Now, what did you see today?"

The man looked Leonard in the eyes. "No comment."

"When you saw this man being killed in front of you, can you tell me the first thought that ran through your mind?"

"No comment," he said and winced.

"Did you know Arthur Goldstein? What was he like? Can you give me a description of his work habits? Did he have a family? Where did he go for lunch?"

"I didn't—" Sneery looked up. "No comment."

"I'm not asking you to elaborate. I just want to know what you saw."

"No comment."

"Can I at least get your name?"

"No comment."

"Good," Leonard said. "I can't underscore the importance of this detail: When you're accosted by the media, make sure those are the only words that leave your mouth. Don't give them the satisfaction."

The man rose and Leonard escorted him to the door before handing him a business card. "Pinnacle's HR department will be in touch about those counseling services. You have a bright future ahead. Good luck," he said and extended a hand.

The man lingered in the doorway, then left without saying a word. Leonard returned to his desk and clutched the receiver. More tufts of carpet became visible to him now, ripe succulents rippling with flavor.

"One down," he said to Armitage. "Send in the next witness."

The red flags flapped into view the moment she came through the door. She was heavyset and padded across the room in a gawky shuffle, appeared unkempt, dowdy, a vagrant who'd been scrubbed down and sent back on the streets. She wore an olive sweater pocked with bleach spots and emerald slacks whose waistline lacerated her torso at the navel. Three different handbags were strapped across her shoulders, each spilling over with books and Tupperware containers. She had a high, gummy smile, a neck stacked with jowls, and cheeks blistered with uneven applications of rouge. Her hair was a sheaf of golden wisps, giving her head the appearance of a crushed dandelion. It was difficult determining her age; she had the fashion sense of someone stricken with dementia, but her gait and cheerful readiness belied that presumption. As she positioned herself to sit, Leonard noticed the laminate—"Der Zeitgeist: Kamera Betreiber"—still affixed to her sweater.

"Christ, what a day," she said as she fell into the chair. In her hand was a half-eaten roast beef sandwich.

"Patty," Leonard read from the folder. "Patty Pachis." He let the words turn over his tongue, testing their sound.

"That's the name they gave me," she said and gave a wide smile, all gums. Her eyes ranged around the room. "What happened to your window?"

"A bird hit it."

Leonard handed the woman a business card. She held it between her fingers and made a phlegmy gasp.

"So, what's a crisis communicator, anyway?" she said.

"I'm in the reputation business. My job is to help people who've been hurt by scandal, and to minimize the potential damage a crisis could cause their personal or company brand through outreach to the press and public."

Her eyes held a look of rapt stupidity, a domesticated animal that had just been given the number of a combination lock. "Sort of like capitalism's junkyard," she said.

"That's . . . an interesting way of looking at it," Leonard said. "Typically, the larger crisis firms preach boilerplate responses: we're sorry, we'll never do it again, etcetera. I think the best way to combat a crisis is to help clients leverage their individual assets and promote a sort of proactive synergy. Brands can always better defend themselves when they know who they are."

"What a load of crap," she said and bit into her sandwich.

Leonard cleared his throat. "You've experienced a shock today."

"I'll say. I never thought I'd see someone die and pretend to be a German cameraman all before noon."

"You don't look particularly shaken."

She leaned back in the chair. "I definitely was," she said.

"You can take that laminate off. We don't need it anymore."

"I like it," she said. "Is Der Zeitgeist a real TV station?"

"It was a term coined by the philosopher Georg Hegel. It means 'spirit of the age.'" Leonard flipped through his folder. "Pinnacle is in your corner all the way. I understand you're an information specialist in the HR department."

"That's a fancy way to put it. I'm a file clerk."

"Pinnacle is willing to compensate you for enduring this terrible ordeal. You're up for review in two months. I'll take this opportunity to let you know you'll be receiving a promotion."

The woman howled with laughter and a wedge of lunchmeat fell onto the carpet. Leonard felt something squeeze him from the inside.

"Why would they promote me?" she said. "They hate my guts."

"Why do you say that?"

"Because it's true. And I hate them too."

"I want to run through an exercise," Leonard said. "The press wants to speak with you. And if they call or stop you on the street, the only thing I want you to say is 'no comment.' Let's try it. For everything I say, simply repeat, 'No comment.'"

Patty smiled enthusiastically.

"What was the victim like?" he asked.

"Never met him."

"What did you see?"

"Someone getting crushed like a bug."

"What do you think was going through his mind at the time of the accident?"

"The elevator floor?" She slapped her knee and roared, which came out with a wet snort. Leonard slammed his palm against the desk.

"Geez, just playing around," she said. "I figured if you're charging these guys a hundred bucks an hour or whatever, we should at least have some fun on their dime."

"We charge three hundred an hour," Leonard said.

"That's a lot of dough to tell someone to say 'no comment.'"

"There's more to it than that."

"Like what?"

Leonard's face grew hot. "You're wasting my time. More importantly, you're wasting your employer's time. In case you haven't noticed, time isn't their best friend right now."

"You're getting testy!" she said.

"I'll be forthcoming," Leonard said. "I find your lack of empathy . . . alarming. The man who died today, his name was Arthur Goldstein. He was your coworker. He had a family."

"Empathy? You care more about what I say than how I feel after seeing something like that."

"I care," Leonard said.

Her tongue rolled into the back of her mouth. "He was looking at me," she said. "As if I could help him. I reached out, tried to grab him. It happened so fast—"

"Now we're getting somewhere," Leonard said. "We're not asking you to forget what you saw. All we're asking is for you to omit those details when someone asks . . . for the time being."

"You want me to lie."

"We're not lying. We're managing the conversation." Leonard cleared his throat. "We're not asking you to turn off your emotions. We're simply refining dialogue. Perhaps it would be better if I explained it this way," Leonard said. "Corporations . . . *companies* are like people. They have personalities. The job of PR is to evaluate the public's opinion and help companies shape their personalities so it works in accord with that opinion."

"You make it sound like some kind of story."

"That's exactly what it is."

"But companies aren't people. They don't have personalities."

"That's your opinion," Leonard said. "And an incorrect one."

"Why?"

"Because you're wrong," he said. "Because smarter people than you have been saying what I've been saying for years. There are books on this sort of thing. Go to a library sometime."

She giggled. "Listen to you," she said. "Do you talk like this at home?"

"I'm not at home," Leonard said. "I'm trying to do my job. And my ability to do the job is one reason I'm not a file clerk."

"I don't plan on being one for long."

Leonard rose from the desk. "Where are you going with this?"

"I'm saying I can go downstairs and tell thirty reporters that the victim's name was Arthur Goldstein, and I saw his legs get sucked through a crack the width of a deck of cards, and you and my company want me to stay quiet about it—"

"There would be consequences," Leonard said. "I can pick up the phone and tell Pinnacle you're not willing to cooperate. They'll fire you, and they'll sue you into the ground."

"They can't sue me for telling people what I saw."

Leonard straightened himself. "Look, Patty, it doesn't have to be this way. You can play by the rules, and everyone wins."

"Maybe I think this process is disrespectful to the man who died today."

"I doubt that's your concern."

"Okay, then, what's in it for me?"

He leaned in. "I can make it worth your while." His tongue flattened and rested between his teeth. "Trust me."

"That sounds nice," she said. "But maybe I just don't like nice."

"But you have a choice. And choices give us power."

She folded her hands. "It's funny," she said. "We talk about the choices we make like they come from the things we've learned. But if you think about it, a lot of our decisions are just animal instinct. Maybe I came out wrong. Maybe I'm just a bad person."

Leonard squinted. He detected something else now, some darker agency. This was a different game.

"Excuse me for a moment," he said. "I need to make a phone call."

Leonard closed the door and raced down the aisle until he found an empty cubicle. He picked up the phone and dug Feinblum's business card out of his pocket.

"We have a problem."

"What kind of problem?" Feinblum said.

"One of your employees, the file clerk. She doesn't want to cooperate."

"Why? What's she doing?"

"As your counselor, I have a professional obligation to inform you—" Leonard paused, weighed his words carefully. He didn't want his client to think he couldn't handle her. "The subject refuses to follow my protocol for denying comment to the press."

"We'll fire her."

"You can't," Leonard said. "At least not now, not while this story is hot. If the media finds out you've terminated an employee who witnessed the accident, this story grows a second pair of legs. I'll need some time, a few days at least, to get her as far away from the scene, from anyone with a press deadline, as possible. It works in your favor that this accident occurred on a Friday, because it's hard for the press to break news over the weekend. In the meantime, I'm going to need leverage."

When Leonard returned to his office, Patty was sitting behind his desk.

"Get out of my chair," he said. "Now."

"Geez, sorry," she said and hobbled back to her seat.

"I have good news," he said and leaned against a shelf. "Aside from that promotion you'll be receiving, Pinnacle has also agreed to give you five thousand dollars."

"Oh, bribery!" she said, and clapped her hands. "I can't wait to tell the press!"

Blood gathered in his head. "You're telling me five grand isn't enough?"

"Maybe I just like seeing you squirm."

"I know why you're trying to wind me up," he said. "You want to cast the illusion that you maintain control of this situation."

"That's not why I'm doing it at all."

"Then why?"

"You're fun to tease. I'm surprised you don't click when you walk."

Leonard threw up his hands. When he composed himself, he whipped around, clawed at the desk, and stared at her for a long time. Silent treatment. It had always worked with his mother.

"What are you thinking about?" she asked.

"A few things."

"Do you think I'm ugly?"

The question surprised him. "I think you're repulsive," he said. "Detestable. You look like a flea market with legs. You look like everything I hate."

"Well," she said. "I believe that's the most honest you've been all day. No worries, I have a thick skin."

"Most reptiles do."

Leonard returned to the window. Already the crowds had thinned, and the flow of bodies had resumed on Madison Avenue. A bustling stream of suits spilled over the pavement, and a torn strip of police barricade tape wavering in the breeze from a bus-stop post was the only remaining evidence that anything had happened on this corner several hours before.

"Let's get real," Leonard said. "Let's put it all on the table. What do you want?"

His eyes clapped on hers, and for a moment Leonard noticed movement back there, turning gears, a mind calculating a next step.

Patty smiled. "How about dinner?"

Chapter 4

The restaurant was designed in haute minimalism, everything white and fashionably austere yet abated by a salon serenity, nanoglass floors imparting the sensation of seeing the world through wax paper. Waitstaff, affecting the roles of biomedical researchers, wore lab coats and carried plates with curatorial care. The art-gallery crowd, small, delicate men and women, eyed everything with rehearsed judgment.

Leonard glanced furtively at the woman before him. Patty's face was in her plate, engaged with an appetizer of seared calamari and baby octopus dusted with pine nuts and currants. She rocked in her seat as she ate, the German press laminate still affixed to her chest, and sang praises for the dish's craftwork as though translating flavors into song.

"This is just divine," she said. "Sinful."

"I take it you've been here before?" Leonard said.

"Are you kidding?" Her mouth, fully open, resembled the underbelly of a lawn mower. "I can't afford this place."

"The hour-long wait was annoying. I guess we're lucky to get a table at all on a Friday," he said. "I was impressed by how many restaurants you rattled off when I asked where you wanted to go. You're quite the gourmand."

"I read reviews. It's a passion." Patty smiled, revealing a wall of gums. Soon her main course arrived, a braised lamb shank with truffled polenta. The lamb had a crisp skin and cherubic interiors. She bent over the plate and went to war with it. Leonard squirmed, looked away.

"You sure you don't want anything?" she asked.

"Not hungry," he said. "You know, I'm actually in hot water for being here. I'm supposed to be at Pinnacle's press conference, which is happening as we speak."

"See, I don't think that's true," Patty said. "I'm guessing your top priority is to keep me away from anyone with a camera or a microphone, to keep me happy."

"Is it working?"

"What's your deal, anyway?" Patty wiped her mouth. "I mean, what's your crisis?"

"What?"

"I'm just curious how someone becomes good at this sort of thing. Are you super detail-oriented, or just really good at manipulating people?"

"There's no point psychoanalyzing me," Leonard said. "Our time together is nearly up. For God's sake, why are you still wearing that press badge?"

"I like it," she giggled. "And you sound awfully confident about the job you're doing. I can still go to the press."

"I'm resolutely aware of what you can tell them. Problem is, after tonight your story won't have nearly as much urgency. The victim's name is being released at the press conference. And tomorrow is Saturday. Do you have any idea what weekends are like in a newsroom? If you're lucky, you'll get a classifieds editor on the phone. By Monday, there'll be another local tragedy, a shooting or a crane accident or a subway jumper, and the media's bloodlust will find another target."

Patty shrugged and resumed eating, her fingers muddied with lardoons of sauce and gristle. A busboy arrived and cleared the table, and Leonard's gaze turned to a candle between them, which glowed faintly from the depths of a slender glass. Patty asked for a dessert menu, and Leonard dipped his finger into the glass, removed a hot thimble of wax, and slipped it into his mouth. It was warm and tasted of vanilla bean and, faintly, brook trout.

"There's another angle here," Patty said.

"What do you mean?"

"I've been thinking about it. I'll bet you're trying to bilk Pinnacle for more Benjamins."

"Why would you say that?"

"Because it makes sense. I don't know if you realize it, but your office is a dump. The place stinks, literally."

"So?"

"So, there's no way my company is a regular client of yours. This job fell into your lap. Besides, I could tell by the way your coworkers were going on about it in the break room. I can see why you'd want me to believe everything's business as usual, but I think you hit the lottery this morning."

"All of my clients are important to me."

"See, you're not even a good liar," she said. "Let's say I go to the press anyway, that I sacrifice everything just to throw a monkey wrench into your plan. Worst-case scenario, I lose my job. You lose the best client you didn't even earn."

Leonard crossed his legs. "What would you gain by doing that?"

"Fun times?" she said.

Leonard shook his head, adjusted himself in the seat. The tables were closely spaced Lucite cubes, and the dubious functionality irritated him.

"It isn't true, you know," Patty said. "What I said earlier."

"Regarding what?"

"The accident, that guy in the elevator. I was so horrified, I got physically sick. I cried for an hour in that basement, nonstop. I was hyperventilating. You can ask the cops. You can ask the guy who was in there with me."

"Then why'd you put on that show in my office?"

"I was afraid you'd take advantage of me. I guess that's what I'm used to. I was a temp for six months before Pinnacle gave me a full-time job, and the only reason they hired me was because the lady who had the position got cancer. That was six years ago. The pay is awful. They won't give me a raise. I work at a horrible job with horrible people, filing records for a company whose executives make more money in a day than I'll see all year."

"My heart bleeds," Leonard said.

"Not that I expect anything else. I've never had good luck. My mom died when I was little. I never had anything, and I've watched people like you my entire life with all this money and privilege treat the city like a giant playpen—"

"You don't know me," he said. He unfolded and refolded his napkin. "I asked earlier. What would make you happy?"

"What do you got?"

"Nothing that could fix you."

"I don't care what you think about me," she said. "I like myself."

"Then you have bad taste."

"Tell you the truth, I was thinking I could get into your line of work someday. Maybe you could give me some pointers, show me how to get my foot in the door."

"Please."

"I even have a project we could work on. If you want Pinnacle's business, maybe we could help each other out. There's some big news coming down the pipe no one's supposed to know about."

"That's exactly the kind of help I don't need."

"I'm surprised," she said. "I thought some insider info involving my company that's going to be front-page news in a couple months might, you know, be something you'd be interested in."

"Okay, I'll take the bait," Leonard said. "Say I'm interested. What are we talking about?"

"I have documents, lots of them. Emails, memos, that sort of thing."

"What sort of thing, Patty?"

"Wouldn't you like to know?"

"Actually, I wouldn't. And what's the catch, anyway? Why would you share something like that with me? What do you get in return?"

"Like I said, you could show me the ropes, tell me what the business is about. I mean, you could buy me dinner sometime—"

"I'm a busy person. I can't take time out of my schedule to feed your childish vision quest to become a PR pro."

"Maybe we could do lunch, a business lunch."

"No."

"That's a shame." She balled her napkin, tossed it onto the table. "I mean, even if what I have doesn't amount to anything, what do you have to lose?"

"Sorry, Patty. I'm just not interested. But your behavior baffles me. This afternoon Pinnacle offered you five thousand dollars, which you summarily refused. And now you want to engage in a horse trade for a free meal and some shop talk."

"Well, sure," she said. "I'm very career-oriented."

Leonard looked around the room. At the table next to them, a pie-eyed woman with a face paralyzed from Botox sat with an older man. She nodded at everything he said, attempted pained conversation between sips of wine.

"A month ago, I decided I was going to kill myself," Patty said. "I bought a bottle of sleeping pills, even did research on what kind kills you quickest. I had it all planned out. I was going to leave a letter for my father, take myself out to dinner, and spend all the money I had on a meal I could never afford, then I'd go home and down a handful of pills with a bottle of wine."

"This is boring me," Leonard said.

"I'm not saying I was going to do it today or anything, but it was going to happen, honest to God. Then, this morning, I overslept and got to work fifteen minutes late. I guess I shouldn't have cared about being written up, considering I planned on cashing in my chips anyway, but then I stepped onto the elevator with a man who got crushed to death before my eyes, and later I realized it was a sign. This is a new beginning. My new life starts today."

"And what does that mean?"

"This whole thing, me and the elevator, me and you, the fact I have all this incredible material on your dream client. This is fate. It was destined to happen. We could do something really special together."

"I have to say, your story strikes a chord," Leonard said. "Where do I sign?"

"I can't tell if you're being sarcastic or sincere," Patty said.

"Then I guess you have your answer."

IT HAD RAINED, AND REFLECTIONS OF TRAFFIC SPREAD IN BUSY FINGERS over puddles as they walked to the corner, stepped tentatively over terrazzo mosaics of busted cobblestone.

"Where do you live?" Leonard said as he hailed a cab. Fear lanced through his stomach when a network news van jockeyed into the middle lane of the street. Then the light turned green, and the van continued on.

"Queens," Patty said.

Leonard gave the driver forty dollars. He leaned into the rear window after Patty slid inside and handed her his cellphone. "Call yourself so I have your number."

"Okay," she said as she fumbled with his phone.

"Remember what I told you earlier. The only comment is 'no comment.' If a reporter bothers you, I want you to tell me immediately. Otherwise, don't call."

"Fine."

"The work I'm doing for your company, it's serious," Leonard said. "No more games. No threats."

Patty rolled her eyes as she handed him the phone. "Don't worry."

"I'll check in with you sometime next week. Of course, if you change your mind and decide to kill yourself, that's fine too."

He was surprised to hear her roar with laughter as the cab pulled away.

BY THE TIME HE RETURNED HOME, HE WAS EXHAUSTED. HE OPENED A CAN of garbanzo beans as he looked over a breathless press release Frazer Rae's team had assembled that afternoon, then shook several spoonfuls of detergent into the can, which produced a lumpy gruel whose flavor he found clumsy and misguided. At eleven o'clock he turned on the television and watched the replay of the evening news and inched up the volume as the screen cut to a shot of Pinnacle CEO Graydon Trotwood, sweating as he stood on a makeshift dais that had been erected on the sidewalk. A heat lightning of cameras flashed as Trotwood reported the day's events, spoken in the measured sotto voce of a public-radio fundraiser. His eyes had it, Leonard decided. They bore the distinction of a natural leader. Even in these delicate moments, he maintained a regal stoicism, a confidence that seemed intrinsic to his being. As Trotwood's statement approached its apex, there was a catch in his throat, eyes brimming tears as he trailed off. He held the silence just long enough to make it seem as though the effect hadn't been rehearsed before he looked directly at the cameras and, as the crowd stirred, uttered the name of his fallen employee, Arthur Goldstein, and shared his story with the world.

After the news conference was over, Leonard drew the blinds and stared into the fish tank, and an irritable feeling came over him. By some left-footed reasoning he'd envisioned a golden egg in this account he'd stumbled onto, but no, come Monday he'd be back to pitching ramen-profitable companies and corporate dead-enders whose careers had been sidelined by bad behavior. Leonard surveyed his apartment; papers were scattered over the couch, and the state of his floors distressed him. He disrobed, stepped into the bathroom, and, for the next half-hour, lay in the tub with the water drawn up to his chin. Failure had its own distinct presence, arrived like bad weather. Several minutes later, he raced across the apartment with a towel draped around his waist, picked up the phone, and dialed Patty. She answered on the first ring.

"I suppose I could squeeze you in for a business lunch Monday," Leonard said. "On the condition you supply me with those materials we discussed. I want documents, real ones."

"You'll get them," she said. "You won't be disappointed."

"Pick a place and get back with me."

"Perfect!" she said. "It's a date."

THE WEEKEND CRAWLED BY. ON SATURDAY, HE VISITED A PET STORE ON Broadway, looked over rows of cichlid tanks, and bought a bottle of water conditioner and a jar of tropical flakes. Then he walked to the men's health clinic, signed in, and sat in a waiting area alongside bodybuilders, off-the-clock executives, and white-knuckle alcoholics before he was called into an exam room, where a nurse injected 150 mg of testosterone cypionate into his left buttock, followed by a sinus shot (methylprednisolone and dexamethasone), and a lipotropic cocktail of amino acids (methionine, inositol, chromium, L-carnitine) as well as B vitamins, choline, dexpanthenol, and vitamin C. He stopped at the alternative health store, browsed aisles containing herbs and oils and mystical palliatives for arcane disorders, pills promising to transform men's genitals into charging rhinos, and purchased an all-natural gastric reflux medicine. Then he went to the organic market and left with basil-scented hand soap, a bottle of aromatic bitters, and a jar of artisanal cornichons. He ate the cornichons for dinner with an hors d'oeuvres fork as he watched television, and, when he grew bored, wet a rubber spatula, dipped it into his box of detergent, and set into a fit of licking. He fell asleep on the couch that night as the city rumbled outside his window.

On Sunday, Leonard outlined a thought leadership campaign for Pinnacle that focused on earned media spots in the ad trades. That evening, he gorged on pimiento olives and fabric softener, left the apartment, and walked to the train. It was pouring by the time he arrived in Koreatown, where crowds threaded up the sidewalks as Leonard slinked past restaurants, electronics outlets, and nail salons before he pushed against the steel door of an unmarked business whose windows were papered over with yellowed classifieds. An intercom buzzed him in to a second unmarked door, and he descended a dark stairwell patterned with patches of lavender light and passed a glass façade before entering the spa lobby, where a small woman with a downturned mouth scrutinized him from behind the desk.

"Hello, Mr. Leonard," she said.

"Hello, Ajumma."

The woman took Leonard's hand and led him to a changing room that smelled like a gym sock and gave him a towel, a robe, a pair of slippers, and a locker key attached to a nylon lanyard. Alone, he disrobed and slipped into the sauna before making a trip to the steam room, followed by a hot shower. Sweating, his anxiety enervated, he sat in the robe on a bench by the door and waited.

His heart thrummed when he saw her through the mineral streaks in the glass. She introduced herself as Amy—she'd been Heather last time—and guided him down a labyrinthine corridor that throbbed with lavender pulses. In a tiled stall he lay on a foam table, where she poured buckets of lukewarm water over his back and administered a table shower, lathered him with soap, and scrubbed his perineum and anus with a bath sponge before hosing him down with a handheld shower nozzle as he stared at a hexagon mosaic pattern on the walls. She toweled him off and led him down another hallway, where his eyes began to play tricks on him in the diffuse light.

The massage room hummed with chamber music and smelled of jasmine. He waited for his eyes to adjust, then scanned the counters for cleanliness. He slipped off the robe, wrapped the towel around his waist, and lay on a heated table, his face cradled inside a horseshoe-shaped pillow. She hovered over him and with oiled, baby-smooth hands made gliding strokes along his lats, then slipped south and worked his hamstrings with fluid runs, brushed his arms with quick wringing motions.

"Haven't seen you in a while," she said as she made circling patterns over his deltoids.

"Sure you have," he said.

"Of course," she said coquettishly. "You are so tense." She knuckled his trapezoids, the outline of his shoulder blades. "You are under stress?"

"Always."

"What do you do?"

"I work in PR. We talked about this for an hour, just two weeks ago."

"Okay," she said and spread the skin at the base of his head. Her technique was horrible and often painful; she dug her fingers into his flesh as though kneading dough. When she sank her elbows into the small of his back, Leonard squeezed his eyes shut and pressed his forehead into the table. "Turn over."

Leonard faced the ceiling and she peeled off the towel. "Deep breaths," she whispered as his scrotum unfurled down his inner leg. She palmed his chest, ran her fingers along the divot between his pectorals, then began working the base of his flaccid shaft, manipulating him into arousal with an adagio of soft strokes before running up and over the frenulum with her fingers and returning south again with calculating, liminal pauses. He tried to quiet his mind, concentrated on the music's dulcet sounds, a faint industrial murmur somewhere in the walls. His nose itched, and he fought back the impulse to scratch it.

"Please," he said. "Put the gloves on."

"I remember you now," she said as she crossed to a workstation in the corner.

When she returned, she positioned herself over his stomach, cleaved a latex-gloved hand behind his neck, and, with the other, slipped between his legs and continued working him, shifted her weight, switched hands and gripped his ass, pulled herself closer and buried her face in the contours of his clavicle, bit his neck. His breathing increased as she brought him to tumescence, and his hand, in an uncoordinated effort to touch her, fumbled in the towel before roaming over her ass and thighs, finding purchase between the buttons of her blouse, where he dialed his thumb around the radius of her nipple. She offered a rehearsed, prolonged moan as she continued pounding at him, and soon he was apprised of a revelation there in the dark, a low warmth that began in his feet and crept into his calves before branching into his fingers. A deep pressure welled inside, and his cock began to contract as he passed a threshold from which he knew he wouldn't return, and an acute sense of impending doom moved over him because everything seemed on the verge of spilling out and he grew desperate to hold it in yet somehow keep the sensation going forever at the same time. He thrashed like a fish on a line, saw a flash of color, bolted upright, and released with a spasm and a pained, muffled bleat, then collapsed and his head sank into the pillow and the world became still and irreducibly quiet as oblivion loomed in the strobing darkness and the air in the room chilled his tingling skin. He felt empty, like he would have to build himself up again from nothing, though everything seemed clear to him now, moderated by a dull shame. There were no more mysteries of the body, he thought, only transactions, a ventriloquism of the appetites. Entertainments to smooth the unruly features of daily life. She pressed a hot towel around his member and climbed onto the table, wrapped herself around him, and cradled his head.

"Can I stay for a minute?" he said.

"Sorry," she whispered. "I'm supposed to go on my break."

HE ARRIVED AT WORK EARLY ON MONDAY MORNING, GATHERED NEWSPA-pers from the lobby, and scanned headlines in his office, clipped and collected the features bearing Arthur Goldstein's photo, which had been distributed to the press by Frazer Rae's team on Friday. He checked his cellphone, found a text from Patty with an address for a restaurant on Forty-Second, called the restaurant and made a reservation for that afternoon. On the television, CNN reported an eight-magnitude earthquake had struck China's Sichuan province. Details were forthcoming, but a school building had collapsed, possibly leaving hundreds of children buried in the rubble. The anchor said it was the country's worst earthquake in at least thirty years, with early estimates of a death toll expected to exceed sixty thousand. Leonard spent his remaining time at his bookshelves, slipping splinters of wood into his mouth, flavor echoes of orange rind and hickory. Then the Todds arrived for the day's meeting.

Crisis: A local radio station had been accused of murder after a woman died by suicide following an on-air prank call. The show's DJ had called the victim, a 46-year-old caregiver and mother of two, telling her she was being deported to her native Guam. Convinced it was true, the woman killed herself the following day. The story outraged the public, the show's advertising roster dropped by sixty percent, and the FCC had opened an investigation. *Strategy:* Put the DJ on the talk-show junket to express "deep regret." After his media tour is over, terminate the show and fire the host. Enact a review of company policies and enforce a station-wide elimination of on-air prank calls. *Crisis:* After establishing a donation drive, an independent bookstore announced via social media it had recently turned down a branded sponsorship offer from a multinational oil-refinery company in the interest of maintaining "local integrity." Donations to the bookstore flooded in from locals supporting the business's resolve, but when news of the announcement reached the oil company's communications department, a press statement was issued claiming it had never offered financial assistance to the bookstore, and, in fact, doesn't participate in sponsorship programs. Now the bookstore's supporters were up in arms, with many demanding a return of their donations. *Strategy:* Issue a press release stating the post was an exercise in satire, meant to draw awareness to the perils of corporatization. *Crisis:* A recording-industry trade group wanted to promote its message regarding the economic impacts of illegally downloaded music. *Challenge*: The campaign's core audience—teens and young adults—comprised the demographic most likely to participate in illegal downloads. *Strategy*: Go guerrilla. Plaster college campuses with handmade flyers featuring a photo of a female student and the words "Stolen iPod! Reward offered!" Attach a row of tear sheets to the bottom of the flyer with a website, where curiosity seekers can contact the victim. When consumers go to the site, they'll discover a blog, wherein the victim candidly confesses much of the music she lost on her iPod was obtained illegally. After several days of updates— make sure to include photos of the victim; she should be pretty, preferably blonde—the iPod is safely returned, and the victim is compelled to share her learned lesson: that music piracy, like theft, is wrong.

Once his team was gone, Leonard opened his desk drawer, grabbed a stack of brochures, and stuffed them into an unassuming mailer envelope. He headed for the bathroom, which he was thankful to find vacant, entered the last stall and closed the door, sat on the toilet, and listened to the hiccuping sound of a dripping faucet and singing pipes within the walls. He perused a brochure for a gated community named Rose Brook Estates, scrutinized condominium models, chapel windows, and paver patios, postcard views of sun-drenched lawns bordered by lattice fences. He set the materials down and tore several flakes of toilet paper from the dispenser, slipped them into his mouth, and rolled them over his tongue, tasting murmurs of apple and rose. He pressed his forehead against the cool steel partition of the stall, let the wad settle into a pocket between his gum and cheek, and closed his eyes.

He awoke to the sounds of splashing. He stepped out of the stall, where Griffin Cruz, Travel and Tourism lead and newly minted Senior VP, stood primping in front of the mirror. He dressed with a predilection for line and order, his jacket, tie, and collar heavily starched and liberated from the slightest wrinkle, the cuffs of his monogrammed shirt taut with the wrists, as though they'd been grafted to the skin.

"Ahoy, Lundell," Cruz said. He had wild eyebrows and an aquiline nose, a high forehead and a gleaming fin of moussed hair. "Who's going bankrupt this week? Whose sex-tape nightmare will be gracing the headlines? Inquiring mind over here."

"Move, peon," Leonard said as he stood over the sink. On the counter was a nest of toiletries: a pocket comb, a curling tube of toothpaste, a spool of floss. He detected faint hints of musk, noticed a peacock-blue bottle of cologne under the soap dispenser.

"Bit of excitement Friday," Cruz said. He stood so close the tips of their shoes were touching; Leonard caught a whiff of antiseptic, the sweet rot of halitosis. "Fresh fish, Lundell?"

"New client in the pipeline. You'll hear about it soon."

Leonard threw open the bathroom door and Cruz followed into the break room, a sour parlor of lemon linoleum, cornsilk wallpaper, and lime overheads. At a table, two young account executives sat tapping on their cellphones. On the television above them, a news anchor held a baby panda in a diaper and teased it with a leaf before the animal bit her finger.

"Listen, Lundell, I wanted to powwow." Cruz set his toiletries on the counter, opened a pea-colored refrigerator, and began rummaging through the crisper. "I've got a new concept I was hoping you could vet for me. This is cerebral stuff. I'm going to boil the ocean with this one."

"Let me guess: staycations? Babymoons?" Leonard said as he eyed Cruz's neglected cologne. "Enlighten me on the vapid leisure campaigns the industry is spinning this year."

"You're behind the times. Why are you so mean, anyway?"

"Congrats, Griffin," one of the account executives said and slipped on his jacket.

"Semper fi, Griffin," said the other and squeezed Cruz's shoulder.

Leonard's face reddened. The account executives left, and he felt a weltering anxiety in his chest. "I heard about the promotion," he said between his teeth. "Felicitations."

"Ha, thanks. I'm moving into Goodfriend's old digs at the end of the week. We're going to be neighbors."

"Wonderful."

"I'll admit there's a certain sense of foreboding, taking a dead man's office. You get any of those coffee mugs Goodfriend gave away before he bought the farm? I've got a World's Number-One Dad I'd be willing to trade if you have anything with a motivational quote."

"I got nothing," Leonard said. "Sorry to disappoint."

"So, we're rebranding the travel division under this new psychology platform, ergo the reason I wanted your help reading the tea leaves. Brace for it." He held up his hands, correlated his thumbs and index fingers to suggest a box, then affected a duck's bill with his lips. "Basically, we'll be

pitching travel as therapy, health over indulgence, experience over destination, wanton use of the word 'journey,' etcetera. We've got this nutcase
shrink on board who thinks travel reverses signs of aging. Real froufrou
stuff, works great with the cleanse-and-colonic crowd."

"Sounds idiotic."

"I'm thinking about calling it Rejuvacation. Also: Sabbaticure,
Pharlough—"

"Travel has always been therapeutic," Leonard said. "Your idea presents
a distinction without a difference. It's a concept that insists on itself."

Cruz smiled and straightened his tie. Under the track of fluorescent
tubes, his face appeared jaundiced, the color of boiled cabbage. "I'm also
thinking about appending my title in light of the promotion," he said.
"What do you think about Senior Vice President and Brand Evangelist."

"Why?"

"Just to do it. Travel isn't blessed with the same rococo ring as crisis
management."

Griffin was a former shoe-leather lobbyist who'd worked for a K Street
government relations firm during the early days of the Bush Administration. He'd left Capitol Hill under shadowy circumstances—or was run out,
depending on who you asked—and landed on Madison Avenue, where he'd
found an unlikely home pitching evergreens in the travel and tourism sector. He'd joined the firm only a few years ago but had skyrocketed through
the ranks, walked between the raindrops to establish the travel unit as one
of the agency's largest practice areas. Cruz signed more retainers than anyone else in the office, and the Gurney principals loved him for it, currying
an internal favoritism that Leonard both understood and resented.

Cruz opened a cupboard, removed a Styrofoam cup, and walked to the
water cooler. As he bent over, Leonard dashed to the counter, grabbed the
cologne, opened its cap, and held it to his nose. Horse and tack room leather.

Cruz turned and reached for his toiletries, causing Leonard to drop the
envelope, its contents scattering across the break room's laminated floor.

"What've you got there?" Cruz said.

"Nothing. Reports," Leonard said as he clutched brochures to his chest.

Cruz bent over and picked up a tract that had sailed under the table.

"Rose Brook Estates," Cruz said. "Lanchester, Ohio." He lifted a hand to his mouth to conceal his laughter as he leafed through the booklet. "Sounds . . . pastoral."

"I'm buying a condominium for my mother. Satisfied?"

"Well, the worm has turned," Cruz said. "Onward and upward."

"THIS IS HARDLY WHAT I WAS THINKING WHEN I SAID BUSINESS LUNCH," Leonard said as they crossed the restaurant's chandelier-bedecked parlor.

The open basilica layout was a retrospective in dining clichés: ivory walls featuring paintings of vineyard arbors, flanked by soaring Greek columns and vases spilling over with fronds. The room was inhabited by stately-looking men who Leonard imagined spent their free time being painted beside library fireplaces.

"The tuna tartare is supposed to be heavenly," Patty said as she fell into her seat and flipped through the menu with childlike anticipation.

"I'm not hungry," Leonard said.

"Geez, don't you eat? No wonder you're so skinny."

Leonard studied her. "Fine," he said and picked up the menu. It was leather-bound and Bible-heavy, detailing items that read like archaic forms of punishment. Soon a milk-skinned waiter hovered over them.

"I'll have the porcini-rubbed Delmonico," Patty said and clapped her hands.

Leonard huffed and settled on the first familiar option that availed itself. "Cedar-planked salmon."

Patty rolled her eyes after the waiter left. "Don't you know anything?" she said. "Salmon is the most boring thing you can get in a restaurant. There's nothing chefs can do with it."

"Sorry to disappoint," he said. "Do you have those documents for me?"

Patty rifled through one of her bags, then laid a battered camcorder on the table. She pressed a button and a red diode flashed, positioned the device so its lens eyed Leonard's face.

"Why are you recording me?" Leonard said.

"A precaution, geez. The other day you said my company would fire me if I told anyone about what I saw—"

"I never said that," he said, looking to the lens.

"Yeah, right. If we're going to discuss anything involving my job, I need a record of it."

"Absolutely not. I'm not playing this game."

"Why?"

"Because life isn't a spy novel, Patty. Because I've been hired to protect—" he cupped his palm over the lens, grabbed the camera, and engaged the stop button with his thumb. "I'm supposed to help your company's reputation. If there's something out there that could subvert that reputation, I need to know about it. We had a deal. I buy you lunch, you show me those documents."

"Fine, take a look." She leaned over, reached into her bag again, and placed a manila folder stuffed with a slipshod stack of papers on the table. Leonard removed the binder clip and thumbed through several sheets, inspected the contents as though he'd been handed foreign currency. Most of the pages consisted of printed emails, back-and-forths between Pinnacle's senior management discussing Europe's largest advertising conglomerate, Publique Groupe S.A., and draft notes regarding a meeting the month prior with the multinational holding company. Much of the correspondence outlined what appeared to be a proposed merger. He skimmed over several more pages, fidgeted in his chair.

"Where did you get this?" he said.

"Wouldn't you like to know?"

"And this is everything?" He closed the folder and covered it with his hands, felt a heat in his chest, and realized, for some unknown reason, his nose was whistling. "I mean, it's not a big deal, Patty. Agencies merge all the time."

"Looks like a big deal to me," she said. "If Publique acquired my company, wouldn't that make us the biggest ad agency in the world?"

Entrees arrived. Leonard stared at the wedge of salmon, lively pink, wading in a pool of leeks and cream. He speared the meat with his fork, and sections of flesh flaked off into his mouth. A sugared glaze browned and hardened the surface; it was warm and buttery and tasted of white wine, garlic, and, faintly, lemon peel. He fought back the urge to vomit and, after enduring several bites, returned his attention to the documents before him, tried to ignore the animal thrashing sounds, the sucking and smacking that came from the other side of the table.

"Do you mind," he said, "not chewing like that?"

"Like what?"

"With your mouth open." He reached for his fork, picked up a knife. "You eat like you were raised by wolves."

"No, I don't."

Leonard draped his napkin over the plate, bolted from the chair, and wedged a handful of bills under his plate. He grabbed the folder and held it tightly to his chest.

"Where are you going?" Patty said.

"This business lunch is over. Our time is finished."

"But we haven't gotten dessert!" she said. Several patrons began to stare.

"You haven't given me any real information on my client," Leonard said. "You haven't provided anything that could help me manage and protect Pinnacle's reputation. I'm afraid we have nothing more to discuss."

"I cooperated with you," Patty said. "I could've given this stuff to some reporter, just like how I could've talked to them about what happened Friday."

"If you want to keep your job, I highly advise you avoid doing that," Leonard said. "As far as the elevator accident is concerned, the press isn't interested anymore. Did you even read the papers? The media have all the facts they need. They were contacted by our co-counsel during the press conference while I was across town stuffing your face. They have other stories to busy themselves with now. There was an earthquake in China, didn't you hear? Almost eight magnitude. The story has grown cold, Patty. They've moved on, and so have I."

"But there's stuff in those documents, big stuff. You just have to look."

"Take solace in this: The real winner here today is you. I hope you're happy. You've gotten another free meal out of me."

He shoved his way past tables and confused waitstaff and picked his pace up to a sprint when the exit came into view.

"Wait, I need those back—" Patty began, but he was already at the door.

Chapter 5

S ure you don't want anything?" Jack said as a cheerless waiter refilled coffee.

The Williams Club dining room was tempered by soft orange light. Every detail, from the masonry fireplace to the framed photographs of Williams College alumni, made it seem like a gift shop of its halcyon past, nostalgia hour for the establishment's white-shoe clientele, none of whom appeared a day younger than seventy.

"I hate it here," Leonard said and straightened his silverware. Even in a restaurant this exclusive, they couldn't grasp the gravity of order.

"I pay monthly dues," Jack said and fumbled with his hearing aid. "Thanks for agreeing to meet me. Sorry I couldn't do it this afternoon. I have a dentist appointment. Do you floss, Leonard? It's very important for gum health."

Jack spoke brusquely, usually out of the side of his mouth. He articulated ideas in a confusing language of antiquated WASP colloquialisms, was wont to air undeveloped political opinions, and was obsessed with cancers of the skin. Around the office, he advocated bizarre social axioms, thought chewing gum should be outlawed, and considered it low-class for men to urinate while standing. As Leonard looked the old man over, crumbs ringed around his mouth, it occurred to him how slowly he moved, limited to an almost childlike range of motion.

A ceiling fan stirred the smell of wood soap across the room. On a television above the bar, a news anchor discussed the effects JPMorgan Chase's credit default buyout of Bear Stearns would have on the markets.

"They say we're headed toward a recession," Leonard said.

"It's a bull market. Our problem is PR's become a bad word," Jack said. "The industry used to be about building relationships. We knew reporters' birthdays, their anniversaries. Nowadays it's all about getting your clients to avoid the press. No one cares about the art of conversation anymore."

"Why should they? The profession's been overtaken by marketing."

"Same thing happened in the sixties when the ad agencies bought up all the small shops. Why care about the work when the holding company's stock price is all that matters?"

"You think the good days are behind us?"

"Young men think about the future, old men think about the past," Jack said. He stared wanly at the fireplace, which Leonard found odd, considering it wasn't lit. "I guess when things are happening, it's always different from after they happened. Live, die, and forget it all, right?"

The statement left Leonard with an unattributed feeling. "Well, we didn't get everything we wanted," he said and set his elbows on the table, "but Pinnacle is officially a client."

"You did good, kid. That CMO called today—"

"Feinblum."

"Said there was a development over the weekend. Apparently, the *Times* tracked down one of our elevator witnesses. Squirrely guy? Graphic designer?"

"Hugh Sneery."

"Scuttlebutt has it he gave more 'no comments' than Eliot Spitzer in a sex probe. They didn't get a word out of him. He wouldn't even confirm his name."

"Great news," Leonard said, half reclined now. "Now we need to talk."

The old man tented his fingers and looked Leonard over with a sort of tense resignation, as though he'd been asked to solve a riddle.

"Let's say after this job is done, I get Pinnacle as agency of record," Leonard said.

"Good one," Jack said.

"Hear me out. We become Pinnacle's AOR. Crisis, media relations, corporate branding, the whole shebang."

"Get to the point."

"Senior Vice President," he said.

"No," Jack said. "You can't say that."

"Too late. We'll have to argue about something else."

"We can't call you Senior VP. Griffin Cruz has that title."

"Then there will be two of us. I want what you promised me six months ago."

"That's too many cooks in the kitchen. I'll put you in the cards for a promotion next year when we're on top again, when some new retainers put us back in the black."

"You say that every year," Leonard said. "We just billed a client ten grand for a few hours of work. Make it happen."

"As an SVP, you'd be responsible for making sure our clients and account teams are getting quality service. It's a demanding job."

"I'm up for the challenge," Leonard said.

"And if I say no?"

"Then I walk and leave the Todds to fumble this ball."

"They're neophytes," Jack said. "You're the only seasoned crisis pro we have."

"You'll get a letter of resignation Friday," Leonard said. "I'll give you until the end of next week to wrap a bow on things, tie up loose ends."

"Next week?" Jack said. "Kid, none of this is necessary—" The old man was a series of clumsy gestures, appeared controlled by remote departments, invisible marionette wires. "Yeah, okay," he said. "It's a deal."

"So, that's a yes? And I can get it in writing?"

"You got it, kid. Fine." The old man exhaled, gave an uncommitted glance around the room, crossed his arms. "It's been a good six years."

"Seven years," Leonard said.

"Seven good years. Remember when I hired you?"

"How could I forget? It was a historically bad morning."

"You had no references and barely any experience to speak of."

"In your defense, I was the only one who showed up for the interview. Lower Manhattan was on fire, after all." Leonard set his palms flat on the table. "Of course, if I'm going to hold an executive position, I'll need a raise—"

"I hope you're enjoying this," Jack said. "Four percent. Current standard."

"Five and a half," Leonard said. "Raises don't come around often."

Jack stood and shook Leonard's hand and reached for his jacket, accidentally slapping his coffee mug onto the floor. "Damn."

A busboy wheeled a mop bucket into the room, followed by a procession of waitstaff who got down on their knees and scouted for shards with dust pans. As a jug of bubblegum-pink floor cleaner was poured into the bucket, phantom aromas began kicking in Leonard's sinuses: fruit, flower, and cask.

"By the way," Jack said. "Frazer Rae called and said he wants you to stop by his office."

"What for?"

"Didn't say. Probably just wants to trade notes and talk shop. You saved his ass, cooling the situation on such short notice." Jack patted his pockets, scanned the table. "Have you seen my glasses?"

"They were on your head a minute ago." Leonard reached inside the old man's jacket and found them, lodged in the bottom of the breast pocket.

"I lost a hearing aid last month," Jack said. "Two pairs of glasses this year. I'm losing everything."

LEONARD WALKED BACK TO THE OFFICE AND CLOSED THE DOOR, OPENED his desk drawer, and removed the folder he'd taken from Patty the day before. It was the second time that morning he'd paged through its contents, and the pages felt heavy in his hands, something better handled with gloves. He perused memos and dozens of emails, including a curious correspondence between Pinnacle CEO Graydon Trotwood and his French counterpart, Publique Groupe's René Martin. All signs indicated this was real: Publique, Europe's largest advertising conglomerate, was attempting to acquire a majority stake in one of the top ad holding companies in the country. The merged entity would create the largest advertising combine in history. It would change the industry forever. Pinnacle would need media training for a transaction of this size, not to mention guidance managing stakeholder perceptions and the SEC review process. He could craft an elevator pitch with a list of every service he could think of, set up a meeting with Pinnacle senior management, and get in on the ground floor before any agency in town.

Leonard dug into his breast pocket for his pen and jammed it into his mouth, slapped the speaker button on the telephone, eyed the blinking green diode.

"Armitage," Leonard said. "I need you to get on the horn and set up a powwow with Pinnacle as early as possible, ideally next week."

"Next week might be short notice," Todd Armitage said. "Is this a catch-up meeting?"

Something was wrong with the connection, and his voice sounded textured, rattled like loose hex nuts on a dashboard.

"Proposal for agency representation," Leonard said. "Nothing I say leaves this conversation."

"Hoo boy. What's the campaign?"

"Listen very carefully." Leonard opened his drawer and raked around for a bottle of hand soap. On the television, a report featured a list of breakfast foods that cause cancer.

LEONARD WANDERED INTO A PET STORE ON LEXINGTON DURING HIS lunch break and perused azure glass aisles. The store was practically empty, somewhat strange given the time of day, and the selection was impressive, a rare quality in pet stores that didn't specialize solely in aquatics. Besides the usual feeder fish, the gouramies and mollies and tetras, they had a prodigious assortment of saltwater fish, as well as Central and South American cichlids. He toured through the network of corridors as though lost in a dream, stopping whenever something caught his eye.

A rash spread over his face when he saw Patty making small talk with the cashier. She wore an ill-fitting floral romper, and a wide-rimmed nylon sun hat obscured her eyes.

"What the hell are you doing?" Leonard said as he stamped up the aisle.

"What a surprise!" Patty said.

"Drop the act," he said as she followed him behind a partition that separated the aisles of tanks from the rest of the store. "Why are you here?"

"Just in the neighborhood." Patty stopped and tapped on the glass, sending a school of fish into a scattering retreat. "What are these?"

Leonard stared at her. "Chocolate cichlids," he muttered.

"Are they friendly?"

"They're fish. What do you care?"

"Maybe I want a pet."

"You can't start with those," he said. "They get a lot bigger, probably thirteen inches or so. And you can't have any plants in the tank. They eat everything."

"They're beautiful."

"Their heads turn gold when they get older." Leonard walked up another aisle, this one housing larger tanks with bigger fish: oscars, blood parrots, and red terrors.

"What's this one?" Patty said.

Leonard sighed. "Blue acara. They're territorial. And they breed like crazy."

"How many fish tanks do you have?"

"One," he said. "I used to have more."

"I always imagined guys in your circle spend their money on hookers and cocaine. You just look at a bunch of fish."

"Is that supposed to be an insult?"

Patty followed him to the front of the store. In a massive tank near the entrance, a fish floated lifelessly in a corner as a swarm picked at the carcass, tiny elastic mouths revealing hundreds of pinlike teeth that ripped chunks of white flesh from the bone, the surrounding water a soup of meat and cartilage.

"That's gross," Patty said.

"That's nature," Leonard said.

Outside, Leonard stole up the sidewalk, reached the corner, and stepped into the street, but the rushing traffic prevented him from crossing.

"Hold up," Patty said as she approached, wheezing. "You doing anything right now? Maybe we could grab a bite—"

Leonard grabbed her wrist and pulled her behind a newsstand.

"Hey, what gives?" she said.

"You've been following me," he said.

"Okay, fine. I want those documents back!"

"What, like you didn't make copies?"

"That isn't the issue. It's my property!"

"Listen to me, you window-licker." He brought his mouth so close to her ear that his lip grazed the lobe. "There will be no more speaking between us, you understand?"

"Geez, you're being mean!" she said.

"I think you have the social graces of a stray dog," Leonard said. "I think if we lived in a civil society, there'd be someone to take you into an alley and have you shot."

Patty's eyes pulled back, and her mouth fell open. "I'll tell everyone about you," she said. "I'll tell that journalist, the one who was asking questions—"

"One step ahead of you, Patty. The *Times* got to your coworker over the weekend. He shut the story down."

"But this guy wasn't with the *Times*," she said. "He said he was with the *Register*. And he wasn't asking about my company or anything that had to do with the accident. He was asking about you."

Leonard locked up, felt his left calf seize in a death cramp. "When?" he said.

"This morning. He said he was going to call you," she said. "Geez, relax. Let go."

"And how did he know you had ties to me?"

"How should I know?"

"Where did he find you?"

"Right outside my building."

"So, what did you tell him?"

"No comment, just like you said. Then he gave me his card and told me to call if I changed my mind."

Leonard released his grip. "Let me see it."

She sunk a fist into her purse and produced a creased square. Leonard noticed the blue type, the familiar serif font: "Noah Sundermeyer, Business Reporter, the *Register*." He stuffed the card into his pocket.

"I need to know everything," he said. "I want to know every question he asked."

"Not much—"

"Patty, this is important. I have to find out why this guy knew to contact you, because he probably plans to write on the accident at the Pinnacle building."

"Then why was he asking questions about you?"

"I don't know. But Pinnacle is the common denominator here, so it's a logical assumption the accident is the angle he's after." He turned his back to her and ran his fingers through his hair. "We'll need to talk," he said. "We'll sit down and discuss exactly what he asked."

"Sure, we can meet for dinner—"

"No more goddamn dinner," he yelled. Passersby began to stare.

"So what do I get in return?" she said. "You're playing me along. You threaten to get me fired, then you steal my documents, and now you get all aggressive on me."

"Tell you what," Leonard said. "Come to my office later today, and we'll go over everything. Then we're going to call this guy, and you're going to tell him you don't know me. After that, I'll get you anything you want. Restaurant of your choice. Dinner, dessert, the works."

"Promise?"

"Scout's honor."

Leonard raced back to his office. He foraged through a drawer crammed with moist towelettes, found a box of erasers, and fled to the break room, where he ate them over coins of dill pickle from a jar he stole from the refrigerator. Then he licked petrified crumbs off the caramel-colored vein of sealant that lined the windowsill. He returned to his office and tried to work, found himself concentrating on the muffled chanting, the din of telephones that hummed from the pods outside his door. His head was inside his filing cabinet when the telephone rang, the emerald flash of the console lighting up the darkened corner like a firefly.

"Leonard Lundell?"

"Speaking."

"My name is Noah Sundermeyer. I'm with the *Register*. I'm writing—"

"Let me stop you there," Leonard said. His nerves had him shaking, and he found himself gripping his chair for support. "I have no comment. I have nothing to say."

"It's strange someone who specializes in public relations would offer 'no comment.' You realize 'no comment' sends the message that you're hiding something, right?"

"I'll take that under advisement, but it's all you're going to get." Leonard retrieved his pen from his pocket, stuck it in his mouth, and began to gnaw.

"Could you just help me with a few details? I spoke with a Pinnacle employee this morning, a woman by the name of Patty Pachis, and asked her—"

"No comment," Leonard repeated and hung up the phone.

Leonard felt hot flashes and turned up the air-conditioner unit. In minutes he was cold and draped his jacket over his shoulders. He opened his internet browser and googled the reporter's name. Only a handful of articles appeared; Leonard skimmed an insipid and unnecessarily lengthy feature regarding the construction of a shopping mall in Staten Island. Sundermeyer, just the sort of WASPy bawl Leonard associated with business reporters. He was young, Leonard decided, had probably been on the job only a few years. Anglo, upper-middle-class upbringing, reasonably educated, though certainly not Ivy League. Spends weekends in sports bars, celebrates "casual Friday" with eager readiness.

Knuckles rapped on the doorframe.

"What do you want?" Leonard said.

Leonard closed his browser as Todd Armitage entered the office. "That weird girl, the elevator witness. She's here, said you two have a meeting?"

"She'll have to wait. Keep an eye on her, will you?"

Once Armitage was gone, Leonard dug in his pocket for Sundermeyer's card and picked up the receiver.

"Sundermeyer," the voice on the other end said.

"Sundermeyer, this is Lundell at Gurney PR. We just spoke."

"Glad you called—"

"I've only got a minute." Leonard walked around his desk, sat on the edge of it. "I don't know what you want. I'm an honest person. I make an honest living. And I don't know why you were talking to that woman about me, but I'm asking you to leave her alone. She has problems." Leonard dipped into a whisper. "She hears voices, has conversations with inanimate objects. Not exactly a quotable source."

"I never said I spoke with her about you," Sundermeyer said, "so I'll take it you've communicated with her since. How do you know this person?"

"She's a friend," Leonard said and resumed chewing on his pen.

"Really?"

"Yes. Please, leave her alone."

"Incidentally, did she know the Pinnacle employee who died in the elevator accident last Friday?"

"No. She wasn't even in the building."

"See, I know that's not true. Police reports are public," Sundermeyer said. "And then, yesterday, I saw her going into a restaurant on Forty-Second with you. That's how I put the two and two together. Is Pinnacle a client of yours?"

"You were following me?"

"I saw you on the street, Lundell. Is Gurney PR Pinnacle's agency of record, or does this fall under a project account—"

"You need to get your facts straight," Leonard stammered. "Pinnacle is a client of Frazer Rae and Associates. I don't divulge who my clients are."

"If you don't want to go on record, could you at least help me confirm a few details?"

Heartburn clawed at Leonard's esophagus. He looked down at the pen in his hand and noticed the butt had been gnawed flat.

"Right now, I've got that you've been with Gurney since 2001," Sundermeyer continued, "but I don't know where you were stationed prior to that. The only matching Leonard Lundell I even found a record for is from a small town in Ohio, and this guy was enrolled at Ohio State for a few years in the nineties, but I'm not sure—"

"Just leave me alone," Leonard said and hung up the phone.

Todd Armitage reappeared in the doorway with a puzzled look. "I don't know where she went," he said. "She disappeared."

"Then find her!"

The phone rang again. Leonard ignored it, left his office with Armitage, and followed him up the aisle of cubicles and into the foyer. He crossed the entire floor, peeking into offices, checking the break room and the stairwell. As he passed Jack Gurney's opened door, he noticed a salvage yard of books scattered across the floor, the old man on all fours, muttering to himself as he crawled among them.

"What are you doing?" Leonard said.

"You know, kid, I've been thinking," Jack said and dialed up the volume on his hearing aid. "PR needs a library."

Leonard looked around the room. A pyramid of books in every corner below a perimeter of shelves still swaddled in plastic stretch film, now semi-filled with columns of color-coordinated volumes. Aside from that, the office was the same as it had always been, stowaways of paperstuffs and dust, a decomposing musk that smelled like old bills. Post-it notes everywhere, detailing instructions on everything from how to use the computer and the fax machine to reminders to turn off the lights.

"Think about it," Jack said. "A free resource where the community can browse books and trade publications about the industry."

"I don't know if people go to libraries anymore, Jack. I mean, the internet . . ." Jack flipped through several pages of a yellowed journal, nodded and muttered as a bridge of eyebrows flattened across his face. "Where did you get all these books, anyway?"

"I had them shipped from home. I've been collecting them since I opened this place, back when the B. Altman department store was down the block." Jack resumed sifting among the pile. "Believe it or not, our industry used to have a library, at the Public Relations Society of America's headquarters on Third Avenue—"

"I've actually got an emergency situation right now," Leonard said. "Have you seen a large woman wandering around?"

"Large woman? No, what does she look like?"

"Never mind."

Maintenance workers were standing in the doorway when Leonard returned to his office. Inside, the telephone continued to ring.

"Work order, chief," a fireplug-shaped man said and waved a pink insertion order. "We're here to replace the window."

The men began ripping out the steel window frame with crowbars, and Leonard returned to the hallway and continued his search for Patty, inspected the conference room and the utility closet and scouted through cubicles. When he returned to his office, his eyes caught a blinding flash as the men hoisted the fresh pane of glass into place. He sat at his desk after the men left and turned on the television. A poll showed twenty percent of Americans believed Saddam Hussein had been responsible for the September 11 attacks. The phone rang again.

"I already told you," Leonard said. "No goddamn comment."

"Leonard?" A familiar voice that took several seconds to register: his brother, Norman. "I've been trying to call you. Don't hang up."

Leonard pushed the receiver against his temple until it hurt. "What do you want, Grandma? I'm working over here."

"Stop calling me that," Norman said. "Listen, something bad has happened. Mom's in the hospital."

Leonard placed the phone down and leaned forward, set his elbows on his knees. He'd forget most of the details later, like the flutter of arrhythmias he felt in his chest as he loosened his tie and tried to breathe, how the room's modified lighting conditions, the way the sun filtered through the new window, made his domain seem distressingly foreign. He recalled only the bouquet of pencils that taunted him from the coffee mug on his desk. He grabbed at them and bit through each neck furiously, gorged as yellow chips flaked over his lap and onto the carpet. Paralyzing flavors, a lupine fragrance not unlike dandelion greens, crisp and bright, a crack of light under the door in a dark room. It wasn't until he'd eaten through six of them and sat gasping for air that he heard a faint rustling from the far side of the room, the yawning of the opening closet door.

He went white when Patty, pale, ghostlike, materialized in the dark. A pillar of shadow fell across the room as the door swung open and she moved toward him, as if hovering above the floor, the camcorder in her left hand drawn to her chest, its scintillating red eye transfixed on the busted thicket strewn over the desk. Leonard shivered and bolted upright, flapped his hands, and made a whipsaw motion for the desk, winched down gripping the edges, steeling himself for what might happen next. The terms of the room changed: The floor met him at an obtuse angle, and the walls began to turn as Patty prowled around the desk and drew the camera to his face, and the hairs on his arms bristled when she placed a calming hand at his shoulder and his eyes turned aslant and his mouth gaped, where a chewed nub of eraser fell from his tongue.

"Well," she said. "That's not something you see every day."

Chapter 6

Atmospheric pressure felt like hands pressed against his temples. Oxygen in the cabin was thin and recycled, as though he was traveling in the trunk of a car. Leonard unbuckled his seatbelt and slapped at the controls on the overhead console, twisted the air nozzle until a dry heat that smelled like rubber scudded over his hairline. An infant screamed amid the tree line of heads several rows away. Somewhere, a pair of headphones blared. He fidgeted in the seat and grazed the moist arm of the woman seated to his left. She was middle-aged and courageously obese, with thick gills of fat that draped over the armrest between them. In the seat to his right, a man chewed on his tongue as if it were a lozenge. Leonard craned his head and looked out the window. Patches of bruised earth between the clouds revealed a wrinkled mountain range, topographic maps of nowhere.

A flight attendant inched up the aisle with a beverage cart. Leonard returned to his book, a dog-eared copy of Hegel's *Phenomenology of Spirit*. He'd read it years ago, and something about its central thesis had seemed apropos when he freed it from his shelf that morning, but he'd just read an entire chapter and hadn't understood a word, and any thematic connection it had with the present was lost on him now. The infant continued to cry. Leonard adjusted himself again, the armrest knifing into his ribs, looked for his seatbelt, and discovered half of it wedged under the woman's right buttock. She rustled in her bag before producing a Tupperware container, opened it, and removed a wet chicken leg. Leonard had been watching this woman eat for more than an hour; since they'd boarded, he'd tallied potato chips, a wheel of cheese, carrot sticks, glued clusters of raisins. She turned to him, arched her eyebrows, and waved the leg. Leonard shook his head, and the woman honked in contentment.

"Sir," the flight attendant said. "Please fasten your seatbelt."

The man to Leonard's right continued to gnaw on his tongue, and he'd now curled his hand into a sort of functionless paw and began thumping his chest.

"Would you like a slice of pie?" the woman asked. "It's brambleberry."

"No, thank you," Leonard huffed.

He returned to Hegel, but the environment was hostile to heavy reading, so he set the book down. There should be rules, Leonard decided, an aptitude test travelers complete before boarding airplanes, a dry run to determine if they possessed the skills needed to occupy close quarters with others. There should be reasonable physical boundaries, an industry-standard measurement for seat width established by an aviation oversight committee, and passengers whose girth violates these delineations must purchase seats in business or first class. There should be assigned seating charts, an easy-to-follow, color-coded system separating parents with young children from the rest of the cabin. Anyone who violates the rules of airplane decorum should be removed from the plane immediately, their money refunded. No exceptions.

"I also have a cobbler," the woman said.

He closed his eyes and tried to relax. Inevitably, his thoughts returned to the events of the previous afternoon. Sleep the night before had been impossible: No position was comfortable, the room was either too hot or too cold, and car horns, stray voices on the street seemed amplified, clamored for his attention. He woke early with a sour stomach and a drumming anxiety, the weight of yesterday still on him, dead on his feet yet rattled into a state of alert.

THE COLOR HAD FALLEN OUT OF HIS FACE WHEN PATTY STIRRED IN THE closet, and a chill came over him as she unmoored from the shadows and drifted toward the desk. He girded the chair as she stood over him, distinctly remembered experiencing the sensation he was falling as his eyes rested on the camcorder lens, now taking a blue crescent of skyline. Patty flicked at the splintered shavings of pencil on his desk before letting out a plaintive sigh.

"Leonard, what were you doing?"

Six floors below, bodies crawled along Madison Avenue. Their movements from this distance spoke less about some fabled energy of the city than caged anxiety.

The words tumbled out of his mouth. "I don't know what you're talking about."

"Leonard." She sat on the edge of his desk, craned her head around the camcorder, and studied him. "I just watched you eat six pencils."

"No, I didn't."

"Yes, you did."

In hindsight, he would regret what he did next, not just because it was a flagrant violation of his oft-repeated cardinal rule of crisis communications—*always respond quickly*—but because it was a grossly incriminating move. He leaped from his chair and dashed to the door, swept past interns and file clerks and printers shucking reams of paper, passed Wanda Markowski, who shook her head in silent judgment, Griffin Cruz, who lounged in the recess of the water cooler, and Jack Gurney, who was still on the floor in his office, sorting through his collection of books. "Hey, Leonard! Hey, kid!" He bypassed the elevators and made for the stairwell, and his bones took on weight, legs couldn't carry him fast enough as he descended the six flights, fell into the lobby, and breached the avenue, where he was swallowed by the rush-hour crowd.

He dodged sky-gazing tourists, busking musicians, knots of suits as he fought his way up the sidewalk. The spine of the avenue blazed in the kaleidoscopic glimmer of dusk as he skipped into the exchange of traffic and ran until he reached Forty-Second, where he crossed Grand Central, entered the plaza of an office building, and collapsed onto a vacant bench. He felt deflated, unwound, a machine running on bad software. He recalled his second rule of crisis communications: *identify vulnerabilities, and respond accordingly.* There was a calculus in every dilemma; all he needed was the right combination of words and he could devise an explanation. But every exit seemed beyond reach; there was just the hammering anxiety, the slot-machine sounds of traffic, a low rumbling beneath the city he wondered whether its inhabitants noticed anymore. He was staring at the soft white underbelly of an incoming crisis, in utero, incubating and taking weight.

"Funny thing you saw back there," Leonard said when he returned to his office twenty minutes later. His tie was missing, and his shirt was untucked and blotted with sweat. Patty was seated behind his desk, tapping a button on his keyboard with her thumb. "It was an exercise," he said, "a radical trust-building exercise I'm devising for a client. The idea being, if you can trust in yourself, you can do anything, bite through a pencil, for example, shred phonebooks with your bare hands—"

"Nice try." Patty swiveled his chair, revealing a snaking trail of tooth marks along the arm pads.

Leonard stood sweating under the hectoring hum of the overheads. He recalled his third rule of crisis communications: *appeal to human emotion.*

"My mother," he said. "She's in the hospital."

"Why do you do it?" Patty said.

She spoke brusquely; there was an air of authority in her voice he hadn't previously detected, a clarity in her expression, an intent.

"Do what?" he said.

He tentatively eyed the camcorder on the desk, then sprang for it and wrested the memory card from its plastic housing with his fingers. He ran to the window and, after some effort, managed to pry it open, defenestrated the card, and watched it waver with the breeze as it drifted into traffic.

"I already uploaded the video," Patty said. "Take a look for yourself." She turned the computer screen toward him, which was open to a video-sharing website. "I haven't posted anything yet. I'm waiting, Leonard. Why do you eat pencils?"

Sweat pooled under his eyes. He felt naked, critically exposed. A numbness came over him, and a crude mantra played in his head, a string of shapeless ideas that resided in the suburbs of language, something he'd either improvised on the spot or had committed to memory in the fog of childhood: *run to the fields, race toward the horizon, find the tall stalks and hide.*

"Because I like it."

WHEN THE PLANE SKIDDED ACROSS THE TARMAC, LEONARD JERKED IN HIS seat and realized he had, in fact, fallen asleep. He scavenged through his duffel bag and drained the remainder of a Pepto-Bismol bottle, looked to the expanse of green earth outside the window. The cabin door opened several minutes later, and he smelled spirits of Ohio air. After retrieving a carry-on bag from the overhead compartment and waiting for the waddling herd to disembark, Leonard walked the carpeted corridors of Port Columbus International Airport and looked for his brother.

He found Norman standing next to a payphone in baggage claim. He was slightly taller than Leonard, slightly heavier too, had a firm belly and a doughy, naïve face that deducted several years from his age. He dressed as though he'd meant to make fun of himself, wore tapered chinos and a lime polo shirt, and sported a ridiculous new addition since their last meeting: an off-center mustache that studded above his lip like an enlarged eyebrow.

"Hello, Grandma," Leonard said and extended a hand. "Long time."

They walked outside, past the smokers' corral and across a macadamized roadway toward the parking garage. The family vehicle, a navy minivan riddled with dents, was parked in the taxi lane with one tire over the curb.

"Like my mustache?" Norman asked and unlocked the passenger door.

"I don't." Leonard sat in the back and tossed his bag into the bucket seat beside him. "Sorry. You look like a child molester."

It was a forty-minute drive from Columbus to Lanchester. The skyline disappeared in the rearview and soon they were in a yellow stretch of suburban half-country, passing car dealerships and amphitheater-sized churches, roadside gambrel-roofed barns that sold fireworks or pornography.

"A broken ankle," Leonard said. "That's it?"

"She tripped over something and fell."

"Why the hell did she stay in the hospital overnight?"

"They wanted to keep her under observation," Norman said. "I think she had a panic attack or something. The doctors wanted to be sure she didn't have a stroke."

"You've really got your thumb on the pulse, Grandma. You're supposed to be watching out for her."

"I've got two jobs. I haven't lived in the house for a year. I can't monitor her twenty-four/seven. What am I supposed to do?"

"Who even drove her to the hospital?"

"I think it was Mr. Roe. He was out walking his dog—"

"Then there's your lack of communication skills," Leonard interrupted. "I just dropped four hundred dollars to fly here on a day's notice. For a goddamn broken ankle."

"The hospital called me, and I called you. I didn't know the details at the time. And please, don't say the Lord's name in vain."

"Whatever," Leonard said.

Though they'd been raised in a secular household, toward the end of high school Norman had begun to take an interest in spiritual matters, and, as time progressed, his theological pursuits evolved into a commitment to the church. His strong academic performance was rewarded with a scholarship to attend the Moody Bible Institute in Chicago; but, as it turned out, the job market for pastors was anemic, and soon after graduation Norman returned home, where he eventually found part-time work as a chaplain at the local glass factory. He'd always hoped the vocation was something he could nurture into a full-time career, but to Norman's chagrin, few workers at the factory sought spiritual solace. Once he'd moved into an apartment of his own, he'd been forced to take a second job in telephone sales at the JC Penney catalog center in Reynoldsburg to pay the bills.

The rest of the ride was spent in silence. Leonard opened the window, the van filled with the beetroot smells of summer, and soon he was besieged by a field recording of childhood memories: daylong bike rides over hot tar roadways, freshly cut grass, the evensong of crickets in nightfall's lavender gloaming. His nerves began to flare as they approached Lanchester's city limits. They merged onto Memorial Drive, the town's thoroughfare, and passed familiar sights: box retailers, outlet malls, payday-loan operations, fast-food chains offering post-war adaptations of American fare.

"My apartment's over there, just past Wheeling," Norman said. "You can come over this weekend if you want. I have an Xbox."

"I suppose there's a silver lining to this," Leonard said. "It's just another reason the house needs to be sold. Did you look at the brochure I mailed you for Rose Brook Estates?"

"I don't know why you're so adamant about selling the house."

"Because the place is falling apart. Because Mom can't take care of herself, which is grossly evident after this recent episode. Because you don't live there anymore, and now she's alone, which makes the situation even more urgent. Because I pay the bills and the mortgage, and that means I say the house goes."

His brother reached into the cupholder and pinched a discarded foil gum wrapper. He wadded the wrapper and massaged it with his fingers, rolling it around in his palm until he'd shaped it into a ball that settled between his forefinger and thumb.

"You're still doing that thing," Leonard said, "with the paper?"

"What are you talking about?" Norman said.

LANCHESTER HOSPITAL SMELLED LIKE DISINFECTANT AND FLOOR WAX. They wandered the halls until an information desk directed them to the third floor, where they passed an octogenarian engaged in a robust discussion with a potted plant before they found their mother's room just after the visitors' lounge. The facilities were surprisingly modern, far nicer than the ecru-colored hospital rooms he'd previously visited, and had all the appointments of a hotel: a desk, a modular sofa, a large window that supplied plenty of natural light.

Leonard parted the privacy curtain and found his mother on the bed watching television. She was a large, soft-looking woman with a waxy face and thin, hoary hair that resembled the strands of notebook paper left discarded behind the spiral. Her right leg was wrapped in a navy boot cast and elevated on a cluster of pillows.

"Oh Leonard, baby," she said. "I'm so glad you're home."

"It's good to see you, Mom."

"You're so skinny." She hugged him, kissed his cheeks, pawed at him as if he was a missing pet. It occurred to Leonard how much older she looked than the last time he'd seen her, and he wondered what age did to a face, if it took you away from the person you were, or if it slowly revealed the person who'd been there all along. In the light, her fingernails resembled the keys of an antique piano. She smelled of lotion.

"This is my older boy," she said to a doctor who stood at the foot of the bed. "You think my other son is weird, wait until you meet this one."

"Your mother was in quite a state when she was admitted yesterday," the doctor said. He was a short, stout man with a face like an aged sausage. "She was unable to reach a phone, and no one discovered her for some time. She wasn't fully responsive to our questions when she arrived, so we decided to keep her overnight for observation, to be safe."

"I fell in the kitchen," she said. "I couldn't move for two hours. If Harold hadn't been on his evening walk, I might still be there now."

"Is she okay?" Leonard said. "I mean, did you find anything abnormal?"

"Everything's fine," the doctor said. "Normal blood counts, good urinalysis, good thyroid, good general chemistries. Her lipids showed elevated triglycerides, which probably just reflects the fact that she'd eaten before she was admitted."

"I made a quiche," she said.

"We also discovered her vitamin D levels are low."

"Low vitamin D," Leonard repeated. "How much is this going to cost us?"

"I suggest she take a thousand IU of vitamin D3 every day," the doctor said. "You can buy it at any pharmacy."

His mother moved her mouth in a hesitating way, as though she was chewing something. "This is what it takes to get my boy to come home," she said. "He's so highbrow in that city, he doesn't visit his own mother for two years. He ignores my calls."

"I wasn't ignoring you," Leonard said. "I've been busy."

"And now he wants to throw me out of my own home."

"All right, Mom," Leonard said.

"The ankle has a hairline fracture," the doctor continued. "It could take between six and eight weeks for the bone to heal. She'll need crutches, and I suggest she keep the leg elevated whenever possible. As far as rehabilitation, there are physical therapists who can help with range-of-motion exercises. I've also written her a prescription for Percocet. If anything changes, if she becomes lightheaded or faints again, you should call an ambulance—"

"I'm sure she'll be fine," Leonard said.

Twenty minutes later, after their mother dressed and rounded up the complimentary lotions and soaps in the room and stowed them in her bag, a nurse arrived with a pair of crutches, followed by an orderly who carted her in a wheelchair to the elevator.

"Two hours," she said and shook her head. "All alone for two hours."

They pushed their mother through the lobby and across the parking lot, where, after some effort, Norman and Leonard managed to lift her into the van.

"I thought I would die," she said. "Truly, I did."

AFTER A TRIP TO THE PHARMACY, THEY ARRIVED AT THE HOUSE, A BEIGE split-level punished by time. Calcium deposits crusted over the windows and rivulets of rust stained the vinyl siding under sagging gutters. In a neglected square of yard bordered by a hedge of thin bushes, Leonard noticed the lawn mower lying on its side in high reeds of grass.

"Is that where the mower goes now?" Leonard said and stepped out of the van.

"Give me a break," Norman said. "It died on me the other week." He opened the van's sliding door and unbuckled his mother. "Wait here a minute," he told her. "We have to clear some things out of the way before we can get you in."

Leonard pondered the statement as he made his way to the garage door, which was where they'd always entered the house growing up. Norman took the steps to the porch.

"That door's locked," Norman said. "Mom uses the garage for storage now." He opened the storm door, frosted with dirt, unlocked the front door, and put his shoulder into it. "You have to push," Norman said and threw himself against the door, which resisted against something heavy on the other side.

Leonard squeezed his way into a dark foyer and waited for his eyes to adjust. When the mountain range took shape before him, the air in his lungs slipped out. He felt an itch in his socks.

"Now you see why I moved out?" Norman said.

Leonard found a crude walkway and lumbered across the room. He slid on a spillway of newspapers, braced his hand against what he assumed was the wall, and fell through it. When he reached the window and drew back the curtains, the living room was enveloped in midday light. Before them were canyons of lamps and air-conditioning units and box fans, a thicket of dining room furniture, teetering stacks of old magazines, board games still wrapped in cellophane, a half-dozen tiki torches, and dune after dune of clearance-item clothing, most of it still bearing tags.

"It's even worse than I thought," Leonard said. "It didn't used to be like this."

"You haven't been home in two years," Norman said.

"Where did all this stuff come from?"

"She buys it, or people give it to her. I don't know. She just comes home with it."

For as long as Leonard could remember, their home had been cluttered. "Cozy," his mother called it. She'd always had a difficult time letting things go, held on to Leonard and Norman's baby clothes long after it became obvious she wouldn't be having more children. The attic filled with cribs and old furniture and discarded toys, and then the same thing happened to the garage. She'd ensconced the behavior under a hobbyist's umbrella. "A collector," she called herself, a term Leonard found odd, considering nothing she collected possessed any value. By the time Leonard was through with college, the house had become an outright mess, but the armchair psychologist in him saw her compulsions as a coping mechanism, a way of offsetting the sense of loss she'd felt after losing her job at the Goodyear plant in Logan. He hadn't heard about any developments since his last visit, so he'd assumed the behavior had hit a period of stasis. But what stood before them was far worse than anything he could've imagined.

Leonard shuffled his way into the kitchen. It stank of sour milk. A hill of sweaters canted over the breakfast bar, and wholesale boxes of dried goods and pyramids of canned goods occupied most of the floor space. The pantry was inaccessible, the doorway buried behind stacks of Styrofoam coolers and Tupperware. On the floor before the oven was a salvage pile of pots and pans and baking sheets.

"Here's where she fell over," Norman said.

"It's no wonder she got hurt. She was under this heap for two hours." Leonard walked to the window, opened it, and slipped on a cookie sheet. "This is unacceptable," he said. "You're supposed to watch out for her."

"What can I do?" Norman said. "I work. I live on the other side of town. And I still stop by several times a week, always."

"You could've intervened," Leonard said. "Had it occurred to you to make her stop?"

"She won't let me throw anything away." He fell into a whisper. "I even have to sneak the trash out at night."

Something twisted in Leonard's stomach.

"You could've done something too, you know," Norman continued. "It's easy to move a thousand miles away and pretend to be oblivious to this problem while I'm left to deal with it. It's not like you didn't know what was going on."

"Well, I'm here now, and I'm putting my foot down. This is a wake-up call, and it's precisely why I want to sell the house. She falls again, and maybe next time someone won't be there to find her. Where's she getting all the money to buy this stuff, anyway?"

Norman gave his brother a dead stare before shoving his way back through the living room.

"Oh, Jesus," Leonard said and cradled his face in his hands. "That was for her living expenses!"

"Leonard, please."

"I've spent tens of thousands of dollars to provide for her, and I come home to discover she's squandered it on a house full of garbage. How am I supposed to feel?"

"Leonard, stop yelling. She'll hear you."

"She's cut off, do you understand? I'm canceling the checking account. I'm setting up a new account before I leave, and the only person who gets access to that money is you. And I want detailed monthly expense reports on everything. I'm calling a real estate agent and putting this house on the market, and we will move her into that gated community."

"Getting rid of the house won't change her behavior."

"Like hell. She won't have anywhere to store this junk."

"It doesn't work that way," Norman said. He stared into a corner of the room. "Personally, I think she does this as a way of dealing with the uncertain things. You know, like death? It's her way of exhibiting control over her mortality."

"That's very perceptive, Grandma. But the house still goes, and so does everything in it. And if you want to prevent another trip to the hospital, I need you in my corner when I broach this conversation with her."

Norman kicked a cast-iron Dutch oven at his feet. "Yeah, okay. Sure, Leonard."

"Come on," Leonard said. "Let's bring Mom inside."

FOR THE NEXT HOUR, THEY WATCHED TELEVISION TOGETHER IN THE downstairs den. Their mother sat in the recliner, her casted leg elevated on a stack of phone books and newspaper coupons that flapped under the ceiling fan. Norman heated leftover quiche in the microwave; Leonard later watched him eat three plates of it. As she took her medication with a can of diet soda, their mother filled them in on the latest celebrity gossip: Madonna and Guy Ritchie's marriage was in trouble, and though there hadn't been a formal announcement, Angelina Jolie's baby bump was clearly visible. Their mother possessed an infuriating propensity to rhapsodize for endless stretches about nothing. It occurred to Leonard now, as it had growing up, that her conversations occupied a curious metaphysical dead zone: He could tune out anytime he wanted, go to the bathroom, run errands, take a nap, and when he resumed listening, invariably she'd still be prattling on about the same item as when he'd left. Some mystery neighbor was always dying of cancer. An outlet store on Memorial Drive was having a sale on some worthless tchotchke she didn't need. Gas was either very affordable or outrageously expensive. At any given moment, a "nice quiche" was baking in the oven.

"What do you plan to do while you're in town?" his mother asked.

"Bit of this, bit of that," Leonard said.

"I was going through some boxes the other day and found your old spoon, the one you used to chew on? I put it in your room, next to your chemistry set."

"I don't know what you're talking about." Leonard looked to the far wall, where he was sure he heard scurrying mice. "Mom, we need to talk. This latest incident has cemented my decision to sell the house."

"I told you on the phone a month ago. I don't want to move."

"And I'm telling you, Rose Brook Estates is a palace. It's a nice gated community not far from Norman's apartment. We can plan a visit while I'm here if you'd like."

"I saw the brochure. I saw all of them. I'm not moving. My entire life is here."

"I'll pay for everything," Leonard said. "It's not an issue."

"Money's got nothing to do with it."

"You're right. This is a matter of common sense. This is about maximizing a potentially narrowing timeframe—"

"What about my collectibles?"

"You can keep them. We'll put them in storage."

She shook her head, lips clasping shut like a leather cigarette purse. "Absolutely not."

Leonard looked to his brother. "We're afraid you might get hurt again," he said. "What if you fall down next time and no one's there to find you?"

"This has nothing to do with any accident," she said. "You've been on a campaign to sell this place for years because you're embarrassed of the house you grew up in, and you always have been."

Leonard turned to Norman again, who was looking at his feet, where a bruise of mold had formed in the carpet. The lack of recourse confirmed his brother didn't have any truck in this issue, which put him on their mother's side by default. It was Leonard versus them, like always.

"It's funny," Leonard said. "That providing for you is your basis for attacking me."

"Now you're just making things up," she said. "You're the one attacking me."

"We've had this conversation a dozen times," Leonard said. "These weren't the terms of our arrangement. I don't send you money every month so you can stack the walls with trash. This . . . nesting of yours has to stop, and getting you out of here is the only way I know how to do it. And because you clearly can't help yourself, I'm stepping in to help you."

"Oh, Leonard, you're making me upset. I'm just tired of talking about it. This is my home, and I don't think you have a right to tell me where to live."

"And I think this aggrandizement of your civil rights somehow being violated is a convenient deflection of the choices you made that led us to this impasse."

"I don't understand a word you just said."

"It means we're selling this house, and you're moving into an apartment that better suits your needs, and that's final."

A trough of tears lined her eyes, and the living room grew quiet. When he'd first gotten the job, Leonard had been proud of his ability to support his mother. Doing so was still important to him, though admittedly it had assumed an obligatory role in recent years. He'd hoped to convince her that moving was in her best interest, but now that they'd had their words, it dawned on him that by strong-arming her, he'd unwittingly validated whatever paranoid beliefs she'd had as to why he'd wanted to sell the house in the first place. It wasn't the path he'd envisioned this conversation taking.

Eventually she returned to the television and began scanning channels. The news reported John Edwards had officially endorsed Barack Obama. A Florida company had initiated a "mandatory fun" policy. An entertainment network was airing a show that detailed the ten deadliest shootings in American history. Norman disappeared and returned with a chess board. Leonard had become an enthusiast during college, but he was out of practice and Norman began wiping the board with him. Several moves before checkmate, Leonard noticed their mother had dozed off. He leaned over and tapped his brother's leg.

"Come with me," Leonard whispered.

IN THE DRIVEWAY, THEY REMOVED THE BENCH SEAT FROM THE MINIVAN and drove across town to Walmart. As they crossed under the store's atrium and nodded to an elderly woman in the greeting station, Leonard took notice of his fellow shoppers. It was all coming back to him: leather-skinned women who bore an alarming resemblance to Larry Bird; burly men who dressed like pubescents at summer camp; overweight couples who, oddly, all wore running shoes. These were incurious people, Leonard decided, and they tolerated their lives here because they knew nothing but their own experiences. Impossibly, they all seemed happy, vibrating with an addlepated joy that made him feel like even more of a stranger in this town. Everyone was just so goddamn happy all the time, and Leonard didn't understand what there was to be happy about, didn't know whether they were oblivious to the way the world worked, if occupying oneself with religion, as Norman had, or collecting junk, as his mother did, or careers or children or any other temporary distraction somehow made the ineludible complexities of life more tolerable, or if they'd stumbled on some arcane mystery he was too dumb to figure out.

Leonard found the most expensive lawn mower in the store and pushed it to the checkout counter. The sun was giving out by the time he and Norman lifted it into the van and crossed town again as Leonard read aloud directions to Rose Brook Estates. His stomach sank when they pulled into the parking lot. The complex didn't resemble the brochure photos at all: Quaint triplex carriage homes were replaced with a browning row of box units bearing hanging flaps of busted siding; the serene fold of manicured landscaping was actually a scrub of yellow lawn hemmed by a bare mulch line. The picket fence in the brochure had been outright Photoshopped; instead, a chain link perimeter lined the community, and a naked headless Barbie doll hung between chinks in the front gate above a wreath of gnats that circled a puddle in the lot.

"I don't know," Norman said. "It looks sketchy."

"It's fine," Leonard said. Two pickup trucks idled in the parking lot, the drivers engaged in some sort of argument. A large man, clearly inebriated, exited his vehicle and began yelling at the other, repeating the phrase "Sorry don't fix my truck."

"I think one of the guys at the glass factory lives here," Norman said.

"Perfect," Leonard said. "She'll have a family connection."

"I'm pretty sure he has a drug problem."

The men in the parking lot continued to argue. The larger one now had his arm inside the truck and gripped the smaller man by the collar.

"Things got bad after Mom was laid off," Norman said. "I don't think she had time to listen to her own thoughts when she was pulling double shifts at the Goodyear plant."

"She used to have these lapses of lucidity," Leonard said. "You remember those fly-by-night purging sessions that happened once a year? I guess I was hoping something like that would've occurred while I was gone, but it would've stuck this time."

"It's been years since she did that," Norman said. "Remember when she threw out the glasses because we didn't have a matching set?"

"Sure," Leonard said. "I'll never forget my first bowl of Mountain Dew."

"Funny how Mom thought I was going to be the breadwinner. What a joke that was."

"You're doing fine," Leonard said.

"It's amazing how far you've come. Dropping out of school and moving to that city without a plan or a job lined up."

"It wasn't easy," Leonard said.

"How'd you get that gig, anyway?"

A squad car tore into the parking lot, and a brief struggle ensued after a police officer grabbed the man standing outside the truck and put him in a chokehold before planting him onto the pavement. A second officer exited the car, placed a knee in the man's back, and called on a portable handset for backup.

"I guess we can look at a different community," Leonard said as Norman started the van.

They drove out of the parking lot and followed the road until they reached the lights and traffic of Memorial Drive.

"Town isn't what it used to be," Norman said. "Meth is a big problem now, and there's a lack of jobs after the Goodyear plant closed. The glass factory is the biggest employer the city has left."

"What can you do?" Leonard said.

"Pray."

"Has it ever occurred to you to pray for something short-term first, to see if it works?" Leonard said. "Like better facial hair?"

"I pray for you too," his brother said.

NORMAN DROVE THEM BACK TO THE HOUSE BEFORE TAKING HIS OWN CAR home. Inside, Leonard found his mother still seated in front of the television, occupying the recliner like a dent.

"Come sit with me, baby," she said as he appeared in the doorway.

Leonard staggered to the couch and braced himself for the long haul. They watched a show that documented medical surgeries in gruesome detail. During an operation for a peptic ulcer, he found himself turning away.

"That's the duodenum." She took a sip of diet soda as a surgical tool tugged on a bubblegum-colored strip of tissue. "It's a common procedure."

"I have to lie down," Leonard said. "I have heartburn."

"Put baking soda in a glass of water. I have some in the pantry," she said as Leonard made his way for the stairs. "When do you leave?"

"Sunday."

"You know you could always move back," she said. "You could get a job in town and meet a nice girl."

Leonard sighed. "We've been through this."

"I'm sure it's exciting living in that city," she said. "What with your career in the RP—"

"PR," he said. "I've told you, I work in PR."

"It's criminal how much they make you work over there. Careers aren't everything. You'll realize it when you're my age."

"I'm not moving back, Mom." Leonard paused, worried his mother would cry again. It was perplexing: He'd always assumed he was good at his job because he was attuned to people's needs, yet he was fully unequipped to deal with their emotions. Tears, any sincere admissions of hurt, made him immensely uncomfortable and sent him seeking flight, as though something would spill out of them and contaminate him. It was just easier to work from some distance, to offer advice as opposed to comfort. "I got promoted at work," he said.

"Oh?" she sniffed. "That's nice."

"Senior Vice President of Marketing Sentiment and Brand Enrichment."

"That sounds impressive."

"Good night, Mom. Try to rest. Don't put too much pressure on your ankle."

"Leonard," his mother said as he moved into the doorway. "I'm proud of you, son."

"All right," he said and left for his room.

THAT NIGHT, LEONARD SURVEYED THE RELICS IN HIS BEDROOM: THE travel chessboard on the nightstand, the high school quiz team plaque on the wall, the chemistry set on the dresser, covered with a fur of dust. The room held a musty, cellar smell but otherwise remained untouched, the one corner of the house his mother hadn't filled. In the closet, he found several aquariums as well as disassembled water filtration systems and pumps and motors. He opened his duffel bag, removed a packet of swabs, and set upon wiping down the room's surfaces. When he was finished, he stripped the bed of its sheets and comforter, threw them into a corner, and spread out the new sheets he'd bought at Walmart.

His eyelids were heavy as he lay down, yet he found himself staring at the perimeter of brown mold that circled the light fixture on the ceiling, feeling trapped, a prisoner in his body, unable to climb out of his thoughts. On the dresser, he noticed the wooden stirring spoon he used to bite as a child. He picked it up, examined its edges, notched with tooth marks, brought it to his nose, and licked its distressed handle. He locked the door and turned off the light and stuck the spoon in his mouth and chewed on it in the dark before he eventually drifted into a fevered half-sleep.

. . .

"YOU DON'T EAT ANYTHING ELSE?" PATTY HAD ASKED. IT WAS A DUMB question, the sort of question that didn't necessarily want an answer, but she kept saying it, repeating the words over and over.

"Of course." Leonard rocked in the chair. The aisle outside the office was a factory of ringing phones and idle chatter, and he found himself zoning out, listening for patterns in the noise.

"But you don't like it. You like pencils."

"Pencils, soap, carpet, whatever." It was a strange sensation, saying it out loud like that. Putting it into words made official what had always felt like an interior experience, gave it legs. "As it turns out, you can have a secret in plain sight as long as no one's looking."

"Have you always done it?"

"Not always. Look, I'm not interested—"

"What triggers it?"

"Nothing. Everything. I don't know."

A colonnade of whiskey-colored light bisected the room. Leonard looked out the window, concentrated on the hushing waves of Midtown traffic.

"What's wrong with real food?" she said.

"It doesn't taste like anything."

"What do you mean?"

"I can't taste it anymore. It doesn't taste like anything."

"Nothing?"

"Nothing."

"Like, nothing at all?"

"Nothing. It tastes like absolutely nothing."

LEONARD AWOKE IN A PANIC. HE CREPT DOWN THE HALL AND INTO THE living room, inched his way through the dark until he found a mineshaft between the mounds of junk, descended the stairs, and tiptoed into the den. Relieved to discover his mother had gone to bed, he crossed the room and looked out the window to the dark reaches of the backyard. Then he turned on the lamp and examined his mother's recliner. Quietly, he pulled it away from the wall, then tipped the recliner so its legs were facing him and knelt to examine its wheelwork of springs. For years now, Leonard had been slowly devouring his way through the centerpiece. The project had begun after college, during a stretch when life had become unbearable. It'd been two years since he'd seen it, two years since he'd tasted its coddling fibers, but it gave him solace to know it was still there, stowed away in the shadows of the den, brewing in the varietals of time. Picking through its chewed underbelly with his fingers, he caught the fusty stink of the aged fabric as he stuffed handfuls of yellow foam into his mouth. Occasionally a crumb would fall onto the floor, spalls of potato chip or ossified flecks of popcorn. He ate until he was satisfied and sated, the moist cheese piquancy of its sponge cake innards singing on his tongue, horribly aged but packed with a mellowed rustic flavor he'd remembered, the soft pink rot of home.

"I SEE WHERE THIS IS GOING," LEONARD HAD TOLD PATTY. "YOU'VE GOT video. You're going to blackmail me."

"Blackmail is a strong word."

"No one will believe you," he said. "They'll think you faked it somehow. Besides, no one cares enough about me to give it the time of day."

"Right," Patty said. "It's not like a certain journalist who writes for the *Register* has any interest in what you do behind closed doors. And neither would my employers, for that matter."

"I handle crises for a living. I can talk my way out of this."

"What would you say?"

"I don't know yet," he said. "Ideally, it'll involve wiping that stupid smile off your face."

"I've never met someone so unaware of himself. I guess it makes sense."

She looked him over, leaned back in his chair, and placed her feet on his desk. "You're just like me."

"I'm nothing like you."

"Nope, you're just like me," she said. "We're tenders from the same cutlet."

"There are ways we can handle this," Leonard whispered. "I have money."

"I don't want your money."

It was a mad game of chess with this one. Every exit that came into view was closed. Worse, she knew it.

"I asked before. What do you want?"

"What I'm about to suggest might sound strange," she said, "but, given what we have here, I think it'll make sense. Now listen closely. I'm going to tell you exactly how this is going to work."

Chapter 7

"One bite," Patty said. "That was the agreement."

Leonard shuddered as he inspected the dish, oily ringlets of calamari in a congealing dross of battered crumbs and paprika aioli. He fidgeted in the booth, gave a defeated sigh, lifted his fork, and speared a cluster, brought a shoestring of rings forward, dangling, to his mouth.

"I can't," he said and pushed the plate away.

"I got the most boring appetizer on the menu so you could try something."

"No one's stopping you," he said. "Dig in."

Patty crushed a wedge of lemon over the bowl, extended a glistening wall of gums, and took a knot of rings with her teeth. She bit delicately, retracted, chewed. Leonard heard gerbil-like nibbling, followed by the clamp of her jaw, which caught with a slight clicking tension like a bent spoke. Her eyes closed, she appeared distant and content, a daydreaming child.

The restaurant was outfitted in the likeness of a yacht cabin: stainless-steel grab handles affixed to walls, orbicular windows resembling portholes, a webbing of monofilament gillnets serving as curtains. The low-ceilinged dining room was rimmed by a bar decorated with aged naval maps and leather pilots' chairs. Sniffy bartenders wore matching admirals' hats.

"I think they're going for a nautical theme," Leonard whispered.

"Don't make fun," Patty said. "This place is popular. We might see a celebrity."

Thankfully, they'd been seated away from the arterial traffic of the bar, in a chesterfield banquette booth behind a fiberglass bulkhead partition that separated the kitchen from the dining area. Leonard brooded for a moment before returning his sights to the barnacle seated before him. She'd dressed idiotically, as always, and had apparently made an effort to spruce up for the occasion in a pleated skirt, a brocade vest bearing a floral pattern, and knee-high moosehide mukluks. The calamari had edged a corner of her lipstick off-center, so her mouth was now curled into an imbecilic grin. A confetti of batter gathered in the creases of her napkin, which she used as a bib.

Entrees arrived: for Patty, a sautéed dorade with grilled baby leeks in a dill and asparagus velouté; and for Leonard, a lobster risotto served in what the waitress had described as a "mercifully light" tomato and coconut reduction. He scrutinized grains knighted with stalks of pink flesh, picked at a curling finger of lobster, and held it to his nose. It smelled briny and unreasonably oceanic. He forked a piece of meat, plunged it into his mouth, and turned it over with his tongue. The flavor was untamed and misguided, creamed rubber coached with butter and salt.

"Don't make that face," Patty said. "If you weren't going to eat, why order it?"

"Because I wanted this exchange to look as normal as possible."

At the bar, stiff mannequin men and waifish plasticine women conferred with forced cheer. They were in character, fortified with wine and pretending to be interested in what the other had to say.

"Where were you this weekend?" Patty asked.

"Out of town. None of your business."

"Visiting your sick mother?"

"As luck has it, she's not sick. Like I said, none of your business."

"Sor-ry. I just thought we'd get to know each other."

"We're not doing small talk, Patty. You reminded me of the rules in your phone call, so I'll return the favor. I do this thing for you, and you keep your mouth shut. In case you hadn't figured it out, I don't want to be friends."

She took a sip of water and sank in the chair, her face doughy and colorless. A stern light on the wall cast a halo over her thinning hairline.

"Believe it or not, I find you interesting," she said. "But I think maybe you have something against women."

"Whatever."

"And I'll bet you don't have many friends."

"I have plenty."

"What do you do with them? For fun, I mean."

Leonard threw up his hands. "We blackmail each other for free food. We do it all the time because that's completely normal behavior," he said. "Do you have any idea what a loser you are? What is it about this ritual that gets you off? What pleasure could you derive from conning strangers into taking you to restaurants?"

"I seem to remember asking a similar question about your own . . . proclivities."

"We're not talking about me," he said in a low tone.

"This condition you have. I've heard of it."

"No, you haven't," he said. "I know what you're talking about. It's not the same thing. Out of curiosity, where's the video?"

"I told you, it's on a server. There's no way you'll find it."

"And you haven't shown it to anyone?"

"Nope."

A kohl-eyed waitress arrived with a dessert menu.

"We'll take the check—" Leonard began before Patty snatched the menu out of the woman's hands.

"Oooh," she hooted. "They have a chocolate tartufo ice cream!"

Leonard returned his attention to the roar coming from the bar. There was an infectious energy to it, the wild rhythm of their easy laughter.

"You realize this thing we have, it won't last," Leonard said.

"I'll be the judge of that."

"It'll be over before you know it."

"You seem so sure."

"I'll put this in language you can understand," Leonard said. "The fact that being a file clerk has been your life's greatest achievement isn't a coincidence. I fix reputations for a living."

Patty's dessert arrived and she went in again, closing her eyes at the taste of it.

"You know, Bill Gates said if he had only two dollars, he'd spend one on PR," Leonard said. "The fact is, a crisis can actually help someone like me."

"That's ridiculous." A pebble of ice cream on Patty's bottom lip began dripping into the cracks of her chin.

"It's true. Jack Kennedy said that crisis, when translated into Chinese, becomes two characters. One represents danger, and the other represents opportunity."

"Is that Mandarin or Cantonese?"

"I don't know," Leonard said. "It doesn't matter. The point is, I can take a reputational attack and redirect it into a branding opportunity. All I need is time to evaluate the internal logic of the problem at hand." He took a long pull of wine. "I'm going to survive this temporary inconvenience. Then I'm going to bury you."

The waitress returned with the bill. Two hundred and thirty dollars. Leonard found his wallet and slapped it onto the table. "Three restaurants a week," he muttered. "I can't afford this."

"I'm sure you'll make do," Patty said.

A confluence of clouds drew over the buildings as they walked north, navigated around beaten trash cans, couples holding hands, joggers in neoprene outfits. They stepped over worn nubs of cobblestone, passed a block of drab, rude-looking storefronts, most of them shuttered and lit by dim, absinthe-colored bulbs. The air held the odor of smelted iron. Then the sky grew dark and it began to pour. Leonard ran for the subway entrance and made it halfway down the steps when he turned to see Patty, still standing in the rain-lashed street.

"I'll text you directions for the next restaurant in several days," she yelled.

"Whatever," he said and ducked into the tunnel.

AT HOME, IN THE KITCHEN'S SOUR LIGHT, LEONARD AGAIN LEAFED through his files on Pinnacle's planned merger with Publique Groupe. One memo suggested restructuring the French conglomerate's marketing units under a series of specialty hubs, wherein Graydon Trotwood would be installed as CEO of the newly reorganized Americas marketing region. Leonard considered the scale of what he was dealing with, then closed the file and went under the sink in search of a snack.

From the very beginning, he'd been aware of the obvious course of action available: He could turn the documents over to Pinnacle and divulge to them how Patty had attempted to leak sensitive internal information on the company. The gesture might put him in Pinnacle's good graces, and there was little doubt she'd be fired as a result. But it strained credulity to assume they wouldn't ask why he'd postponed disclosing Patty's theft for so long. His complicity in holding on to the merger documents without informing his client made him his own liability, and this lapse of foresight had the potential to give away his intention to use the files as a means of pitching them his services. After cycling through the facts, it was clear this route was too risky, was out of the question.

Worse, Patty now had video evidence of him engaging in his most secret act. Of all his vulnerabilities, this one was clearly the most portable, and though he didn't know what level of conviction she held to her threats, blowing the whistle on Patty could provoke her to go nuclear and release that video to everyone: his colleagues, that journalist at the *Register*, his prized future client. The board was set in such a way that virtually any outcome would produce a win for her, while only a very limited and narrow range of options could conceivably benefit him. If Leonard wanted Patty off his back, if he wanted her to disappear, he needed leverage, collateral. He'd have to get personal.

He stayed up late that night, conducting research. An internet query revealed a dozen people in the country named Patricia Pachis, but none appeared to be the woman he was looking for, and none of the search results, aside from a fifty-two-year-old pediatrician living in Peoria, Illinois, yielded any substantial information at all. He perused social media pages and performed a search on the cellphone number she'd given him, but nothing materialized. It was as though she didn't exist.

ANXIETY WOKE HIM THE NEXT MORNING, AND A DULL HEADACHE CLUS-tered behind his right eye as he took the train to Midtown, walked to work, and hid himself away in his office. He logged in to the firm's LexisNexis account and searched city newspapers, combing articles, marriage announcements, and crime blotters for Patty, but there was nothing. He opened a new browser window and had begun another internet search when the Todds arrived for their meeting.

Crisis: A recently constructed apartment complex in Brooklyn's up-and-coming Bushwick neighborhood had run a print-ad campaign many considered offensive. The management company behind the development— "Bohemia," where a two-bedroom unit cost $3,500 a month—referred to the neighborhood as a "new frontier" and likened its lessees to "settlers" and "pioneers," statements some residents of the mostly Hispanic community said employed colonialist language. *Strategy:* Ingratiate locals to the development with a viral campaign. Hire a local crew of graffiti artists to devise a tag-style condo logo alongside Sandinistaesque revolutionary iconography, and have these designs spray-painted on partnering businesses throughout the neighborhood. *Crisis:* A local meteorologist was the subject of attacks in the form of crude and misogynistic comments regarding her weight that were posted to the news station's Facebook page. When the woman logged on to the forum and responded to the remarks, she was fired for violating the broadcaster's policies. Now the public was furious that the meteorologist had been terminated for standing up for herself, and the National Association of Journalists had joined the fray, giving the story ink in prominent news outlets. *Strategy:* Rehire the employee and suggest she host a televised special on online bullying. *Crisis:* A city councilman was embroiled in scandal after it was discovered he participated in a bizarre compulsion of taking photos of his bowel movements in public toilets. A strange website had appeared months prior, allegedly featuring daily ejecta in various johns around the city. When news of the site began making circles, savvy viewers noted a *whois* lookup traced the site to the politician's address. As rumors circulated regarding the identity of the person behind the site, one astute web user noticed a reflection of the politician's face could be seen in a toilet's aluminum handle. When a second reflection surfaced in another toilet entry, professionals were brought in to analyze the photos, which they determined to be legitimate, and calls demanding the councilman's ouster poured into his office. *Strategy:* Hold a press conference and announce you're seeking counseling.

LEONARD LEFT THE OFFICE DURING HIS LUNCH BREAK AND WALKED TO the police precinct, a brutalist slab of a building on Third Avenue. At the front desk he was given a form and directed to a bench in the lobby, where he sat next to an elderly man with wild eyes who whispered insults to himself. Leonard looked over the form and began to fill in the fields: name, address, occupation. White space anchored the sheet below an area labeled "detail of event." He bit his pen as he deliberated a strategy; he wanted to choose his words carefully, calibrate his statement for impact. He enumerated everything as it had happened, from the beginning, then began questioning the unnecessary exposition, not to mention the additional pages he'd need if he planned to document every event that had occurred in the last few weeks and decided it would be better to begin with the inciting dramatic action that had provoked his complaint. Words to consider: harassment, fraud, blackmail. Anxiety stirred in his gut, and that's when he considered the grotesque stalemate of his situation. Patty hadn't committed a crime. Sure, she'd made vague threats against his reputation, but what exactly would he tell them, that he was being coerced into buying dinner for someone because she'd caught him eating pencils? There was an inscrutable, almost artistic symmetry to it: The whole thing made absolutely no sense to anyone but the two parties involved.

Ten minutes later, a police officer ushered Leonard into an office that smelled of burned coffee and water damage. A middle-aged detective with tired eyes and bad posture sat behind a steel desk.

"Can I help you?" the man said.

"There's this woman," Leonard said and looked at the unfinished form, now furled in his hand.

"Yeah?" The detective lifted an eyebrow.

"Never mind."

LEONARD SPRINTED BACK TO THE OFFICE, BREACHED THE BREAK ROOM, and ransacked the cupboards for soap. Empty-handed, he tapped into his reserves, discovered a travel-sized bottle of shampoo in his desk drawer, and fled to the bathroom, where he turned on the taps and left the water running as he huddled in a stall and sucked on the bottle until balloons of color filled the room and he felt a deep pressure release beneath his ribs.

He resumed his online search for Patty, purchased and downloaded proprietary software that guaranteed the largest collection of address records and employment histories for U.S. residents. The database offered the same entries for Patricia Pachis he'd found in prior searches, but his heart thrummed when he noticed an unfamiliar addition, a listing for a thirty-six-year-old woman who lived in Queens. He clicked on the listing and saw a phone number, then consulted his cellphone and confirmed the match. But that was all the information the listing offered. Leonard closed his browser window. Then his telephone rang.

"Mr. Lundell?" the voice said. "Noah Sundermeyer. I wanted to give you another chance for an interview—"

"No goddamn comment," Leonard said and swiveled his chair. He blinked several times and ran a hand through his hair. "I told you already."

"It's interesting," the man said. "You teach people how to communicate with the media, yet you won't talk to me."

"You've highlighted this paradox before. Duly noted. The fact is, I can't talk about my work. Reporters like you would have a field day if I named some of my clients."

"Any chance you could help me clarify several facts? Previous work experience?"

"Not going to happen."

"How about an anecdote on life in the crisis field?"

"Nope."

Leonard opened a new browser window and punched "Noah Sundermeyer" into an image search and refined his earlier assessment as he scrutinized the gallery of photos, the stupid face that smiled back stupidly. He was very young, mid-twenties at most. Latent protestant upbringing, unmarried but has a girlfriend, some office prole with a predilection for romantic comedies and brunch.

"Right now, I've got nothing to work with," Sundermeyer continued.

"I stopped listening to you several minutes ago." Leonard looked at the clock: four-thirty.

The man prattled on with questions: memorable campaigns, notable account wins, where Leonard had graduated from college. Leonard's jaw tightened. He sat there stimming in the chair, shaking his crossed leg as he chewed on his pen. He switched grips on the receiver and brought a knee to his chest to deaden the involuntary movement.

"Hello?" Sundermeyer said.

"Don't call again," Leonard said and hung up.

He sat there and chewed on the pen as he stared at the phone. Seconds later, a shadow sprawled over the bar of light under his door, followed by a knock.

"Got our Pinnacle meeting on wraps," Todd Armitage said from the doorway. "They confirmed. Monday afternoon."

"Monday?" Leonard said. "A little soon, don't you think?"

"You said next week," Armitage said. "By the way, Pinnacle's crisis guy called. Said he wants you to come in for a powwow."

"Frazer Rae," Leonard said. "Jack already told me. I've been meaning to circle back."

"Guy's a little persistent, no?"

"His textbook has been required reading in university communications courses for decades," Leonard said. "Call him and confirm."

"No need. He said to come by his office anytime." Armitage shrugged. "Anyway, I'm off to the bar. For what it's worth, Pinnacle sounds excited about the meeting."

Leonard returned the pen to his mouth and stared at his computer screen. He debated calling Sundermeyer back, then tasted something, felt the run of ink on his chin, and leapt from the chair, threw the pen in the wastebasket, and raced to the bathroom. As he washed his mouth out in the sink, the door opened, and footsteps clapped against tile. Leonard looked up to see Todd Shillenburg facing a urinal.

"Hey, Lundell," Shillenburg said.

"Todd," Leonard said and moved to the towel dispenser. "Scuttlebutt says the boys are getting a drink after work."

"Sure," Shillenburg said. "We do every Thursday."

"Mind if I join?"

THE BAR WAS A BUG JAR OF A PLACE, OUTFITTED WITH BOILERPLATE INTE-riors: mallard-green walls, ceilings veined with exposed ducts, shelves show-casing sports memorabilia. A congress of vacant, sallow-faced patrons who all looked like they had the flu. Leonard found the three Todds huddled in a booth near the bathrooms, ties undone, sleeves bunched at the elbows.

"Gentlemen," Leonard said and sat.

Everyone was looking to the television. The news was broadcasting Sen-ator Obama speaking at a campaign stop in Minnesota before crossfading to footage of Senator McCain at a fundraising event in Louisiana. The ticker at the bottom of the screen announced that by a narrow margin, Obama had secured enough pledged delegates to become the presumptive Democratic nominee.

"That settles it," Todd Shillenburg said. "Hillary's out, Obama's in."

"This is crazy," Todd Armitage said.

"He'll never win," Todd Colton said.

A waitress appeared, and Leonard inquired about a wine list, provoking silence to fall over the table.

"You hear the new buzzword this week?" Todd Colton said. "The one they're pushing in fashion PR to keep people buying in this shit economy?"

"Do we have to talk shop every time we go out?" Todd Armitage said.

"Frugalista," Todd Colton said. "It's recession chic. Think thrift stores, recycled materials, coupon campaigns."

"Frugalista," Todd Shillenburg said. "Jesus. That's worse than Baby-moons."

"Ever wonder why so many PR pros are such bad communicators?" Todd Armitage said.

"I find myself asking the same question," Leonard muttered.

"It's the colleges," Todd Colton said. "Too many bad programs."

"It's the big shops. They don't give new hires adequate training anymore," Todd Armitage said. "Account executives today are basically glorified telemarketers."

"You got your start at Waggener Edstrom, right, Lundell?" Todd Colton said.

"Burson-Marsteller," Leonard said.

"The reason people fail in this business is because they aren't good storytellers," Todd Shillenburg said. "They're oblivious to the fact that the best pitches are tailored to a current event, not their client. There's a formula to it. You can turn anything into a headline, guaranteed."

"Here we go," Todd Armitage said to Leonard. "You heard this shtick before?"

"Are we making a bet?" Leonard asked.

"Give me a product," Todd Shillenburg said. "I'll pitch you."

Todd Armitage stared him down. "Dog food," he said.

"Dog food?" Todd Shillenburg said. "Fine. Give me a publication."

"*Forbes*," Todd Armitage said.

Todd Shillenburg closed his eyes. "Money angle," he said. "A recent rise in global food prices has hurt not only grocers and shelf prices, etcetera, but is also affecting the cost of dog food. Your client—insert dog food company name here—has research showing Americans are now paying, on average, ten percent more on pet supplies than they were a year ago. Offer a list. *Forbes* loves lists."

"Okay," Leonard said. "*Time*."

"Health angle," Todd Shillenburg said. "For the doctors' offices, because they're the only ones who subscribe to *Time* anymore. The rise in popularity of organic foods has compelled pet food manufacturers—insert dog food company name here—to sell organic pet food. Incidentally, your client also has a brand of dog food that's one hundred percent organic. Have the art department throw together some asinine infographic on the history of canine domesticity."

"CNN," Todd Colton said.

"Scare tactic." Todd Shillenburg stared at the ceiling. "China's recent food recalls portend a possible pet food contamination. However, your client—insert dog food company name here—has a website showing a list of common toxic chemicals found in pet food, none of which, incidentally, are found in your client's product. Bonus sidebar: celebrity angle. Offer a photo gallery of stars and their dogs."

"Nice," Leonard said.

"It's not rocket surgery," Todd Shillenburg said. "Reporters love to pretend we're the bane of their existence, like they'd be a phone call away from the next Watergate if we didn't harass them with pitches. If we're so bad, why do they depend on us for half their leads?"

"Deadlines have a lot to do with it," Leonard said. "They have a slow news day and they're expected to produce copy."

"Deadlines, my ass," Todd Shillenburg said. "Reporters are lazy. They take stories from us because we do the work for them."

"Still, earned media from a journalist is more valuable than a marketing campaign any day."

"What you see on the nightly news is the end result of a business transaction," Todd Shillenburg said. "There's no such thing as news anymore, just creative methods of marketing. We're behind the façade, pulling the strings of news theater, directing the migration patterns of information. And that, gentlemen, is the beauty of PR."

"You like your job," Leonard said.

"You kidding? It's the best gig in the world." Todd Shillenburg swallowed a mouthful of beer and looked at his watch. "I have to go. Dinner plans with the wife."

"Bound and hagged, Shillenburg?" Todd Colton said.

"Shut up, Colton," Todd Shillenburg said.

"I'm leaving too," Todd Armitage said.

"I have another one for you," Leonard said as Todd Shillenburg rose from the booth. "Let's say someone's blackmailing your client, threatening to go to the press. What do you do?"

"Shit, Lundell, you lead the team. You tell me."

"But I want to know what you think," Leonard said. "I respect your opinion."

Todd Shillenburg cleared his throat. "I'd need more information. What did your client do to be blackmailed in the first place?"

"Let's say he has . . . a strange appetite."

"He's a pervert," Todd Shillenburg said. "That's easy. Rally your allies in the press and get in front of the story before the blackmailer can. Then work internally on damage control. Why am I telling you this?"

"He's not a pervert. He was just . . . caught doing something he shouldn't be doing, and the person who caught him is threatening to go public."

"Okay, I get you. Your client can't talk because he did something illegal."

"It isn't illegal."

"Then what's the deal, Lundell? If someone's blackmailing your client and he didn't do anything wrong, he shouldn't be talking to you. He should lawyer up and call the cops."

"Let's say the police would never listen to him."

"Why not?"

"Because it's too strange. And besides, he's not being blackmailed for money."

"I don't get it," Todd Shillenburg said. "It doesn't make sense."

"It doesn't make sense, Leonard," Todd Colton said.

The team left and Leonard stayed in the booth, watching television. A study had discovered people with an acute sense of smell were more likely to endorse authoritarian governments. Eventually, he rose and ambled through the crowd. Before reaching the door, he spotted Griffin Cruz sitting at the bar, dressed in resort casual—magenta oxford, tapered khakis, boat shoes—and revealing a recently acquired tan.

"I'm surprised to see you in a place like this," Leonard said.

"Everyone from work comes here. Except you," Cruz said. He sipped a lime-colored drink from a lowball glass. "Have a seat."

"I was just leaving."

"What were you and the frat boys yammering about back there? Let me guess: 'rally our core demographic,' 'look at our research,' egregious use of the phrase 'power lunch'?"

"If you have so much antagonism for this line of work, why don't you quit?"

"Because I like it," he said and smiled. Leonard had never noticed the curiously poor condition of Cruz's teeth. A browned, splintered incisor that resembled a pistachio shell breached his lip. "You were asking the plebs for advice—"

"What did you hear?"

"Not much. Why don't you tell me what's wrong?"

"Not going to happen."

"You're not still sore about me getting that promotion?"

"Are you kidding?"

"Some things are bigger than you," Cruz said. "I might be able to help."

"Doubt it. I fix people's problems for a living."

"You spin tedious clichés so our barons of industry can maintain their con act over the bovine masses who buy their products. No offense, but it's a ridiculously low bar to clear. I'm guessing your troubles are more . . . existential in design? You know what your problem is, Lundell?"

"What?"

"You're too textbook, too old-school. Reporters have been replaced by bloggers with high readership and no scruples. There's a nation of citizen journalists sitting in their parents' basements, waiting for their fifteen seconds. It's scorched earth out there, and everyone's reputation is a target."

"You think I don't know that? People like me have been shaping public opinion a lot longer than bloggers. You're just trying to pass off cryptic babble as some sort of platitude."

"Anytime the system is disrupted, the rules of engagement change. I think when it's your turn in the barrel, you'll realize that your crisis toolbox could use a few more tools."

"You want to help me? Fine." Leonard grabbed a cocktail napkin from the bar and scribbled Patty's name and phone number on it, folded the napkin, and stuffed it into Cruz's palm. "You still got the hookup with that analytics firm in D.C. you told me about?"

"I know a guy," Cruz said. "His agency creates predictive modeling for political campaigns based on data he collects on every single living adult in the country. He sells the stuff to politicians, super PACs, research companies. Apparently, they're able to tell what presidential candidate someone supports based on their shopping habits."

"Anything he could find. A criminal record or employment history, parents or siblings or a credit report or previous cities of residence. I'd appreciate it."

"No problem. Might take a few weeks. This person giving you a hard time?"

"Something like that. Do me a favor and keep this between us, will you?"

SUMMER HAD ARRIVED, AND THE DAYS ACQUIRED AN EXPANSIVE, EX-hausting quality. It was still early when Leonard left his office, but already the city was simmering, and he knew that by afternoon the heat would be oppressive, the streets sweltering with rage. Sweat clawed down his back as he crossed Park Avenue and surveyed addresses for his destination. He found it easily enough, a beige brick building with an unadorned exterior, the office sandwiched between an accounting firm and a chiropractor's practice on the third floor. A small, cramped space, devoid of the white-shoe furnishings he'd envisioned, a waiting room that resembled a retired couple's home, rose-gold carpeting and mirrors in garishly baroque gold frames. A chinless woman sat behind the reception desk.

"Leonard Lundell to see Frazer Rae," Leonard said and toweled sweat from his forehead with his sleeve.

The woman disappeared, and Leonard took a seat under the slipstream of the air-conditioning unit. A grid of commemorative plaques was arrayed across a wall, most of them from the seventies and eighties, industry awards and accolades recognizing mundane achievements. On the coffee table, a Silver Anvil award from the PR Society of America was preserved in a glass vitrine.

"So, this is the man who stopped a falling elevator." An older man in a steel blue suit stepped out from behind a heavy door, walked with a gait that dipped at the left knee, and grabbed for Leonard's hand. He was short and broad-shouldered and shaped like a fist, had skin that shone with a bronze luster and a high-fade haircut that held wisps of gray near the temples. "Please, come in."

Rae's personal office was bathed in amethyst light, the result of a panel of stained glass that hung in the window. More gold-framed mirrors, a gold-leafed chiffonier that doubled as a fully stocked bar, a cherry-stained mahogany table with gold line inlays. Leonard sank into a wingback leather couch as Rae stepped to the chiffonier and jogged his fingers across a fleet of glass necks.

"Libation?" Rae said. Leonard shook his head as the man filled a rocks glass with scotch. "How are things at Gurney?"

"Fine."

"And how's Jack?"

"Same."

"I've known Jack for years. He's crazier than a shithouse rat." Rae crossed the room and leaned on his desk. "I wanted to commend you personally on the work you did keeping those Pinnacle witnesses quiet. You saved me a lot of heartache. I'm sure you heard, but I was shanghaied and waylaid, not in Shanghai per se but Dulles Airport."

"My pleasure," Leonard said.

"Trotwood is a star in front of the camera. The press conference my team assembled went off without a hitch, and our side of the story was in every paper by Monday morning."

"I saw," Leonard said.

"There's still talk of a lawsuit, but—and hey, this is completely off record—we think the family might settle. The press didn't get one interview out of those witnesses, thanks to you, and now they've got earthquakes, tsunamis, bank collapses to busy themselves with. And, of course, this election. Never in my lifetime did I imagine . . ."

"It's going to be interesting," Leonard said.

The man took a drink and leveled his eyes at Leonard.

"I'm a dinosaur in this industry," Rae said. "I got my start in the seventies, when crisis communications had a backbone, when reputation management didn't mean calling Al Sharpton for mea culpas every time a celebrity used a racial slur. I worked the Challenger disaster, the Pan Am bankruptcy, Exxon Valdez, New Coke."

"That's very impressive," Leonard said.

"I singlehandedly managed to convince an entire nation of newspaper reporters that Liberace wasn't queer."

"I'm familiar with your work," Leonard said. *"Public Relations Fundamentals* was on my nightstand for years. You have this way of crafting a crisis-response narrative that's both appropriate yet always completely unexpected—"

"I'm a Black man with an office on Park Avenue. Every day of my life has been a crisis." He walked to the window, opened it, and perched himself on the windowsill, then lit a cigarette and waved smoke at the skyline. He removed a handkerchief from his breast pocket and dabbed his forehead with it. "You know, this profession is full of snakes. Nothing is sacred to some people: not accountability, not even the respect of their fellow practitioners."

"Isn't it the truth," Leonard said.

Rae threw his cigarette into traffic and fidgeted on the windowsill, as if plagued by cankers. "You're a real worm, you know that, Lundell?"

"Sir?"

"I didn't call you here to blow smoke up your ass. I know what you're doing. You're trying to steal my client."

Leonard stiffened in the chair. "The thought hadn't occurred to me."

"You think I was born yesterday? El Dorado falls into your lap, and you're going to close the books once the campaign is over? I've been Pinnacle's chief crisis counsel for twenty years. I don't care how many elevator accidents you work. You think some flack from a press release mill at the bottom end of Madison can handle a Fortune 500 company?"

"I swear, I—"

"And I don't appreciate Jack telling my client I'm washed up. Don't think I didn't hear that one."

"Sir, I'm not Jack's keeper."

"I will unequivocally whoop his elderly ass, and you can tell him that, verbatim."

"I'm not trying to steal your client, sir."

"You're a goddamn liar. And you're not even a good one." Rae swept across the office and opened the door. "Just remember we had this talk."

Leonard found it difficult to move. He remained in his seat and studied the man's demeanor, the flared nostrils, the deep grooves in his temples, a chest that heaved with heavy breaths.

"Everyone knows you're the go-to guy for reputation management," Leonard said. "Actually, I came here hoping I could get some advice, for a client."

The man clenched his jaw. "Advice? Are you kidding?"

"He's being blackmailed," Leonard said.

"Blackmail." Rae appeared to recoil in the doorway, a hermit crab caught outside its shell. He closed the door, then crossed the room and picked up his drink, sat behind the desk, and folded his hands. "Okay, let's dance," he said. "This person. What's he being blackmailed for? Fraud? Prostitution?"

"It's nothing like that. What he did, it's not illegal."

"Okay, personality crisis. Infidelity? Gay desires?"

"It's not that, either. But yes, this person has a secret, and someone found out about it, and now that person is threatening to tell the press, his clients, the competition, his coworkers, virtually anyone involved in his professional life."

"What's the price of the hush?"

"I don't follow."

"Cut the shit, kid. How much money is this person blackmailing you for?"

"None. Nothing."

"So, this is purely an issue of threatened slander."

"Yes."

Frazer crossed his legs. "Contrary to what crisis pros will tell you today, our line of work isn't supposed to be apology theater. PR is a natural function of transparency."

"Right."

"Silence concedes the accusation. So, come clean. Neuter the opposition by going public with whatever it is you're being blackmailed for. Get it out before they can."

"He can't."

"Why not?"

"He can't call the bluff because it's too outlandish. No one would believe him."

"If no one would believe you, who's to say they'd believe the blackmailer?"

"Because this person has video evidence. Also, this person . . . she . . . has a professional connection with one of his clients. He can't antagonize her if it risks the possibility she might divulge this information to them. So, for the time being, he's forced to play her game."

"Curious symmetry," Rae mused.

"There's more. A reporter is in the process of digging up dirt on . . . my client . . . and, by an incredibly bad stroke of luck has now met the blackmailer. They've been in contact at least once."

"Has she shared this video with him?"

"Not yet."

"Double knot." Frazer closed his eyes, then reached for the handkerchief. "Any practitioner will tell you, the safest route in PR is to tell the truth and take the hit. But there's still one option behind the emergency glass."

"What's that?"

"Hit back. Attack the adversary, destroy your opponent's credibility. Record that person making these threats against you, either over the phone or with video, and document them doing something even worse than what you've done. In effect, blackmail the blackmailer."

"I thought about that. I don't think it'll work."

"Why not?"

"This person, she has the moral compass of a psychotic child. She's shameless, impervious to embarrassment. She routinely engages in debasing and abjectly self-degrading acts of behavior in public. She has nothing to lose because she exists solely for the purpose of antagonizing others so she can experience bursts of short-term pleasure. Also," Leonard paused, "the one thing my client has on her is something that, unfortunately, also happens to involve him."

Rae looked him over. "Anything else?"

"I think that's about it."

"I'll be honest with you, kid. I'm having a hard time figuring out the interpersonal calculus here. You won't tell me why you're being blackmailed, aside from telling me it's not illegal and you're not being blackmailed for money. Now you tell me the blackmailer has safeguarded the initial blackmail with a backup blackmail, and this person's lack of redeeming social value somehow renders her immune to the universal follies of reputation damage. I simply don't understand the terms of engagement here. I'm sorry, I can't help you."

"Is there anything else I can do, given what I've told you?"

"I'll tell you this. Don't engage this person any longer. You'll only invite further transgression."

"That's another problem. This person is forcing engagement at regular intervals, per the rules of the blackmail."

"Then things are only going to get worse."

Chapter 8

Leonard scrolled through the gallery on his browser, clicked through a slideshow of thumbnail images showcasing airy, whitewashed interiors, model homes boasting vaulted ceilings and ivory wainscoting. Exteriors with wide overhangs and steeply pitched gables, generous yards bordered by fits of perennials. A young, tortuously Anglo couple frog-marched a child through what appeared to be a topiary garden flanked by irrigation ditches. Superimposed over the image, a stylistically inappropriate yellow brush font read "Mango Cove." Leonard shuffled through the images a second time, then picked up the phone.

"Hello?" Behind the voice, a battery of video-game gunfire.

"Grandma, I emailed you a link to another property. I need you to check it out."

"I'm kind of busy," Norman said.

"It's Saturday afternoon," Leonard said. "Humor me." An exasperated huff followed by prolonged silence. "Well, what do you think?"

"The names of these places are ridiculous. Mangos don't even grow in Ohio."

"Completely immaterial," Leonard said. "This place has an electronic gate. There's a community swimming pool. It's more money than I'd care to spend, but the investment is worth it. I think this is the one."

"It's nice, I guess," Norman said.

"They call it a lifestyle community. Please use this term when speaking with Mom about it. The language is important."

"I'm not one of your clients, Leonard."

"I need you to do the work, Grandma. Have you done what I asked, with the trash?"

"Been loading up the car every night, mostly with stuff from the garage. You were right, she hasn't noticed."

"What about those part-timers at the glass factory, for the gig we talked about?"

"I've got three guys on board, might be able to get a fourth."

"Good. I'm calling the appraisal agent and setting up an appointment, and I'm buying a plane ticket next week. In the meantime, I'm researching dates for the Muskingum County Flea Market, so I'll need you to figure out a day we can get Mom away for a few hours."

"She's going to hate you for this, Leonard. She'll hate us both."

"Things will be tough for a while, but we have to remember apologies are the engine behind every resolution. We'll get through this. You'll see."

Leonard reached for his ream of documents, opened his notepad, and resumed working on his upcoming presentation for Pinnacle. Soon he was under the kitchen sink digging for his box of detergent, which he was disappointed to find empty. He shook the remaining crumbs into a ceramic ramekin, rummaged under the sink again, and resurfaced with a bag of aquarium salt. He chose hand soap for a condiment, for the zest of its mints, and with his index finger whipped the concoction until it gelled into a curding pudding crowned with caviar beads of salt. He extended his tongue into the foaming bowl and immediately drew back, a sour report that mortified his senses, the herbaceous flourishes of the soap a poor cover for the salt's alloy profile, which stung his tongue and made him feel as though he'd placed it on a nine-volt battery. The adventurous new textures more than compensated for the dish's lacking complexity, so he licked the bowl several more times before the program became too rank, too uncivil, and then he ran back to the kitchen and washed his mouth out over the sink.

THE RESTAURANT'S INTERIORS WERE CATACOMB-DARK, AND IT TOOK several minutes for Leonard's eyes to adjust. The only light source consisted of several flickering gas lanterns affixed to meat hooks on the far side of the room and a glowing hearth in the middle of the dining court, a fire pit gated with wrought iron where a sweating pig turned on a spit. The air smelled of wood smoke and hickory, and from the reaches of the kitchen he could see an industrial smoker piled with smoldering lunkers of brisket. He crossed a bare cement slab floor and, beyond a row of lizard-skin banquettes, noticed the arched, low-ceilinged passageway, a warren of candlelit alcoves.

He parted a velvet curtain and found Patty seated at the bar, drinking from an oversized tulip glass festooned with fruit. She wore high-waisted shorts and a crop top that appeared several sizes too small.

"Incredibly, you're just as ugly in the dark," Leonard said.

"Nice to see you too."

"Let's get this over with."

"I'm so excited," Patty said as the hostess led them to a half-moon booth. Patty fell into the seat and clapped her hands. "Can you believe this heat? They say it's going to be high nineties all next week."

"I don't have time for pleasantries," Leonard said as he consulted the wine program, "but there are a couple things I need to ask. First, any word on that reporter Sundermeyer? Has he called?"

"Haven't heard anything from him," Patty said. "Not once."

"Are you sure?"

"Of course I'm sure. Has he called you?"

"Two days ago. And he called the week before, too."

"Why didn't you tell me?"

"Because it doesn't concern you." Leonard caught his reflection in an antique mirror that had lost most of its silver. Several sets of eyes flashed in the dark, silhouetted epicures feasting by candlelight. "Second order of business. Have you abided by the rules of our arrangement?"

"You mean, have I told anyone you eat pencils? You're being paranoid." She hid herself behind a novella-length menu. "I hope you brought your appetite," she said. "This is authentic Texan cuisine."

"With an Upper East Side price tag," Leonard said. "The people in this city throw money at things in the hopes it'll allow them to participate in some authenticated experience. They don't realize that once you begin valuating experiences, you turn them into another product."

"But that's what you do, right? Like, you'll tell a company to call something artisanal or handcrafted or whatever so people will forget how prefab it is."

"You're confusing PR with advertising," Leonard said. "The latter is about selling something. Admittedly, PR has taken on a marketing role in recent years, but it's mainly concerned with influencing public opinion by using the media."

"Yeah, okay," Patty said. "Totally different."

A waiter wearing a gingham shirt and bolo tie stood over the table. Leonard scanned the menu and ordered the least predatory-sounding item he could find.

"It *is* different," Leonard said after the waiter left. "PR is about starting conversations so companies can gain public trust. It's about using thought leaders to influence consumers' attitudes so brands can find leverage within those attitudes."

"So, the idea is to come up with an identity for the brand, but pretend the brand is its true identity?"

"Not exactly."

"But that's what you said. There's just something so degrading about it," she said, "tempting people with shiny things that confer social status."

"I thought you said you wanted to get into this business. Degrading to whom?"

"The only thing you're good at is keeping people in the dark. You engage in this passive-aggressive pimpery where a brand means one thing in a boardroom and something else in the outside world. That's why you think it's acceptable to say idiotic things like 'thought leaders.' You guys aren't leaders of anything. All you're doing is lowering the standards. You're just making boring things acceptable." Patty took a histrionic breath and picked up her glass. "You're an emotional terrorist."

"I suppose you're the enlightened one here? A layabout with impulse-control problems who's weaseled her way into a quick scheme that will inevitably end in disaster?"

"Sounds like someone else I know," she said.

"Don't try to manufacture some false equivalency between us. I've worked for everything I have, and you have to blackmail people for meals. People pay me for advice, and society avoids you at all costs. I'm a professional, and you're a deranged pig."

"There you go, trying to rationalize your mediocrity again. At least I like myself."

"Congratulations. That and a dollar will get you a bag of chips."

"You can't even have a normal relationship with a pencil," she said.

Their entrees arrived. On Patty's plate was a smoldering locker of braised ribs encrusted in a resinous glaze, served unnecessarily over a sheet of butcher paper and alongside a heap of duck-fat fries drenched in a Cajun rémoulade. Leonard had ordered the catfish; it was broiled to a medieval char and arrived with a wheel of cornbread and a tangle of coleslaw submerged in mayonnaise. He cleaved off a section of fish and inspected it before forcing it into his mouth. He chewed slowly, then reached beneath his tongue and removed a residual bone.

"So, have you looked at those files?" A ring of BBQ sauce had formed around her mouth.

"Yes. Several times."

"My God, the marbling," she said. "It's as though I'm an infant being cradled in my mother's arms."

"I already told you," Leonard said. "There's nothing I can do with them. I don't want to bother going into specifics."

"Why not?"

Leonard took several sips of wine. "Out of curiosity, where did you find those documents, anyway? How in the hell did you obtain personal emails from René Martin of all people?"

"Funny how you want to talk about something you can't use."

"He's one of the wealthiest men in France. I'm curious."

"I found it on a copy machine," she said.

"I don't believe you," Leonard said. "And it's one reason why I won't touch it."

"Or maybe that's what you want me to believe," Patty said. "You're up to something. I know you are. That mind of yours, it's always spinning."

"You should realize telling me about those files widened your perimeter of liability."

"What are you talking about?"

"Here's a tip from a pro, Patty. When you have a secret, keep it that way. Every person who has access to your missteps exponentially increases the chances of your downfall. You made a fatal error when you tried to blackmail the same person to whom you supplied leaked documents. I could tell Pinnacle everything, and you'd be fired. I'm the biggest liability you have."

"Convenient, considering I'm yours."

"I protect the world from people like you. Right now, you need my cooperation as much as I need yours. You want to release that video of me? The temporary embarrassment I'd feel pales in comparison to the pleasure of taking you down."

"But you wouldn't do that," she said. "There's too much at stake, with what you stand to gain by having my company in your pocket."

"You seem so sure."

"I am. We're locked in a stalemate."

Leonard stared at her, leaned forward, and set his arms akimbo on the table, a mock attempt at interrogation. His elbow edged his glass over, and when he went to save it, the glass struck his foot, sending a spray of wine across the floor. He dove under and felt his way in the dark on all fours, chased the rolling glass until his cheek struck something moist, a bare leg.

"Bet it smells like Christmas at grandma's down there," she said.

"You're disgusting."

. . .

LEONARD SPENT THE REST OF THE WEEKEND GOING OVER PAPERWORK he'd neglected, compiling and comparing notes, drafting and revising and refining the presentation for his Monday meeting with Pinnacle. On Sunday afternoon, he took a trip to Koreatown, and that evening, he rehearsed his presentation as he licked a stick of deodorant. He worked until he was cross-eyed and nodding off over his laptop, and just as he was drifting overheard a report on the television regarding a psychological bias that often occurs among intelligence analysts called mirror imaging, wherein analysts mistakenly assume their subjects possess the same general perspectives as the professionals analyzing them. Leonard inched up the volume, and an idea struck him that was so obvious, he became furious with himself for not thinking of it earlier.

HE ARRIVED AT THE OFFICE EARLY ON MONDAY, TURNED ON THE TELEVIsion, and picked through the Pinnacle files one more time. At nine o'clock, he reached for the telephone.

"Noah Sundermeyer."

"Sundermeyer, it's Leonard Lundell."

"For someone who doesn't want to talk, you call me a lot."

"Quid pro quo for you. Instead of publishing an article about an accident that happened weeks ago, how'd you be interested in a real scoop?"

"You want me to spike my story in return for an exclusive? I can't do that."

"I'm offering you breaking news that's going to do a hell of a lot more for your career than something no one will read that's going to run opposite the classifieds."

"Let me guess, exciting agency client announcement? Industry award win? I swear, you PR people think everything is news."

"You near a fax machine? Give me your number, and I'll send the first several pages. If what I'm sitting on doesn't blow your hair back, feel free to include this exchange as my quotable for your article, and we'll call it even."

The idea was simple: If he leaked the Pinnacle/Publique merger files to the *Register*, the resulting crisis could force management's hand in hiring Leonard as their counselor. He'd pitch them on his expertise in handling merger rumors at the meeting they'd scheduled later that day, placing him in the default position of being a natural fit for the job once the story broke. The leak would have the added effect of getting Sundermeyer off his back; and of course one of the major marks Patty had on him would also get rubbed out, as going to Sundermeyer with the video would be ineffectual once Leonard had him in his pocket. He was writing his own ticket with someone else's pen. Insofar as plans go, it was unassailable, foolproof.

Outside the office he heard a squalling wail of children. A wide-eyed girl, no older than four, cheeks spackled with what appeared to be blue frosting, punted a cupcake into the carpet as Leonard crossed the hall. A russet smoke of hair danced over the wall of the fax center, and Leonard reached a clearing in the cubicles to see Wanda Markowski hunched over the photocopy machine. She wore a slender charcoal pencil skirt, the notches of her exposed spine like the perforated border of a coupon. There was a shrill uproar behind them, and they turned to see a stampede of children racing through the aisle, several parents giving chase. A nearby cubicle wall was festooned with balloons, the desk below set with a spread of confectionery provisions and plastic cups.

"Haven't seen you in a minute," Wanda said as Leonard slid in next to her at the fax machine.

"I've been here," he said. He took a cover sheet from the drawer and scribbled on it, fretted the pages into the upright tray, punched in the number, and heard the trill of the machine as it scanned the content. A child was wailing somewhere among the cubicles, amid ringing phones and the delirious chatter of account pitches. "What's up with all the kids?"

"It's Bring Your Mistake to Work Day," Wanda said. "We decided it was a good idea to turn the office into an asylum for pint-sized psychotics once a year. Feeling overjoyed yet?"

She followed him as he fled back across the aisle. A passel of children cut them off in the hallway, and a young boy darted between Leonard's knees and latched on to his calf. From inside his office door, he could already hear the phone ringing.

"Do you have a second?" Wanda said. "There's something I wanted to talk to you about."

"Sorry, can't." A young account executive, no doubt the boy's mother, peeled the child off Leonard's leg. "I'm in the middle of something."

"I only need a second—" Wanda began as he closed the door and streaked to his desk.

"Is this real?" Sundermeyer said when Leonard picked up the receiver.

"Sure is. And there's a lot more where that came from."

"I can't breathe," Sundermeyer said. "I'll have to talk to my editor. I mean, I don't usually write hard news."

"You do now. And you'll get everything, on the condition you tell absolutely no one where you got it."

"I don't reveal my sources," Sundermeyer said sternly.

"Good man. I'm sending everything over now."

Leonard grabbed the rest of the files, and then the door behind him opened. "What are you doing?"

"Uh, meetings?" Todd Armitage said as the team filed into the room. "You forget?"

"Of course not."

A young man strolled in with the group, holding a stack of the day's papers. He was short and wiry with a face like bad taxidermy, wore a cheap shirt and a frayed army jacket and had a wispy mustache, a subcutaneous lump in his cheek. He set down the papers and discreetly spit into a twenty-ounce soda bottle.

"Check out the mongo," Todd Colton whispered.

"Who's that?" Leonard said.

"New gofer," Todd Armitage said. "Colton scared the old one off."

"Say there," Todd Shillenburg said. "Meet Leonard. He leads the crisis team."

"Hello, sir," the man stuttered. "Thomas Chessel, but everyone calls me Beau."

"Why?" Leonard said.

"Beau's a better name." He spoke with an ambiguously southern accent and sounded as though he were carrying marbles in his mouth.

"Where are you from?" Leonard said.

"Obion County, Tennessee," Beau said. "Just arrived three months ago—"

"You can't wear that jacket to work, Beau," Todd Colton said. "We do biz caj around here. Also, ditch the spittoon. Now, we're going to need plenty of coffee for this meeting—"

"Yes, sir," the man said and fled from the room.

"Did you have to humiliate the guy?" Leonard said. "Go ahead and get started. I have some business I need to take care of."

Leonard jogged back across the aisle and fed the sheaf of documents into the fax machine, and as the scanned pages danced over the carpet he noticed a simple gesture in the clouds, strokes of sun that bled between them and spilled through the windows, setting planks of light along the cubicle walls. He experienced an ineffable sensation, a fleeting glimpse of his life from the impossible vantage point of some not-too-distant future, as though the rest of him were out there just ahead of himself, watching the closing distance.

LEONARD WAS SHAKING WHEN HE ARRIVED AT THE PINNACLE BUILDING that afternoon. He took the stairs to give himself time to rehearse talking points and disembarked on the sixth floor out of breath and delirious from the heat. He passed employees on autopilot, many wearing earbuds and looking to their phones, eyes avoiding other eyes. A receptionist led him into a well-appointed conference room with floor-to-ceiling windows and a table stocked with elephantine high-backed chairs. Feinblum occupied a corner chair, wore heavy-lidded eyes and a wireless headset emitting a blue light. Two stone-faced men of uncertain allegiance sat across from him, each handling identical flap-over leather briefcases. They followed Leonard with itinerant eyes as he crossed the room shaking hands, locking stares with Frazer Rae, who offered an impish grin from the end of the table.

"I'm assuming you two know each other?" Feinblum said. Neither man said anything. "Will Roger or Wanda be joining us?"

Leonard cleared his throat. "Just me," he said.

Feinblum offered a tentative, mouth-closed smile. "I suppose we should begin. Why did you call this meeting?"

A company of eyes set on him. Leonard blanched, then returned to Rae, whose grin had metamorphosed into a bare-toothed sneer. Leonard strode to the window and examined the skyline in the fatigued summer light, gave a subtle cough as he fought back the urge to vomit, turned, and forced a smile as he made slow, measured steps back toward the table.

For the next thirty minutes, he spat through an impromptu presentation, first rehashing his media training campaign for the Pinnacle elevator witnesses before clumsily segueing into a general discussion on the importance of crisis management. He would later recall very little of what he'd actually said, but he distinctly remembered falling back on every marketingese superlative, every boardroom bromide in his armory, cribbed from a war chest of industry boilerplate he'd amassed going back to his earliest years in the business. His thoughts lacked logical coordination. Sentences were broken up by disfluencies, collapsed into disjointed phrases, a language liberated of rhythm, emphasis, clarity, coherence. His throat constricted and words eluded him; he repeated himself and neologized phrases. Composure grew difficult, his forehead prickled with sweat, and his skin felt irritated, began to itch. The others looked at him askance, and the room grew acutely quiet, occasionally broken by coughs or a fidgeting of legs. Feinblum's brow appeared permanently knotted. He seemed stricken with a sort of vexing concentration, less interested in the content of Leonard's speech and more focused on assaying the years he'd squandered, how better served his life would've been in any other line of work than the one he'd chosen. Only Frazer Rae, who reclined and sucked through his teeth, seemed amused by the spectacle. On the ceiling, Leonard noticed the winking light of a smoke alarm.

"Is that it?" Feinblum said when the presentation was over. The two supplicants on the other side of the table chuckled, a gesture that assured leadership they were in on the joke.

"Yeah, I think so," Leonard said and wiped his forehead.

The group stood and summarily filed out of the room. Leonard held the door open, though no one acknowledged the gesture. Entering the hallway, he felt a hand on his shoulder.

"Can I have a word?" Rae said. They moved into a corner, where the carpets were paneled with light from the midday sun. "This move was embarrassingly transparent, Lundell. I hope you realize that."

"I don't know what you mean," Leonard said and set down his briefcase.

" 'Diversified synergy'? That was the most ad hoc presentation I've heard in thirty years. Why did you call this meeting today?"

Leonard blinked several times.

"Don't want to tell me? Fine, here's my theory: You wanted to pitch your services to my client in the hopes they'd ink a partnership with your agency. You just didn't plan on me being here."

"I wanted to get them up to speed on our elevator witnesses," Leonard said. "Something wrong with checking in?"

"For work that was invoiced weeks ago." Rae dabbed his head with his handkerchief, set down his own briefcase next to Leonard's, and took to pacing. "You're in the wrong league, kid. You don't know what the hell you're doing. You have no strategy. You act impulsively. You obfuscate, you mistake ineptitude for sagacity, you rely on misdirection over long-term solutions. You're precisely the reason our profession gets no respect today.

Public relations is supposed to be about providing transparency, but for you it's just another tent to peddle your cheap, carny-grade chicanery."

"Are you finished?"

Rae's lips tightened. A wheelwork of wrinkles radiused at the corner of his eyes. "And I thought of something else. You know what brings down a man's empire more than anything?"

"Surviving on laurels from two decades ago?" Leonard said. "Traveling out of state without a cellphone?"

"One bad decision on top of one piece of damning content. It's funny, why would a person who's connected to one of your accounts be blackmailing you?"

"Excuse me?"

"The other day in my office. You said your blackmailer is connected to one of your accounts. Why would that be? Have you been doing something with one of your clients you shouldn't have? Stuck your nose where it doesn't belong, perhaps?"

"I haven't done anything wrong," Leonard said.

"There has to be a reason this person is blackmailing you now. It could be a coincidence, but we don't like coincidences in this line of work, do we? I'll tell you, it's quite a coincidence all this trouble began after you started crafting a reputation salvo for Pinnacle."

"Who said it did?"

"The first rule of crisis management is to mobilize a rapid response. You've got the look of a man being held over a fire. Quit hiding the ball, Lundell. What do you have on my client?"

"Nothing," Leonard said.

They locked eyes, Rae stepping toward Leonard until their shoes touched. A single tear of sweat made its way down Rae's face.

"It's over, Leonard. You should do the honorable thing and fall on your sword. If you don't tell me what you have on my client, so help me, I'm going to be your shadow, a rock in your shoe, two eyes over your shoulder every waking minute of every day. And I'll find out what this alleged video of you is all about. Be a man, for once in your life."

"I don't know what you're talking about," Leonard said, "but I don't like your tone."

He grabbed his briefcase and shoved past Rae's shoulder, then stormed down the hallway, passing aisles of cubicles and the reception station. It wasn't until Leonard had left Pinnacle headquarters and returned to his office and was rocking in the elevator as it shuttled through the guts of the building that his thumb grazed a divot in the briefcase handle. Curious, he set the briefcase on the carpet. A familiar exterior contained strange additions: edges tooled with wear, the grain cowhide appearing thinner than he'd remembered. There was a small tear in the stitching he'd never noticed and a paracord fob on the zipper of the peripheral storage pouch. He threw open the briefcase, and its contents, four dog-eared early editions of *Public Relations Fundamentals*, spilled to the elevator floor. Then he screamed.

LEONARD RAN BACK TO THE PINNACLE BUILDING WITH THE TASTE OF blood in his mouth. Rae was nowhere to be found, of course, so he made a futile call to the Frazer Rae and Associates office, where the receptionist promised she'd relay Leonard's message when Rae returned. Eventually, Leonard returned to his building again and dialed Noah Sundermeyer.

"You've got to eighty-six that story," Leonard said. "I'm begging you."

"Why, what happened?" Sundermeyer said.

"I made a terrible mistake. I never should've sent you those files."

"Relax. I'm not quoting you. My source is unnamed."

"You don't understand. My career is on the line."

"What kind of trouble did you get yourself into, Lundell?"

"Someone knows I had those documents," Leonard whispered. "I'm going to be turfed for this. Please, you have to kill it."

"I can't kill the story. It's been filed, it's been edited, it went through fact-checking. Production just sent proofs an hour ago. We're live tomorrow morning."

"You wrote the whole thing already?"

"We're competing with blogs over here." Sundermeyer quieted. "We got the front page."

Leonard swiveled in his chair, noticed the stack of Pinnacle meeting notes on his desk, and swept them into the wastebasket.

"Fact-checking," Leonard repeated. "Out of curiosity, what did Pinnacle's communications department say?"

"What do you think?" Sundermeyer said. "They said 'no comment,' just like you."

AT HOME THAT EVENING, LEONARD ATTEMPTED SEVERAL MORE CALLS TO Frazer Rae's office, then raided the kitchen cabinet under the sink and scattered its contents over the floor. He hadn't gotten around to buying another box of detergent, and he wasn't about to degrade himself with aquarium salt again, so he foraged on his knees until he found a discarded duster can used for cleaning electronic equipment. He held its straw nozzle to his nose, sniffed anodyne gas, then depressed the plastic actuator and sprayed the payload into his lungs before his head made a lateral whip, and he pirouetted in a fit of sneezing. The sensation—chaotic, redemptive—hit the back of his calves first, then seized his face and assailed his senses, left him blinded by a riot of light. He jammed a knuckle over his right nostril and blew a yarn of snot into the sink, then found a paper lunchbag in a drawer and discharged the duster until the bag was soaked with a champagne broth, clasped it over his mouth, and inhaled. He staggered there for a moment, lightheaded, and soon was scarfed in a warm interstellar cloud of color, a dizzying euphoria where, for a moment, he thought he could taste the glimmering baubles that now patterned the walls, a synesthesia so distinct it was as though he'd witnessed new colors being introduced to the world. Then the floors began to tilt, and he acquired tunnel vision and was besieged by dissociative thought loops. He stumbled to the bathroom, splashed water on his face, and turned on the shower taps, disrobed, and stacked his clothes on the toilet. He hunkered over the sink and stared at his reflection. He was surveying the ruins clearly now. Patty's knowledge of his secret and his inability to reel in Pinnacle as a client weren't the problem. He simply wasn't good at his job. Wisps of vapor scattered across the mirror. He stepped behind the frosted glass partition and sat on the shower's warm tile floor, got on his knees, picked a worm of green grout between the tiles with a fingernail, held it to his nose and sniffed, a spoiled stink of aged prosciutto. The steam grew heavy, coalesced into a cocoon enveloping him, and he imagined hiding in a dense fog, a place where no one would be able to find him.

DINNER THAT NIGHT WAS IN BROOKLYN. LEONARD EXITED THE TRAIN, crossed well-lit storefronts and roaring bars and mid-rise apartment buildings, and continued walking until signs of life disappeared. Soon, he found himself in a wasteland of scattered warehouses and vacant lots cordoned off with chain link and concertina wire. The street dead-ended with a screen of rebar poles, and he looked out over the black, enameled span of water swelling and stirring against a cragged sweep of shore. From across the river, wisps of fog gauzed between buildings in the silver nimbus of downtown skyline. The air smelled foul: diesel exhaust and industrial solvents.

The restaurant, housed in the former site of a sugar refinery, sat beneath the steel gossamers of the Williamsburg Bridge. A procession of twenty-somethings queued down the sidewalk, and Leonard cut through the crowd, scanning a faux-thentic industrial tableau, as predictable as he'd envisioned: shiplap walls featuring apocryphal advertisements for bygone brands, a squadron of rough-hewn plank benches lit by exposed-filament bulbs, smug mission statements written in chalk on sandwich boards, detailing the establishment's tireless dedication to social responsibility. He found Patty seated on a bench near the bar.

She wore a floral muumuu and sun hat, an ivory-colored shawl draped over her shoulders.

"You look like a cafeteria lady at a funeral," Leonard said and sat.

"Always the gentleman," she said.

"New rule. From now on, we do this only in the city. It took me forty minutes to get here."

"You're the lucky one. I waited in line for an hour. I just got our seats five minutes ago."

"I don't know if you picked up on this, but waiting hours to eat haute cuisine referred to in hushed tones by Brooklyn's nouveau riche isn't one of my pastimes."

"This building has a lot of history," Patty said. "Back in the eighties, artists used to squat here and pretend they were factory workers."

"And now the yuppies are squatting as artists. The cycle completes."

"Cities are the new suburbs. Here, try this." She passed a votive glass filled with a milky liquid. "It's called a White Guilt."

A waiter wearing tan jodhpurs and paddock boots restlessly hovered over them.

"I'll have the tuna carpaccio," Patty beamed before turning to Leonard. "It's supposed to be delish."

"Glass of malbec," Leonard said as he eyed the menu. "And the po'boy sandwich. The one you sell for eighteen dollars."

The waiter rolled his eyes and left. Across the street, a former loft was being refurbished into another chic eatery. Leonard watched as two men hoisted into place a vintage tin sign that read "Delicatessen," while another with an airbrush painted what appeared to be faux rust onto stars of metal filigree above the doorway.

"We should talk," Leonard said and rapped his knuckles against the table. "Things have taken a turn."

"What happened?"

"I'll be straight with you. I lied. Those Pinnacle files, I'd planned on using them."

"I knew it!" she said. "I told you that you were a bad liar."

"Do you have any idea of the implications of Pinnacle joining forces with a French ad agency?" He paused, adjusted his silverware. "I thought I could use those materials to pitch my services to Pinnacle, but someone got in the way, someone very powerful. He's an obstacle I can't get around, so those files are now useless to me."

Patty grew quiet, contemplative. "Oh, well," she said. "Not a big deal."

"Actually, it *is* a big deal. We could be in serious trouble. I have a powerful enemy who now has material on me that, believe it or not, is potentially far worse than any video you could've shown my clients or employers. For once, you're the least of my worries."

"So, this person saw the files?"

"Yes. I mean, he has them."

"That was stupid, Leonard. Those files were for your eyes only. I figured you'd do something with them, but I didn't want you sharing them with the world."

"He tricked me," Leonard said. "Believe it or not, he stole them."

"Ironic. That's how you got them from me."

"It gets worse."

Her eyebrows jumped. "How?"

"This morning, right before the files were stolen, I leaked them to that reporter."

Patty shot up from the table and glowered at him. "You did what?"

"My reasoning was that it would make Pinnacle's public image during the pending merger a more urgent matter, which would light a fire under their asses to hire me. It was a good plan. I just didn't foresee a third party stealing the files and being able to link them to me."

"What does this mean?"

"It could mean a number of things. Here's my prediction: As of tomorrow, Pinnacle is going to find out I've been nosing around in their affairs. Not only will I never work with them, but they'll probably inform my superiors, and I'll have to dig my way out of it, which is going to take some finesse."

"What about me?"

"You'll probably be fired."

"You screwed up, Leonard. This guy is going to take us both down."

"Like it or not, we'll have to come up with a story together, one that corroborates," he said. "We can't let people draw their own dots. You'll need to let me devise a plan."

"No way. You want me to share your risk, but you want to control how the risk is handled. I don't think so. I swear, sometimes I think I'm better at this than you are."

"This might not be your fault, but it is your problem," Leonard said. "We're circling the drain here. In a few hours, both of our careers will be on the line. How would you advise we handle this?"

"All I did was give you a few documents," Patty said. "You're the one who's in danger of having the whole world find out what a fraud you are. I'll just deny everything. And if you try to link me to those files, I'll lie."

Leonard dug his fingernails into the table. "It's not that easy," he said. "You can't lie your way out of everything."

"Seems to work for you," she said.

Their food arrived, and Patty commenced gorging, eyes closed, an enthralled knitting of lips, fingers knuckle-deep in a ramekin of a longan and mission fig compote. "Decadent," she moaned. "So tender, so moist."

Leonard looked to his plate, thumped a mealy bun, then picked at the side dish, a crude slaw referred to on the menu as "moonshine pickles."

"Every time I've tried to fix things, I've only made them worse," he said. "First I was blackmailed while working for a client I wanted but never got. Then a writer was trying to slander me, and when I tried to fix it, the competition got worse material on me than you did. And now I'm forced to find a way out of the mess I started in order to get myself out of the mess I was in in the first place."

"Maybe you just make bad decisions," Patty said, her mouth crammed with food.

"I realize now my biggest mistake was thinking I was good at my job."

"Listen to you," she said. "You're self-absorbed but self-loathing. How weird is that?"

Leonard's face flared. "I hate my job." He leaned over and began licking his napkin. When he grew bored with this, his tongue began roving over the wooden grain of the table. "I hate my goddamn job."

"Taste good?" Patty said.

"Go to hell," Leonard said. He began gnawing on the corner of the table with his bicuspids. Behind the hard fender of its exterior, an amber, resinous warmth, apple butter and cardamom. The waiter appeared with Leonard's glass of wine, stood over the table as Leonard chewed, and rolled his eyes. Leonard stood and took the glass from the waiter's hand, the man's eyes widening as Leonard bent over and licked his tie.

"Leonard," Patty whispered. "You're embarrassing me."

Leonard swept his plate onto the floor. He didn't know why he did this; it was unrecognizable behavior, like discovering a photo of his younger self he'd never seen. There was a terrible crash, and the restaurant went mute, and a cadre of busboys scurried out from the corners to sweep up scattered edibles and fragments of porcelain. Patty bolted up from the bench, and Leonard rushed around the table and fumbled for her shoulders, pushing her back into the seat. Then he leaned over and spoke in a low register, barely above a whisper.

"You want decadent? From now on, if I have to suffer your plebeian ideas of urban sophistication, you're going to have to deal with my own eccentricities. You aren't the only one capable of bad manners."

"I want to leave," Patty said.

"No. Eat," he said and brought her plate toward her.

Patty's face turned up and lost several shades of color, her eyes resembling the quivering whites of an egg. Leonard picked up a glass carafe. As he made to throw it, she winced.

"Eat," he repeated, and held the plate under her chin.

Red-faced, Patty looked to her plate, leaned over, and clamped down, whimpering softly like a child as she shuffled stores into her mouth. Leonard drained his wineglass, as a flock of busboys wended around them, then cleared the table of its remaining tableware and bread, before tossing the carafe, which managed to bounce twice before shattering near the restrooms.

"What's going on?" a woman said from a neighboring table.

"I don't know." Her companion sighed. "I can't tell what's real and what's an art installation anymore."

Chapter 9

L eonard sat in his office the next morning and studied the *Register*'s front page. The article had Sundermeyer's handiwork all over it, was written without a trace of authorial ambition and assembled with a kind of inscrutable idiocy, a series of half-realized ideas shaped by incompetent hands. The first three paragraphs had been lifted wholesale from the materials Leonard had sent him. What followed was a breathless, nauseatingly flattering summary of Publique Groupe's history that had obviously been cribbed from a Wikipedia entry and seasoned with weasel words and sycophantic clichés, at one point even suggesting Pinnacle CEO Graydon Trotwood had been seduced by the "Gallic charm" of Publique chief René Martin. As far as Leonard could tell, the only real work Sundermeyer had done was to cite a disinterested analyst who pegged the deal at thirty billion. He skimmed the article once more before tossing it into the wastebasket, and then his eyes rested on the telephone, as they had for most of the morning.

The door swung open. "You all right?" Todd Armitage said. "Why are the lights off?"

"I'm fine." Leonard opened a drawer and popped several antacids into his mouth. "Let's get this over with."

Crisis: An upscale department store had been accused of harassing Black customers. Customers alleged that on two separate occasions they'd been targeted by the store's security personnel; and during one incident, police had detained a customer because security suspected he'd purchased items with a stolen credit card. Civil rights leaders now threatened to stage a protest in front of the store. *Strategy:* Hire sensitivity experts to conduct a thorough review of the company's policies. Offer a nationwide promotion to celebrate Black History Month. *Crisis:* A year after a woman was killed in a car accident, the victim's family attended the vehicular manslaughter trial brought against the defendant. As it turned out, both parties had used the same insurance company, and the family was shocked to discover the company had brought in a team of high-profile lawyers to place blame for the accident on the victim. Days later, a story broke in a national daily with the headline: "Woman Pays Insurance to Defend Her Killer." *Strategy:* Apologize, dovetail crisis plan with legal strategy and focus on a settlement with the family. *Crisis:* A humanitarian organization hired a celebrity spokesperson to drive pledges for an international fundraising campaign to buy mosquito nets as a means of offsetting malaria outbreaks in sub-Saharan Africa. The widely publicized campaign trumped expectations, raising more than five hundred thousand dollars. Months later, however, rumors spread that many of the nets purchased went missing after arriving at the Lagos airport and had since resurfaced on the black market, where they'd been repurposed as wedding dresses. *Strategy*: Rehire the celebrity to raise awareness for a donation drive to buy wedding dresses for young women living in sub-Saharan Africa.

The team took a break, and Leonard turned on the television. A commercial promoted a reality show featuring the wives of white-collar criminals. The news returned with an announcement that July was Buffalo Wings Awareness Month. Beau, the new gofer, entered the room with a vacuum flask of coffee and settled into a vacant chair.

"Big news this morning on the Pinnacle front," Todd Armitage said.

Leonard stared at his phone, the slate-gray receiver resting in its cradle.

"I just want to know how the *Register* broke the story," Todd Colton said. "No one reads that rag."

The news now reported a movie star had plowed her SUV into a Beverly Hills storefront window while intoxicated. The room exploded in exhortations for Leonard to change the channel.

"I could work this gig for a hundred years and never understand why celebrities trash their reputations when they know it'll haunt them forever," Todd Shillenburg said.

"They do it to elevate their brand," Todd Armitage said. "Fact attack: A huge amount of the celebrity scandal you read is planted by the publicist."

"I heard about that," Todd Colton said.

"Ask a gossip reporter," Todd Armitage said. "You think it's a coincidence the Paris Hilton sex tape showed up a week before her show debuted? I've got a buddy in Hollywood, this former agency ham-and-egger who opened his own publicity shop. He hosts these sponsorship parties where he pays a celebrity wrangler to secure B-list attendees and makes them pose for photos with his client's product, usually a soft drink or something. These has-beens don't give two shits sideways what they're promoting as long as they're being paid, and my guy sends the pics to the society-page editors with a quote and files it with the client as a media impression. He's made a living doing this."

"Goddamn. That's brilliant," Todd Colton said.

"Celebrities are placards for product placement," Todd Armitage said. "They use the headlines to stay relevant. I'll bet you that celeb's publicist told her to crash her car."

"You call that making a living?" Beau said. Leonard's copy of the *Register* now lay unfurled in Beau's lap, and Leonard noticed the assistant had drawn several penises over Sundermeyer's cover story. "Shit, my daddy pulled twelve-hour shifts at the Reelfoot packing plant for thirty years. Weekends, nights, you name it. Hell of a lot harder than sitting in an air-conditioned office and saying 'think outside the box' over and over again."

"I'm sorry the chicken hatchery offers a more rewarding career experience than a Madison Avenue agency that's been in business for forty years," Todd Colton said.

"All's I'm saying is no one ever wrote a good song about losing their PR job," Beau said. "Why are you getting riled?"

"Because you're the fucking help, and you aren't fucking helping," Todd Colton said. "Now why don't you step lively with my coffee?"

Leonard's mind returned to the *Register* article. He looked to the telephone again. Almost on top of the thought, it rang.

"I need everyone to leave," Leonard said. The group rose and staggered, far slower than he would've liked, into the hallway. He slammed the door behind them and tentatively picked up the receiver.

"Leonard Lundell?" A somewhat familiar voice—older woman, polite but solicitous—was enough to confirm the call had nothing to do with the *Register* article. Then he remembered: He'd scheduled a phone meeting with a Lanchester appraisal specialist.

THE REST OF THE DAY WENT BY WITHOUT INCIDENT. LEONARD SCHEDuled an inspection date with the appraisal agent and researched real estate agents specializing in Lanchester-area properties. He bought a plane ticket and emailed Norman with an update on his progress, then watched a report on TV about a new emotion-sensing technology that gauged consumer product loyalty (top sentiment-earners were potato chips and cologne). Eventually his anxiety dialed back; no one called, and no one stopped by his office to discuss the *Register* feature. Somewhere in the lacuna of quiet a thought occurred to him: It was his birthday. He'd forgotten.

He was sifting through paperwork that afternoon when the phone rang again. He grabbed for it and heard static. Seconds later, a faint voice broke through before disintegrating into pulses, blips in a scanning radio dial.

"You're a dead man, shit bird, you understand?"

"Excuse me?" Leonard said. "Frazer? Is that you?"

"You put a red rag under the bull's nose . . . that phony meeting . . . classic!" There was a long-distance delay between sentences, and then the signal broke apart again, and the words disintegrated and became unintelligible.

"I don't know what you're talking about, but I'm having a hard time understanding—"

"Quit playing dumb, you son of a bitch. I had you pegged from day one. How'd you do it? How'd you know that story was coming out in the *Register*? How far upstream does this red herring swim?"

"What?"

"Was someone really trying to blackmail you? That's what I'd like to know. And have you pulled this kabuki dance before? I'm going to find out if that person really has any dirt on you, and then I'm going to ruin you, you understand?"

"I'm hanging up," Leonard said. "I want my briefcase back."

Leonard walked to the end of the hall, to the office just before the stairwell. He paused and considered going back, then squeezed his eyes shut and rapped furtively on the door's metal frame.

"Oh, so now's a good time?" Wanda Markowski was perched in the chair in front of her computer, which was playing a video of a cat scratching a mirror.

"You said you wanted to talk yesterday."

"I did, I do. But I've added an item to the list." She fanned a folded copy of the *Register*. "Assuming you heard?" Leonard studied her posture. She seemed irritable and guarded, even more so than usual. "I take it this complicates your plans?"

Leonard stiffened. He fought the urge to pick at something with his fingers.

"Why did you have a meeting with Pinnacle yesterday?" she said.

"Tying up loose ends. Typical courtesy call. How did you know?"

"Cut the shit. How's your pipe dream coming along to extend their contract?"

"Honestly? I've hit a few snags."

"Color me surprised. What did they have to say about the merger?"

"Nothing. I'm as shocked as you are."

She gave him a hard stare, appeared on the cusp of saying something, but rolled her eyes instead. Then she took off her glasses, leaned forward in the chair, set her elbows on the desk, and steepled her fingers against her temples.

"You all right?" Leonard said.

"Truthfully, I'm exhausted." Wanda pumped a bottle of sanitizer and wrung her hands. "I have a headache. I'm doing this ten-day cleanse, and I've had nothing but lemon water and cayenne pepper for a week. But I feel great," she said. "Really, really great."

He'd never noticed the antiseptic, waiting-room sterility of her office. It smelled like a new shower liner and was bare, completely unadorned save for a beige floor lamp and particleboard bookcase. Not a houseplant, a painting or photo, a single accent detailing her personal interests, a life outside the office.

"That dirt-eater Beau, our new account assistant," he said. "How did we hire this one, anyway?"

"I'm not sure," Wanda said. "I think Roger was drunk. Why?"

"I want to fire him."

"For what reason?"

"He's insubordinate. Rude. Do we have anything on his record?"

Wanda consulted her keyboard. "Says he was written up for carving 'Whitesnake' into a desk." She leaned back, studied him. "You can't fire him. I won't let you. He's got a face only a mother could love, but, believe it or not, he's good at scheduling meetings."

"Fine," Leonard said. "Any chance we could get caller ID installed on the phones?"

"No. Why?"

"Just talking out loud." Leonard stood and made his way to the door. "No reason."

Wanda narrowed her eyes. "I'm assuming you've noticed how bad Jack's gotten?"

"He's seventy-eight years old," Leonard said. "Do things get better?"

"He's decompensated. Roger heard him talking to himself the other day. And we're not talking casual chin music. These were full, longwinded conversations with himself."

"Okay. Where is he?"

"Right now? In catatonia, in his office. Where else? Look, Roger and I had a talk about this. We're thinking about asking him to consider taking some time off. You and Jack have always been . . . close. We thought you might run the idea by him too. Mention he might want to plan a trip, start doing some work from home. He owns three of them, for Christ's sake."

"This business, it's Jack's life. It's all he's got."

"And he's pissing all over the legacy he worked forty years to build. You heard him during that meeting with Pinnacle. I'm surprised he didn't botch the deal. All that constant talk about how PR isn't marketing, how the ad conglomerates are buying all the shops, blah, blah, blah. And now that damn library he's hoarding in his office."

"I see what's going on." Leonard shot a wry smile. "So, our resident persona non grata warms to the idea of being out of the office, and then you'll suggest he work from home full-time. Sooner or later, you'll ask him to retire. You want to tell the guy who founded this company to bow out, you'll have to do it yourself. I'm sorry. It's not in my job description."

Wanda's movements grew stiff, and a hatch of lines etched out across her face.

"Why do you always have to stir the turd, Leonard? What is it about this job that makes you so antagonistic? Do the thoughts and feelings of your colleagues simply not register to you, do you lack such basic decorum you never consider the effects your actions, your words have, or do women in positions of authority occupy a special target for your contempt? And why, for the love of God, are you constantly testing my patience?"

He got the feeling this speech had been loaded in the chamber for some time. In truth, he hadn't intended to be so churlish. The words just sounded better that way.

"Fine. I'll talk to him. Meeting adjourned?"

"You could've saved us a lot of trouble and agreed to it the first time," Wanda yelled after him. "Honestly, I'm jealous of people who don't know you."

He passed Jack's office on his way to the cubicle court and, out of curiosity, peered in. The old man was reclined in his chair, mouth agape and stuttering snores. A brickwork of books lay strewn across the floor and fortressed the walls, half the room slitted with light from the afternoon sun that cut through the blinds. Leonard crept in, side-stepped between the stacks, took a knee, and tried to decipher a spine. Then Jack shook his head, muttered something unintelligible as the folded hands in his lap twitched, and Leonard thought the old man had woken up, but he resumed snoring, the coinlike buttons on his navy jacket rattling with every breath.

DINNER THAT EVENING WAS AT A MIDWEST-THEMED RESTAURANT IN Chelsea called Heartland. Patty said she chose the venue after reading a review in one of the alt weeklies that'd been written in the form of a confessional, wherein the author professed being "addicted" to the meatloaf. The dining hall was a cynical interpretation of rustic charm, corduroy couches and walls junked with a tapestry of pastoral clichés: rusted biscuit tins, antebellum farming tools, gas station signage, and, predictably, a taxidermy deer head. Behind a corrugated-steel bar, bottles sat stashed on plumber's-pipe shelves alongside garden gnomes and bygone gewgaws.

"I thought you'd appreciate it here," Patty beamed, "being you're from the Midwest."

Leonard inspected a small toolbox on their table, which held napkins, silverware, and condiments, then eyed a plaster statue across the room of a beer-bellied man wearing a T-shirt that read "Don't Blame Me, I Voted for Bush."

"Actually, I find it offensive," he said. "No one back home nails washboards to their walls."

"Do you miss it?" Patty said as she pondered the menu.

"I left for a reason."

Leonard's phone buzzed. He read the message, then commenced typing: *Thanks, Grandma. Bought plane ticket. Appraiser meeting Sept 2, same day as flea market. Remember to get Mom out of the house.*

"Any word on whether that person who took those files spilled the beans?" Patty asked.

"Nothing yet."

"What's his name, anyway? I feel I should be in the know."

"It doesn't matter. There's nothing we can do but wait."

"It's just, you know, I'm affected by this too."

"Look who's gotten concerned all of a sudden."

"I read that story in the *Register*," Patty said. "Everyone in the office is talking about it."

"Oh? And what are they saying?"

"Honestly, a lot of people think they're going to lose their jobs."

"Mergers and acquisitions can lead to layoffs, but Pinnacle's a Fortune 500 company. I did research—"

"Then you'd know Pinnacle is broke. Shareholders have been pressuring the company to sell for years. We stopped hiring. Everyone's expected to do more with less. Did you even read about Pinnacle's last earnings report? Management moved the shareholder meeting to a hotel in Florida, and they held the meeting at eight in the morning so the press wouldn't be there to report on how badly Pinnacle missed its revenue targets."

"Maybe I should've dug deeper," Leonard said. "This is news to me."

"How do you think Pinnacle is going to handle the rumors?"

"Hard to say," Leonard said. "Scandals that ruined careers twenty years ago, like coming out as gay, don't register today. The only thing that's certain anymore is, thanks to the internet, crisis has a long shadow. Everyone's a target."

At the bar, red-faced men screamed over a baseball game on television. Food arrived, Patty clapping and squealing at the sight of her plate, meatloaf alongside a hummock of mashed potatoes. Leonard's phone buzzed again, a call from his mother.

"Geez," Patty said. "You're blowing up tonight."

"True story," he said. "Today's my birthday."

"Happy birthday," she said. "How old are you?"

"Thirty-two."

"What was your childhood like?"

"A series of humiliations." Leonard stowed the phone in his pocket. "It doesn't matter. What happened in the past never does."

"I don't know how you can say that. We are our histories. I think time gives us perspective."

"A true understanding of the past requires the knowledge we had at the time we experienced it, which is impossible," Leonard said. "So, reliving those moments with what we know now in no way grants perspective and is a pointless endeavor." Leonard paused, rearranged his silverware. "Our memories are constantly changing based on our current perceptions. With every replay the original signal gets weaker. We get diminished returns until you can't separate what's real from what's made up. Our pasts are our fictions."

"And now you've got me all pensive with my meatloaf," she said. "That might be the most depressing thing I've ever heard. I don't know about you, but this is the happiest time of my life."

"And you think I'm depressing? I'm interested in tomorrow. I'm concerned with what's to come."

"Well, maybe the opposite is true too," Patty said. "I mean, everything you said about the past also applies to the future."

"No, I don't think so," Leonard said. "How?"

"Because we create these phony ideas of what our lives will be like based on our expectations. It's like we see how other people live and assume the same is going to happen to us. Isn't it more likely that things will be just like they always were?"

"Not necessarily."

"Why not?"

"You have a myopic worldview, Patty. You're too cynical. We don't know what's going to happen in the future. There's a difference."

Patty held a corner of the tablecloth to her mouth to conceal her laughter. "You know, I have a theory."

"A theory for what?"

"An idea, based on all the things we've talked about these last few weeks."

"Don't embarrass yourself."

"The people in your line of work have been so brainwashed into thinking everything needs to be some committee-approved sound bite, it's never occurred to you to tell the truth for once," Patty said. "You guys put on this façade where you avoid sharing what's on your minds. Doesn't that contradict what you're supposed to do? If you really want to do something interesting, instead of telling people what they want to hear, you could open a business where you tell people what you think of them. Truth is a valuable commodity. These days, being honest is a kind of transgression."

"And you're a paragon of honesty, aren't you? What you said is very poetic, Patty, but your idea isn't practical as a business model."

"Why not?"

"Because it doesn't take into account how people operate. We're motivated by unmet needs. People don't settle for who they are, or what they have, or what they can afford. We're concerned with becoming our idealized selves, not the people we're forced to live with."

"Like pretending to be a successful PR executive and not someone who sits at home eating soap?"

"People want things, and companies produce goods and services to meet that demand. It doesn't matter if it's pornography, or a bigger house, or a sandwich, or the illusion that we're someone else. That's our world. It's not complicated."

"Did you just equate pornography with a sandwich?"

"Pornography is just another word for what you don't have."

Leonard's phone buzzed in his pocket. He looked at the screen, then swiveled in his seat to answer it.

"I'm still in the office," Todd Armitage said. "Bernie Feinblum from Pinnacle just called. Senior management has fangs out. They want to have a meeting. He says it's urgent."

A swelling panic came over him. "I'll have to look at my schedule," Leonard said. "I could probably squeeze them in Thursday—"

"You don't get it," Armitage said. "They want to see you now."

"It's eight o'clock," Leonard said.

"Like I said, they told me it's urgent."

LEONARD ARRIVED AT THE PINNACLE BUILDING THIRTY MINUTES LATER. A sour anxiety welled in his stomach as he listened to the seashell echo of his footsteps across the empty lobby, boarded the elevator, and debated how he'd respond in the inevitable event that Pinnacle management confronted him for leaking internal documents to the *Register*. His mind drew a blank, at a loss for an exit strategy. A lone idiot voice spoke inside his head: deny everything.

When the elevator door glided open on the sixth floor, Leonard felt a natural inclination to hide. He crossed a dark corridor and navigated mousetrap hallways past a gallery of vacant cubicles where a single tubular bulb flickered just before the far wall. Outside, the wind between the buildings soughed against the glass, and Leonard considered how no one thinks about what happens during the hours after everyone leaves an office, how places all have their own unique echo, a kind of voice when people aren't around. A thread of light ran under the conference room door. Leonard entered to see Bernie Feinblum occupying the same corner chair as before, tie undone, sweating under the lights like a rotisserie chicken. Sitting at the head of the table was Pinnacle CEO Graydon Trotwood. The late hour had democratized the executive, who'd dressed uncharacteristically in an absurd rayon sports shirt decorated with palm fronds. Leonard expected to see something in the man's face he could decode, but his expression, plaintive and reserved, belied the urgency of the situation. He was a difficult man to read, and Leonard decided this quality probably contributed to his success. His hands were on the table, fingers knit together like the interlocking teeth of a zipper.

"I got here as fast as I could," Leonard said. "By the way, I'd like to apologize for my ramshackle presentation the other week. I've been under a lot of pressure—"

"Take a seat, Leonard," Trotwood said. A deferential smile graced his face.

Leonard shuffled into a chair, adjusted himself, and crossed his arms. He felt trapped, unprepared, outnumbered. "What's going on?"

"It's been a long day," Trotwood said. "I cut my vacation short and flew in from Turks and Caicos this afternoon to work damage control. I'm sure you saw the story in the *Register*?" He motioned to a newspaper strewn across the table.

"I did." Leonard fidgeted.

"This wasn't a company announcement under embargo," Feinblum said. "Our writer here had to dig deep, which is what journalists do, of course, but this isn't exactly a top-flight publication."

"Did you see the writing?" Trotwood said. "Gallic charm, my ass."

Leonard was sweating now, dry-mouthed. The mantra returned to him: deny everything.

"And then, something else happened," Feinblum said. "Last night, hours before the *Register* story dropped, Frazer Rae got off an airplane in Paris. He went to Publique Groupe's headquarters and demanded a meeting with René Martin."

"And apparently, after a night of harassment, René relented," Trotwood said. "Details of their meeting are still somewhat unclear, but the long and short of it is Frazer tried to counsel him on how to buy us out."

Leonard cleared his throat. "Why would he do that?"

"We don't know," Feinblum said. "But apparently René laughed him out of the room. Then his people called us. They said Frazer had heard scuttlebutt on some merger deal in the works between the agencies and wanted to switch teams. He even produced documents."

"What kind of documents?" Leonard said.

"Emails, meeting notes, the same materials quoted in the *Register* story that hit newsstands hours after their meeting," Feinblum said.

"Quite a coincidence," Trotwood said.

"Take a look. René's people faxed some of it to us." Feinblum slapped a ream of papers on the desk.

"So, this is actually happening?" Leonard said as he pretended to read through the documents. "A merger with Publique?"

"Not officially," Trotwood said. "There was no formal agreement, just early discussions. It was nine months out, at least. Given the time it would have taken federal regulators to approve a deal this size, maybe a year."

"It's just . . . I know the agency isn't doing well," Leonard said.

"We're doing fine," Feinblum said. "Our second-quarter earnings were lackluster, but the economy sneezed this year, and several of our agencies fell short of expectations. We believe there was an opportunity to integrate both companies' offerings—"

"Jesus, Bernie, give it a rest," Trotwood said. "He's not a shareholder."

"Have you confronted Frazer about this?" Leonard said.

"Are you kidding? It's the first thing we did after René's team called," Trotwood said. "We've terminated our contract with him, effective immediately."

"Frazer is no longer handling crisis for your agency?"

"He's history," Feinblum said. "Honestly, he's been on his way out for a long time. Who doesn't carry a cellphone in this day and age?"

"Jack was right," Trotwood said. "He's washed up."

"Funny thing is, Frazer doubled down when we asked where he got his information," Feinblum said. "He said someone gave it to him."

"Who?"

"He said he got it from you," Feinblum said.

"That's a lie," Leonard stammered. "I barely know him. Besides, I don't have access to what goes on here. I couldn't have given him this stuff if I'd wanted to."

"That's what we said," Trotwood said. "But why would he implicate you in this?"

"I don't know. I won't try to explain someone else's fiction," Leonard said. "The easy answer is Frazer was caught with his hand in the till and whipped up an ad-libbed story to get you off his back."

The men were quiet.

"It's all conjecture; I have no way of substantiating any of this, but have you considered maybe Frazer leaked those documents to the *Register*?" Leonard continued. "Think about it. He has this years-long relationship with you, has all kinds of access, and somehow gets hold of info he's not supposed to have. So, he tips off the press to shake some leaves and goes to France with the hopes of catching the next moving train. But Publique throws your Benedict Arnold under the bus, so he cooks up this wild story about getting the merger files from me so you'll let him crawl back."

"But why would Frazer blame you?" Feinblum said. "That's the part I can't figure out."

"It makes perfect sense," Trotwood said. "Frazer is threatened by Leonard. After all, he's the first PR pro besides him to handle reputation work for us in nearly twenty years."

"So, what now?" Leonard said.

"Short term? We're taking the red-ink bath," Feinblum said. "René was apoplectic when he saw the *Register* article. Any plans of a merger are scrapped."

"It's a failure," Trotwood said. "One giant, expensive failure."

"What's your strategy?" Leonard said. "How are you going to play this out?"

"It's not an easy needle to thread," Feinblum said. "We put together a press release to quell the anxiety. But the long view remains uncertain."

The men looked Leonard over.

"How would you like to pick up some work for us?" Trotwood said. "We'll need a new reputation counselor, after all."

Something crept across Leonard's face. Bewilderment, beatitude, he wasn't sure, but he was lightheaded and struggling to put thoughts into words. "Yeah, sure. I think I could handle that," he said.

"Good," Trotwood said. "We'll be in touch."

Outside, Leonard stood on the corner and watched the wandering crowds, garlands of light that snaked in curvilinear lines across the buildings' filing cabinets of glass. This was strange new territory: He couldn't remember the last time he'd been happy about anything and wasn't entirely sure how to process it. It was dark now, and everything had softened, though a faint light cindered along the scattered animal shapes of clouds above the steel range of skyline. He checked his phone for the time. He knew he should probably go home, but it was still early, and now he felt energized and ornery. He paused, recalculated, then turned and headed south on Madison, toward Koreatown.

SUMMER WAGED ON. THREE TIMES A WEEK LEONARD MET PATTY AT A restaurant of her choosing, where she gorged until she was satisfied. In time, the strange language of these encounters became familiar, the notes and rhythms of each evening another version of itself, variations of a theme as they consumed their way through the city's most hallowed eateries. At Café Dauphine, he recalled seared langoustines swimming in a Riesling and butter broth. At Barrio, medallions of ginger-glazed lamb and confited onions paired alongside roasted artichokes anointed with red wine aioli. Identidad was renowned for its broiled branzino sautéed in champagne and tomato, Le Saint Régis had silken pillows of lemon curd foie gras terrine jacketed in herbed chèvre and poached fig, and Suganoya served pitch-perfect fronds of fluke sashimi embroidered with poppy seeds and bathed in chive oil and uni butter. The rustics of Enoteca's potato tortelli bolognese imparted a warmth of the past, Viña's pork and chive dumplings with spoonable nubs of spiced pear were positively transportive, and Savoy's bold, byzantine medley of quivering quail eggs over blooming roses of tuna carpaccio was nothing short of subversive with its astonishingly intricate phrasing of flavors. They managed their routine with martial order, assembling at dusk and canvassing the city's culinary troves under blue roaring half-nights, and that phantasmagoria of memories where pasts become fictions eventually began to acquire the unmistakable element of narrative, shuttled him out of the treadwheel cycle of the present and toward some strange, rudderless future where life as he'd known it would never return.

Patty's hunger never wavered. She arrived at each meeting ravenous and always ate beyond her appetite, sometimes ordering seconds, even thirds, and often finishing in cold sweats and laboring for breath. Already during their brief time together, Leonard noticed she'd begun to take on size, and by late July her frame revealed inchoate signs of metamorphosis, the addition of folds near the joints, a cavernous dimpling at the knees, bunched rolls on the back of her neck resembling a package of hot dogs. The boundaries between her chin and neck disappeared, her gait slowed to a shuffle, and she was forced to update her wardrobe with loose-fitting shirts and sweatpants. She complained of gastric ulcers. Leonard wondered if there was a limit to her gluttony; he imagined her confined to a wheelchair or medical bed, her stomach swollen and stretched to the point of immobility. He pondered the ceremonial aspect of it, what equanimity the mealtime ritual provided her, and wondered if she was like him, if her behavior was a sublimation of a similar impulse, if it satisfied a deep urge, offered some relief from the heat of everything, triggered a hidden, almost hallucinatory sensory area of the brain she could visit to suppress the disquieting discomforts of daily life.

A subtle, cynical symmetry had begun to develop between them, but on a Monday afternoon in early August he received a phone call from Bernie Feinblum that rendered all other inquiries immaterial. Details were sparse, but apparently Graydon Trotwood had just exited a boardroom meeting with a major airline that was interested in retaining Pinnacle as its global advertising agency of record, although the company was facing an injunction from the Justice Department after a fleet of its planes revealed long-time manufacturing defects in their electrical systems. Feinblum wanted to know: Could Leonard kick around a few strategy ideas within the next week? Leonard said he'd have a proposal by the next afternoon.

. . .

THE DINING SCENE THAT NIGHT WAS SOMBER. THEY'D MET AT AN ALL-organic, all-locally sourced eatery in NoLita called Hush, a spare, colorless space that smelled of tea tree oil. A large window framing traffic offered a stark contrast to the dining room's funereal volumes, a silence broken only by the occasional cough or the sounds of warring silverware against porcelain. Patty had briefed him on the concept prior to their arrival: Guests were forbidden from speaking with one another upon entering the premises; restaurant rules stated patrons had to endure their meals in complete silence. Leonard was incredulous. Sure enough, on the back of a cream-colored menu card the chef offered a mission statement articulating his philosophy, suggesting our modern social treatment of mealtime and its environmental distractions—chatter, background noise, music—distorts the palate, and his restaurant, allegedly inspired by Buddhist monasteries, enforced a mandatory code of silence as a "radical reclamation of the dining experience." Leonard rolled his eyes, flipped the prescript over, and scrutinized the menu before checking off the least infuriating item he could find. A gaunt waiter wearing a black rubber apron bent down and took their menu cards, then left without saying a word.

"Hate to break the rules, Patty, but we need to chat," Leonard said. "These past several months have been interesting, but I wanted to let you know this is the last meal we're going to have together."

"You've said that before."

"Shhhh," a young couple chorused from the next table.

"It's different this time," Leonard whispered. "The circumstances surrounding our . . . relationship have changed. I'm no longer in the same position I was in several weeks before, even several days before. As a result, I can now safely let you go without fear of reprisal."

"Sir." The waiter perched above Leonard's ear. "Please refrain from speaking."

"You know, I used to think you were a simpleton," Leonard said after the man left. "I now see my biggest mistake was underestimating you. You're quite clever."

"Care to elaborate?"

"I never believed for a second you wanted to get into PR. But then something dawned on me. All that dirt you had on Pinnacle. You knew damn well what you were giving me."

Glasses of wine and salads arrived. Leonard picked at a plate of rambling greens and sprigs of purple cress. It was terrestrial and dry and left him wanting for soap.

"You deliberately saddled me with that information because you knew somehow I'd spread it into the ether, which would damage your company's credibility and reputation. You planned it from the first time we met."

"What if I did?"

"Right, exactly. Because you ended up with something bigger. And once you got dirt on me, you ditched your initial plan for a long-term con. Out of curiosity, where did you find those documents? How in the hell did you obtain personal emails from René Martin, of all people?"

"I told you. I found them on a copy machine," she said.

"Sure," he said. "Whatever your plan was, it backfired. I'm going to let you in on a few insights. One, you remember the guy I told you about, the one who rooked those documents? He took the fall for me. Two, his blunder has left a new position open, one I've been enlisted to fill. Your attempts to ruin me have only made me stronger."

"Well, congratulations," Patty said. "You accidentally fell into an account you didn't deserve, deliberately screwed up your life even worse in the process, and then accidentally didn't get caught for it. I think you should consider two things. One, you're an idiot. Two, you owe me for your successes as much as your missteps. I'm sure you'll snatch defeat from the jaws of victory again next week."

"Say whatever you want. This game is officially over."

"Sir," the waiter said. "If you don't stop speaking, I'm going to ask you to leave."

"Then ask, you pretentious asshole," Leonard said as the man stormed off.

"You're wrong," Patty said. "I still have the video."

"Go ahead and broadcast that video to the world. It's the only collateral you have, and it no longer matters. You and I are responsible for killing a thirty-billion-dollar mega-merger between two of the largest marketing conglomerates in the world. Do you have any idea how much trouble we'd be in if they found out? We're implicated in this together, which means we're effectively at a stalemate, which means you can't bother me anymore. The only reason we dodged this bullet is because of me."

"So, why didn't you sell me out? Why didn't you tell them I gave you the documents?"

"Because, halfwit, then they'd know I had something to do with it."

"I could still tell Pinnacle you had those documents all along. I could tell them you're the one who gave them to the *Register*."

"Of course you could. Aside from the fact that you'd be implicating yourself, I have a solution for that as well. I'll lie. Plausible deniability, Patty. Look it up. The second reason comes in the form of another secret I'll divulge. Ready? Pinnacle is going to be my client. And in the spirit of telling the truth, per your little speech the other night, if you don't leave me alone after this evening, I'll tell them, in no uncertain terms, that you were responsible for those documents seeing the light of day, and you gave them to me because you wanted to hurt your company's reputation, and I held on to them for safekeeping and planned on telling them about it until someone stole them."

"That's not the truth at all," she said.

"Your word against mine. Who's keeping score?" Leonard paused, took a sip of wine. "I will then recommend to my client a course of action that includes having you fired and calling the police to bring charges against you." He dipped into a whisper. "I'll even make a few things up. You might want to consider heading for the exits."

The words seemed to wound her, left a mark on her face. "You're pressuring me to quit my job?" she said. "That's extortion. Several weeks ago, you said we had to work together. You said we had to come up with a corroborating story."

"I changed my strategy."

"I thought we were becoming friends. Now you're screwing me."

"Not with a ten-foot pole." Leonard stood and shoved his chair out with his legs. "It's over, Patty. My feet are going up on the desk, and you're going out on the curb. Now if you'll excuse me, nature calls."

Leonard passed the open kitchen, a harried staff that worked in silence, and walked a dim, whitewashed hallway lit by brass candelabras. He found himself shaking as he urinated in the bathroom sink, rattling in the triumph of vindication. Soon he noticed the yawning door of a utility closet. He washed his hands and swept the door open with his foot to discover a clandestine housekeeping station dispatching hopeful smells, the hard stink of chemical cleaner. A metal locker stockpiled a bounty of tonics: soaps and polishes and solvents and a battered cardboard box storing clumping dunes of detergent. He brought a thimbled finger to his lips; it smelled like a dryer sheet and tasted faintly of egg. He continued picking through the wares until he spotted a beaten jug that lay in a dripping utility sink. The label was curled back and sodden with moisture, but the word "soap" was scrawled in black marker over a strip of masking tape, so it seemed discreetly potable. He unscrewed the cap and peered inside. The liquid was viscous and chartreuse-green and yielded a sweet, heady smell that aroused his appetite. He tipped the jug, decanted its syrup into the cap, and licked it. The first taste hit him like a musical note; it had a revelatory flavor profile, syrupy but somehow astringent at the same time, pickled beets and sugar water and dry vermouth. He drew the jug to his mouth and took several sips, sucking on its plastic lip as though he was aerating a fine wine, then went back in with spirited gulps.

By the time Leonard returned to the table, he felt like he was walking on the heaving deck of a ship. Main courses had arrived and appeared underwhelming; the gorgonzola butternut squash ravioli Patty had ordered sat in a lagoon of oil. Leonard's throat was numb, and his mouth held a metallic taste, and now the room was assailed with colors. He felt drunk, febrile, confused. He heard singing birds.

"You don't look so hot," Patty said.

"I'm fine," Leonard said and fell into his seat. A wave of nausea came over him, and he gripped the table in an attempt to regain composure. Across the restaurant, phantasm shadows scurried in a corner. He tried to unfasten his tie but had difficulty rallying the bureaus of coordination. Corporeal forms in the carpet made themselves known. His fork and knife began conspiring.

"Drink some water," Patty said and handed him a glass.

"Try the flan! Try the flan!" the fork said.

Leonard leaned over and vomited a chute of olive-green liquid into the aisle. Then the muscles in his back went slack, and he tipped over. The room riffed with patrons' screams, followed by panicked hushes. Leonard felt tile in his cheek, saw a blurred panorama of faces, and struggled to move, to no effect. Then Patty hovered over him.

"Don't leave," he said. The last thing he saw were silver crescents of traffic reflecting in her eyes.

Chapter 10

A canvas of ivory wall tempered by sour light. A spare, dull-looking room scrubbed of its history, a pair of ecru doors tattooed with curious hieroglyphs of shadow from an assembly of branches outside, faint smells of cresol, peppermint oil, and disinfectant. The world moved into focus as he inspected his surroundings, turned from the abstract to the specific like the dilating eye of a projector. A bedside table furnished with mauve plasticware, an IV pole on dry-rotted rubber wheels saddled with a pouch of fluid. A park lawn framed by the open window and a breeze that tousled the curtain, which brought a spray of sunlight into the room, traces of fresh asphalt and grass. From the hallway, disembodied voices and intercom rabble, wheels scuffing linoleum.

Leonard stirred in bed. Patty was seated in a chair at the edge of it and seemed directed by restless movements. Her gaze wandered and met his, and then she ran into the hallway.

A doctor entered seconds later, followed by a gray nurse who pushed a computer console on a plastic cart. The doctor was middle-aged and had small eyes that didn't appear to blink for extended periods.

"Good morning, Mr. Lundell," the doctor said. "How do you feel?"

"Resplendent."

The man leaned over and shined a light in Leonard's right eye, then his left. "Can you tell me your full name?"

"Leonard James Lundell."

"Good. And do you know what day it is?"

He looked around. "How would I?"

The nurse furiously typed something on the console.

"Can you tell me where we are, Mr. Lundell?"

"Beefsteak Charlie's. How long have I been here?"

"Since yesterday evening. I was hoping you could tell me."

Leonard looked to Patty. She stood in the doorway with her arms crossed, her face empty and raw.

"What happened?" Leonard said.

"You drank antifreeze, ethylene glycol. Not your brightest idea," the doctor said. "You're lucky to be alive. As you may have figured out, antifreeze is highly toxic. We don't know exactly how much you drank, but I've seen five ounces kill someone."

Leonard tried to sit up but felt a stabbing pain in his groin. Only then did he discover he was wearing a tie-back hospital gown. The fabric was stiff, like a motel bedsheet.

"Receiving medical attention after intoxication was paramount. You can thank your girlfriend—"

"She's not my girlfriend," Leonard stammered.

"We gave you fomepizole, which blocks antifreeze from being absorbed into the system. I understand you had a few glasses of wine with dinner. Believe it or not, this may have bought you some time. Interesting fact about antifreeze poisoning: Before the medical world came up with an antidote, treatment used to involve giving patients ethanol, because it has an enzyme that metabolizes antifreeze. We used to get people drunk." The doctor smiled. "In the meantime, I took the liberty of leaving you some literature. We have several psychologists on staff. It might be a good idea if you spoke with one of them."

"Why?"

"Standard procedure in these situations."

"What situation is that?"

The doctor's demeanor possessed a dimension of rehearsed diplomacy. "How would you describe your mood lately?"

On the counter beside the bed, Leonard noticed a brochure bearing clip art of an elderly man seated alone at a kitchen table. The brochure was titled "Coping with Depression."

"I'm not suicidal," Leonard said. "When can I go home?"

"I can't overstate the gravity of leaving antifreeze consumption untreated," the doctor said. "Everything from metabolic acidosis, which can cause hyperventilation, to acute renal failure, loss of kidney function. That's what we're testing you for now."

Leonard closed his eyes and drew a breath. Patty crossed the room and took his hand like a concerned guidance counselor.

"You should sue!" she said as Leonard pulled away. "What the hell is a restaurant doing with antifreeze, anyway?"

"To answer your question, I don't know when you can leave," the doctor said. "You may need hemodialysis while your kidneys recover. We need to monitor your kidney function and make sure there isn't any damage. Oh, as you can probably tell, we put a catheter in to monitor urine output."

The doctor stepped around him and consulted the console. "I should also let you know we discovered some . . . anomalies in your physiology. You have scarring on your trachea . . . and what appears to be a severe case of acid reflux."

"I'm on an experimental diet," Leonard said.

"Not anymore. For the foreseeable future we'll have you on a steady regimen of hospital food. It's terrible, by the way."

The nurse strode up beside the bed with the console. "Mr. Lundell, we retrieved some personal information from your wallet. But we need a few more details." She consulted the monitor. "Your friend here says you're a professional liar."

"I work in PR," he said.

"I need a contact name. A family member, someone we can call."

"I don't have anyone," he said.

"Acquaintances, friends?"

Leonard looked to Patty and closed his eyes. The nurse took Patty's information, and in several minutes she and the doctor were gone, leaving Patty and Leonard alone in the room.

"Can you believe it?" Patty said as she approached the bed. "I saved you! I saved your life!"

"You should've let me die," Leonard said and looked to the window.

HE AWOKE THAT AFTERNOON TO THE RATTLING COILS OF THE AIR CONDI-tioner, a patter of rain against the overhang. His esophagus was swollen, and his mouth tasted foul, dried blood and rust. Everything ached. He turned on the television and scrolled through the channels. Gunfire had been exchanged between separatists and Georgian forces near the South Ossetia border. United States unemployment had reached its highest level in four years. A recent study had found that the more TV news viewers consumed, the more uninformed they were. A nurse delivered lunch: a desiccated chicken breast, a spongy clod of broccoli the consistency of wet newspaper, and, as a grace note, a completely reasonable-looking cup of chocolate pudding. Leonard secured listing arrangements with the Lanchester seller's agent and called Todd Armitage to relay the news that he was out of pocket, telling him he'd been hit by a car. Then he called Bernie Feinblum about the airline strategy he'd failed to send Pinnacle and left a message. Terror struck him when he realized he hadn't fed his fish in two days. He called a neighborhood locksmith and asked if he could access Leonard's apartment and drop flakes in the tank. The man hung up on him.

No one called, and no one visited, except Patty, who arrived unannounced that afternoon to antagonize him. She wore a flowing tie-dye muumuu and gold lamé shawl, as though an animal had tangled itself in someone's clothesline and wandered into the hospital.

"What are you up to?" she said as she picked up the remote and began surfing through the channels.

"Suffering. What does it look like?"

"Turn that frown upside down. You're a white guy with money in the bank. How many problems do you have? And you're alive!"

"Are you kidding?" Leonard said. "Here's how I see it. Pinnacle wants to hire me as their reputation counselor, and after all the work I do, I wind up here, away from the office, unable to take a meeting and without the notes I prepared for a very important account. Do you have any idea how bad this looks, what it could mean if they find out I'm in the hospital for drinking radiator coolant?"

His cellphone rang, and he regarded it pensively.

"Is that them now?" Patty said.

"It's a real estate agent. I'm buying my mother a condo."

"And all this time I thought you were a self-absorbed windbag. That's really nice, Leonard."

"You don't know the backstory," he said. "Listen, I was hoping you could do me a favor. This might be wishful thinking, but along with . . . everything else you know about me, I'd appreciate it if you could keep the incident in the restaurant last night between us."

"I don't know," she said and sat on the edge of the bed. "You weren't very nice to me. Let's see if I remember it all: You're going to tell my bosses about those documents you stole from me, and you want me to quit my job or you're going to tell them to fire me and call the police. Am I forgetting anything?"

"I've been under a lot of stress." Leonard bristled. "I'm willing to recognize your . . . beneficence in bringing me here. What can I say? I misspoke. I'm sorry. Suffice to say, I won't be telling my client anything."

Patty shrugged her shoulders. "Promises, promises."

"What do you want me to say? I can't get rid of you no matter what I try. Aside from losing my job or moving to a different city, it's clear you're going to be sewn to my hip for the foreseeable future. The whole goddamn thing is futile."

"Listen to you."

"It's true. I manage uncontrollable situations for a living, and I can't put my shoulder to the wheel when my own life goes off the rails. Eat your heart out, Ivy Lee."

"I don't know who that is."

"Was. Press agent for the Pennsylvania Railroad. J.D. Rockefeller hired him to clean up the Standard Oil Company's image. He basically created PR."

"What happened to him?"

"Oh, he ended up doing stateside PR work for the German company that made Zyklon B for the gas chambers. When he died, he was being investigated for circulating Nazi propaganda."

"Great role model your industry has," Patty said. "See, I guess that's why I don't take your saber-rattling personally. All this pseudo-rationalizing of yours reminds me why you're so successful at what you do but also a complete failure as a human being."

"Thanks."

"Every person I know . . . they make mistakes. Maybe they're not total failures, but their faults are endearing. So much for people being brands, right?"

"This nonsense again."

"People are complicated. Brands are just names people use to separate one dumb product from the next. Brands are about one thing, but people are about a million things." She began drawing circles over the floor with her feet. "So, you can walk the earth a confident man, Leonard Lundell. I won't tell a soul. Consider this one on the house. Water under the bridge. Kindness of my heart. Because at the end of the day, your professional talents aren't the problem. Your personality is."

"I appreciate it," he said. "But there's another favor I need to ask." After a few minutes of detailed instruction on how to feed his fish, as well as directions for checking the nitrous and pH levels, he gave her the keys to his apartment. Then, on one of the bedside brochures, he wrote out a list of books he wanted her to retrieve.

"Done," Patty said. "Can I have your chocolate pudding?"

"Sure." Leonard slid the cup toward her.

Leonard asked Patty to buy him a notepad from a neighborhood pharmacy. When she returned, he promptly told her to leave, and for the next hour sketched out a few ideas for Pinnacle's airline account based on what he could remember from the notes he'd drafted at the office the day before. By sunset, his tongue and lymph nodes had swollen, and a burn radiated from his windpipe to his stomach. That's when he discovered the efficacy of the morphine drip button, and for the next hour he floundered in half-consciousness, the pain in his esophagus coming and going as he watched shadows rise and collapse on the wall in dusk's waning light. Darkness fell and time became impossible, and that night he was plagued with fevered dreams involving a field that grew turds. The stalks were harvested by scythe-bearing peasants who collected and distributed the turds in muddied cornucopias to a nearby village, and the village's residents feasted on them over wine and cheese like a delectable fruit.

ON THE SECOND DAY, LEONARD CALLED THE PROPERTY MANAGER AT THE Mango Cove Lifestyle Community in Lanchester to discuss his mother's move-in date. Nurses came and went, and the doctor paid his visit. Leonard called Bernie Feinblum again and left a second message. Then he slept and dreamed he was general manager of a fast-food restaurant called Risky Burger. That afternoon, he counted the ceiling tiles as he listened to faint moans within the walls. A TV program provided an overview of rare diseases.

There was a knock at the door, and Roger Lawton eased into the room with full beads of sweat on his forehead. In his tapered slacks and collared purple shirt, he looked like a stage actor who'd settled on playing Roger's part in a small-town community-theater production.

Roger casually inspected the room, spotted the chair, and seemed to deliberate sitting in it before shuffling to the window. "Hell of a view. Bet you never imagined you'd have real estate this close to the park." He looked Leonard over. "You don't look like you were hit by a car."

"Word gets around," Leonard said. "For the record, I wasn't. Hallermann-Streiff syndrome just isn't something I care to explain over the phone."

"That sounds serious." Roger pulled the chair up bedside and fell into a whisper. "I left the office early to see how you were doing, as well as to congratulate you. I spoke with our friends at Pinnacle, the CMO—"

"Bernie Feinblum," Leonard said. "Why are we whispering?"

"They said you were game to idea-jam crisis strategies for an airline who might retain Pinnacle as AOR."

"We're not going snowboarding, Roger. I'm trying to keep Pinnacle as a client. What else did he tell you? I've been waiting for his call."

"You did good, Leonard. I'll get the team up to speed and build out something skeletal in terms of a deck structure—"

"You didn't answer my question. Why were you talking to my client?"

Roger snorted. "People talk. Agencies talk. Bernie came by the office, and Wanda and I took him to lunch. What's the deal?"

Leonard struggled to sit up. "The deal is this is my account."

"And your accounts are my business." Roger's red face wagged in the dull light. Leonard could tell he was getting angry, bargaining with himself to maintain a conciliatory tone.

"You came all the way to the Upper East Side to tell me you're satisfied with my performance? What's going on?"

A lizard's tongue darted from the corner of Roger's mouth. "You know what my family did in Texas, back in the seventies?"

"No idea."

"We had a chain of filling stations," Roger said. "We lost everything in the oil crisis."

"And then you got into PR? Hell of a change."

"Well," Roger said and smiled. "Point is, we failed because we refused to adapt in a disrupted market. There's going to be a lot of changes at the agency. That's why I wanted to let you know you won't be alone when it comes to signing big accounts like Pinnacle. We're going to put together a transition team so we can get some sense of flow—"

"No," Leonard said. "My team works alone. Why do you think we get so much done?"

"Not anymore. I've got a new guy coming onboard who'll be shadowing the crisis division so he can coordinate your work with our other practices."

"What's wrong with the team I have?"

"Nothing, but you know as well as I do that the agency structure has evolved. The days where we used to meet with clients and figure out how to juggle our work with their ad partner and social media agency are over. Everything is integrated nowadays. Clients want a one-stop-shop that can do everything from digital media to web design to reputation. They want the talents of large and small agencies in one."

"Okay. So what?"

"So, this guy's got agency experience. He's also got a law degree. He's smoothly transitioned a number of blue-chip accounts. And he's a really nice guy."

"You realize 'nice' is a coded way of saying there's nothing remarkable about him, right?"

"We need integration management. If we're going to be pulling in the big players, we need a deep bench of talent, specialists who can coordinate our best practices and collaborate with clients' outside agencies. We need to be forward-thinking, innovative. We have to engage with consumers in more experiential ways or we'll be left behind."

"Doing what other agencies are doing, by definition, isn't innovative," Leonard said and crushed the morphine drip button. "We're a PR firm. You know how Jack feels about the idea of us pretending to be an ad shop."

A nurse entered the room with a tray containing dinner.

"Doubt I'm going to get a better segue than that," Roger said and thumbed his watch. "We're going to be working with Jack in the near future, and discussing, in the most equitable way possible—"

"A trip, I know. Wanda told me about it several weeks ago."

"Jack's almost eighty. He needs to begin filing for retirement benefits. Social Security would net him two grand a month. Also, if he starts the registration process for Medicare, it could save us about ten grand for the fiscal year. We'll pay the supplementary plan, of course."

"Jack's not like the rest of us. He's not working toward retirement. He's working because he likes work." Leonard paused. "I guess I'm confused about what you're getting at. Wanda was talking about Jack taking time off. What you're saying sounds like exile."

"Don't use a loaded term, Leonard."

"I'm pretty sure you can't make someone retire."

"Jack will remain with the firm in an advisory role. We're not making him do anything. The company is simply undergoing a leadership transition process that's been several months in the making."

"So, Jack is out? Funny how I was never told about this."

"You're not senior management," Roger said. His face reddened again and now, oddly, he was smiling, that effete deflection people exhibit when they fall down in public and want to convey the impression that they're not hurt. "The things I'm telling you today aren't suggestions, Leonard. They're not up for debate. Our agency has been treading water for years. Several months ago, we were thinking about leasing out part of the office to a goddamn travel agency to save on rent. We need to think about the future."

Leonard wanted to say something repudiating in response, to highlight Roger's casual relationship with facts, to remind him that getting rid of the agency's founder wouldn't erase any kind of real debt, meaning Roger should probably devise a better excuse if he wanted to adequately explain the reasons behind his plan. It occurred to him he could always do what he did with his mother and disabuse Roger of this particular idea while reminding him of his past victories. Roger wasn't Leonard's mother, however; his ambition made him dangerous. But he was also stupid, which meant he had a habit of revealing his hand. It was simply easier to smile and plan a response from some distance.

"I appreciate your candor," Leonard said and played the morphine button with his thumb. "But if you'll excuse me, I need to get some rest. See you in the office next week."

After Roger left, Leonard rose from the bed and began pacing. Eventually, he picked up his cellphone and dialed Jack Gurney. "They're flinging shit inside the monkey cage again," he said. "They want you out."

"Who?" Jack said.

"Who do you think?" Leonard said. "Your second and third banana, Wanda and Roger."

"How are you sure?"

"Because pronouncements of trustworthiness always imply inverse intentions," Leonard said. "First they casually suggest you take a sabbatical. Spend time with family, plan a getaway to Saint Maarten. Then they start talking retirement. This is sabotage. They're plotting your exit strategy. You can't let them do this to you."

He could hear Jack shuffling around. A slammed door, a buckling chair, desk drawers opening and closing.

"I've been thinking about taking a trip," Jack said. "This cruise line is offering a seven-day voyage where travelers get to participate in social impact activities at ports of call in Central America. You know, help residents install water filtration systems or work with a women's co-op that recycles paper products. I guess a lot of folks don't care about that sort of thing, because the cruise line had to cut the prices in half so they could fill the ship. It's a real bargain. They don't like empty ships, Leonard."

Leonard huffed. Having a conversation with this one was like chasing a loose balloon. "The other principals want you to walk the plank. And now Roger's talking about outfitting the office with marketing buffoons. All the things you worried about, they're coming down. The knives are out."

"I don't know," Jack said. "I spoke with Wanda and Roger over the weekend. Maybe taking some time off is a good idea."

The phone was a cold fish in his hand. "Now you tell me. Just don't sign anything. And if they give you any forms or documents, I want you to tell me about them immediately."

"Fine. I haven't been in the office all week. You haven't noticed?"

"What? No, I—"

"I've got some family issues going on. My daughter's back in town."

"You sound thrilled."

"She gave me a lot of trouble. I'm not going anywhere, Leonard. This won't be permanent. I'm just going to take some time to decompress. You've got to see these new additions I've got for the library. You ever read about astronomy? There's an article in *Astronomy Now* that says a German supercomputer estimates there might be as many as five hundred billion galaxies. Five hundred billion, Leonard. Puts all these fears about the economy into perspective, huh?"

LEONARD LAY IN BED THAT EVENING, PROSTRATE WITH BOREDOM. ON the television, President Bush was calling on Russia to end its military campaign in Georgia. A cooking program shared recipes created by prison inmates. He called Feinblum again; still no answer. Patty returned with his books and proceeded to badger him with useless information. An artisanal cheesemonger had opened a pop-up shop inside a former subway newspaper stand. A regional dish known as Chicken Ronkonkoma was gaining popularity across parts of Long Island. A new farm-to-table restaurant in the West Village, called Reparations, featured waitstaff that inconvenienced white patrons in an effort to remind them of their socioeconomic privilege.

Once Patty left, Leonard picked over the books she'd brought him. Darkness began to settle, and he turned to the alarm clock on the table, a split-flap LED display beside an analog AM/FM receiver, its safety-orange dial somehow uncommitted to any familiar anatomical scheme or shape, like a letter that hadn't made it into the alphabet. He was struck by a singular idea, something so obscenely unpalatable it defied casual explanation, but now that the idea was there, he was helpless to it, so that even trying to unpack the notion was enough to leave his stomach aching in anticipation. After several minutes of deliberation, he left the bed and retrieved his keys from his pants, then pried his mailbox key into the clock's plastic faceplate until he'd cracked it open like an oyster, disassembled the radio face with his fingers, and plucked the plastic tab from its innards. Later, as he chewed on the orange dial and leafed through Thomas Hobbes's *Leviathan*, he mused over the ameliorative spell reading provided and wondered why he so rarely engaged in the activity anymore. At one point, he came across a passage he felt compelled to write down, but his notebook was out of reach, and he didn't feel like getting out of bed, so he read it twice and convinced himself he'd memorized it, even if a part of him knew the words would be out of his head by the time he turned off the light: "Appetite with an opinion of attaining is called hope; the same without such opinion, despair."

That night there were dreams again. The first was a montage of quick images, random frames of a night terror scene that involved his teeth falling out. Later he dreamed he was in the house in Lanchester, and he was young. A river ran between the hillocks of junk in the living room, where a giant snake had lived for years and grown to incredible size, feeding off the piss and shit and bathwater.

The final episode arrived in the small hours before dawn and was less a dream than a revived memory he'd long consigned to oblivion. He'd awoken to screams from the alarm clock. A pale light skimmed the wall behind a curtain. Outside, rain pelted the lawn as he listened to the distant bells of Orton Hall. Details began to take shape in the gray: a black torchière floor lamp, a pyramid of textbooks under a snow of dust on the hutch, a particleboard bookcase, an Ohio State wall calendar, a perfunctory print of Magritte's *Son of Man*, clumsy attempts at transposing the comforts of home abroad. A roommate's bed that was, thank God, currently unoccupied. He listened for sounds of occupancy, sat up, and looked for the telltale bar of light beneath the bathroom door. A dull pain clustered behind his right eye, and he rolled over, but by nine-fifteen forced himself up and began stumbling through the dark, where he felt a violent rousing before vomiting in the trash can he'd placed bedside. Then he returned to the cradling folds of the covers and fell asleep.

At ten-thirty he threw down a cocktail of decongestants and antihistamines, left Bradley Hall, and crossed campus's wasted landscape in a blind march. It was a cold, colorless morning, sheet-metal skies draped with trails of drifting smoke. For the better part of a week a snowstorm had churned its way through Central Ohio, but the night before a warm front had moved in, coating the campus in a glaze of ice. Mirror Lake was still rimmed with frost, but the sidewalk before it was a pond of slush blocking his path, so he turned back, navigated his way around the banks, and made his way onto the Oval, an eleven-acre egg-shaped lawn in the middle of campus surrounded by a perimeter of laboratories and leaning oaks. The ground was glacial, sheeted with snow, as though the earth had been scorched by some great blast. As he skated across a sidewalk stained with salt and littered with a flotsam of cups from the Saint Patrick's Day celebrations the night before, he slipped on a glassine patch of ice and went down, paws in the slush, and commenced a wheezing fit, confused and delirious and numb from the cold but somehow still burning with fever. He fought himself up and continued, where he was buffeted by winds, and a low chattering in the naked trees followed him as he walked under the colonnaded entrance of the undergraduate center.

His fingers were blue by the time he signed in and found a seat in the waiting area, a lifeless room with camel-colored carpets, chairs littered with AOL trial CD-ROMs. He felt heat flashes and was jittery from the anti-histamines, so he reached into his coat pocket, found his favorite pen, and slipped it into his mouth, which always calmed him. A radiator hammered to life. Several students hunched over desks in a corner with their backs to him, shoulder blades quivering with the sceptering movements of pencils. A girl sat beside him and grazed on a bolus of bubble gum. On a television bolted to the wall, the news reported President Clinton had signed legislation banning federal funding for research on human cloning. Investigators said they believed a personal dispute was behind the death of Notorious B.I.G.

Twenty minutes later, a small man called Leonard's name from a cubicle. The man blinked excessively and had a nose with sunken pores that resembled burned Styrofoam.

"How are we, Leonard?" He sounded as though his nasal passages were obstructed.

"Fine. Actually, I have the flu."

"Now, that's a bum deal." The man sneezed into a handkerchief, then leafed through a sage folder. "I see you're a sophomore, twenty years old, major undeclared. You live in the Bradley honors dorms . . ." He trailed off. Behind him, a cloth doll of Ohio State's mascot, Brutus Buckeye, was crucified to the cubicle wall with pushpins. "Doing anything for spring break?"

"Nope," Leonard said.

The man coughed. "I see you're missing a statistics final right now. Any comment?"

"Yeah," Leonard said. "I think I want to drop out."

"Today's the final. Deadline to drop the class was seven weeks ago."

"I want to drop out of school. How do I do that?"

The man squirmed in his seat. "That's a big step. Are you sure it's the right decision?"

"Positive."

"And what do your parents think about that?"

"My mom . . . I don't know. I haven't told her."

The man turned toward the wall, cradled his face in the handkerchief, and thrashed in a sneezing fit. When he recovered, he returned to the folder. "I'll be honest. This is a large university, and, as you can imagine, we get some bad eggs, but your high school transcripts were impeccable. You had an SAT score of fourteen hundred. You received a merit-based scholarship from this university that allotted funding for two academic years . . ." He placed his finger on a page, blinked several times. "I also see you received an external scholarship in the amount of two thousand dollars, from this Appalachian group?"

"The A Plus Program," Leonard said. "It's for high school students of modest means who exhibit academic merit."

"I'm at a loss here. Anything you want to explain regarding why you'd like to leave this institution?" The man resumed shuffling through his papers. "You were doing swimmingly during your freshman year, though your recent performance has revealed . . . anomalies. Specifically, I'm seeing a troubling attendance record this quarter and grades from the fall term that reveal . . . noticeable neglect. Intro to Bio, Anthro Two. For someone of your talents, these aren't particularly difficult courses."

Leonard looked outside. Two students held hands as they crossed the lawn. The sun was hidden, and the sky looked like the frayed edge of a burn.

"As you were informed upon admission," the man sniffed, "students who receive a merit-based scholarship are required to maintain a minimum three-point GPA each quarter. Based on your most recent performance, based on the fact that you're missing a final as we speak, I hasten to guess your GPA for the term will fall short of this, and the university will be forced to rescind this gift. I'm sure this must be devastating news. Though be it an unfortunate feature of bureaucratic necessity, it's not my department. But if you'd like to make a further inquiry into their decision, you may take it up with the Office of Scholarship at any time. I guess that's not why you're speaking with me today."

Leonard remained silent.

The man laid the folder across his legs. "Here's what I can do. I'll lift the restrictions on your account so you can register for spring quarter classes. Over the break, you can sign up for your FAFSA, and though your loans might disburse a little late, they'll come through. You'll need a co-signer, so that means your parents—sorry, your mother will need to be apprised of what's going on." He clenched the handkerchief and wiped his nose. "Now, the big stuff. The university understands things happen. In extenuating circumstances, such as illness or a family death, or any hardship that may have hindered your academic performance, you can appeal your grades to the academic board. Considering this is your first offense, I'm going to recommend we replace your failing grades with incompletes. I'm doing you a favor, and it isn't something I can do again. Take the incompletes and carry on or keep the failing grades and remain on academic probation. The choice is yours, but if you choose the former, it will mean winter quarter, for all intents and purposes, never happened."

Leonard shook his head and returned his gaze to the window.

"In the course of filing your appeal, you'll need to write a letter of intent to the academic board. I suggest you work the heartstrings. I highly suggest you mention that you had the flu during finals. One more thing. We'll have to find you new housing. It's not a big deal. We'll get you a room somewhere, but some of the students in Bradley . . . they're sensitive about the stock of their fellow residents."

"The stock?"

"They want to maintain a certain tone." The man crossed his legs and coughed. "You've gotten awfully quiet. How do you feel about all this? I'd appreciate your input on the things we've discussed."

"I guess I've been depressed," Leonard began. "I mean, I was upset about being sick during finals. It's terrible luck. But I've had a few days to think this over, and now I've taken it as a sign."

"A sign for what?"

"To quit," Leonard said. "I realized I wasn't missing classes because I was depressed. I was depressed because I don't like my classes. I don't like being here. It feels like I'm at a party I was never invited to. This university is the cause of my problems. It isn't the place for me."

"Of course it's for you. You're a bright young man. Why wouldn't it be?"

"Because I don't know what I want to do. That's why I need to leave, to figure things out."

"That happens. That's natural," the man said and flipped through the file. "That's why we let students explore their passions. I know you haven't declared a major yet, but have you taken any classes you found . . . inspiring? I see you've taken a number of philosophy courses. Is this something you've considered majoring in?"

"Maybe."

"Why philosophy?"

Leonard shrugged. "It interests me."

"I'm just trying to get a grasp of this situation. I want some insight into your thought process."

"I took some classes I liked, I took some I didn't like, and most of the latter I took because I had to. I just can't wrap my head around the hurdle of electives this school forces down our throats. We have to take an entire year of a foreign language. We have to take a year of science. There are math electives, history electives, humanities electives, and now there's a diversity elective I just found out about several months ago. I don't see the utility in wasting my time studying material that isn't germane to my needs."

"And what are your needs exactly?"

"I don't know, that's what I'm telling you. But the premise here is this institution is the authority in guiding me toward finding out, which I find insulting."

"But don't you think that's the point, that we're trying to show you what's out there? Education has its own value. It's an investment. We provide the skills that make people erudite, well-rounded members of society."

"See, I thought we came here so we could get a job," Leonard said. "Universities sell a lifestyle. It's a great profit model, but you're preparing us for a future that doesn't exist."

"Society benefits from people like you being educated."

"But if you don't know what you want to do, it's an expensive way of finding out."

"That's why we provide scholarships, so we can narrow the gap of opportunity. You're a sophomore. You're halfway there."

"Who finishes school in four years anymore, given the electives we have to take?"

"That's why you take out loans," the man said.

"So, I get the job to pay off the loans I took out to get the job. In my opinion, this system is creating more inequality than it's fixing. It benefits only those who can afford it."

"If you're going through a rough patch—" the man began and folded his arms. "If you're depressed, we have an excellent staff of counselors. You're on the student health insurance program, so it's free. It's okay if you need to speak with somebody. And I should mention that enrollment in our counseling services will help your intent letter to the academic board. It will make your claims appear sincere. I can set up a meeting today, this afternoon."

"You're an academic counselor, not a therapist."

"I'm saying this because I want to help. You'll have a hard time finding a job without a college degree."

"That's my problem. Besides, my family, none of us went to college. We're poor."

"I was too," the man said.

"It's embarrassing."

"Yes." The man seemed to wander off, then set a hand on Leonard's shoulder. He was irritated by the maudlin effect and understood it was more for the man's benefit than his own. "You're a bright kid, you've got your own way of thinking. Maybe you're right, maybe this isn't the place for you. Here's my advice: Take some time off, try things out, get a job, do what makes you happy. Enjoy yourself. Whatever it is, I'm sure you'll be fine."

"I have a feeling you're not supposed to tell me that."

"Sure I am. Good luck."

ON THURSDAY MORNING, A CAB MET THEM AT THE HOSPITAL ENTRANCE. It was an overcast day, the sky ashen and shawled with blustering milky clouds that resembled the nucleus of an ice cube. Patty and Leonard spent the ride in silence. Leonard felt brittle and empty, like his insides had been scooped out. When they arrived at his apartment, Patty helped him out of the cab, walked him up the steps of his building, and unlocked the door. Inside, he took a cursory inventory of the living room, peered inside the fish tank to make sure everyone was accounted for.

"Something to eat?" Patty asked as she rummaged in the refrigerator. "Maybe some ice cream?"

It was as though she'd moved in. Empty cartons of carryout food on the coffee table, discarded bodega bags on the floor, curling copies of *Gastronomica*, *Bon Appétit*, and *Food & Wine* splayed across the couch.

"How much do you pay for this place, anyway?" she said when she returned to the living room with a bowl. She fell onto the couch, feigned a yawn, and dug her heels between the cushions.

"I need sleep," Leonard said as he surveyed the room. In the kitchen, a puddle of water pooled under the refrigerator. "I plan to go back to work Monday."

"Are you crazy? You nearly died. The doctor said you need to rest for at least a week."

He shuffled across the apartment, down the hallway past the bathroom, where a ball of towels had been stuffed between the toilet and shower. The bed had obviously been slept in, the mattress appearing as though it had taken a cannonball. An oversized bra lay on the floor by the closet. He blinked several times as his mind reeled to account for the violation of her unmonitored presence, the things moved from their proper place, curious fingers rooting through his possessions. His sanctuary defiled, blankets and cushions contaminated by stray hairs and bodily crumbs. He was skirting on the edge, just barely holding on, trying to breathe under the unusual cruelty of it.

Heavy footsteps behind him. "Hey," Patty said. "You know, I've been thinking: your lifestyle, the things you've been eating. It isn't healthy. You need to take your life back, Leonard. Your tomorrow starts today."

"Get out," he muttered.

"I can only show you the door. You're the one who has to step through." She stood there filling the hallway, blocking any chance of an exit. "But first I was thinking, maybe we could go out and celebrate—"

Leonard fished in his pockets. He hadn't worn his pants in five days, and it took an inordinate amount of time to find his wallet, lodged under a wad of moist towelettes.

"Here's a hundred dollars," he said. "Go find the nearest buffet and stuff yourself. Leave me alone, and don't come back."

"There's this new gastro-pub downtown—"

"Get out!" he screamed. His hands went wild, and a rope of snot dropped from his nose as he chased her down the hallway. Patty made a strident cry and her hands slapped at the air as she fumbled for the knob and fled into the hallway, where he slammed the door behind her.

With the apartment empty, he returned to the bedroom and took in the mess around him, tried to calculate the inestimable amount of time it would take to sanitize the room, return a sense of order to this space, rid it of the stink of her. His throat still hurt, his arm was sore from the IV, and now his head throbbed. He sat on the bed and tried to get it all sorted out, then lay down and watched the pale slip of light that danced on the wall, just as it had in his dream. Listening to the whispers of traffic, he drifted behind the curtain of sleep.

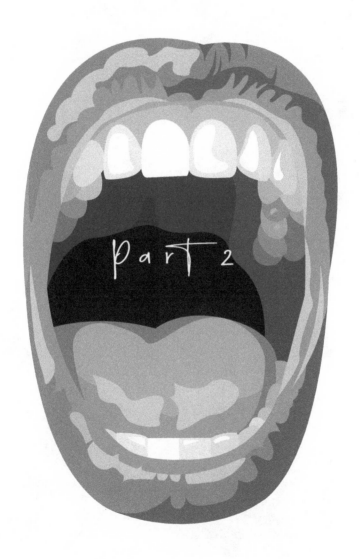

part 2

Chapter 11

He needed a job. He'd been out of school for weeks and was broke. When the university shut down for spring break, he found off-campus housing through an ad in the classifieds and depleted his savings on the security deposit and first-month's rent, as well as a phone line and a TV and a twin-sized mattress he'd found at the Salvation Army, then lugged his belongings from Bradley Hall to an unfurnished studio beneath a laundromat on Chittenden Avenue. The apartment resembled a bunker, had asparagus walls and a ceiling braided with intestinal bands of exposed piping that made the room constantly hot. A single window, lined with iron bars and just inches aboveground, overlooked a brown courtyard strewn with beer cans. He wasted hours stretched out on the mattress among the ruins of cardboard boxes and milk crates, watching TV or reading books as he chewed on his favorite pen, rarely getting dressed and avoiding the outdoors for days at a time.

There was an undeniable freedom in having no plans to speak of, because no matter what he did, he couldn't disrupt a future he hadn't made. He'd always valued the concept of work more than school, of being self-reliant in the present as opposed to investing years in a career that might not pan out. He just didn't know how the process was supposed to begin. His job history at this point consisted of a part-time shift at Burger King during high school. He was inexperienced and unskilled, hopelessly unemployable. He'd tried to navigate the local career market, applied for the most remedial positions in the service industry, at restaurants, grocery stores, car washes, anyplace parading a help-wanted sign. He took home stacks of applications each week but never got an interview, not even a callback.

He was scanning the help-wanted section of the *Columbus Dispatch* with a Magic Marker, perusing ads for dental assistants, truck drivers, and egg donors, when he came across a listing that read "Telemarketing. Experience Not Required." No address, no description, not even a company name. The slippery details were a giveaway, an apparatus of pyramid schemes and the get-rich-quick infomercials on late-night TV. He circled the number anyway. After all, he was desperate.

"We're not hiring," a man said. He told Leonard to try again in several months and hung up.

Leonard redialed the number, insisted he'd read the ad in that day's paper, and said the man was either lying or the *Dispatch* owed him a refund.

"Persistent," he said. "You passed the test. How about you come in tomorrow, say two o'clock?"

The office was in Whitehall, a quiet township on the city's east side, and it took him an hour to get there by bus. Leonard had never been to the area before, and when he arrived at the office, a derelict industrial building in a flex park clustered with low-slung warehouses, his first instinct was to turn around. A single window beside the front door framed a poster of a man in a bear costume with the acronym BAD spelled out across the chest. At his feet knelt a group of smiling children, each carefully picked for racial variety. A script font anchored at the bottom of the poster read "Bears Against Drugs."

Even with the overheads it was dark inside, the blinds twisted back to ward off natural light. Everything in the office appeared exhausted: threadbare carpets scarred with runs and stains, ceiling tiles tanned from moisture damage, wood-paneled walls studded with nicks and taped down where entire sections had peeled back. The air was warm and stale and smelled of burned coffee and cigarettes. There were two rows of three desks, half of them vacant, the rest occupied by employees chatting on phones.

"You'll start tomorrow," a man seated at the front desk said. He was short and shaped like a decorative gourd, wore clothes that were ordinary and lacked effort. "Shifts are six days a week, four o'clock to nine o'clock weekdays, nine o'clock to one o'clock Saturdays. Morning shifts are optional for earners. Pay is minimum wage or commission, whichever is highest at the end of each week." He paused before delivering a line that sounded rehearsed. "I think minimum wage is insulting."

It felt strange that they'd skipped the traditional hiring formalities, the interview, the callback, the W-2, so Leonard asked if he should fill out an application. The man sighed, removed a sheet of paper from the fax machine, and slapped it on the desk. Leonard wrote down his name, address, and Social Security number, and the man stuffed it into an adjacent filing cabinet.

"Name's Dean," he said. "Welcome to Helping Hands."

AS DEAN EXPLAINED THE NEXT DAY, HELPING HANDS TELEPHONED AREA households to raise money for the Ohio Troopers Association, a fraternal group of highway patrol officers that promoted the police unit's image through charities. Officers also occasionally visited elementary schools dressed as the OTA's mascot, an anthropomorphic bear named Teddy Trooper, in an effort to warn kids about the dangers of drug abuse. Helping Hands funded the OTA's efforts by selling jarred food products made by a family cannery in rural Tennessee. The biggest seller was the Appalachian Jelly Set, a gift box containing an assortment of homemade jams, jellies, and preserves. A single box retailed for thirty-five dollars.

"Finest quality jellies you can find," Dean said. "And"—he leveled a finger—"the proceeds keep kids away from drugs. Always remember to say that. We keep kids away from drugs."

Helping Hands offered other products: there was the Appalachian Breakfast, a four-bottle assortment of syrups; and the Appalachian Mustard set, which consisted of a peppercorn mustard, a honey mustard, a horseradish mustard, a jalapeño mustard, and a cryptic variety titled Appalachian Dijon.

"Always use the word Appalachian," Dean said. "Sounds cultural, you know?"

On his first day, Leonard would be working with Earl, a lumbering man who smelled like couch leather. Earl's head was a pink dome flanked by wisps of cottonlike hair, and Leonard envisioned scenarios in which he moonlighted as a mall Santa. Earl wore a jacket decorated with commemorative veterans' pins, and his desk was adorned with wartime insignia from the Korean, Vietnam, and Second World Wars. Next to his telephone stood a figurine depicting the flag-raising at Iwo Jima.

As Earl explained it, telemarketing was all about increasing your odds. It didn't matter what the product was. Delivery was key.

"Talk about the jellies like they've already bought them. It's simple psychology, and it works."

Earl said a telemarketer has, on average, six seconds after someone picks up the phone to deliver a pitch that results in a sale. It might seem like a short amount of time, but for the true salesman it's all he needs. To demonstrate this, he held his pinky finger to his mouth, his thumb to his ear, and threw himself into a frenzied hypothetical pitch.

"I'll go ahead and put you down for a box of our famous jellies. Not a jelly man? No problem, how about I get you in for an order of our syrups." Earl laid down the imaginary phone. "It's that simple," he said. "If you've got the right attitude, you can sell pork rinds to a Hasid. I could sell homeowner's insurance to a Mexican."

A Latino delivery driver stepped into the office from the adjoining warehouse and glared at Earl, now howling and slapping the desk. He picked up his phone and dialed a home in Pataskala. A woman answered.

"Is your mother home?"

Leonard could hear the woman laugh. Earl spoke softly, affecting his language with bucolic charm. He reminded her that the proceeds fund an anti-drug program. His use of the word "children" was excessive. She wasn't buying it. Earl shifted gears and began discussing the quality of the product:

a family recipe, homemade. He was mid-sentence when she thanked him for his time and hung up. The two sat in silence.

"You come from a military family?" Earl asked.

"No."

"Anyone in your family been in the military?"

"I had a great-uncle who was in World War Two," Leonard said.

"Good man," he said and slapped Leonard on the back. "I was born June six, nineteen forty-four. You know what day that was?"

"D-Day?"

"Goddamn right," Earl said and took a sip of coffee. He pulled a referral card from his desk bearing the name of a Masonic lodge in Groveport. "These boys order a few boxes of jellies every six months for their charity breakfasts. If my memory serves me right, it's that season again."

"And there's no season like jelly season," Dean interjected from across the room.

Both men laughed.

Earl called the lodge and was thrown into lively chatter with a man on the other end of the line. Earl asked how the man's wife was doing, his business. He gave Leonard a wink and flipped the card over. Written in pencil was a jumble of random information: "Hanoi '72," "auto parts store," "grandson."

"Isn't your grandkid's birthday coming up?" Earl asked.

Earl made the sale. Three orders of jellies and a box of syrups later, he staggered from his seat and slapped four carbon-copy sales tickets onto Dean's desk, each detailing customer name, address, phone number, and method of payment.

"Cha-ching," Dean said.

"Always know your customer," Earl said when he returned. "I keep a running tally of any information I can get. I know where they work. I know their kids' names. I know their pets."

This, Earl said, was why repeat sales are key.

Earl said Leonard should make a call on his own, passed him the phone and a sheet filled with numbers. Leonard's palms were clammy, and the receiver stuck to his cheek. The line rang, and a woman answered. Taking a cue from Earl, Leonard told her she sounded young for her age.

"Idiot," she said and hung up.

The rest of the evening went like this. Some were polite enough to let Leonard rattle off a ten-second spiel before announcing they weren't interested, but most hung up as soon as they realized Leonard was selling something. Some were worse: A man in Reynoldsburg cursed him out for interrupting his dinner, and a woman in Pickerington screamed so loud it caused a ringing in his ear. By the end of his shift, he hadn't made a single sale.

THAT NIGHT LEONARD GAVE HIMSELF AN ULTIMATUM. HE HAD UNTIL THE end of the week to get better at the job or, if he didn't get fired first, he'd begin looking for work elsewhere. Sitting on his bed, he composed what would become his first telemarketing pitch. It was rough but offered promise, a combination of his own words along with phrases he'd lifted from Earl's calls earlier that day:

> Hello, this is Leonard from Helping Hands. We're collecting money for the Ohio Troopers Association, who, as you may know, teach children the dangers of drug abuse. In order to raise money for this cause, we're selling jars of Appalachian jellies and the proceeds go to help this charity. Can we count on you today to help some children in need?

He arrived on the second day, found an empty desk, unfolded his pitch, and hit the phones. He ran through the same rebuttal with each call, discovered a dance in the words, a swing and cadence in the sentences. Most stayed on the phone longer than the day before, some even thanked him for his time, but two hours later he still hadn't sold anything. He placed his head in his hands. Phone sales was a foreign language, an impossible code to crack. At the next desk over, he listened as a coworker sold one box of jellies after another.

"It's not about the money. These jellies are an investment. I'm going to tell you something I haven't told anyone: Last week I gave up my commission because the state wants to quit funding this program. That's how much I believe in Bears Against Drugs."

This was Monty. Monty was surly and gaunt, had a leathery, cracked face with an orange hue that reminded Leonard of a baseball mitt. A cigarette between his teeth at all times. Listening to him on the phone, Leonard found his delivery impeccable. He was personable but manipulative, casual yet attentive to detail. Like Earl, Monty used an arsenal of brogue to appeal to his audience. Unlike Earl, Monty was actually good at it. For the better part of ten minutes, Leonard heard Monty become an elderly southern man, a starched-collar executive, each syllable limned with a preacher's flair, every word tailored to identify with whomever he imagined was on the other end of the line.

"Pull their heartstrings, and you'll get them every time," he told Leonard as he filled out a sales ticket. "I'll make a housewife cry if I need to. I have before."

As Leonard later learned from Dean, Monty was an ex-convict who'd recently finished serving several years in prison for robbery. He'd held odd jobs, but a criminal record made finding stable work difficult. Dean had taken a chance and hired him, and the decision paid off. Monty consistently outsold everyone else in the office; some weeks he sold more than all the other telemarketers at Helping Hands combined, a fact he was wont to broadcast.

"I'm the reason this place pays the bills," he once told Leonard. "I make commission all week, every week."

Monty was proud of his jelly-selling prowess, among other laurels: his former business ventures, his travels, his myriad romances. It took Leonard all of five minutes to realize Monty was full of shit. Leonard had known people like him his entire life in Lanchester. The man was born poor. He lied because it was the only time he wasn't invisible.

Then there were Monty's spiritual beliefs. He borrowed freely from whatever religion sounded good to him at the time, co-opting a half-dozen cultures' sacred texts into a contradictory web of mantras and maxims. He offered conflicting Taoist and Islamic parables as advice. His desk was a confusing shrine of New Age, Hindu, and Egyptian religious symbols.

"I'm Native American and proud," he said as he positioned a cast-iron Shiva figure next to his Rolodex. "My grandmother was one-eighth Cherokee, and there is definitely a spiritual element to the work I do."

Monty's spiritual beliefs apparently allowed a moral respite each time he got on the phone. He told customers a hundred percent of Helping Hands's profits went to the OTA. He said Helping Hands had been raising money for decades, though the office had been open for only a year. Leonard once heard him tell a customer the jellies would be delivered by a highway patrolman. And while his desk was hardly within earshot of Dean's, the obvious question was no longer whether their boss knew Monty was lying but for how long he'd been turning a blind eye to it.

Leonard picked up the phone and dialed a number in Bexley. A man answered, and Leonard delivered a solid pitch before the man interrupted, announced the world was ending, and suggested they pray together.

Across the aisle, Monty began filling out another sales ticket. He got up from his desk, poured a cup of coffee, and shook his head as he listened to Leonard's spiel.

"How's that pitch working out for you?" he said once Leonard got off the phone.

"Honestly, I'm having a hard time."

"No shit. You read from a piece of paper when you talk to your friends?"

Leonard called a home in Powell, and a middle-aged man answered. Leonard glanced at the pitch but abridged its content, abbreviated words. He felt Monty's eyes on him and folded the paper. The man hung up.

Leonard dialed another number, and a young woman answered. He looked at his pitch; Monty grabbed it and threw it in the trash.

"Hi, I'm calling with Helping Hands," Leonard said. "I'm sure you've heard of us . . . we've got a program where we send highway troopers to schools to teach kids about drug abuse. Here's the deal: We're giving away boxes of homemade jellies, syrups, mustards . . . stuff you can't buy in a store. It's free of charge, our way of saying thanks for helping a great cause. All we're asking in return is a suggested donation."

Monty snapped his fingers to notify Dean. Scrambling for a pen, Leonard began filling out a sales ticket. When he put down the receiver, the office erupted in applause.

"Cha-ching," Dean said.

Seconds later, from across the room, Earl made another sale.

"Cha-ching," Dean said again. "Gentlemen, we're in the midst of a jelly frenzy."

After the sales tickets were tallied, Dean unlocked a glass display case by the door and removed a set of the mustards, then produced a box of crackers from the filing cabinet. The men gathered around his desk and opened the jars, and Leonard helped himself to a generous portion of the Appalachian Dijon. It was terrible.

LEONARD MADE EIGHT SALES BY THE END OF HIS FIRST TWO WEEKS, AN acceptable start, according to Dean, and enough reason to keep him on board. This was considerable consolation, as Leonard had seen three other employees come and go during this time. He never went back to a paper pitch. He made his calls as personable and anodyne as possible, maintained control of the conversation, and kept various details vague: The price of the jellies and any details about the company were withheld unless someone specifically asked. He also decided, against Dean's wishes, to showcase the company's variety of products from the beginning so as to widen appeal. He realized many of the things people did were not out of want or because they had pragmatic reasons for doing them, but simply the result of a conditioned social reflex. That's why he began referring to the jellies as a "gift" instead of a purchase, a reward for their donation. People were easy to figure out: It took only a few seconds to guess a person's gender, age, and race, a few more to gauge their economic background and interests. In doing so, Leonard learned to contour his language to the person he imagined he was speaking with, but he also discovered how to discern potential customers from non, thereby eliminating the time he spent running through rebuttals. The best calls were the housewives, usually in the hours before their husbands came home. As long as their favorite shows weren't on, they were easy to talk to, and Leonard could get them to pony up to anything if he pushed the charity hard enough. The worst calls were always men, especially during dinnertime. The most unpredictable calls were the shut-ins. If he gave them the chance, they'd talk until they dropped, and their enthusiasm would lead a lesser salesman to believe he was going in for the close. More often than not, they just wanted someone to talk to, and by the end of the conversation he'd have nothing to show for it but wasted time.

HE GOT ALONG WITH HIS COWORKERS. DEAN AND MONTY WERE FORMIDA-ble chess players, and sometimes Dean closed shop early so the three could get in a few rounds. Monty had become an enthusiast in prison, and his hours on the board showed. Dean was unbeatable. His moves were deceptively simple; he'd develop his bishops before his knights, ignored the center of the board, and made advances that temporarily strengthened Leonard's position before he'd clean house with moves so elementary, he may as well have been playing against a child. Dean brought a new psychology to the game, waited patiently, baited his opponents, and let them assume they had the upper hand. It was as though he was working off some invisible grid, the outcome decided before the pieces were brought into play.

They argued politics and discussed current events. There were stories. Between Earl's Vietnam tales and Monty's self-aggrandizing diatribes, it became hard, sometimes impossible, for Leonard to get any work done. The worst were Monty's "left for dead" anecdotes, absurd yarns of indomitable will and triumph in the face of low-stakes adversity: scuffles in disreputable taverns, intricate webs of conspiracy spun by bowling-alley vixens with names like Rhonda and Destiny, each saga a wearingly familiar variation of the last.

"Don't mess around with a married woman," he told Leonard one day.

"I'll try to keep that in mind."

"I courted a married woman for a while. It was great, until her husband got hold of me." He took a drag from his cigarette. "He hit me over the head with a wine bottle. Drug me into a tool shed and kept me tied up for two days."

Monty would improvise a new version of these stories whenever the need for attention arose, often adding crucial details he'd conveniently left out during previous accounts. His entire life was this way. There was an invocation of fiction whenever Monty shared his memories; nothing was real, aside from how he felt at the time he revisited them. In a way, Leonard admired the concept, the idea of living with your own version of the past, remembering things not as they were but as they should've been.

A month into his job, Leonard was averaging two sales a day. Overall, activity remained sporadic; sometimes he could sell four boxes of jellies in a shift, other times he'd sell only one. He was living on four-seventy-five an hour, hardly a living wage, and it was insulting, just as Dean said, especially given the amount of work Leonard was putting in. While his frustration fueled an obsession with improving performance, it also spoke to the company's obvious limitations. Telemarketing is a game of numbers. The more calls you go through in an evening, the better your chances of making a sale. And while having a good pitch increases the chances of getting to the dotted line, you eventually find yourself thinking about what you can do to increase pitchable calls. Leonard discovered other telemarketing companies hired agencies to supply them with household data. These are the leads, the prospects arranged by demographic and income. Most telemarketers have a computer that displays this information; they have a name to go by, an idea of who they're talking to, and, depending on the quality of the leads, this variable can make a measurable difference in the amount of product a company turns over. Helping Hands, on the other hand, was cold-calling in its most primitive form. Employees were supplied each day with a sheet containing four rows of chronological digits ranging somewhere between 0000 and 9999. At the beginning of each shift, Dean decided what areas of town they'd be calling and wrote the three-digit prefix at the top of each sheet. The result, while cost-effective, wasted a lot of time. After weeding through the disconnected numbers, fax machines, and modems, it could be five minutes before Leonard spoke with an actual person, let alone delivered the magical pitch that would sell a thirty-five-dollar box of jellies to support a charity no one had heard of. He was at the mercy of chance, searching for patterns in chaos, signals in a landscape of noise.

LEONARD HAD BEEN ON THE JOB FOR NEARLY TWO MONTHS WHEN DEAN shook his hand one Friday night as he handed out checks. Leonard had made commission. It was nearly two hundred dollars more than his usual pay, still not great money but a milestone nonetheless. Several weeks later, he hit commission again. By late June, he had earned commission two more times.

This professional watershed occurred around the time Leonard began to bite things. The habit materialized inconspicuously; he'd always possessed an oral fixation, never left home without his favorite pen—the Pilot Precise V5 Rolling Ball, Extra Fine—which was lodged in his mouth at all times. But this was a different animal. He was now driven by an intemperate urge to assault random objects with his teeth. Cellophane wrappers, discarded plastic milk-jug caps, the ribbed edges of Styrofoam cups—they demanded his attention, satisfied some cathartic compulsory lever he couldn't refrain from pulling. Leonard reasoned the eccentricity was a natural reaction to the work environment; he was the only one in the office who didn't smoke, and, like cigarettes, his nibbling dialed back the anxiety, eased the stress of the sale. He found a conspicuous surrogate in the plastic caps shielding the heads of the screws that lined the underbelly of his desk. He'd pop the caps loose with his fingernails and set them dancing in his mouth as they prodded his gums, a ritual he enjoyed so much, he found he couldn't speak on the phone without them. After he'd stolen all the caps from his cowork-ers' desks and worn them down to wads, he trekked to a hardware store at the northern edge of campus and bought several replacement boxes. Habits were simple things, routines that developed naturally in the course of set-tling into a life. The subject of the world was always us, so it made sense that in navigating the intricacies of the human experience, we discovered things about ourselves we wish we hadn't known. It wasn't until he made his way to work on a southbound COTA bus with the bag of screw caps he'd planned to eat that he wondered how responsible we were for our eccentricities, or if they'd been set in the foundation before the footings were poured, as though by some cruel feature of fate, a part of growing up meant realizing there were things about ourselves we'd never be able to fix.

LEONARD'S PERSONAL CRISIS ALSO MATERIALIZED AROUND THE TIME Helping Hands got the first of several visits from the Columbus Police Department. Local TV news outlets had begun reporting on an alleged rise in fraudulent telemarketing operations in the city; apparently, a call center on the north side had been phoning area homes to raise money for an apocryphal strip of private highway in Delaware County. The Better Business Bureau notified police, but only after the operation had bilked twenty thousand dollars from local residents through ran-dom cold-calling. These stories clearly amounted to a sore spot for law enforcement, because now they were making a dedicated showing of doing something about the problem.

"If keeping kids off drugs is a crime, then I'm guilty," Dean said. "It's those other telemarketing outfits that should be scared. You think the

Police Athletic League helps kids? We put officers in the classroom, where it counts. I've had kids tell me Bears Against Drugs saved their lives."

Dean offered variations of this Barnum act anytime someone in the office asked how these developments might affect business. Leonard wanted to believe Helping Hands was a legitimate operation, just like he'd wanted to believe Dean was unaware of Monty's unscrupulous sales tactics. He'd wanted to believe its products were made by a family in the Tennessee foothills, even as he watched delivery drivers affix phony stickers to boxes in the warehouse. Maybe he even wanted to believe they were helping the community in some way, but the longer Leonard worked at Helping Hands, the more bothered he became by several details that never made sense. Dean lived in motels. He never stayed at the same motel for more than a few weeks' time, and some nights he slept in the office. He kept boxes filled with his belongings in the warehouse, and it wasn't uncommon to see ironed shirts hung across the blinds. Leonard also found it strange that he was always paid by personal check, and taxes were never deducted. Then there was the charity itself. Ohio law required that charitable organizations give a minimum of thirteen percent of their profits to the causes they promote. Leonard didn't know how much Helping Hands contributed to the OTA, and Dean was adamant that if Leonard was asked to provide proof of affiliation, he give customers the telephone number of a retired sergeant named Elkinberry who'd vouch for their standing as a legitimate fundraiser.

"Do not . . . I repeat . . . do not give them the OTA phone line," Dean said. "The secretary is a wingnut, and she probably doesn't remember who we are."

The nightly news was poison. Every time a story broke about another busted telemarketing ring, the office suffered. Customers began asking for proof of Helping Hands's affiliation so often, Leonard began working Elkinberry's telephone number into his pitch. Deliveries plummeted, and Leonard went back on minimum wage. Dean blamed a lack of "real news" for the ongoing coverage. Earl blamed the liberals in City Hall. Monty threw a chair across the room when he received his first minimum-wage check.

Then a Helping Hands delivery driver was pulled over by the cops. He was detained for only a few hours, but his paperwork must have piqued their curiosity, because soon the office was getting weekly visits from detectives who wanted to look at everything from donation receipts to the payroll. The stress became palpable, and this was around the time Leonard discovered toilet paper, light and hazy, with its perfumed cotton candy skin. At home, he began keeping a roll bedside, slipped squares under his tongue and pulped them with his teeth as he watched TV. He couldn't chew toilet paper and talk on the phone at the same time, so at work he stole for the bathroom at every opportunity, sat on the commode, and sucked on a fist-sized biscuit as his eyes rolled back and took blood-colored snapshots of his retinas.

Curious, Leonard decided to call Elkinberry's number, figured he'd introduce himself, and the two could chat about their mutual work for the OTA. The line rang a few times before Leonard noticed a simultaneous ringing in the warehouse. He'd heard that phone before and guessed it'd been set up for delivery calls. He hung up and redialed, and once again the warehouse phone began to ring. It was all coming together. They were piggybacking onto a preexisting charity they had no affiliation with, selling junk products no one would otherwise buy. Sergeant Elkinberry didn't exist, Dean was a crook, and for the past three months Leonard had been working as a con artist, and he'd been too naïve to know it.

He needed another job. He set up an interview with AmeriCall, a national telemarketing agency that ran a Columbus outpost from an office park on the north side. AmeriCall sold discounted magazine subscriptions and gave a percentage of each sale to the Special Olympics. As familiar as the concept was, AmeriCall couldn't have been more different from Helping Hands: The office was sterile and governed by corporate protocols, the company enforced a business-casual dress code, and there was a strict no-smoking policy in the building. AmeriCall also utilized a national database of computer-generated leads, was aligned with a legitimate charity, and the product was affordable and easy to sell. And the job paid seven-fifty an hour, as well as a commission on each subscription sold. Looking over the script, Leonard gave the HR director a sample pitch from a telephone in the conference room. They hired him on the spot.

Dean took it hard, as Leonard knew he would, and leaned heavy on the histrionics when Leonard broke the news the following day.

"Do you realize what you're doing? They take away your soul in those places! You're going to be their lab rat, sitting in a cubicle all day. Stay here in the trenches where your work counts!"

His afternoons now belonged to AmeriCall, but by the end of their meeting, Dean had nonetheless persuaded Leonard to stay on several days a week. Better wages aside, AmeriCall, like every other telemarketing shop in town, didn't hire full-time, so Leonard agreed to come into the office for two or three hours in the mornings before slogging across town to his second job. Leonard was disappointed with himself for giving in so easily; the entire point in quitting Helping Hands had been to distance himself from its mounting legal problems. So, he promised himself the arrangement would only be temporary. In the meantime, the extra money didn't hurt.

On his first day at AmeriCall, Leonard was given a headset and a clipboard that contained his script as well as a list of computer commands. He sat beside an acne-scarred man who wore high-index prescription lenses and introduced himself as Isaiah. Leonard looked over the script; it read like it'd been assembled by a team of lawyers. The idea was absurd: Here was an easy-sell product, endorsed by a well-known nonprofit and marketed to high-income households, and the company was neutering itself by making employees deliver a second-rate pitch. Glancing over the rows of cubicles, he realized AmeriCall had worked its way around this problem. Quantity over quality: this was how the big boys played the numbers game.

From the other side of the cubicle, Isaiah made a sale.

"Schiller the killer!" a supervisor roared from a dry board on the far side of the room. He clapped enthusiastically and slashed through a bundle of tally marks next to Isaiah's name.

Leonard strapped on his headset and pressed a button on his computer. The screen displayed the name of a man in Kentucky with the last name Jones. Several seconds later, a voice was speaking into the receiver.

Hello, Mr. Jones, I'm calling on behalf of AmeriCall Corporation. We have some amazing news for you today! We would like to give you some great savings on your favorite magazine subscriptions, titles such as *Time, Life,* and *TV Guide*! We would like to offer you a four-year subscription to these titles and many more with savings of up to fifty-two percent off the cover price. Best of all, fourteen percent of the proceeds will go directly to the Special Olympics!

The man hung up within seconds. Meanwhile, Isaiah Schiller had made another sale. Leonard glanced at the board. The guy was a machine, maybe even better than Monty. Leonard pressed the button, the computer dialed a number, and a man in California answered. This time Leonard ad-libbed, decided to plug the charity in the beginning and offered a choice of a two-year subscription instead of the four. He kept his language informal, glancing at the script only when he needed pertinent information. By the time the man hung up, Leonard had sold a two-year subscription to *Rolling Stone*.

"Lundell, doing well!" The supervisor marked a tally next to his name.

Seconds later, Leonard's computer screen went black, and another supervisor holding a cordless phone leaned into the cubicle. "I was listening to your call on our monitoring system," he said. "You're deviating from script, violation of company policy. Don't do it again."

Leonard dialed another number, and a woman answered. He glanced up the aisle, and his eyes met the supervisor's, the cordless pressed to his ear. Leonard read the company pitch verbatim, and the woman hung up.

The AmeriCall supervisors were the bane of Leonard's existence. Most were OSU business majors; they had names like Trevor or Chad, and many belonged to the same fraternity. They spent their days chanting idiotic rallying cries from the dry board or roaming the aisles between the cubicles, randomly eavesdropping on employees' calls with their cordless phones. They were lazy, and it took Leonard only a few days to realize how to get around them: He noticed his phone made a subtle clicking sound each time one of them patched into his line. As long as their eyes weren't aimed in his direction, he was free to deviate from the script as much as he liked. If he heard a click in his earpiece, he simply switched back to the company pitch and took the loss.

"Lundell, giving them hell!"

The sales began pouring in. A month into his job, Leonard was one of the top sellers in AmeriCall's Columbus branch. He bought new clothes, ate at restaurants on the weekends, began to own things. He was even able to buy a junker car so he no longer had to take the bus to work. And as much as he loathed them, the supervisors grew sycophantic once corporate began praising the office in light of Leonard's performance. Schiller stopped him in the break room and asked for his secret formula. Leonard told him the truth: After learning how to use random numbers to sell a thirty-five-dollar box of jellies, pitching cheap magazine subscriptions to America's upwardly mobile was easy.

Between both jobs, Leonard was averaging forty-four hours a week, a punishing amount of time for anyone to spend on the phone. And it was then, sometime during his second month at AmeriCall, he discovered the wonders of laundry detergent. The experience was exhilarating. Powdered detergent electrified his mouth, stung as it dissolved over his tongue and laid bare a library of unexpected varietals; depending on the brand, he'd encounter everything from rose to peppermint to vinegar-cured chalk. At home, he'd dip his wetted fingers into the box and lick thimbles candied with tiny confectionery crystals. He began bringing Ziploc bags to the office, stowed them in his pockets, and tried to ignore the increasingly suspicious eyes of coworkers each time he wandered away from his cubicle for the bathroom.

As his financial situation improved, Leonard began cutting back his hours at Helping Hands: first to three days a week, then two. The police, for the time being, had let up on their investigation. Still, the ordeal had devastated the esprit de corps; sales were down, a delivery driver had quit, and morale around the office was low. Leonard didn't plan on being there when the cops came back around, so he set a date to meet with Dean and officially quit Helping Hands for good. It was during that week, however, that Leonard stumbled upon something that changed his telemarketing career forever. Because AmeriCall was a national company, its offices were forced to plan their calls in accordance with the time zones. At eight p.m., the computers switched from Eastern and Central time to Pacific so employees wouldn't disturb households that went to bed early. In the half-hour immediately prior to the switch, supervisors purged the cache of local calls that remained on their servers. The result was a barrage of solid Columbus leads. At seven-thirty each night, Leonard began jotting down customer information in a notebook as it appeared on his screen. The next day, he took the notebook to Helping Hands and began dialing the numbers. It was like putting on an old jacket and finding money in the pockets. By the end of the first night, he had a stack of completed sales tickets, some from the same customers he'd sold magazines to the night before. He was making commission from the same families twice, stealing leads from one company and using them to make commission at another. He'd finally discovered a shortcut in the numbers, a foolproof way to outmaneuver the system.

"Cha-ching," Dean said. "This is beyond a jelly frenzy! It's a jelly nor'easter, a jelly monsoon, a jelly tsunami! I don't know what they're doing to you in that cubicle farm, but the kid is back!"

Commission was easy with the new leads, and soon Leonard was filling out eight or nine sales tickets for each three-hour shift. To keep Dean from growing suspicious, Leonard would hold on to some of his tickets for several days before turning them in. If sales were slow, he'd reach into the drawer and pull out another ticket, thereby ensuring his commission for the week. The plan seemed ironclad, and in the weeks that followed, as Leonard continued to steal more leads from AmeriCall, his sales at Helping Hands increased as his hours continued to dwindle. He was showing up only two days a week, usually only several hours a shift, and still selling more than anyone in the office. Most of the time, he was the only one making commission. Dean didn't seem to care where the money was coming from; he approached Leonard's sales with the same don't-ask-don't-tell that had characterized his relationship with Monty, but the rest of the office grew quiet every time he filled out a sales ticket. Monty stopped speaking to him altogether.

Leonard's hours at Helping Hands dropped again, to only one day a week. He began calling the stolen AmeriCall numbers from his apartment, hitting *76 on the keypad to keep the calls from being traced. He made his sales and turned in his tickets when he showed up for his weekly visits. One Friday morning, when he stopped by the office to pick up his check, he noticed the place was empty. No one was there except Dean, who sat at his desk, playing a one-man game of chess.

"We're in trouble," he said.

Apparently, Monty had tried to go into business for himself. Unbeknownst to Dean, he'd set up a small operation with several friends in Grove City. The script was familiar: Monty leased out a cheap office, acquired a few phones, and hired a skeleton crew at minimum wage. He picked a local charity, in this case the Grove City Fire Department, and started calling area households. He was in business for only several days before the office was raided by police. The incident made headlines. Monty was in jail again, and a paper trail of sales tickets, call logs, and stolen office equipment led the police back to Helping Hands. Dean had sent Earl and the remaining delivery driver home for the day because he didn't see the point in doing business when everyone was so upset.

"We're going to make it through this," he said. "We'll be back on top, and it's going to be raining jellies all over Columbus. We'll hire a new staff, maybe get a new office, but everything is going to be just like the old days. I want you to be in on this. Please tell me you'll be in on this."

There were a lot of things Leonard wanted to say, but in the end he only suggested they play a game of chess. It was rough going as usual. Dean advanced his knights quickly and did a lot of damage, but Leonard was onto his plan and gained control of the center of the board before taking Dean's queen two moves prior to checkmate.

"I knew what you were doing the whole time," Dean said as he advanced a pawn.

"What do you mean?"

"Stealing leads from that corporate gig and using them here."

"How?" He took Dean's bishop with a knight. Dean countered by taking the knight with a pawn. It was an even trade, depending on the type of player you were.

"Because a month ago you gave us a bad address for a customer in Worthington. Our delivery driver showed up at a vacant house, so he called the number on the sales ticket. Those corporate databases are good, but they're old. People move, you know." Toward the end of the game, there was nothing left but several pawns and a knight. And Dean still managed to win. He always won. "You're not coming back, are you?"

Leonard didn't say anything. Dean gave him his paycheck, and then he unlocked the display case and removed several boxes wrapped in cellophane. "Here," he said. "A memento of your time in Appalachia."

Dean walked Leonard to his car, and they shook hands. When Leonard reached James Road, he pulled into a grocery store parking lot. He drove behind the store, got out of the car, and threw every box of jellies in the dumpster.

LEONARD WAS SITTING IN HIS AMERICALL CUBICLE A MONTH LATER WHEN a supervisor told him the manager wanted a word. When he finished his call, Leonard removed his headset and strolled to an office at the end of the hall. A Trevor and a Chad were seated in the corner, and his stomach seized up when he registered the obvious, winking tone of their somber faces. He was busted. Somehow, the company discovered he'd been stealing their leads. Leonard didn't know how they'd figured it out, but he hoped they'd read his last rites and show him the door, and the police wouldn't have to get involved.

"Have a seat," the manager said. "Do you know what this is about?"

"I have an idea."

"Good." He opened a manila folder and leafed through several pages. It was a file Leonard had never seen before, a spreadsheet summary of his sales history at the company. "You haven't been selling many four-year subscriptions lately. Do you mind telling me why?"

"Excuse me?"

"You're the best seller we've got. And here you are, pitching one-years all day." The man set down the folder. "We told you in training that your pitch is supposed to lead with a four-year sub. If you don't make the sale, you rebut with a three. One-year subs are an absolute last resort."

"Well," Leonard stammered, "why push them for four-year subscriptions when I can take them easier for a one and move on to the next call?"

"That's not our philosophy here," he said.

"Most people don't sell half of what I do. Sometimes I'm the only reason this office makes quota at all."

"Exactly," he said, "and that's why we're counting on you to come through with the fours. You're a superstar doing bare minimum. I know you can do better. Right now, your performance . . . it's not working for us."

"I'll see what I can do," Leonard said and stormed out of the office.

As he sat in his cubicle and strapped on the headset, Leonard could feel the anger roll against him. The room felt hot, and he became aware of a slight ringing in his ears. His computer dialed a number. He drew short breaths, and his temples throbbed. His knuckles were burled around the edge of the desk. The computer dialed another number. He acquired tunnel vision, stepped outside himself, felt weightless yet oddly still in control, senses acute, a mind operating on autopilot. And when nine o'clock came and the phone lines died and employees removed their headsets and the supervisors assembled around the dry board, Leonard had made a branch record, with fourteen four-year subscriptions. The supervisors surrounded his cubicle and showered him with whistles and cheers as Leonard pushed past them, rebuffing high-fives. He clocked out and left the building and walked to his car. He drove out of the parking lot and never went back.

Leonard returned to Helping Hands the next day. He didn't see the idea of asking Dean for his job back as a mark against his pride; he was too high on nostalgia during the trek across town to consider any effects the move had on his dignity. Dean had taught Leonard everything he knew about sales, and he owed him another shot, felt obligated in a fundamental sense to return the favor of giving him a chance when no one else would. The experience had corrected Leonard's vision, disproved a long-held belief that he wasn't good at anything, that he had no discernible talents. It was as though he'd emerged from some machine recalibrated, reimagined for purpose, and maybe he wanted to believe they could make it Dean's way, moving from town to town, selling some throwaway product for ten times its worth with a ragtag crew of lunatics and criminals, running a racket with the wind in their faces and, hopefully, more than a few steps ahead of the law. When he parked the car, he couldn't help but notice how desolate the lot was, more quiet than usual. Approaching the front door, he realized the lights were off. The door was locked, and the Bears Against Drugs poster was missing from the window, replaced with brown butcher paper. He stood there for a minute as autumn sunlight played across the face of the building, listened as a breeze whispered in the doorway. They had closed shop. Dean had moved on.

Chapter 12

Leonard exited the subway station, threaded into the crowd, and hurried up the sidewalk in a lopsided keel. It was a hot, restless morning, the sky empty and irradiated with sun, anodized windowpanes glinting light as he dodged suits and tourists. A shear of heat whipped over the avenue, smells of charring meats, hot trash, exhaust. Twisting sleeves of steam flanked traffic, as though a fog had sprawled over the street, as he started up Madison's gray corridor, where he embarked on the last leg of a route he'd made every day of his working life for the last seven years.

As he quickstepped over a bay of vents, he was reminded of the familiar background props, cameo characters reprising their roles in the daily scene: a bent trash can on the corner of Forty-First, a bronze siamese standpipe crowned with pigeon spikes, mailboxes badged with stickers. Mystery puddles he swore hadn't budged all these years, collecting a turbid flotsam of cigarette butts and receipts and wrappers. A broken chessboard of sidewalk, several wedges nudged skyward by underground roots that had somehow survived beneath it all. They were everywhere if you looked hard enough, those ballasts of place, old friends anchored in the earth. The mob crested at the intersection when he arrived at the most familiar of them all, his office building, its sooty exterior now ensconced in a ramshackle sidewalk shed, the first three floors caged behind pylons of scaffolding, an appearance that augured a place in critical disrepair.

The air in the office felt different. The terms of the room seemed altered somehow, controlled by foreign agency. Leonard crossed the center aisle between the cubicles, paused, offered cutaway smiles to passing coworkers, and came to a full stop. Unfamiliar faces in the hall, drifting vapors of industrial solvent, the whimper of an unfolding ladder. He turned and felt a dart of panic when he saw Hector, the janitor, disassembling the Gurney Public Relations lettering from the lobby wall.

"Welcome back." Todd Shillenburg met Leonard outside his office door. "You don't look like you were hit by a car."

"What the hell's going on?" Leonard said.

"What do you mean?"

"The sign, genius. Why's it being taken down?"

"You didn't hear?"

"Hear what?"

"Pinnacle. They're buying us out."

Leonard fumbled with his keys, anchoring himself on the doorknob. "Hilarious."

"Press release goes out tomorrow. Some of the trades already have a draft under embargo. I can show it to you if you'd like. Conference call with Pinnacle shareholders this afternoon."

"Oh, Jesus, you're serious," Leonard said. There was a tension in his chest followed by dizziness, the onset of vertigo. He closed his eyes as the blood rushed to his head, saw copper-colored flashes over the back of his eyelids.

"It's been under the carpet for a minute," Todd Shillenburg said. "Why do you think that CEO's lapdog Feinblum has been in Roger's office every week for the last three months? My guess is they've been eyeing us ever since you worked that elevator salvo back in the spring."

Leonard kicked open the door. Shillenburg followed, and others appeared behind him: Todd Colton, along with a younger man Leonard didn't recognize who settled into a vacant chair in the corner. He had a small head and sharp features, efficient eyes that scrutinized everything.

"Hey, Lundell, feeling better?" Todd Colton said.

Leonard began pacing the room. "How did Jack allow this to happen? There's no way he'd sell out to a conglom."

"Moot point," Todd Shillenburg said.

"How so?"

Shillenburg and Colton exchanged a wary glance before Shillenburg passed Leonard the press release. It was boilerplate insofar as media statements go, loaded with the usual bombastic superlatives and equivocating jargon, trivial details disguised as weighty issues, turgid claims on how an agency merger would "foster cross-agency collaboration, expand Pinnacle's integrated service offerings with an increased focus on recruiting top talent," blah, blah, blah. Wanda Markowski and Graydon Trotwood both offered lengthy quotes, formal expressions of high praise for the entities with which their respective agencies would merge. At the bottom of the release, it stated Gurney PR Founder Jack Gurney would remain onboard as Chairman Emeritus while the agency underwent a management succession plan, with Jack eventually leaving the agency by January 2009, at which point he would endeavor to dedicate more time to his passions in the library sciences.

"What's this?" Leonard said.

"Jack's retiring or something," Todd Colton said. "I mean, not retiring per se, but taking a limited role. You know, basically retiring."

"I think he's in the Dominican Republic right now," Todd Shillenburg said. "I heard he's on some chichi humanitarian mission to help this indigenous lesbian commune turn recycled paper into trinkets for tourists."

Leonard grabbed the first thing within reach, a Styrofoam cup, and threw it against the bookcase, but the cup fluttered to the floor and didn't convey the intended pathos. His temples throbbed, and he became aware of a slight tingling in his fingers.

"You want us to leave for a bit?" Todd Colton said.

"What else happened while I was gone?" Leonard said. "How much more bad news is there?"

"I think that's it," Todd Shillenburg said. "Guess you picked the wrong time to be in the hospital."

"Thanks for keeping me informed, idiots."

"Calm down," Todd Shillenburg said. "We figured it was best not to bother you."

"Didn't you get hit by a car?" Todd Colton said.

"You could've called, sent a text message. Email. I would've come down for a meeting," Leonard said. "By the way, the release doesn't say what our agency will be called now that we've been conglommed. Any clue on the absurd portmanteau they're giving us? Pinnacle Strategic Engagement, perhaps?"

"Oh, I hate that," Todd Colton said and thumbed through a stack of paperwork. "These agencies rebrand with a new fad moniker every couple years. My money's on Pinnacle Marketing Solutions."

"Pinnacle Integrated Communications," Todd Shillenburg said.

"I love it when they make their entire name lowercase," Todd Colton said. "Or when they remove the spaces between the words."

"This should rustle some jimmies," Todd Shillenburg said. "I hear there's a fashion PR shop on Lafayette that changed its name to a symbol."

Labored groans pitched through the room, a bray of titters and hinky laughs.

"Sorry to disappoint, but it's nothing that exciting," the younger man seated in the corner said. He leaned back and chuckled with an effrontery that suggested he'd known the group for years. "The agency will maintain its branding. Gurney PR: A Division of Pinnacle International."

Leonard closed his eyes and mouthed the words, then returned his attention to the man. "And you are? Sorry, pal, this is a private meeting."

"Just repeating what Roger told me," the man said.

"Leonard, meet the new guy," Todd Shillenburg said. "An envoy from our overlords at Pinnacle. He's going to be shadowing our meetings from now on. He's got a law degree."

"Beveridge," the man said. He rose from his chair and extended an enthusiastic hand. "Todd Beveridge."

"Roger told me you were coming," Leonard said. "Of course, he conveniently failed to mention you were a Pinnacle staffer. No offense, but crisis management might not be in your wheelhouse."

"I was on the crisis team at Burson-Marsteller for two years before I jumped ship for the ad world," Todd Beveridge said. "I guess I bounced back."

The man possessed a despairing quality of boardroom civility, as though he'd taken a course on superficial charm. He laughed compulsively, which always bespoke a troubling character flaw.

"Honestly, this is the best thing that's happened to us," Todd Shillenburg said.

"Are you kidding?" Leonard said.

"I'm totally not. No one respects this agency. We're mismanaged, the offices are ugly, the building's old, and our boardroom looks like a place where Charles Dickens goes to fuck. With any luck we'll be folded into one of Pinnacle's PR units by the end of the year, and we can get out of this hole."

Leonard felt a buzzing in his pocket, a text from Patty: *Can u believe it? We're going 2b coworkers!*

"You should worry about how an agency with Roger and Wanda at the helm is going to affect our work," Leonard said. "Which reminds me, any good news? Client wins, RFPs, RFQs, anything? And where the hell is Todd Armitage, anyway?"

Radio silence in the room. "Guess we forgot that one," Todd Shillenburg said.

"Guess so," Todd Colton said.

"My God, what now?" Leonard said.

"Armitage quit. He's gone," Todd Shillenburg said. "Got a job repping food brands at Pollard PR."

"Food PR, figures. With all the other twinks," Todd Colton said.

"Guessing y'all heard?" Beau the assistant stumbled into the office, red-eyed and furious. He slammed the vacuum flask of coffee on the desk and capered around the room, a burlesque of knees and elbows. "This is some bullshit. One month I've been here, and you don't have the stones to tell me I'm about to be voted off the island. You riled the wrong dog, boy."

"Christ, put the lotion in the basket already," Todd Colton said.

"This ain't no joke. I've been watching the news every day. The banks shit the bed, and now our superiors are sinking the ship to save themselves. They'll be punching tickets by Friday, mark my words."

"They teach you about mixed metaphors under the stairs?" Todd Shillenburg said.

"My understanding is there will be no staff changes as a result of this merger," Todd Beveridge said.

"Bullshit," Beau said. "Yankee food processor said the same thing twenty years ago when they come to Tennessee and got up with the Reelfoot packing plant. Then they caught wind of how much folks was being paid and started handing out pink slips. My daddy was hung out to dry with three hundred other people, and we've been poor as field mice since."

He paced the room, eyes down, hands balled into fists. Then he paused near the desk and cracked his knuckles, made a sharp clicking sound with his tongue. Leonard caught a whiff of him; he smelled like a wet ashtray. "The only reason I came to this town was to earn some scratch to send back home. I managed a salad bar in Times Square for three months before I got this gig. You have any idea how dehumanizing that feels, overseeing a team of vegetables?"

He said "feel" as though it rhymed with "pill." He reminded Leonard of every man he'd known growing up in Lanchester, a directionless rube who was always one lotto ticket away from freedom. Leonard felt a mystery heat in his chest, furious at this raging lummox taking up space in his office. From the corner of his eye, Todd Shillenburg and Todd Colton were squirming in their seats, barely able to stifle laughter.

"You can bet if they're going to pick off Jack, then someone like me will be first to go in the barrel," Beau continued. "Laugh it up, I suppose this is what I get, listening to y'all insult me all the time. You play bullshit games, you win bullshit prizes. You boys'll step on my back so you can keep moving up the imaginary ladder. Lord knows you ain't got nothing better to do than see who can be tallest dwarf. Snakes in the grass, every one of you. You ballwashers can kiss my entire ass."

There was a shuffling of feet, a kicking of chairs, and Leonard caught a fleeting glimpse of Todd Shillenburg and Todd Colton making a half-assed attempt to intercede as he grabbed Beau by the shoulders, spun him around, and pushed him through the door, whereupon Beau grappled in the doorway before Leonard hoisted him by the collar of his army jacket.

"Walk," Leonard said as he lockstepped with him down the aisle. Several heads cropped up over the cubicle walls to watch the commotion. Then they reached the foyer, breached the doors, and stumbled toward the elevator bay.

"What are you doing?" Beau said. "Why're you so angry?"

"You're fired." Leonard opened the stairwell door and shoved him through it. "Don't come back."

Leonard's collar was ringed with sweat when he returned to the office. Oddly, he felt better.

"Was that necessary?" Todd Shillenburg said.

"Are you kidding?" Leonard said. "Did you hear how he was speaking to us?"

"Seems kind of cruel," Todd Colton said. "You want us to give you a minute?"

Leonard sat behind his desk. His cellphone buzzed again, and he fumbled in his pocket. Another message from Patty. "Don't be ridiculous," he said and shut off the phone. "Let's get to work."

Crisis: A regional fast-food restaurant was censured in the press after its founder publicly espoused a series of anti-gay sentiments during a recent radio interview. Protests were later held outside the company's headquarters, with boycotts against the restaurant staged in several states. *Strategy:* Rally your core demographic. Reiterate the company's Christian principles, hit conservative talk-show circuit, appeal to the First Amendment and family values. Offer a weekly promotion where customers who recite a to-be-determined biblical verse get a free sandwich. *Crisis:* A national insurance agency had run a series of televised advertisements commending the bravery of residents affected by a recent hurricane. Last week, however, a newspaper reported the company had simultaneously denied claims from homeowners whose property had been damaged in the storm. *Strategy:* Pull the ad. Respond to press with reasons for the denials, citing a computer processing error that affected some East Coast policyholders. Release a new campaign apologizing for the oversight and again commending residents' bravery. *Crisis:* Some parents were convinced an electronic workbook programmed to educate children about planets wasn't enunciating the intended phrase "this is Venus," but was actually saying "kiss this penis." The allegations fueled human-interest stories in papers and on nightly newscasts around the country, and many retail stores had pulled the item from shelves. *Strategy:* Double down. Hire a linguistics expert to verify the book is uttering its professed expression.

The team took a break and looked over reports as Leonard flipped through channels. A nature program discussed the top five wild animals people fear most. A study revealed shoppers shown images of car crashes were more prone to exhibit impulsive behaviors. A marketing agency had issued a white paper claiming it had discovered "brand triggers," or a set of universal associative cues companies can use to elevate their brand's presence in consumers' thoughts. The news recapped Senator Obama's acceptance speech at the Democratic National Convention in Denver, then cut to announce Senator McCain had selected a running mate, Alaska Governor Sarah Palin.

"This broad is batshit," Todd Colton said as the woman waved on the screen. "She looks like a tweaker on Thanksgiving."

"This is McCain's attempt at currying support with the housewives to combat the idea that he's Bush Part Two," Todd Shillenburg said. "It's a brilliant move, and it's the first shot in the arm his camp has gotten since the race started."

"She's a dullard," Todd Colton said.

"She's tits on a ballot. McCain's lucky to have her," Todd Shillenburg said. "Obama has marketing appeal. That's what you need to win elections nowadays. Imagine Obama on a T-shirt and compare it with McCain. The guy's face looks like my scrotum."

"The marketing model has changed," Todd Beveridge said from the back of the room. "At Pinnacle we saw it years ago. Clients were saying they didn't just want ads; they want market research, outcomes measuring, content development, media training. They don't want to referee conversations between agencies anymore, and PR firms are uniquely positioned to respond to this because they're basically doing anything you can think of nowadays short of buying ad spots."

"We know," Leonard said. "What do we get in return for merging with an ad agency?"

"Bigger clients, better resources for design and production. Deep contacts and industry expertise. Superior analytics," he said. "We did a Facebook experiment this year that showed emotional states can be spread between users without any written cues, simply by exposing them to content expressing a particular emotion."

"That sounds like brainwashing," Leonard said.

"We call it emotional contagion," Todd Beveridge said and smiled. "Did you know there's a PR agency uptown that offers stand-up comedy training? Buddy of mine runs the program. His title is Chief Laugh Officer."

"God, he's a complete ass," Todd Shillenburg whispered.

"He'll fit right in," Leonard said. He turned on his cellphone; a third message from Patty.

As the men gathered their things, Todd Beveridge lingered before sheepishly approaching Leonard's desk, then leaned uncomfortably close and laughed in such a way that Leonard considered he might have a learning disability.

"Nice riffing with you today. I wrote a couple notes, legal pointers," he said and passed Leonard a sheet of paper. "It's just . . . I couldn't help but notice a few red flags in the language."

Leonard looked at the sheet, lashed with ink.

"Then there's that strategy for the insurance company. It assuages the client but completely ignores public sentiment—"

"So?" Leonard said.

"Not to get all inside baseball on you, but from now on we have to make sure all quotes are cleared internally before they're issued," Todd Beveridge said. "And I think it's prudent to remember that while positive coverage is key, we can't advise anything that would get our clients into any further trouble, re: the hurricane. We can't tell our clients to lie to their customers."

"I'll keep it in mind," Leonard said. His face darkened, a bruised hue. The man left, and Leonard balled the paper and threw it in the trash. Then he read the last text that Patty had sent him. *This company sux, but now that we're working 2gether could u sign my petition to hire an exec chef 4 the cafeteria? Emailing u the dets now k thx bye.*

That afternoon, Leonard crossed the hall to Jack's office and opened the door. To his surprise, the room was almost entirely vacant: The wraparound bookshelves were dismantled, and the desk, the computer, all signs of Jack's forty years of residence moved out. All that remained was an empty filing cabinet, several piles of residual paperwork, and a dust outline where the desk had been. On the cabinet he found an olive hanging file folder, bound by rotting rubber bands, stuffed with photographs and brittle clippings. Leonard sat cross-legged on the floor and picked through it as he registered the room's familiar cellar smell, dusty and damp at the same time, the decomposing musk of old newspaper. There was Jack, clearly sometime in the seventies given the attire, standing with his late wife, Sophia, on the roof of the St. Regis Hotel during what must've been one of the Arthur W. Page Society's fabled banquets; middle-aged Jack, in the throes of the eighties as noted by attendees' hair, at a National Investor Relations Institute conference; nineties Jack, thinning and gray now and looking like he'd shrunk at the shoulders, at the Financial Writers Association's annual "Financial Follies" ceremony; eighties Jack again at the George Polk Awards; nineties Jack at HSMAI's Adrian Awards. A newspaper clipping dated 1965 captured Jack at the bar of the old Overseas Press Club that used to overlook Bryant Park. He would've still been a financial reporter at the *Journal-American* at this time, his future only beginning to stretch out before him. A curled Post-it note fluttered by with the air-conditioning's breath, and it dawned on Leonard that there was an organizing principle at work here, a thematic symmetry that spoke not only to this empty room but to the current state of the company. What had always been was gone, and Leonard resented the fact that everyone else in the office was blind to this simple tragedy. The impermanence of everything just seemed cruel to him, and though he'd spent the sum total of his adult life wanting more than what he'd had, now he just wished things could be the way they used to be. A nagging sadness overtook him, which he fought resentfully as he tucked the folder under his arm, stuffed the Post-it note in his mouth, and chewed it as he turned off the light and closed the door.

Leonard gritted his teeth as he walked the halls. The Gurney PR sign was gone from the lobby wall, and all that remained was a crude memento mori: vacant screw holes stained with peach-colored rust and a faint outline of the logo where the sun hadn't reached the paint. He shoved open the lobby doors, where he found Wanda Markowski waiting for the elevator. She offered a strained smile, and Leonard considered at that moment how everything she did was for show, how she was the sort of person who was constantly aware of how she was being perceived. Unfortunately, her face had always been her worst enemy, imparting a dispassionate honesty that belied every pretense.

"I was out for only a week," Leonard said.

"Okay?" Wanda said as she stared at the bay of doors. "I hope you're feeling better, by the way."

"I want you to know I find this very cute, orchestrating a buyout while I was in the hospital."

"Christ, why does everything have to be about you? Everyone else is happy with this partnership." Floor numbers flashed on the elevator console, and she pressed the button several more times.

"Out of curiosity, what did you get out of this deal?"

"Soup to nuts? Real stock, phantom stock, a nice bonus. Career stability with a chance to grow at a major agency. Why?"

"Pretty convenient Jack's out of the picture, just several weeks after you intimated you wanted him gone."

"You got us, Leonard," Wanda said. "It was a cloak-and-dagger cabal to weed out Jack and subvert some authority you don't have. And we would've gotten away with it, if you hadn't untangled this tempestuous web of lies and deceit, every strand of which conveniently leads to you. Happy?"

"Pinnacle posted big losses last quarter, and for some reason they're buying a mid-sized agency that's swimming in debt. Sound strange to you?"

"You're an M&A expert now? Here's an inconvenient truth for you: This deal has been in the making for months, well before you worked with Pinnacle on that elevator accident. How do you think we got their CEO into our boardroom to begin with? You actually believed Roger when he told you we just ran into them on the street?" She pressed the elevator button again. "I suppose I should mention that the work you did for them actually sweetened the deal, because Pinnacle has always wanted to add a crisis practice to its toolkit. They consider you their beacon in the fog and thought it was awfully nice of you to step in and offer your help after they fired their last counselor. I guess you could say you had a hand in taking us to the dotted line."

Then the elevator arrived, and Wanda stepped inside it, where she remained quiet until the doors closed.

OUTSIDE THE SUBWAY STATION, LEONARD'S SHADOW STRETCHED LONG against the pavement. It was still warm, but there was an amber tint to the light now, new smells on the breeze, a slight, early crisping that signaled an inevitable change of season. He passed a chalk-colored quad on Park Avenue and the usual neighborhood habitués, tourists, identical elderly women walking identical dogs. Block after block of luxury apartment buildings bearing Anglophile names: The Worthington, The Bedfordshire, The Prescot Regis. He'd received a voicemail, not from Patty, thank God, but from the Mango Cove Lifestyle Community property manager, confirming they'd received Leonard's deposit. On a tree-lined street he came upon Jack's townhouse, a neo-Georgian with a mansard roof and arched windows barred with ironwork. The interior appeared to be under some capacity of construction: plastic sheeting was draped over a window on the first floor, and a utility van sat idling at the curb. Men in splattered painter's garb filed out of the heavy wooden front door, which stood wide open.

He walked under the foyer's vaulted entryway and into the parlor. He hadn't been inside the home in several years, but it appeared unchanged, minimally furnished in boilerplate patrician stoicism: Gainsboro gray walls bordered by colonial wainscoting, a glass-beaded chandelier centered above the central staircase. The living room doorway was sectioned off with a plastic curtain, and he'd managed to plant a foot on the first stair when the curtain peeled back and Lila Gurney stepped out, her hands crusted with paint.

"Dad isn't here," she said.

Behind her, from the opening in the curtain, Leonard caught a glimpse of the living room's herringbone floors and several canvases on easels, each covered with plastic sheeting. "What's with the construction?"

"We're giving the house some light updates," she said. "New drywall, new paint. I'm converting the dining room into an art studio and moving Dad's office upstairs." She paused. "Mom always said this place looked like a museum. A place where you weren't allowed to touch anything."

"They moved Jack's stuff out of the office. I was worried."

"He's fine, but you have to leave. He can't see visitors." She blinked as she said this, corrected her posture. "Besides, he's at a doctor's appointment."

"He isn't on a cruise?"

"No, why would he be?"

Leonard tossed the folder of photos he'd brought onto an accent table beside the living room doorway, where a bronze statuette of the Greek goddess Demeter surveyed a pile of mail. "He left these. I figured he might want them back."

She followed him outside with several of the photos in her hand. It had been years since he'd seen Jack's daughter. She was somewhere in her forties, attractive under certain lighting conditions, a reedy build and skin on the albinism end of the color index, hair dyed jet-black, the auburn roots clearly visible. She dressed with a kind of performative nonchalance, wore a sequence of mismatched layers that sufficiently covered every inch of her frame save for her hands and face. She appeared sophisticated by default, deliberately constructed to recuse herself of any allegiance to gender, and the result was intriguingly maladroit, a librarian who'd been forced to take a job at a gas station.

"Happy to be back in town?" Leonard said from the steps.

"What are you doing here, Leonard?"

"I wanted to see your father. Roger and Wanda didn't send me, if that's what you're asking."

"I wouldn't care if they did. Dad can't see anyone. He isn't well. I'm sorry."

She lit a cigarette and exhaled defensively, a flurry of ashes dancing between them. Leonard had had few interactions with Lila. She'd been away from the city for years, though he'd gathered plenty of stories in the interim. She'd attended various universities and trade schools on and off for decades, had made financial commitments to become everything from a chef to an acupuncturist to a veterinarian, though insofar as he knew she hadn't received a degree from anywhere. In the years since, she'd been arrested several times for occupying various administration buildings in the course of protesting a litany of social issues, and he remembered she'd once traveled the country with a ragtag band of activist busking musicians who referred to themselves as "gypsies," though he was pretty sure they hailed from the Upper East Side. Last he'd heard, she'd joined some yoga cult in the Caribbean, and Jack had been forced to pay for her rescue and subsequent deprogramming therapy. That was several years ago.

"Dad's retired, and he's spending time with me now," Lila continued. "We've spent our days painting together. This is the happiest he's been in ages."

"You're an artist now?"

"I've always been an artist," she said. "I have a gallery show at the end of September, if you're interested. It's part of a collaborative series where I asked children what they think of our war in Iraq, and I translated their answers into paintings. A poet will also be there who creates verse by combining patriarchal doctrines with women's-rights texts."

She unfolded a flyer she'd removed from her pocket and passed it to Leonard.

"Be seeing you," he said and stepped onto the sidewalk.

"You hate art?" she called after him.

"Just artists."

"I'm curious about something." The muscles in her neck clasped and a perplexed wrinkle struck the center of her forehead. "They say we're on the verge of a recession. How does it feel to see it crumble before your eyes, to watch your world fall apart?"

"I don't know. Maybe you could make a painting about it."

"Funny how you can be so cavalier about your impending doom," she said. "Does it always make you feel better to put others down?"

"Sometimes. Pretending they're more important than they are is fun too."

"We live in a world that hands out success to young white men, yet you and your pack of lowlifes become petulant when reality doesn't conform to your bankrupt perceptions of it. You think I don't know why you came here? You want to get Dad back in the game. He wasted the last few years of his life at that agency, and your delusion regarding his current situation shows how utterly, willfully blind you are."

"You sound like a joy to be around, and I'm sure you think this constructed persona of yours makes you interesting, but the truth is I came here because I'm worried about Jack. He wouldn't retire, not like that. Something else is going on. You might not believe it, but he's the only reason I stayed at the agency as long as I did."

She smoked, the breeze tugged at her hair, and the light from the open doorway behind her appeared to get tangled in it. Then she extinguished her cigarette with her shoe, folded her arms, and looked to the street. "Look,

I'm under no obligation to tell you this, but perhaps it will explain my motives. Dad is having a hard time remembering people."

The words took a moment to comprehend, like she'd handed him a passage of text that'd been photocopied to illegibility. "I don't believe you."

"Dad's as stubborn as you are. In fact, he has a kind of strength that's rare and often misunderstood. I know you two were close. I want to tell you grief can be good. Loss can give life context, can give us insight, inspire us to move forward. Loss is like a religion, in a way."

It was strange how she'd wandered into a friendly frame of mind. Then again, self-righteousness typically won the tug-of-war against self-respect.

"Was that a BA in armchair psychology, or did you do post-grad work?" Leonard felt a buzzing in his pocket and looked to his phone. Another text from Patty. "It was nice talking to you."

Leonard walked south. The sky had darkened, and blood-red clouds captured the last straining rays of sunlight. He paused at the corner, debating his next move, but his thoughts promptly returned to Jack. Leonard recalled a story his mother had told him about an uncle who had acquired dementia. Apparently, he'd begun referring to her with his mother's name. In the months before he'd died, he called local businesses at odd hours. He said strange men were coming into his room, described demons drifting out of the vents, crows on the windowsill that spoke in strange tongues. Leonard was struck by a compelling thought, something he wasn't sure he could articulate extemporaneously: whether everyone saw the same things in a person, or if we each saw something different based on what we were used to. He was so lost in the idea, he didn't realize his phone was buzzing. Patty again.

"What the hell do you want?" Leonard said. "You've been calling me nonstop all day."

"I came up with an idea," Patty said.

"An idea regarding what?"

"The merger, genius. I know how we can throw some sand into their gears."

"Sure. I suppose you found another incriminating folder on a photocopy machine somewhere, or you've blackmailed some sap into telling you what Pinnacle's going to do to my company once the deal goes through."

"I'm serious. This is huge. We should talk ASAP."

Leonard cast around for the right response. He hated the fact that after everything, he still possessed an impulse to hear her out, given the celestially impossible chance that she might have a worthwhile strategy for handling this crisis. A superficial reading would be that his sense of judgment had flagged, but the fact remained that he had no ideas left, and no one else was in his corner. After all, they'd just dismantled the largest merger in advertising history. Maybe they could do it again.

"I suppose I could meet for a bit," he said. "Where are you?"

There was no mystery regarding what she would suggest next: There was a secret traveling dinner-party series she wanted to attend, the locations of which weren't revealed until several hours before each event. She texted him a web address, followed by instructions on how he could purchase tickets. Several blocks later he found a printing and copying store that doubled as an internet café, sat at a terminal, and punched in the address of a spare, cryptic site that looked like it had been designed a decade ago. After several minutes of laborious navigating, he keyed in his credit card information. Immediately he received a confirmation email that looked like it had been written by a lawyer. He texted Patty back. Considering that he was still uptown, she suggested they meet at some halfway location and take a cab to the event together. After some hesitation, he agreed.

He entered an unassuming cocktail bar that looked like a funeral home: linear wood-paneled walls, button-tufted banquettes, bar shelves lined with honey-colored bottles alongside a bizarre assortment of old clocks, none of which displayed the correct time. The establishment was devoid of any pretense of contemporary allure, maintained that chimera of authenticity today's consumer so desperately seeks, and yet the place was empty, a diminutive draw compared to the self-labeled "dive" bars around the corner where drinks sold for ten dollars. Leonard sat and exchanged furtive glances with a listless bartender. Several stools away, a middle-aged patron had nodded off. On the television, a news report claimed average U.S. housing prices had fallen more than twenty percent from two years prior.

"Can you believe a Black man might be president?" The man seated at the bar stirred to life. He had diaphoretic skin, a desperate comb-over, rheumy eyes in the shape of half-moons. He wore a department-store suit and looked like he was allergic to daylight, endured nights full of bad times.

"He's great in front of a camera," Leonard said. "He might win, if he has a strong campaign, if he touches on a prescient theme."

"How do you figure?" The bartender exchanged the man's glass with a fresh drink.

Leonard realized he'd crossed into territory in which conversation was now expected. "I'm in public relations," he said, and then, sensing he was under a social obligation to reciprocate, "You?"

"I sell mattresses. Bed frames, bedding accessories, that sort of thing."

"That's interesting."

"It's horrible." The man leaned toward him. "Did you know mattresses gain five percent of their weight over the course of their lifetime?"

"How is that possible?"

"The mucus, all the dead skin. It just collects. I'm here to tell you."

Leonard shifted in the stool. "I didn't know that."

"Mattresses," the man muttered. "They're horrible things."

The man cleared his throat and had begun to say something else, but the television distracted him, and Leonard seized the opportunity and made for the door. His feet hit pavement, and his eyes caught the bronze flash of traffic, and he realized he'd left his cellphone on the bar.

Chapter 13

He sat on a bus-stop bench between a sweating derelict and a man offering an unsolicited evaluation of a female passerby's physique. A livery cab pulled up to the curb as Leonard was relocating himself to the corner, noticed Patty gawking from the backseat window, her face pressed against the glass and a faint ring of what appeared to be confectioners' sugar dusted around her mouth.

"What took you so long?" Leonard said as he rushed into the seat beside her. "I thought you were coming directly from the office."

"I left work hours ago to get a Waggle." She shook a haute pastry box spotted with grease.

"What the hell is a Waggle?" The car lurched into traffic. It had been less than a week since he'd seen her, but she'd gained weight, appeared physically uncontained somehow, spilling out of her clothes.

"Half bagel, half waffle. This famous pastry chef sells them at a pop-up shop near the Flatiron. There's usually a three-hour wait." She clapped her hands. "I'm so excited about tonight!"

Leonard exhaled. "I suppose standing in a depressionesque breadline to buy an overpriced artisanal pastry is a slightly better pastime than dropping a hundred and twenty dollars to eat in someone's apartment."

"You didn't have to come, you know."

They floated south to Union Square, then steered west. Midtown's grid disappeared, and soon they forged through twisted joints of dark streets, passed an arcade of storefronts, before entering a neighborhood occupied by turn-of-the-century tenements.

"So, this buyout of my agency is a disaster," Leonard said. "I'm not going to be Pinnacle's crisis counselor, because who buys the cow when the milk is free, right? Then they bring some yes-man onto my team who's going to be overseeing my work, and now my boss is retiring, who's basically the only ally I had. The entire office, everything I've accomplished is in jeopardy."

"Pinnacle's a shit company," Patty said. "They make us write evaluations on ourselves. How schizophrenic is that?"

"You're my last line of defense. I want to discuss how we're going to cannonball the pool. Whether you realize it or not, a Pinnacle–Gurney merger bodes poorly for you too. If you think I'm bad, wait until you meet Wanda—"

"Oh! This is the place!" Patty said before directing the driver to stop. They exited the cab, and she made a feeble attempt to jog up the sidewalk, her gait accompanied by a wobble. "Hurry, we're late!"

Two stone-faced men wearing suits and sunglasses met them on the corner. "Reservations?" one said before scrutinizing Leonard's cellphone screen. "Do you have the password?"

Leonard bristled as he struggled to recall the password, which had been referred to as a "vibe check" in the confirmation email. "We're here to adopt the ducks."

"Put these on," the other man said and produced two satin sleep masks. "We'll lead the way."

"What's this?" Leonard said.

"Didn't you read the instructions?" Patty wheezed between words as the men led them hand-in-hand down the street. "We're supposed to be blindfolded."

"Why?"

They walked a block and, given the sounds of what appeared to be a steel door opening, took some postern entrance into a building. They were led down a hallway and up a flight of switchback stairs and, just as Leonard began to grow panicked, were ushered into a room brimming with convivial sounds, wafting aromas of food. Given what he knew of the area, the room's acoustics, and its aged brick smells, he figured they must've been brought to a loft of sorts.

Soon a man accosted them, introducing himself as the host. He had a French accent, spoke with a lateral lisp, and said everything slowly, as though he was undergoing regressive hypnosis.

"Thank you for joining us," the man said. "Our collective is embarking on a new conversation about the dining experience. We argue if there's one thematic component that characterizes today's underground food scene, it's storytelling with subversive flavors that provokes us to explore our shared emotional connections between value, authenticity, and meaning."

Leonard drew an exasperated breath. "Why the masks?"

"We're a culture that places too much emphasis on the visual. In the dining milieu, there's the overvaluation on plating and preparation, not to mention the social aspects of restaurant culture: the night out, the nauseating ritual of being seen. In this country, with your celebrity chefs and reality cooking shows, not being able to see one's fellow guests undermines the notion that the communal experience of mealtime is just another capitalistic triviality that matches processed products with processed consumers." He paused. "Make no mistake, what we're doing is nothing less than a form of civil disobedience."

More guests arrived. Patty and Leonard were led to a table, where the host ran through the bill of fare. A Bordeaux was served, along with a parmesan pinacate amuse-bouche, followed by an appetizer: canapés crowned with slices of magret de canard, which, according to the host, had been rested over an apartment radiator to pay homage to the tenement immigrant community's contributions to the city's culinary traditions.

"Delicious," a woman said. "You can just taste the poverty."

After a palate-cleanser sorbet, they were served small plates of lemon curd foie gras terrine wrapped in poached fig, followed by a baby beet salad, and then cocottes of coq au vin. Several more guests milled into the apartment, and, as the group dined, a tapestry of idiotic chatter floated through the room, conversations on everything from famed brunch haunts to superficial assessments of the presidential candidates. A duo of women seated across from Leonard discussed their shared disdain for capitalism before transitioning to the topics of laser corrective surgery and microdermabrasion facials.

Soon the main dish was served, a duck confit choucroute with truffled potatoes. According to the host, the waterfowl had been stolen from a summer home belonging to the Bush family near Kennebunkport, Maine. They were transported to a warehouse in Brooklyn, where an illicit gavage facility was hastily constructed. Preparations were allegedly inspired by the Bush Administration's enhanced-interrogation techniques.

"The ducks suffered terribly," the host said. "They were placed in boxes and force-fed corn for three days before being drowned in baths of Armagnac. To add further distress and disappointment, they were placed in front of speakers and forced to listen to Jacques Brel as we discussed the futility of your war on terror."

"The flavor profile is staggeringly above my head," a man said. "It's creamy, warm, inviting—"

"I need to get my aura unblocked," one of the women across from Leonard said to the other. "A hot yoga session last week put a bad energy in my spine."

"Bright, dissonant, riffing with flavor," the man said.

"GMO labeling isn't enough," another man said. "I want to know my farmer's name, what financial ties he has to big agriculture."

"Did you just gender-assign an entire profession?" a woman asked.

"I am so fucking triggered right now," said another.

"Bold, primitive, aggressive," the man continued.

"Captain Adjective," Leonard snapped. "Do you mind shutting up?"

Instinctively, Leonard leaned over and licked the leather arm of his chair. No one was looking anyway, so he figured he was free to do what he wanted. The chair had been screaming for his attention, and he was pleased to find it salty and warm.

He felt a hand on his shoulder. "How does everything taste?" the host asked.

"Sanctimonious," Leonard said. "Oh, host?"

"Yes?"

"Restroom, please."

The man escorted Leonard down a hall. Inside the bathroom, he took off the mask and checked his cellphone. The Mango Cove Lifestyle Community property manager had left a message saying his mother's unit was ready for occupancy. He'd also missed a call only several minutes prior from Noah Sundermeyer. Leonard turned on the taps to mute the sound. Then he dialed.

"Burning the midnight oil, Sundermeyer?"

"Something you want to tell me, Lundell?"

"Not particularly."

"Word on the street is Gurney PR is folding into Pinnacle. Any comment?"

"I can't. But I'm assuming you've seen the press release out on embargo?"

"You screwed me."

"Are you kidding? I gave you the scoop of your career."

"For a merger that never happened. Now I'm a laughingstock and back to writing profiles for the business section. I'm lucky I didn't get canned. Meanwhile, your agency gets bought out by the same conglomerate. Coincidence?"

"The deal was real, you moron. It was abandoned because of your article, not in spite of it. Listen, it's touching you think I'd waste my time putting together a rumor of that magnitude to hoodwink a glorified stringer at a cops-and-courts paper, but I've had enough experience with the press to know the story is written by the time they call. So, what's the deal?"

"I've got plenty of dirt on you already. Maybe it's time to see if I can grow something with it. You've been warned," Sundermeyer said and hung up.

On the sink was a bottle of organic hand soap. Leonard unscrewed its cap and sniffed, a chamomile fragrance he found humdrum and underwhelming. Soon he was rooting through cabinets, picking through fair-trade lotions, apricot-scented facial scrubs, various balms, and essential oils, looking for the first reasonably comestible item he could find. In a cupboard, he found a box of tangerine-scented candles with a heady scent. He bit one and it crumbled in his mouth; a chalky body, which he'd anticipated, but with surprisingly dexterous flavors, an aromatic assembly of demerara sugars rounded off by a burst of citrus. He managed to swallow one of the candles, filled his pockets with the rest, and, when he was finished, for good measure, returned to the sink, unscrewed the soap's cap, and drained it into the toilet. Then he unzipped his pants, placed the head of his penis flush with the bottle's open neck, and refilled it before returning the cap and placing the soap on the sink where he'd found it.

By the time he returned to the party, guests had been served a chocolate-covered brioche and were waxing rhapsodic about halotherapy and anal bleaching.

"Patty?" Leonard said.

"Right beside you."

"If I stay another minute, blood is going to shoot out of my nose."

"Fine," she said. "I'll catch you on the flip flop."

"We have business to discuss. It's the only reason I agreed to meet you tonight. Step outside with me, or I'll cause a scene."

"A scene?"

"Remember what happened in Brooklyn last month?"

"Leaving so soon?" the host said as the pair lumbered to the door. "There's something on your shirt." He began brushing pebbles of wax off Leonard's chest as he stood in the doorway.

"Guess I figured you were blindfolded like everyone else," Leonard said.

The man rested a hand on Leonard's arm. "I'll send you the cleaning bill for my chair."

THE MEN IN SUITS ESCORTED PATTY AND LEONARD TO THE SIDEWALK. They returned their masks and walked to the corner, where the pavement was mottled with light from the streetlamps.

"Next time I invite you out, I'd appreciate it if you didn't embarrass me by insulting everyone like that," Patty said.

"I've never met such disdainfully arrogant assholes in my life. If there was any justice in this world, someone would dig a hole and throw everyone upstairs in it." He removed a candle from his pocket and began to chew on it.

"Rant to yourself all night," she said. "I have someplace to be."

"If you want to go back upstairs after we're finished and discuss the finer differences between brie and camembert with the cargo cult, be my guest."

"I meant I have another dinner engagement uptown."

"And where are you going?" he said.

"Wouldn't you like to know? Sorry, private affair."

"Another dinner? You just ate for an hour straight. That can't be healthy."

"My body, my business. I think I have a swollen posterior giblet." She chuckled. "Since when do you care?"

"I don't. Just an observation," he said. "Maybe slow down a little, that's all."

"I'm the one who saved your life, remember? And some thanks I get, you being all physically violent with me in your apartment like that. And let's not forget how you wanted to force me to quit my job."

"Quit rehashing old stuff," Leonard said. "The only reason I agreed to meet with you in the first place was because you said you had a plan on how we could pull the brakes on this merger. So, let's hear it. I've been waiting all night."

"Fine," she said. "Remember a few months ago, when you said sometimes an attack on someone's reputation can be an opportunity?"

"Sure. So what?"

"So, I was thinking, what if you open your own crisis shop, but you offer a service where you intentionally created scandals for your clients? Like, what if you start a company where you train people to deliberately do something controversial so the media will pay attention to them?"

"And why would anyone pay for something like that?"

"Because any publicity is good publicity, and maybe they're not getting it through traditional PR because the press thinks their company is boring and not worth talking about, or whatever. But if they're in a crisis, the media will notice, because gossip is all people care about."

Leonard shook his head. "But it doesn't make sense."

"Why not?"

"Because your concept is a service in search of a demand. No one wants people to hate them. Nice try, Patty, but it's a dumb idea." He began to chew on another candle. "That was the big plan? Congratulations on wasting another evening of my life."

"Are you kidding? I'm bringing boom to the room here. I suppose you have a better idea?"

"As a matter of fact, I do," he said. "I was thinking we could write a press release for Pinnacle's shareholders, tell them what a dangerous investment Gurney is. That's enough to rattle any investor. We could distribute it to the newswires. If we do this right, we can get the shareholders to threaten a lawsuit challenging Pinnacle on the terms of the acquisition."

"I'm pretty sure that's fraud."

"It's called spreading a rumor."

"I don't know. Maybe you should let it go," she said. "Have you considered you're putting all your ambition in the wrong place? Think about it. You've wasted years of your life trying to climb the ladder at an agency no one's heard of that's run by people you don't like. All this time, you could've gotten a different job, a better one."

"I don't have time for this," Leonard said. A cab crossed the intersection, and he held his hand to traffic, but the cab continued on, and they were alone again, standing in the shadows their bodies made under the streetlamps.

"I've been listening to you for months now, and I don't think you even know what you want, but I do know you've got this stupid job you keep using to try to find some kind of meaning," Patty said. "I'm pretty sure you'd be happier if you just cleared the deck and found something you're passionate about for a change."

"If it makes any difference, I don't know how much longer I'll be at my job," Leonard said. "I just can't see any other way out of the woods at this point. I guess the silver lining here is there's no scandal you've got that can destroy a client relationship I don't have. Or a career, for that matter."

"So, that's it? You're going to quit?"

"Maybe. I don't know."

"Does that mean you won't tell your bosses about those documents I gave you?"

"Why would I? You're not my problem anymore. And if I'm gone, this game is over."

"One step ahead of you," Patty said. "To be honest, I'm just kind of bored with the whole thing. You're a miserable person. You're judgmental and you've got anger issues and you're not that much fun to be around. You're basically what would happen if Richard III was general manager of an Olive Garden. I mean, you've got an aromatic candle in your mouth, and you think getting rid of me is going to fix what's wrong with you?"

"I guess that settles it." He hailed another cab, and this time it stopped, pulling up to the curb as he stepped into the street. "Well, this is a strange turn of events. If I'd known annoying you would be what inspired you to cash in your chips, I would've tried a lot harder from the beginning."

"Don't worry, you've done plenty," she said. "You truly are a breath of stale air."

"Then this is it?"

"You really think my plan was that bad?" Patty said.

"Honestly, it was even worse than your last idea," Leonard said. "Anyway, it's been interesting, Patty. Be seeing you."

HE WAS LATE GETTING TO THE OFFICE THE NEXT MORNING. IN THE FOYER, he was hit with the ammonia pong of carpet cleaner. The walls had been given a fresh coat of bone white, and the beige cubicles had been replaced with a bullpen-style floor plan, everything open and managed by clean lines, a laboratory sterility. He crossed the room, marveling at its bare geography and inspected workstation tables made of brushed aluminum as he listened to a euphony of keyboards.

Jack's old office had been repurposed somehow, a massive control room window installed along an interior wall. A small staff of men and women sat feverishly typing at twin rows of tables. The only other appointments were four thirty-inch screens mounted on the wall that played a stream of social media conversations and a pair of conical speakers perched in the corners.

"Ahoy, Lundell," Griffin Cruz said as Leonard entered the room. He stood rocking on his heels in front of the control room window, wearing a turquoise button-up and canary-colored tie.

"What's all this?" Leonard whispered.

"New research facility, courtesy of our corporate overlords at Pinnacle."

"They did this in one day?" Leonard said.

"Less, technically," Cruz said. "Contractors pulled an all-nighter after the office closed yesterday. Check it out, they're gathering data from influencers in some Millennial focus group."

The control room window opened into the boardroom on the other side. A teenage boy and girl occupied the table, and Roger Lawton and Wanda Markowski stood over them distributing snacks.

Leonard couldn't help but notice that the party paid him no mind as he approached the window. When Cruz thrust his pelvis at the group, Leonard realized a mirror had to be facing the other side of the glass.

"By the way, I've got another idea to run by you," Cruz said. "Lamentcation. It's a trip someone takes after their spouse dies. Think educated, senior demo of course. Also: bereavaway, widowfari—"

"Shh," Leonard said.

Roger's voice crackled through the speakers. "We're interested in collaborating with an outside collective of spokespersons to boost our online marketing campaigns' visibility. How would you recommend we communicate with bloggers?"

"I don't know," the boy said and rolled his eyes as he checked his cellphone.

Cruz buckled with laughter. Behind them, the frantic patter of keyboards.

"Let's talk about authenticity," Wanda said. "We have a client that produces a popular line of snacks, and they're interested in mission-driven corporate responsibility. What do you think about participating in the message-creation process for a brand dedicated to mindful snacking experiences?"

"They taste good, I guess," the girl said.

"Well, this has been very productive," Roger said and passed out more snacks.

"You've got to see the folks they've scheduled for tomorrow," Cruz said. "We're talking real wackadoos, like some guy who says he can cure prostate cancer by rubbing crystals on your balls, and this group that claims to have sexual relationships with lakes."

"What do you think about all this?" Leonard whispered.

"Millennials?" Cruz said. "An obvious sign of colony collapse disorder. As a species we have ten, maybe twenty years tops—"

"No, this merger. The Pinnacle buyout."

"Don't put your faith in cavemen, Lundell. The markets are just natural selection by other means. In ten years, every flack in Midtown will be working for the same four shops. Oh, by the way, here's that info you wanted. Sorry it took so long."

Cruz removed a slip of dot matrix paper from his pocket. Leonard had completely forgotten about Cruz's offer to have his D.C. contact dig up dirt on Patty. Unfortunately, the contents were sparse, providing nothing in the way of employment history or a criminal record. But there was an address. Leonard looked the information over and stuffed the paper into his pocket.

The team had finished its meeting by the time Leonard got to his office. The television was on, everyone was drinking coffee, and Todd Beveridge was thumbing through press releases from the fax machine as he relayed an anecdote that had the others in fits. Leonard fell into his chair, gave a plaintive sigh, and waited for someone to acknowledge him. Todd Shillenburg was dripping contact solution into his eye, and Todd Colton was leafing through a copy of *Twin & Turbine* magazine. On the television, a psychologist wrote the word "doubt" in Magic Marker on a folding chair and proceeded to shame the chair.

"We need to amend that last account strategy," Todd Beveridge said. "Attacking the blogs that went after our client's clothing line is too aggressive. Accountability needs to be the sine qua non of this response. The last thing we need is a nation of pissed-off mommy bloggers."

"Fuck them," Todd Shillenburg said. "Why does reality have to be sterilized for everyone's consumption these days?"

"Our client's credibility is the problem. They're a sweatshop label," Todd Colton said.

"Exactly," Todd Beveridge said. "A corporate social-responsibility angle would be a better route—"

"How much would you pay for a T-shirt, Colton?" Todd Shillenburg said.

"A plain shirt?" Todd Colton said. "Six, maybe eight bucks?"

"Congratulations. You're the reason we have sweatshop labels."

"About those accounts," Leonard said. "Sorry I'm late, but I'd like to go over them."

"We already did," Todd Beveridge said. "Meeting's over."

"I wasn't here," Leonard said. "Let's run through them again."

"I don't mean to haggle—" Todd Beveridge began.

"What the hell are you doing, Todd?" Leonard said. Instinctively, he slid his arm across the desk, took Todd Shillenburg's contact solution, and stuck it in his mouth. He didn't realize he'd been nibbling on it until he'd punctured the bottle with an incisor and felt saline dribbling over his lip. The flavors were low-key but surprisingly complex, rosewater and cocktail onions.

"Are you chewing on my eye drops?" Todd Shillenburg said.

"No," Leonard said and set the bottle on the desk. "Answer the question, Beveridge."

"The hell you weren't," Todd Shillenburg said. "I saw you. It was in your mouth."

"Gross," Todd Colton said.

"Just spitballing," Todd Beveridge said. "Don't take it personal."

"You're undermining my ability to lead my team."

"I'm offering guidance. What's the problem?"

"Was that really in your mouth?" Todd Colton said.

"You and me, outside," Leonard said. "We need to talk."

"Overreact much?" Todd Beveridge said as they walked the hallway.

Leonard put his ear to Wanda's door and heard peals of laughter coming from inside. He shoved it open to find Wanda and Roger, along with Bernie Feinblum, gathered around Wanda's computer. On the monitor, a video played of a cat chasing its own tail.

"Leonard, Todd," Roger said. "What a surprise."

"Get this clown off my team," Leonard said. "I can't take it anymore."

"Whoa," Roger said. "What's the problem, gentlemen?"

"I don't do paint-by-numbers, just-add-water PR. That's the problem," Leonard said. "I don't do coupon campaigns or tag-sale press statements, and I don't want my accounts being monitored by middle-management toadies to read like elaborate soda commercials for Joe Slackjaw."

"Is there a point to this rant?" Feinblum said.

"He'll stop soon. Just let him go," Wanda said and yawned.

"Get him out of my meetings. Get him out of the building," Leonard said. "This isn't how we do business."

"We're glad you're back, Leonard," Feinblum said. "I've been thinking, maybe you'd enjoy the responsibility of writing an internal release statement for our shareholders before the conference call next week, a sort of primer for what they can expect out of this merger."

"Yeah, I get you," Leonard said. "Some snappy boilerplate with a newsy quote about how Pinnacle is a 'best-in-class communications agency with top-notch talent'? Maybe we could even end it with an idiotic cliché, some-thing like 'finally, a company that cares.' I'll get to work right away." He froze, recognizing the dangerous territory he'd stumbled into.

"This is disappointing," Feinblum said. "I'm not used to being spoken to this way."

"You're being rude, Leonard," Roger said.

"What about our arrangement, Bernie?" Leonard said. "That meeting we had the other week in your boardroom? I was supposed to be your go-to guy. And now you want to keep me busy writing in-house copy for share-holders?"

"But we've still got you, Leonard. And now we've got the Todds, Wanda, Roger, not to mention that genius Griffin Cruz in your travel department. In some ways, you're the reason we were convinced this acquisition was the right choice. Consider it a promotion."

"We don't want to stop you from doing what you do so well," Roger said.

"You don't want to go down that road. Trust me," Todd Beveridge said.

"Oh, really?" Leonard said.

"This is the most unprofessional person I've ever worked with," Beve-ridge said. "Aside from routinely berating and dressing down his colleagues, yesterday I watched him manhandle an employee and physically throw him out of the office."

"I heard about that," Wanda said. "Poor Beau."

"His habit to shoot inside the tent isn't the only thing I find disturbing," Beveridge said. "For years, he's apparently told everyone he used to be an account executive at Burson-Marsteller. Well, I called some of my former Burson colleagues yesterday. They've never heard of him. In fact, I can't find any evidence he's done PR anywhere aside from this agency."

The room went silent. Leonard felt the sour reflux of adrenaline, a tight-ening in his chest. He clenched his jaw and realized he was shaking.

"Don't look at me," Wanda said. "Jack hired him."

"Think about it," Beveridge continued. "Ever wonder why his work de-viates so wildly from the normative protocols? Ever wonder why he's so adroit at crafting unconventional strategies but so combative at the idea of following procedure? He's a fraud."

"These are serious allegations," Feinblum said. "Leonard?"

"Leonard has worked here for seven years," Roger said. "He manages an integral part of our business. I won't have you come in here and attack him like this."

"Don't shoot the messenger," Beveridge said. "Just reporting what I heard."

"Leonard, do you have anything to say?" Feinblum said.

A guttural scream from outside the office interrupted them. The group rushed into the hallway to find Jack Gurney, shirtless and flailing his arms in the windows' affluent light as a diffuse crew of junior staffers formed a perimeter around him.

"Oh, my God," Wanda said.

"This is a function of management!" Jack yelled. A steel pica pole in his hand glinted as he slashed at the air. "What the hell happened to my office?"

He listed and wobbled up the aisle, a trail of discarded clothing—shoes, socks, shirt, undershirt—on the carpet. His skin was pallid, and he had a drawn, displaced countenance, drooping lips and dim, glassy eyes. Shirtless, with his spindly arms and sunken chest, he looked like a melting wax figure of himself.

"Looks like I missed a meeting, Roger! What's in the applecart today for Pinnacle International?"

Employees scattered as the old man advanced. The scene had the effect of democratizing the office; no one wanted to assume the leadership function needed to control the situation. Two young staffers from the creative services department were capturing the spectacle on their cellphones.

"Is he a vagrant?" Beveridge whispered. "Should we call the cops?"

"You've got a lot of irons in the fire, Jack," Roger said. He approached the old man cautiously, adopted a crouched position, extended a hand as though he were coaxing a stray dog. Bernie, meanwhile, had jogged to the nearest desk, grabbed a phone, and began fumbling with the keypad. "Let's step into my office and talk."

"Where's my library, shitbird? You snake, turncoat. Apostate! My empire, forty years of work. This place looks like a goddamn doctor's office!" Jack threw the pica pole against the wall. Then he began struggling with his belt.

"Christ, not the pants," Wanda screamed.

Leonard took off his jacket, draped it over Jack's shoulders, and began walking him back toward his office. In his arms, the old man felt impossibly frail, bones wrapped in loose skin.

"Shame what our world's come to, Leonard," Jack said. "I hired every one of them, and they ran me out of my own company. I leave them to mind the store, and they sell my agency behind my back to a conglom, and now my office is gone."

"Live, die, and forget it all, right?" Leonard said. "I think it's best if we take a walk."

Jack looked at Leonard the way someone looks at a busted clock, seemed to possess a feral inability to comprehend what was being said. Then he placed his head on Leonard's chest and began to weep.

"Leonard, you could've been one of my own. I always told everybody, you could've been my boy."

A dry heat flashed over Leonard's face. His eyes stung, and he had difficulty keeping his head erect. Then a makeshift security team arrived, Hector the janitor and several doormen from the lobby, and they gathered Jack's clothing, hurriedly dressed him, and marched him to the elevators. Eventually the crowd dispersed, and the factory sounds of office work resumed, and the management team who stood milling around was the only reminder of the private tragedy that had just occurred on this patch of carpet.

"Let's go back to Wanda's office," Roger said and set a hand on Leonard's shoulder. "Let's resume our meeting."

Leonard looked up and noticed everyone—Roger, Wanda, Feinblum, Beveridge—staring at him with wide, empty mouths.

It was a strange thing about work: There was something intrinsically rewarding about the prospect of mastering a craft, an appreciable feeling of accomplishment seeing one's labor rendered into a service or product for public use. If you were lucky, you grew to take comfort in the structure of it, got married and shuffled through productive, unexceptional years punctuated by football pools and office gossip and conversations about 401(k)s, met with coworkers for drinks and attended company office parties, not a bad life by any reasonable metric. Problems arose only when your priorities failed to hew to your sleeping colleagues' religious enthusiasm, when you lacked the commitment to define yourself by what you did for a living, and the job you hated consigned you to the lead-footed ennui that came with spending your free time trying to reclaim the lofty idealism you'd had in your youth. It was as though, at some point during early adulthood, a light goes out, and we spend the rest of our years shuffling around in the dark, trying to get it turned back on.

"Leonard?" Roger said. "Hello? You look like you've seen a ghost."

"This job is bullshit," Leonard said. "I quit."

Chapter 14

It was late summer, one of those misleading days that belonged to another season. There was a waning confidence in the light as Leonard exited baggage claim at Port Columbus International Airport. He rented a car and drove south under unremitting gray skies, faint traces of wood smoke and dead leaves on the breeze, passed Columbus's glinting skyline before entering a treeless country of empty fields bordered by steel-lattice transmission towers.

He checked into a budget motel off an exit ramp several miles from Lanchester city limits. His room was neutral and smelled of citrus disinfectant, with tattersall-patterned carpet and oak appointments. A random thought occurred to him, and he dashed to his briefcase for an index card so he could write it down. Several former coworkers had left voicemails in the hours he'd been unreachable, and he'd received an email from HR, reminding him they still needed a formal resignation letter for their records. He scribbled on a second index card, then a third. He adjusted the thermostat several times and stretched out on the bed facing the room's single window, which framed an empty parking lot strewn with leaves.

He scrutinized the notes he'd written and made phone calls, reserved a lease for several units at a local storage facility, and arranged a key pickup for his mother's new condominium. Then he spoke with Norman, and they went through each step of their plan twice. On the television, the news reported that millions had rallied to vote on a new McNugget sauce. During a talk-show segment, a comedian asked people on the street to summarize a current event, and a laugh track played each time the subject invariably failed to construct an adequate response. In the bathroom, Leonard discovered a ridiculous silver paten gifting an assortment of complimentary toiletries: travel shampoos and lotions, a functionally dubious toothbrush shaped like a piece of flatware, and several disks of soap resembling communion wafers, each wrapped in plastic and nested in a bed of haute-cerise craft paper. He unwrapped one of them and let it rest on his tongue. It was dry and had a cheap clay taste, but the fragrance intrigued him, so he broke the soap into several pieces and reconstituted it with water in his palm, discovered bright, assertive flavors bracing with hints of lemon rind and caraway. He managed to eat two of them this way before he succumbed to a coughing fit and had to force down several glasses of water. Then he called the front desk to report that housekeeping had forgotten to leave soap in his room. He stayed up watching television that night and slept poorly.

HE DROVE INTO TOWN THE NEXT MORNING. THE NEIGHBORHOOD WAS just as he'd left it, identical ranch ramblers that huddled close to the ground, modest lawns patterned with miniature trees, everything still swollen a deep green, the air perfumed with the heavy, hazy smells of curing asphalt and grass. A low rumble of lawn mowers in the distance. Memories lingered like a familiar song as he considered the subtle indignities that came with returning home. Home was the genesis for everything that had happened to you; that's what gave it so much power, whether you liked the place you came from or not. It was strange, he thought, the distances we'll travel to remind ourselves why we'd left in the first place.

He parked at the curb several doors down. At nine thirty, he watched his mother hobble from the house to the minivan and drive toward town. He waited, then pulled into the driveway and called his brother, who arrived ten minutes later.

"Flea market is all the way out in Zanesville," Norman said and removed twin buckets filled with cleaning supplies from the trunk. "I told her there was a sale on Native American earthenware. That's her new thing. She'll be gone all day."

His brother's mustache had metamorphosed, taken over his face, drap-
ing down the sides of his mouth with curling tendrils that blotted out his
upper lip, ineffectually tamed with the application of what appeared to be
some sort of oil or wax. A car edged into the intersection, and both men
froze until it made a lazy left turn and continued on.

"I suppose there's still time to turn back." Norman said this in the same
indirect, deferential manner Leonard's former coworkers would use when
they felt strongly about something but didn't want to appear combative. A
passive suggestion dripping with judgment. "This might create more trouble than it solves, you know, like you're attacking the symptom, not the
cause?"

"We, Grandma. We're doing this together," Leonard said and slammed
the trunk door. "And she'll be fine."

They entered the house wearing dust masks, trash bags folded in the
crooks of their arms, forded the hallway's grotto of laundry, and breached
the living room on their knees, surveyed the grove of busted furniture and
lamps that cropped out before them. Precarious towers of filing cabinets
and books and mound after mound of bargain-bin clothing, everything
covered by a skein of dust. There was something about the air in this place;
the room had managed to trap the last remaining smells of the season, and
Leonard lingered there for a moment, taking everything in: the span of
lemon light that crossed the hallway, the musk of aged wood sweating in
the hibiscus rot of late summer, a house charged with stray memories, laden
with the luxuriant weight of the past.

For the next hour they hauled trash to the curb. The deeper Leonard
dug, the more impressed he was by the diversity of artifacts they excavated:
board games and badminton rackets, rotary phones and typewriters. They
found Adirondack chairs and a croquet set, an electric tea kettle, a hydro-
dynamic swimsuit, and a brass bar cart stuffed with old newspapers and
catchpenny trinkets. Moths fluttered as they cleared debris, and the room
plumed with dust. Soon the fleet began to arrive: two U-Haul trucks, several utility vans, and pickup trucks occupied by men in overalls. Leonard

counted eight of them in all, twice the number his brother said had signed up for the job.

"Economy isn't so great," Norman said. "A few guys' brothers asked if they could help."

"Probably for the best," Leonard said as he counted the cash in his wallet. "We'll have to be quick."

They divided the movers into two groups: one to load essential items into a U-Haul that would be taken to their mother's new condominium, the other to pack the remaining hoard into a second U-Haul bound for the storage facility. Leonard and Norman would dictate which items belonged in which vehicle and would also be in charge of loading trash into the pickups, which would have to make periodic trips to the county landfill throughout the day.

The crew worked with rehearsed efficiency, partnering up, dividing refuse from movables, hauling it to the vehicles under a general air of silence. By noon they'd made significant progress; Leonard carted what seemed like mountains of trash, and his arms were sore and his hands were raw and he was pretty sure he'd sprained his wrist moving an air-hockey table to the curb. After clearing most of the living room and kitchen, he transitioned to his old bedroom, where stashed in his dresser he found women's sweaters and baby clothes still bearing tags. He was fisting them into a trash bag when he discovered a drawstring pouch in one of the pockets. Something was wadded inside it, and he opened the pouch and shook several baby teeth into his palm. He vaguely remembered his mother had kept them, some grotesque memento of his childhood. He rushed to the bathroom and flushed the teeth down the toilet, and then he scrubbed his hands vigorously in scalding water. When he returned to the bedroom, he retrieved his old wooden stirring spoon from the nightstand drawer and licked and bit it several times until he was calm.

The appraiser arrived sometime that afternoon. She had thick features and shoulder-length hair that looked like someone had chopped it off in her sleep, and she engaged Leonard with a brand of Prozac-Christian chatter he'd remembered growing up in this town. She seemed puzzled by the presence of the crew but soldiered into the house unfazed, jotting notes on her clipboard in the kitchen as a halo of fruit flies shrouded above her head. She was explaining the protocols of property value assessment when, through the open door, Leonard noticed several movers hauling the den recliner to the pickup bound for the landfill.

"What are you doing?" he said as he rushed down the porch steps.

"Mice got to it," one of the men said and tilted the recliner to reveal its chewed underbelly.

"It stays," Leonard said. "Put it in the storage truck."

Leonard didn't notice the minivan until it was steering into the driveway. He'd always known his plan would yield a confrontational moment, but he'd hoped that by taking a preemptive initiative to clear everything out of the house he could at least give his mother some distance from everything, somehow make the inevitable as painless as possible. All it took was the single-frame image of her face through the windshield's curved glass to realize that the idea had transitioned into failure. And yet he should've predicted it would end this way, because these were the conscripted moments he'd always been forced to endure. The rest of the world seemed indifferent to this injustice; there was just the milling work crew that now stood silent, a driveway dappled with soft patches of sunlight, long whispers from the wind-rustled leaves.

"Norman, there wasn't one piece of Native American earthenware at that flea market!" she said as she climbed out of the van. Her arms were laden with bags, and there was a slight unevenness to her gait. "Leonard! What are you doing home?"

It took her a moment to realize what was happening; Leonard watched her put it all together in slow motion. She stared with walleyed wonder at her son like a newborn seeing everything for the first time, offered a faint smile, a sort of cordial suspicion that reminded him of the adage that people reveal themselves through the smallest details. She wrinkled her nose when she noticed the fleet of vehicles, the beeline of men hauling furniture from the front door, and then the smile disappeared and she looked to her son again, this time with an expression that indicated she was on the verge of losing custody of her senses.

"Leonard, what did you do?" she screamed.

"This is a great opportunity, Mom."

"What did you do?" she repeated. Then she dropped her bags in the driveway and burst into tears.

It was an inauspicious start to the afternoon. They wasted an hour bickering in the driveway, a footless debate that soon boiled into low insults and screaming. Because he'd anticipated her opposition ahead of time, he began the dialogue by laying out, in a manner as dispassionately as possible, several key arguments he'd prepared on index cards at the motel the night before. He argued his mother's living conditions had produced effects that ran counter to the family's objective; that all familial units set goals based on the collective well-being, health, and happiness of its individual members, endeavors that require trust, a sort of political capital to be earned by each party involved. Justifying a continuation of their mother's hoarding while offsetting the effects it had on the household would necessitate an equal counteraction, a larger home, for example, or an annex added to their current one, neither of which they could afford. But doing so would run counter to the reason families—and, indeed, societies—adopt rules to begin with, so a third counteraction would then be required to reinstate a culture of equity while taking into account the family's preferential treatment of her. The idea was to persuade his mother to accept it was impossible for her sons to allow her to continue exhibiting behavior that was antithetical to the family's objective, regardless of how much quantifiable happiness it produced. The logical framework seemed sturdy to him, but he hadn't foreseen his mother's chosen argumentation, which was to avoid articulating her own position or even engage his individual points, and to instead take scenic paths around them, offering an onslaught of ad-hominems that, from what he could discern, centered on the notion that he was unkind and selfish and dishonest, and he'd displayed poor judgment in removing her property from her home without permission. Leonard referred her to the premise of his argument, at which point she broke away in a crying jag and fled into the house, where she locked herself in her bedroom and threatened to call the police. Speaking through the door from the hallway, Leonard reminded her that she'd transferred the title to him years ago because he'd been the one who'd paid the mortgage ever since she'd been laid off from the Goodyear plant. Another hour passed until she agreed to come outside—Norman insisted on piloting the discussion now—by which time the work crew had finished moving virtually everything into either U-Hauls or the trucks en route to the landfill.

The sun was setting by the time they managed to talk their mother into Leonard's rental car, and the family drove across town in a committed silence until the cupolas and colonial gables of the Mango Cove Lifestyle Community came into view. Crossing wrought-iron gates, Leonard marveled at the expanse of lawn that stretched into the distance, twin vine trellises that flanked the parking lot, a decorative garden windmill strangely islanded in the middle of a retention pond.

"Welcome to your new home," Leonard said. From the rearview, his mother sat sullenly in the back seat, arms crossed, staring into the headrest. "There's a swimming pool, you know."

Standing on the unit's portico porch, he made a show of dangling a new set of keys before unlocking the door. The condominium interior was austere, an open white space softened by faux-travertine floor tile and damask wallpaper in the hallway, a tasteful equipoise between decorative and orderly. A new home that smelled of fresh paint and sun. Leonard checked the bathroom and was pleased to discover it had marble counters and a stall shower fitted with rain glass.

"This is nice," Leonard said, flipping the lights on and off. "Honestly, I'm jealous."

He was sore and practically hallucinating from fatigue. All of the furniture had been delivered, but now the challenge of putting it away lay ahead. Their mother sat on the sofa, furious as her sons carted things into temporary homes. Thankfully, Norman discovered a radio and set it on the dresser, a means of breaking the palpable silence. A news program announced Sarah Palin's seventeen-year-old daughter was pregnant.

"I'm not staying here," their mother said.

"Negotiations are closed," Leonard said as he unfolded a duvet and draped it over the couch. He was disappointed to see moths flutter out of it.

"Spend all the money you want," she said. "I'm not staying in this apartment."

"You're staying. We discussed this months ago. I own the house, and you turned it into a sty after I repeatedly warned you." He paused, raked his fingers through his hair, pressed palms into his temples. "Your freedom isn't being taken away. There simply need to be certain modifications made to your lifestyle."

He paced the room, realized he wasn't done getting it out. "Your compulsive behavior has gotten to the point where you've compromised your safety. So, this is your home, and you'd better enjoy it, because it's all your doing."

She began to cry again, hysterically this time, a histrionic spectacle of falsetto keens and moans. There are mental filters, created either out of biological necessity or perhaps a simple fear of ridicule, that prevent most from divulging their entire menu of thoughts at any given moment. No such program existed with Leonard's mother; it was as though there was a tributary transporting an undistilled slag of commentary directly to her mouth, often flowing out before it could be codified into language. In times of crisis, she often sounded as though she were speaking in tongues.

"He's so mean to me. My oldest boy, he doesn't like me."

"Get it together," Leonard said.

"He kicks me out of my own home," she continued. "I don't know why he's so mean to me."

"Mean?" Leonard said. "Like leaving your kids in the car while you went shopping? Mean, like dropping us off at a church we didn't attend because a craft fair across town had a sale on Fabergé eggs? Mean, like those redneck kids who made fun of us when we couldn't afford lunch at school, because our mother spent every dime she owned on patio furniture at the goddamned Kmart? There's a reason we have a superficial relationship, and it isn't simply because your interests are superficial. You embarrass me. You've always embarrassed me."

"That isn't very nice, Leonard," his mother wailed.

"No, it isn't," Norman said.

He charged to the bathroom and turned on the taps. It was an unfortunate outburst, the worst part being his response suggested his motivations were founded in a deep sense of personal injury. True, he'd wanted her to bear some measure of guilt for everything, but now he was the one who felt guilty, and this was enough to make him furious all over again, because she'd been in the wrong, which meant all those old resentments got to keep taking up real estate, would keep boiling over in his mind. With the water still running, he opened the bathroom door and inched his way down the hall, where he listened to them in the adjacent room.

"I want him to leave," she said.

"I know. Believe me, I get it," Norman whispered. "Just one more day."

"I told you, he doesn't like me," she said. "He's never liked me."

Leonard returned to the motel that night. The next morning, he drove to a hardware store on Memorial Drive and made copies of the condominium keys before visiting the post office, where he filled out a change-of-address form. He called the electric company and the water company and the cable company, then he returned to the old house and resumed cleaning. There were still residual items scattered throughout, and it took him nearly an hour to haul it all to the curb. When he was finished, the rooms were bare, only four walls and the stale breadbox smells of an empty house erased of its history. That afternoon he met with the real estate agent. She was in her forties and looked like someone who owned a waterbed. She spoke with a rhotacized impediment, pronouncing every *r* like a *w*. She made giddy squeaking noises as she strode through the house, taking photos with a digital camera. She promised Leonard she could get a good price for the home; she repeated the phrase "great school district" at least six times.

Leonard signed a disclosure statement and was given a listing agreement that he folded and stuffed in his pocket.

He stopped at a grocery store on his way back through town and returned to Mango Cove as though nothing had happened the evening prior, and by late afternoon he and Norman had put together a respectable, albeit meager, abode. Leonard met one of his mother's new neighbors, a middle-aged man who resembled a walrus. The man was walking a German shepherd that appeared emaciated from malnutrition. He told Leonard he'd trained it to bite Black people.

That evening they went to a diner on Memorial Drive. It was the most normal restaurant he'd been to in months, completely absent of ironical flourishes, puce-colored counters, gas-station lighting, and a mirror-backed bar housing Heartland bric-a-brac, nothing about it suggesting anything other than what it was. They sat in a booth the color of smokers' teeth and consulted menus before a bouffant-haired woman took their order. She looked like she'd arrived straight from central casting, a mirror image of every diner waitress he'd ever seen: same clothes, same hair, same voice. An eternal fifty years old. The usual quiet settled over the family. Leonard ordered coffee.

He arranged his silverware as Norman reported trivial goings-on at his job. Several employees had been fired after developing a meth problem. Norman was also pretty sure one of the security guards was hooked on OxyContin. Another employee, who'd managed to clean up several months ago, was trying to regain custody of his daughter because the mother had remarried and the new husband, apparently like everyone else in town, was some variation of drug addict. Their mother turned her back to Leonard in the booth as she listened to her youngest son. They'd always been so chummy, these two, always whispering, always conspiring against him. Leonard watched as she surreptitiously lifted a stack of packets from the sugar caddy and slipped them into her bag.

"How's your job going?" Norman said.

"Funny you should ask," Leonard said into his coffee. "I quit. Just last week."

Their mother gasped, and her eyes widened, the mournful expression she'd worn lifting for the first time in days. Leonard watched his brother's face react to the news, the mustache twitching as he peeled a strip from the paper tablecloth and set to folding it with his fingers. Leonard sipped his coffee. It tasted like burned dirt.

"Great," Norman said. "Wonderful timing, Leonard. Why didn't you tell us?"

"Relax. I'll get another job. I've got several ideas."

"I don't understand," their mother said. "You just got promoted."

"So," Norman said, "what are your plans exactly?"

"Christ, all kinds of stuff. Do you have any idea how many PR gigs there are in that town? The market is booming."

Food arrived. Norman made stertorous breathing sounds through his mouth as he ate a congealed sheaf of meatloaf while Leonard watched their mother use a salad fork on her strip steak, the most expensive item on the menu, he'd noticed, which admittedly was still relatively cheap. His silverware had somehow become uneven again, and he leveled it with his palm. Things were always falling out of alignment when he wasn't looking, slipping out of their proper place and requiring adjustment.

"Were you even planning to tell us?" Norman said.

"Sure," Leonard said. "I just did, in fact."

"It doesn't make sense," Norman said. "Why now?"

"Let's just say I worked long hours for horrible people at a company where I was constantly reminded that my life and career were inseparable, even though I was never allowed to feel I was part of the culture, and thus felt divested from the work and took no pride in what I did."

"Sounds like every job I ever had," Norman said. "Couldn't your existential crisis have waited a few months, at least until we made the first rent payment on the condo you just forced our mother to move into?"

"So I quit my job. What do you care?"

"Because I'm beginning to think your concern for Mom's well-being is bound to the convenience of the situation at hand."

Leonard sighed. He sensed they were headed toward another internecine moment, and he didn't have the energy to argue. He flagged the waitress for the check.

"Leonard will find a way to get it worked out," their mother said. "He always does. He's resourceful."

It was a small gesture but a significant one, though it occurred to him it was exactly the sort of thing he'd say if he wanted to get something out of a client. Families always appeared different from afar, sturdy lacquered things ordered around a shared culture and purpose. In reality, an incredible amount of metaphysical landscaping was required to give the interior dysfunctions a presentable façade. He just felt uncomfortable sitting there, fulfilling his obligations to this domestic compact, and he longed for the ameliorative glow of the television, the dumb blue light of a documentary, a home-improvement show, an infomercial, anything to mute the false sense of fellowship these engagements imparted. Soon the waitress was back with their bill, and Leonard was up and heading for the register. He looked back and caught his mother, hunched over the booth, about to sneak a ketchup bottle into her handbag.

"Don't even think about it," he said.

HE COULDN'T SLEEP THAT NIGHT; A HOSTILE SILENCE THAT MADE HIS thoughts desperately loud seized the motel room. He rose from bed, peered out the window over a vacant parking lot, and watched the twisting lights of the overpass. Minutes later, he was dressed and walking to his rental car. Memorial Drive was deserted, and so was Main Street, where he came upon the ruins of once-familiar childhood haunts—the comic book shop, the music store, the ice cream parlor—now either vacant or boarded up. He tacked south, crossed the Hocking River, and drove past a neglected park and a factory that appeared to have been abandoned decades ago. The storage facility was located on a spare, grassless block between a recycling center and a liquor store. He crossed a lot littered with lottery tickets, found the unit, keyed in the security code, and lifted its steel gate, then flipped on the lights and crawled over a thicket of furniture until he was staring at the old recliner. He made a clearing and tipped the chair so its legs were facing him and felt a frisson of excitement as he knelt and examined its underbelly of springs before picking a stray tag of fabric and placing it in his mouth. A gentle vanilla note, unexpected but buttery and warm with a damp, rustic finish that put pops of color in his peripheral vision. The memories were a wild animal; something sewn into its corduroy skin seemed emancipated now by his roving tongue, a dim playback of holidays and cooking oil and furnace heat and dust, sun-blanched summers and the honey locust smells of afternoons spent on carpets threaded with stray tangles of hair. Snapshot moments recorded in time, secrets trapped like growth rings in a tree trunk, in the walls, the hot stable smells of an old recliner left to age in a basement den for decades. It tasted like home.

It was very late when he returned to the motel and chewed on antacid tablets as he flipped through TV channels. A study revealed eight in ten Americans never forgive retailers after a bad shopping experience. Research suggested affluent Caucasians reported the highest incidence of drug abuse in their youth, yet still achieved the most upward mobility. A celebrity had been kicked out of an upscale restaurant for refusing to remove her hat, a pink beanie bearing the name of a popular cancer charity. Apparently, social media was apoplectic with the news, and at least one famed food critic had suggested a citywide boycott of the establishment. Curious, Leonard powered on his laptop to witness the damage for himself. What was truly offensive, he decided as he clicked through several articles, was how obviously contrived the entire thing was: He could practically see the publicist's hand pulling the strings of TV theater to raise his client's media profile. He remembered the concept Patty had shared with him the week before, a crisis management firm that deliberately manufactures false outrage as a means of promulgating a brand into the national conversation. She'd been correct in a complicated way: It was alarming, the things people elected to be offended about nowadays; it was as though simply being aggrieved automatically adjudicated one's opinions as worthy of being taken seriously. Returning to the TV, he mused over the circus stupidity of it, how the media manipulated the bovine masses' capacity for outrage as a means of peddling entertainment masquerading as news. He let the notion turn over in his mind, and then the idea arrived, came upon him like a tackle in the dark. He dashed out of bed and turned on the lights and set to work on his index cards, and, as the hours passed and the sun rose, he felt truly alive for the first time in a long time, maybe for the first time ever, because even though he wasn't exactly sure how he was going to pull this off, he knew he was going to make a killing.

THE FOLLOWING TUESDAY, LEONARD WALKED A PHENOTYPICALLY FILTHY stretch of Hell's Kitchen that reeked of sewage and rotting fish. He entered an inconspicuous Italian restaurant, retrieved several antacids from his pocket, and scanned a narrow dining room, waiting for his eyes to adjust. Wood cladding floors, obligatory paintings of quaint Tuscan villas encircled by olive trees. A squadron of ceiling fans turned lazily above him. At a small table in the back, he spotted Dennis Taufield, Senior Vice President of Indianapolis-based retailer Value Barn. He was a large man with jowls that hung loosely over his collar. Cellphone aloft, it cast a crescent moon of absinthe light over the left side of his face.

"Been a minute." Taufield stood to shake hands. He had a castrato voice that didn't match his body, and one of those indeterminable accents that sounded southern by default. "Here, I ordered a sandwich," he said and handed Leonard a menu.

"Already ate," Leonard said and sat. A *Wall Street Journal* on the table read: "AIG, Lehman Shock Hits World Markets." Leonard's napkin was creased, and he tried flattening it with his palm, then straightened his silverware, setting the fork, knife, and spoon in picket-fence sequence before rearranging them. "I was surprised to hear from you."

"I'm in town for a conference, fly back Monday," Taufield said. "So, Gurney's crisis wunderkind has decided to hang out a shingle. You've got to open the kimono here. Are we talking greener pastures, or did something bad go down?"

"It's a long story," Leonard said.

"I'm guessing Pinnacle's buyout had something to do with it?"

"No comment."

"Their loss," Taufield said.

A waiter arrived and offered detailed descriptions of the specials before Leonard waved him away with the menu. Then the men stared at the TV above the bar. The news repeated the day's top story, that Barclays had pulled out of a last-minute rescue of Lehman Brothers, forcing the company to file for bankruptcy. A panel of pundits offered the typical wash-and-wear commentary as the screen replayed images of employees leaving offices with boxes in their hands. Many of them were in tears.

"The world as we know it is over," Taufield said.

"They'll bounce back, just like they did after the last crash," Leonard said.

"Hell of a time to start a new venture," Taufield said.

"I guess I'd argue the reputation business is recession-proof."

Taufield's phone buzzed, and he commenced tapping on it. Then he set the phone down and draped his napkin over his plate.

"This new shop of yours. Don't know if you remember why we hired you the first time. Our former VP, the drunk?"

"How could I forget?" Leonard said. "He used to borrow his son's pizza-delivery sign before he hit the bars because he thought driving with it kept the cops from pulling him over."

"Well, here I am again."

"Here you are again."

"Ready to buy the same horse twice," the man said.

"But your reputation isn't in trouble this time."

"What reputation? Our competition has left us in the dust, and we don't have a customer under the age of sixty."

"My mom shops there all the time," Leonard said. "To your point, I suppose."

"They say failing to plan is planning to fail, but we've spent everything we have on marketing retainers. Rebranding, promotions, even this social media stuff. Nothing takes. We haven't been able to achieve relevance with the younger demographic, and our core audience is shrinking. We're a dying brand."

"You're a victim of circumstance," Leonard said. "Shopping habits have changed, and there've been seismic shifts in how media is consumed. Here's the thing: I think we can embrace that disruption and offer a narrative that functions as a comment on these strange times in which we live."

"What do you suggest?"

"Remember last year when that actor did all those TV spots in Japan, the ones where he wore blackface?" Leonard said. "The country lost its mind when we caught wind of it stateside, but he never said anything. No press conference, no apology, no walk of shame, nothing. He didn't even hire PR counsel. Then there was that comedian who hosted the Academy Awards earlier this year. Made all those misogynistic jokes? He never apologized either. In fact, he went on social media the next day and made even more of a pig of himself. A week later, we forgot about it. We simply moved on."

"I don't see where you're going."

"What if we initiated a visibility campaign that made today's audiences do your brand outreach work for you? What if we fabricated a story, an apocryphal controversy, something outrageous, that makes your brand go viral?"

"Don't follow. A story?"

"We deliberately expose you to some salacious crisis situation, and then we mitigate impact by simultaneously developing a response strategy. We provoke, then we engage. And we'll do it over every top-tier media outlet in the country, outlets that were previously unwilling to give your brand coverage."

"Let me get this straight. You want to ruin our reputation so people will pay attention to us?"

"Not *ruin*. The key is to make sure the offense doesn't permanently stick. Ideally, the transgression should be banal enough that your reputation recuperates quickly, and one your target base sympathizes with. In a few weeks, everyone will forget about it, and the company recuperates, but the masses remember the brand."

"But you want to make people hate us?"

"I like to say we're taking advantage of a toxic media environment that cares more about clicks than content, and a voyeuristic mob of embittered consumers whose narcissistic appetite for scandal is a temporary salve for their own personal shortcomings."

"It's incredibly cynical."

"You watch the same TV I do? We live in cynical times."

The man was silent, appeared to be listening for something. "I've never heard of anything like this before," he said.

"That's because I invented it."

Chapter 15

On September 16, 2008, the CEO of closeout retailer Value Barn strolled into an Indianapolis-area Applebee's, sat at the bar, and lit a cigarette. City council had passed a much-maligned—and excessively publicized—ordinance banning smoking from restaurants the month prior, a fact on which the bartender reproved him as she slapped an ashtray on the Formica. To the patrons' incredulity, he continued puffing away, ignored the bartender's repeated demands to leave, and ended up smoking halfway through a pack by the time police arrived. Leonard had prepared several dozen phony letters to the editor of that city's weekly paper in an attempt to simulate grassroots support, names he'd pilfered from area Myspace accounts, but it turned out that step was unnecessary: The CEO's arrest bypassed the crime blotter and went straight to the *Indianapolis Star*'s front page the next morning. By six o'clock, each of the local news affiliates had dedicated airtime to the story. The news spread across social media channels, smokers'-rights advocacy groups began touting the executive as a hero, and, by the end of the first week, senior management reported foot traffic in Value Barn's four hundred brick-and-mortar stores had averaged a twenty percent increase, the highest in six years. And with that successful execution of his first client campaign, the Appetite Factory officially opened for business.

Tapping into the nation's outrage reserves, Leonard created bogus crises for his clients by making them say or do idiotic things, then unmasked them with anonymous scoops to a scandal-hungry press who predictably penned histrionic headlines that manipulated the public's capacity to judge in exchange for clicks, baiting readers to share, post, and hurl abuse at these moral transgressors over the internet, which Leonard used to raise brands' national profile.

Finding business wasn't easy. He scoured the web and compiled lists of public and private companies whose bottom lines had been affected by lack of visibility, cast a wide net to identify dying brands by consulting surveys such as Harris Poll's Reputation Quotient, which ranked consumer awareness of hundreds of U.S. companies, diagnosed the cause of their misfortunes, issued a corresponding outrage narrative, and assembled enough pitches to grace the desk of every corporate communication director in Midtown. He spent his mornings on the phone in his apartment, afternoons with clients at restaurants, nights compiling lists. He worked all hours, discovered a reservoir of energy he hadn't known he had, solved problems in his sleep. By the end of the second week, he'd managed to sign three additional retainers.

Crisis: When the owner of a Miami-based fashion PR firm was busted at a South Beach nightclub in possession of 400 mg of cocaine (Florida's highest possession limit below a felony charge), a media relations campaign tipped off the gossip blogs and celebrity-news outlets to the arrest. Local nightlife circles began buzzing over the publicist's newfound national notoriety, resulting in the agency's retainer of three new clients within days of the owner's release from jail. *Crisis:* A century-old bourbon company suffering a decline in sales announced it intended to dilute its signature single-barrel bourbon as a cost-saving measure. Outrage among the brand's loyalists predictably ensued, with thousands threatening to boycott the distiller. Once the press got hold of the story, the company immediately retracted the apocryphal announcement and vowed to keep the original recipe. *Crisis:* A local storage company kicked off a transit-focused marketing campaign, placing a series of controversially worded advertisements in the city's buses and subway system supporting a state ballot proposition that would legalize same-sex marriage. From his apartment, Leonard called in angry complaints to the Metropolitan Transit Authority detailing how offensive the ads were, even hiring a crew to vandalize the placements on several subway lines. After two weeks, the MTA told the client it was canceling its contract and returning the storage company's money. Leonard then sent out press releases denouncing the MTA's censorship of a company that supported gay rights, providing storyline steroids to the media.

It wasn't like his old job, where client retainers came as the result of a request for proposal or an announcement in one of the trades. Finding work was purely a numbers game: no leads, no contacts, only the dim prospect of pitching strangers a service they'd never heard of and convincing them how they could benefit from a communications strategy that, frankly, sounded ludicrous. He was laughed at or hung up on more times than he cared to count, the retainers were scarce, and it was only an uphill climb once they'd signed the dotted line; his objective thereafter was basically to scam the press for free media impressions by tipping them off to news that had been entirely staged. Still, being in the trenches like that, placing his bets against impossible odds, made the chance of a client win that much more rewarding. It had taken years, but somehow, through the intricacies of fate, he was finally doing what he'd always wanted to do, making a living his way.

Soon the pragmatic concerns began to set in. There was something about second chances, the idea of being on the upswing after a recent defeat, that made you take inventory of the warehouse, in the habits that had set you back to begin with. His work had always consumed him; he'd never had the luxury of a social life or the simple recreations of a drinking problem or an addiction to online gambling. Still, the one comfort he'd allowed himself would have to be reined in if he wanted to stay the course with his newfound progress. So, he cut it all out: the soaps, the shampoos, the spoons of detergent, the pencils and scented candles and stray bits of carpet and paper and everything else. He climbed on the wagon, made a dogged, determined effort to abstain from the destructive habits that had come so close to derailing his career all those months ago. He purged the apartment of toiletries and cleaning supplies and faced a white-knuckle crisis, endured long colorless days broken up by tasteless meals and the monotony of work. Sleep was an ever-present challenge, and when it arrived, he was beset by nightmares. More often than not, he lost himself in the only task that kept the anxiety at bay, pegging away from strategy to strategy, campaign to campaign, job to job. After a week of crushing pressure, he eventually felt a subtle lifting, the gentle high he imagined one experienced after detoxing from a narcotic. The seas calmed, and he faced a clear horizon, the wind at his back, everything flattened out before him. Still, no matter what internal resources he marshaled, he broke into a sweat every time he saw a box of detergent on a store shelf or chanced upon the fragrant, turned-field smells of wood soap in a restaurant. These temptations sang out to him from impossible distances, but he told himself they were an unfortunate feature of the undertaking of going cold-turkey, and that the urges would dissipate with time.

HE LEAPED OVER PUDDLES AS HE DASHED UP THE SIDEWALK IN THE WINDspun rain. It was almost October now, and it had poured relentlessly for the past three days, the gutters clogged and overflowing, streets made churning rivers. His umbrella had fallen apart several minutes before, leaving exposed steel ribs that resembled a cat-o'-nine-tails in his hand, so he threw it into a trash can and charged blindly through the crowd with his jacket over his head until he reached Grand Central. He crossed under the network of archways that led to the station's lower concourse, took the escalator to a basement food court, where, after toweling off in the men's room, he found Todd Armitage straddling a chair beneath a television, which replayed highlights from the McCain/Obama debate the night before.

Armitage sipped a bottle of beer not-so-conspicuously wrapped in a paper bag. His hair had grown out, and he looked like he'd gained a few pounds, wore a wool ash cardigan and a ridiculous pair of moccasin slip-ons.

"You look like you sell inner peace for a living," Leonard said. "How are things at Pollard?"

"My colleagues are nice. There are the usual toadstools, I guess, but it's not like how things were at Gurney. Don't take it personal, but the whole culture over there, those guys, I don't know. Anyway, from what I heard about the buyout, it sounds like we got out just in time."

"What's the verdict on food PR?"

"What can I say, the market hasn't been kind. Folks aren't going out to eat anymore. Everything has a value message. There's even this generic packaging trend, because if something looks too expensive no one will buy it. Forget about influencers and celeb endorsements. Publicity is the last thing on people's minds."

"The casino has shut down. Exhibit A," Leonard said and gestured to the television. A news crawl overlay on the bottom of the screen reported the House was voting on a seven-billion-dollar cash-for-trash rescue bailout package that would buy up bad assets from investment banks in an attempt to stop a collapse of the nation's financial system.

"So, my first job out of college was at this mortgage brokerage in Queens," Armitage said. "We sold home equity loans to people with bad credit, usually through phone calls using sucker lists. One of our most common mailers was these draft loan checks, which basically coaxed homeowners with cash if they refinanced or took out a second mortgage. Of course, if they didn't have money problems, we persuaded them to buy a car, take a vacation, etcetera."

He fidgeted in his seat, the track lighting winking in his frameless glasses. "These loans weren't just subprime; what we were doing was predatory. A huge portion of our outreach was with the elderly, widows especially, and virtually all of it was in Black or Hispanic neighborhoods. Our borrowers had low incomes, poor credit histories, no assets. Interest rates were the lowest they'd been in forty years, but the mortgages they qualified for were double-digits. Of course, the rates weren't adjustable, the loan-to-value ratios were ridiculous, the terms were filled with these unjustifiable fees and stipulations, and the monthly payments were so low it was impossible for anyone to repay the loans in their lifetime. We were locking people into impossible terms and destroying what little equity they had, steering them toward foreclosure with no legal recourse. And it was the easiest gig in the world," Armitage said. "So, I guess I wasn't surprised by what happened on Wall Street. Honestly, I've been waiting for the other shoe to drop for seven years."

His eyes flitted. The TV went to commercial, but his gaze stayed with it. "Anyway, I'm here, so I'm obviously intrigued. But what you said over the phone didn't make sense."

"Think of it this way," Leonard said. "Public relations is a problem-solving endeavor, right? What if it was problem-creating instead?"

"I don't follow."

"We're a culture addicted to moral outrage," Leonard said. "The practice of online shaming has revealed this weird tribalism that demands we throw a new victim into the volcano each week to keep ourselves entertained. What if there was a crisis management practice that deliberately manufactured controversy as a means of elevating brands into the national conversation?"

Todd paused. "Honestly, it screams proof of concept. No offense, there's just not much of a Venn diagram overlap between new ideas and services people are willing to pay for."

"Consider this. We count on a public reaction to our campaigns, right? Problem is, we have to deal with demanding clients and fair-weather journalists who have fundamentally different goals from our own. Thankfully, the media cycle has been disrupted. Reporters can't break the news as fast as a couple of kids on a computer. Journalists are desperate, and for the first time they're a shoo-in, because we're offering an exclusive they can't refuse. All we have to do is create a controlled burn; we persuade the client to do something controversial, based, of course, on a script we write, then we leak it to the media and let the masses gather with their pitchforks and respond with an apology we've already crafted. The story dies in a few weeks, and the client recovers like they always do, but brand recognition remains."

"But why would a client agree to something like that? Companies hate controversy."

"Because they know scandal always trends. Because some of them will do anything to get noticed. You saw it yourself. The opportunity cost is worth it if it means millions in free media impressions. Best of all: no middle management, no corporate hierarchies, no more shoveling shit. It's just us, in the toolshed, doing what we do."

"I appreciate you thinking of me, but, to be honest, I don't know if it's the right fit. I can't just quit my job. Not in this economy."

"That's why I'm offering you a new job," Leonard said. He rapped his fingers against the table. "Let's say we take your current salary and add twenty percent."

"Slow down," Armitage said. "How many clients do you even have?"

"Four. But word's getting around."

"Are you kidding? You've retained four clients, and you think you can pay me almost a hundred grand a year? What if it doesn't work out?"

"For decades our line of work has been poisoned by gray-haired men who've clung onto outdated textbook ideas. Ironic, if you think about it: We're supposed to be the ones who come up with new ways of communicating. And now we finally are. I just cleared ten grand in billing in the last week, all by myself, out of my apartment. Imagine how good business will be once the economy picks up. We're navigating uncharted territory here. This is PR where there is no playbook."

"You might want to pull that cart behind the horse, Leonard. At least the work we did came from a client's need to share their side of the story. You're just trolling people. Besides, what am I going to do, schlep over to your apartment every morning?"

"We'll get an office. We'll hire staff. I'm thinking about bringing Jack on board."

"Jack Gurney? Isn't he a little long in the tooth?"

"Jack's seen it all twice. He's got capital and knows how to start a business." Leonard began to whisper, though he wasn't sure why. "I think he's being held incommunicado. His daughter Lila, I think she's taking his money. She's been pushing this narrative that Jack has dementia."

"How do you know she's not telling the truth? I heard he dropped trou in the office last month, was fending off staff with a ruler?"

"They fired him from his own company. You'd be upset too. Cards on the table, you in or not?"

Armitage took a pull from the bottle and set it on the floor. "It's either a brilliant or utterly crackpot idea. I don't know. Can I think about it?"

"I'll give you a week," Leonard said and stood. "Then I'm taking out help-wanted ads."

"I still don't get it. How do you even find these people?"

"The clients? They're everywhere. Turns out we're all dealing with a crisis in some form or other."

"One more thing," Armitage said. "The Appetite Factory. How'd you come up with that name, anyway?"

"This person I know," Leonard began. "It's a long story."

HE RODE IN A GYPSY CAB ALONG FDR DRIVE THE FOLLOWING AFTERNOON. A promontory of rust-colored buildings rose from the north as they meandered through the capricious movements of traffic, jettying out beyond the roadway and steel quays that notched the spine of shoreline spanning the river. The air chilled and fragrant with the saffron smells of autumn, a confetti of dead leaves and discarded bodega bags danced between vehicles as bands of sunlight fell from the clouds and alighted on gray, shivering waters.

His phone vibrated and he scrutinized the screen. "I'm on my way to a meeting," Leonard said. "Give me the bad news first."

"Unfortunately, the appraisal was . . . disappointing," the Lanchester real estate agent said. "I can fax you everything tonight, but the long and short is they have the property valued at ninety."

"Ninety? As in thousand?"

"This isn't Manhattan, Mr. Lundell. We've got three bedrooms, one bath, seventeen hundred total square feet, and just about every foot of it needs some sort of work. The appraisal showed signs of mold damage."

"Where?"

She paused. "Everywhere. There are several upsides, though. The attached garage, for one. And the lot, which is nearly three thousand square feet. Buyers find that very attractive. Also, it's a good school district."

"What are we looking at?"

"Considering the market, considering the economy, considering the state of the property, I think we need to list this as a project buy, a fixer-upper. Price it to sell at eighty-five and see how people respond."

"That's awfully low."

"Have you watched TV in the last two weeks? This isn't exactly a seller's market. If you want to close quickly, adjusting the price is a good start. The other option is to make repairs and get the house reappraised in a year. People are bound to start buying again—"

"We need to sell now. Put it on the market at eighty-five. But that's as low as we go."

He directed the cab to the curb a block before Jack's townhouse. Lila's gallery event was scheduled to begin in less than an hour; still, he waited on the sidewalk for twenty minutes to make sure he wouldn't run into her, huddling among several trash cans that looked like someone had beaten them with a baseball bat. Soon a copper-colored burn hung where the sun had been, and then soft squares of light began winking on in the windows along the block.

A tired-looking woman with a gray-fringed hairline answered the door. The housekeeper; Leonard remembered her from a holiday party Jack had hosted five or six years before. Several minutes of whispered haggling ensued before Leonard rested a hundred-dollar bill on the door chain.

"She's going to fire me, sir," the woman said. "If Miss Gurney finds out you've been here, she'll call the police."

"Just a few minutes, I promise. Ten minutes, tops," he said as the door closed. "Five minutes." He felt a wave of relief when he heard the chain slide off the lock.

He stole up the stairs and began opening doors, discovered a white tile bathroom outfitted with a vessel sink and apothecary shelving, a guest bedroom with rose-colored linens and a wicker bar cart serving as a nightstand. The floorboards complained as he padded down the hall until he came upon an expansive master, Jack's room, outfitted in the sort of sartorial refinement one finds in living quarters belonging to retirees: an airy space with wainscoted walls and gray brocade curtains and a four-poster bed fitted with plum-colored throw pillows. From a door near the stairs, Leonard heard the ring of a hammer. A gilt of light ran under the door, and he opened it to find Jack Gurney on the floor, screwing together slats of a pressboard bookshelf.

Apparently, the books the old man had been hoarding at the Gurney office had been returned. The walls were lined floor to ceiling with shelves, each crammed with tented spines, many so old their bindings had peeled back like dry garlic skin. Several shelves lay unassembled in a corner among precariously stacked piles of books.

"Young man," Jack said from the floor. He looked unmanageably thin, as though he was disappearing inside himself. He still wore his trademark navy jacket, polo shirt, and slacks, all slightly too big for his shrunken frame. A dime-sized portion of his nose appeared discolored, a mark Leonard had never noticed before.

"It's great to see you," Leonard said as he approached him. The man stalled and looked up apprehensively, a vacancy behind his eyes. "I guess you finally got your library back."

"Yes, sir! Take a gander." Jack toddled toward one of the completed shelves. "It's all here, everything separated into categories. This shelf is dedicated to ethics and investor relations, that shelf has corporate communications, and here's crisis," he said. "We have books on marketing, publicity, media relations, college textbooks, directories from the PR Society, the National Investor Relations Institute—"

"How many books do you figure you have now?"

"Nine hundred and thirty-three. More than a hundred have public relations in the title, almost forty have marketing in the title, and about three dozen mention publicity."

"Impressive." Leonard fondled one of the spines, and yellowed crumbs flecked off in his fingers. He scrutinized the shelf more closely, noticed a Michael Crichton novel among the collection, and then several phone books. "I was worried," he said. "No one's heard from you. I thought you'd been locked up in here."

"Not locked up." He bent over and began hoisting up a finished bookcase. "Little help?"

They walked the bookcase to the far wall, and then Jack began alphabetizing one of the stacks on the floor.

"So, Lila's letting you do this?" Leonard said.

"Are you kidding? She bought the bookcases," Jack said. He began to file volumes on a shelf, then returned to the stacks. "I'm telling you, these are some of the best books on the industry you've never read. The newcomers to this business, these kids graduating with communications degrees, they have no idea. *Always Live Better Than Your Clients*, without a doubt the best bio of Sonnenberg ever written," he said and waved a book. "*The Power House* by Susan Trento, an essential source on lobbying. *You're Too Kind: A Brief History of Flattery* by Richard Stengel. I'm thinking about hitting up the universities. We can invite students in to browse. My plan is we won't charge anyone for the first visit. Of course, you have to pay if you want to take something out on loan—"

"Jack, I didn't come here to socialize. I wanted to talk shop. I wanted to tell you I've opened my own agency."

A long stretch of silence. The old man turned and straightened a shelf. "I think we need to build a seating area," Jack said as he looked around. "Get some chairs, a reading table and one of those banker's lamps, maybe that Wi-Fi everyone's telling me about."

"Think of my new shop as an experiment into the power of irrational behavior," Leonard said. "See, everyone on the internet is offended all the time—"

"*Merchant Princes* by Leon Harris," Jack said as he returned to the stacks. "A classic!"

"This is an entirely new algorithm, Jack. I'm looking at office spaces right now, and Todd Armitage is in."

"Always liked him," Jack said. "Pretty wife."

"That's Todd Shillenburg," Leonard said. "This is a new beginning, and I need staff that can build intellectual capital. I want you to be part of it."

"Oh?"

"We're going to get even with those bastards."

"I don't know what you mean," he said.

"Roger and Wanda. Those clowns at Pinnacle. We're back in business, your business. I'm making you partner, Jack. You're going to be back on top. All we need is a little starter capital, something to get us out the gate, and it'll be just like before, like you never left—"

"I'm sorry. I don't know what you're talking about," Jack said. "Left what?"

"You ran a public relations agency for forty years."

The old man wouldn't hold Leonard's gaze. He kept picking up random books, scrutinizing their spines, rearranging books on the floor. Leonard could tell he was uncomfortable, and this conversation was exhausting him, and that maybe he'd wanted to say something but lacked a social commitment to do so.

"Sorry," Jack finally said. "What did you say your name was?"

LEONARD PLODDED DOWN THE SIDEWALK IN A DAZE, THREADED IN AND out of traffic. The sky had darkened as another storm came in, and as bands of rain pounded at the streets and every surface between, the scattering world blurred into mosaic blots of color, as though he were looking at everything through shower glass. He lowered his head and let the rain batter him as he continued with slow, furtive steps, gripping his jacket and steeling himself from the chill. Several blocks later, he entered a subway station on Lexington and boarded the train, where hunger gnawed inside him.

Back in his apartment, he opened the cabinet under the sink and clawed for the libations awaiting him. He was so hungry he could chew off his eyebrows, and the certainty of his trove being there mollified him, set him licking his palms in anticipation. After scattering everything onto the kitchen floor, he remembered he'd purged the cabinet as part of his recent pledge and sank supine onto the tile, grinding his teeth as he listened to the murmuring rain. He chanced to look into his living room, where, in the aquarium, his favorite yellow fish was bobbing belly-up on the water's surface. He crossed the room and peered into the tank, blew on the water in a futile attempt to revive the fish, then stood there for a moment and watched its lifeless fins sway as an arresting sadness welled inside him. Eventually, he retrieved a net from the closet and scooped the fish out of the tank. Then he cradled it on a bed of paper towels and placed it in the trash.

HOW HAD IT BEGUN, EXACTLY? HE'D NEEDED A JOB. EVENTUALLY, AGAINST all odds—and by lying, of course, and through his regular program of chicanery, an apocryphal résumé filled with professional experience he'd never earned and references that didn't exist—he'd found a position for which he was unqualified and which he hadn't deserved. Along the way, there had been setbacks, watersheds, all the superficial mile markers that demarcate a career, a life boxed into tiny squares. Time rambled on. Moving through those shadowy years wasn't unlike sitting in an unmoored boat: If you neglected to look back occasionally, you might forget how you'd drifted to where you were. How tragic that the human mind wasn't engineered to understand history, that our knowledge of the past was always changing, retrofitted to accommodate our current perceptions of it. That we were unreliable narrators of our own experiences.

And so here he was, performing carnal exorcisms in the dark with a mystery woman who smelled like fresh melon and was always forgetting his name. He wondered how many hours he'd logged down here over the years, in the warm waters of a darkened room beneath the rumble of the city, seeking company and conversation from someone whose manual talents smoothed out the world's rough edges, annealed the internal stresses that came with navigating the fog of consciousness. His thoughts lapsed as she switched positions and did something different with her hands, and soon an image of bobby socks came to him, as it often did during these moments, and he clapped his hand to his mouth as he felt a shudder, saw an electric flash behind his eyelids.

"All finished," the woman said.

Leonard remained on the massage table, contemplating the grueling prospect of rejoining the outside world. "I was wondering," he stuttered. "If you aren't doing anything Saturday. There's this place on Prince Street. Great sushi?"

"I'm working," she said as she wiped her hands.

Eventually he climbed off the table, dressed, parted the beaded curtains, and navigated a dark hall, palming walls that thrummed with sounds from the adjoining rooms. At the reception desk, a young woman stood before a panel of backlit glass, spoke with a droll voice into a cellphone as she absently slid two envelopes across the counter into which Leonard stuffed bills: the first envelope going to the house, the second a tip for the woman in the room. She shuffled over to a small closet, bent over and gathered a stack of towels, then turned her head as Leonard's eyes caught the half-moons of an ass peeking out from beneath her skirt. She smiled, sat on the edge of the table, and continued her conversation as she commenced doing long division with her legs.

"I told you, you can't talk on the phone at work," the proprietor said as she stepped into the room. She pushed past the girl, slapped a ring of keys and what appeared to be a stack of résumés on the reception desk. It was strange, he thought, how much this place operated like a business. He quickly realized how idiotic the supposition was that it could be anything else.

"Hello, Mr. Leonard," the woman said.

"Hello, Ajumma," he said and headed for the door. To his surprise, she followed him outside, lit a cigarette, and shook the pack at him.

"So, what do you think?" she said.

"About what?"

"Don't play dumb. The new girl you were gawking at. You're a business-man. Is she company material or what?"

"She's young," Leonard said after some deliberation. "Probably forming an identity for the first time. Maybe not very receptive to the concept of work? I don't know. I'm guessing annual evaluations aren't something you do."

The woman sighed. "I can't keep quality staff. I think I've hired every failed waitress in the city at some point. It's a burden, on top of everything else that's going on."

"Why, what's that?" he said.

"The landlords want us out because they say we're the reason they can't rent the place next door."

"No kidding," Leonard said. Just then two men stepped into the business with guilty faces. Ajumma stubbed her cigarette out on the pavement and was halfway through the door when a thought occurred to him. "Hey, how much do they want?"

THE FOLLOWING WEEK, TODD ARMITAGE AND LEONARD MET A REAL ES-tate agent on a crowded Koreatown block. He was a small man with a shaved head revealing outlines of male-pattern baldness and an aquiline nose that looked like it belonged to a buzzard. His left arm didn't extend past the elbow, the apparent result of a birth defect. In its place were several pink half-developed thumb-like digits that resembled a mole's paw.

The man led them to a narrow building sandwiched between a law of-fice and a restaurant. A single door from the street brought them into a narrow foyer, which accessed two units inside. He opened the door on the right and ushered the men into a small space that smelled like plaster dust and radiator heat. The walls were riddled with an acupuncture work of pushpins alongside several sun-bleached maps of Queens and Brooklyn. In a windowless second room, separated behind a partition of frosted glass, hunter-green walls were adorned with an assortment of travel destination posters, inspirational aphorisms, and a framed diploma in hotel management from the University of Long Island.

"Looks like the last tenants got out in a hurry," Todd said.

"This is perfect for a small office," the man said. "And you're in walking distance to Penn Station, Times Square, a stone's throw from every amenity Midtown has to offer."

"Seventeen hundred a month," Leonard mused. A pipe rattled above him. On the far side of the room, he noticed an aluminum roaster pan on the floor, presumably used to catch ceiling leaks. "I've never seen anything so low, especially in this part of town."

"The bargain of all bargains," the man said. "It's an unorthodox setup, sharing an entrance with the neighboring tenants, but it's a minor drawback when considering the value."

"It's okay, I guess," Todd said as he opened a closet. "The lighting is terrible."

From the foyer, the door of the adjacent business opened, flooding the entrance with chartreuse light as a woman in a denim skirt stepped out. She peeked into the office, winked, and flashed a smile. Leonard blanched.

"What's next door?" Todd whispered.

"A spa," the real estate agent said after some deliberation. "Nice people. And as it turns out, their busy time is evenings, after I imagine you'd be gone for the day."

"Actually, the lighting's fine," Leonard said and toggled a switch for the overheads.

"Can I speak with you a moment?" Todd said. He gripped Leonard's sleeve and ushered him into the foyer. A middle-aged man in a suit exited the other door and stumbled hurriedly into the street with his head down.

"It's a whorehouse," Todd whispered. "The business next door is a goddamn whorehouse."

"I don't care what it is. You can't find a studio apartment in town for this price."

"That's because other people don't have to share a front door with prostitutes," Todd said. "Look, I quit my agency job because it dawned on me that the work we do is basically born out of contempt, and if I'm going to inveigle people to buy more worthless products they don't need, I'd rather do it without participating in monthly media mixers or listening to idiotic word salad about 'creatives' and 'thought leadership.' So, I'm in. But we can't bring clients to a place like this. It's not professional."

"This is all we can afford right now. Ever since I found out Jack won't be backing us, we've had to cut down our budget. Besides, have you seen our client list? Do you really think they'll be in any position to cast judgment?"

The real estate agent shuffled into the foyer. "Is everything all right?" the man asked.

"It's perfect," Leonard said. "We'll take it."

Chapter 16

They started working before the furniture arrived, hung a dry-erase board on the wall and brainstormed ideas as the paint dried. Each morning they rattled off ideas and mulled over pitching tactics and potential outreach targets. Then one of them hit the phones while the other wrote copy. Afternoons were reserved for client meetings. They worked late nights and weekends, outlining strategies, devising new ways to feed the media's outrage machine. Several weeks went by, and slowly they built their client roster.

Crisis: On its Facebook page, a national sporting-goods store vocalized its support of a bipartisan anti-trafficking bill protecting the children of illegal immigrants, which was expected to be signed by President Bush. The Appetite Factory created dozens of fake Facebook accounts and posted scores of racist statements from those accounts on the retailer's page. The company then launched a response statement extolling the virtues of a nation that values cultural inclusivity, which was forwarded to the national press. Several days later, the Appetite Factory hired a live events group to organize a flash mob of immigrant children on the National Mall, lauding the retailer's support of the measure (Follow-up media pitch: "Six reasons to love this company. Number four will make you cry!"). *Crisis:* A regional chain of sports bars leaked an apocryphal company policy memorandum detailing a "code of conduct" required of employees, which mandated that waitresses wear revealing clothing and affect a demure manner when serving male patrons. The Appetite Factory pitched the blogs with a baiting email subject line: "This is outrageous! I'm offended, and it's not okay!" News of the story, which migrated to the network outlets within days, provoked the usual reader indignation while rallying the business's existing customer base. *Crisis:* An up-and-coming Manhattan restaurant was attacked by an anonymous customer who slammed the business in an online review site, citing the chef/owner's policy of refusing dish-ingredient-change requests. That "review" had been entirely fabricated, of course, penned by the Appetite Factory as a springboard for a promotional messaging opportunity. The chef responded to the review with a sprawling rant on the restaurant's website, claiming a culture of entitled patrons had forced professionals in the culinary industry to compromise their craft (Press release headline: "Someone attacked a local business online. You won't believe what happened next!").

The majority of their core clientele consisted of the expected: fledgling companies or failing brands seeking to innovate themselves out of a death spiral. As word of the Appetite Factory spread, however, they were approached by a new league of patrons: people with too much money on their hands who wanted to become famous. A hedge fund manager contacted them about a series of online videos he'd produced detailing how vaccines cause autism. The scion of a wealthy real estate developer ran a website that she said proved Barack Obama wasn't a natural-born U.S. citizen. It was the kind of work they usually found themselves turning down, but these experiences provided a rare glimpse behind the curtain. Leonard was dumbstruck by the discovery that there were otherwise successful, by-all-accounts well-balanced people in the world who were willing to ruin their reputations and careers in exchange for some attention. As it turned out, there were scores of prospective clients out there, untold millions waiting to distort and re-create reality to escape the lives they'd been forced to endure.

THE RETAINERS GREW, TO THE POINT THAT THE WORK BECAME TOO MUCH for two people to handle. Between finding clients, pitching clients, writing copy, hosting meetings, pitching the press, and tallying media impressions, there either weren't enough hours in the day to commit to the basic

responsibilities of operational upkeep, or they simply forgot. Calls went un-
answered. A pile of bills gathered on the front desk. They neglected to mail
invoices, or take checks to the bank, or add deposits and payroll into the
accounting program. As it turned out, running a business was hard work, a
mildly irritating endeavor on a good day, laden with so many trivial mana-
gerial chores that Leonard felt they could never catch up. When they accidentally double-booked a meeting, they decided something had to be done.

"We need help," Leonard said as a telephone technician tucked wires
into drop-ceiling tiles above them. "This is more work than we're used to."

They had to rewire the office with new Ethernet cables, so he'd called an
IT company the week before. As it turned out, the phone terminal needed
to be replaced too, so he'd also made an appointment with the phone company, and it so happened that both men had shown up at the same time.
Unbeknownst to Leonard, Armitage had also called their internet provider,
because they'd been having issues with their service, so a third man was in
the office, and it was stepladders and ass cracks from the front desk to the
watercooler.

"Whatever happened to that kid Beau?" Armitage said. "Last I heard, he
got sacked from Gurney right after I left."

"Are you kidding?"

"There was a Crime Watch vibe, but he had gas in the tank."

Before long, the IT guy made a comment about the data speed the office
was receiving from the router, which the ISP guy apparently interpreted as
an insult, and the two began having a robust debate on internet bandwidth.

ISP guy: "We deliver a DSL connection of ten Mbps, and if the customer's equipment slows it down, it's on them."

IT guy: "Ten Mbps when no one's online. The SpeedTest I ran showed
a data rate of five megabits. You're throttling the connection."

ISP guy: "The office probably uses a bad DNS server. Or they need to
boost the MTU settings. Look at that old 802.11b router."

IT guy: "That's an 11g, pal. You don't know what the hell you're talking
about."

This went on for several minutes, until one of the men blamed the phone company, which apparently owned the wires the internet providers used to access the building, so now the phone guy had joined the fray, and there were three men yelling at each other in the office and Leonard was convinced it would soon come to blows.

"Guess I'll post something on Craigslist tonight," Armitage said. "Much as I hate the cattle-call interview process."

"Hold off on that," Leonard said. "I might have a lead."

What he did next wasn't entirely legal, but after some deliberation he conjured his best attempt at a southern drawl and called Gurney PR's human resources department. As it turned out, the number was no longer in service, and it took a few more calls to discover the function had been swallowed by Pinnacle's HR department. After being transferred several times, he found himself speaking with a payroll associate, at which point he launched into a tirade about how he'd been fired a month prior and still hadn't received his final paycheck. He heard a furious percussion on the keyboard and decided to dial it up, carping about his lost wages as well as the way the company had treated him, threw in a sick mother for good measure, and, somewhere in between, demanded a confirmation of the phone number and mailing address they had for him in the system, lest they fail to pay him again. He was shocked to discover this tactic actually worked. A few minutes later, he called the number he'd been given, and after some uncomfortable small talk made arrangements to meet with Beau the next day.

BEAU WAS APPARENTLY NOW LIVING IN A BOARDING HOUSE OF SORTS IN Washington Heights. Leonard rode the subway and arrived in the neighborhood early evening, got momentarily lost in its winding network of hills, and watched a drug transaction go down in plain sight. The sun was surrendering beneath the Palisades when he found the address, a clumsy-looking building beside a bulletproofed Chinese restaurant under the rattling girders of the George Washington. An aluminum-framed letter board in the lobby informed him that he was visiting a sober living facility, primarily used, he later learned, as transitional housing for a nearby treatment center. Its residents, as far as he could tell, were dry drunks who bore the dispirited look of having lost everything. The bulletin board stated alcohol was prohibited in the building, and that Sunday worship services, as well as daily Alcoholics Anonymous meetings, were held in the basement. He exited the stairwell on the third floor to handmade no-smoking notices posted along the walls, increasing in frequency as he drew closer to Beau's room: "Smoking on this floor is prohibited!" "Seriously, no smoking allowed!" "Whoever keeps smoking up here is going to be thrown out!"

Beau's room was spartan and small, outfitted with a low bed and dresser with barely enough room to walk between, as well as a worn rattan chair below the window, where Leonard recognized a fax machine and several telephones from the Gurney office cradled in a nest of cords.

"Long time, Lundell." Beau looked Leonard over through the fishbowl bulge of his glasses. He possessed the look of a man cornered, had nervous eyes and a pale, hesitant face and stood against the wall with his shoulders pitched forward, as though he'd break for the door at any minute. He was wearing denim carpenter shorts and, for whatever reason, fingerless tactical gloves.

"How's life treating you?" Leonard said and sat on the edge of the bed.

"Staying busy." He said this in that slow, cynical way that underscored the superficiality of small talk. "I floated around a bit after I left Gurney, did marketing research work, phone surveys. Now I've got a job in customer relations downtown."

"What's the gig?"

"Phone psychic," Beau said. "It's all off the books, under the table, a no-paperwork kind of deal. Nothing too cozy, but it's easy. I basically tell folks what they want to hear. Kind of like you."

"I suppose the city's perfect for it," Leonard offered. "Lots of lonely people, which is funny, considering we all live on top of each other."

Beau apparently missed the ill-conceived attempt at commiseration. "I interviewed with an employment agency in Midtown that staffs media jobs. Took an aptitude test and did pretty good. Supposed to get a callback this week. The psychic gig is temporary, kind of like this place, which I'll admit is a cold cup of coffee. There are amenities, though. I've been going to meetings in the basement."

"I didn't know you had a drinking problem," Leonard said.

"I don't. I just wanted to make friends. The only thing that's keeping me from going back to Tennessee is I don't want people to know how bad I fucked up. There's an entire town waiting to remind me I never should've left."

"I've got a similar story," Leonard said.

"Figured you did. I can tell by the accent."

"I don't have an accent," Leonard stammered.

"Okay, bud."

Beau opened the window and lit a cigarette. He cleared the chair, sending the fax machine and phones crashing to the floor, then leaned back. Slow eddies of smoke stirred around him before escaping outside.

"So," Leonard said. "I wanted to apologize for everything that went down in August. I made a mistake firing you like that. What can I say? Our agency had been bought out, I didn't get the promotion I was promised, and the guy who taught me everything about this business got run out of his own company. I was dealing with personal issues."

"Hey, man, shit rolls downhill. I get it."

"I recently opened my own shop. Todd Armitage is on board, and we need someone who can coordinate workflow and schedule appointments. What I'm really looking for is a seasoned pro who can pitch the press, arrange meetings, all the responsibilities of an account executive position. It's a big step up. You'd be acting as a liaison between clients and the agency, and you'd be making a hell of a lot more scratch than before. You could move into a better place, officially start a new life here. What do you say?"

Beau was quiet for a moment. "Hate to poop in the punchbowl, Lundell, but I've got a few misgivings with the industry that've given me reservations about getting back on the fire truck. Don't know if you're privy to my history, but my first job in the business, the reason I was able to land that gig at Gurney, came from a stint I had on the communications team for a pork rind factory in Tennessee."

"Okay, so?"

"So, I came up with this marketing concept where we created a contest and asked folks to come up with a new flavor. It was huge, we're talking thousands of submissions every week. Of course, they'd already developed the new recipe; the entire point was to boost brand awareness and build our email list, so we just kept it going until someone guessed the right flavor. Well, some bad shit went down. This old guy from Dyersburg, he sent us hundreds of recipes, emailed them to us all day, every day. I guess he had some kind of terminal illness that prevented him from holding a job or leaving the house."

"What was wrong with him?"

"Some old-timer shit. Milk leg, chilblains, grocer's itch. Fuck if I remember. Anyway, right before he bought the farm, he was the one who guessed the new recipe. So, we gave him a plaque and a lifetime supply of pork rinds, which I heard his nephew ended up inheriting. Till the day he died, that poor bastard thought it was his idea, told anyone who'd listen. As he saw it, it had been his crowning achievement. But it was all a lie."

"Sometimes I wonder whether comedy has a place in the world anymore," Leonard said. "I mean, satire seems unnecessary when we're confronted with a parody of basic sensibilities on a daily basis—"

"That shit depressed the hell out of me," Beau said. "And I guess I've had a bee in my bonnet about the business since. Then I started thinking, after everything that went down at Gurney, casting my lot in with those cork-sniffers and having nothing to show for it, maybe it was time I hung up my boots."

"Out of curiosity," Leonard said, "what was the winning flavor?"

"Peaches and pralines," Beau said. "Anyway, I can pitch press like a raped ape all week and twice on Sunday. That's a fact."

"So, it's a yes?"

"Well, if a man don't want to work, I guess he hadn't ought to hire out."

"I don't know what that means."

"Means we should celebrate, and I've got an eighth of downtown brown if you want to toke up. But we've got to stuff a towel under this door. They're going to kick me out if I keep smoking in here."

THE FOLLOWING MONDAY, LEONARD MET BEAU AT THE SUBWAY STATION, and they walked to the office together. It was a cool, sunless morning and the sky looked imposing, clouds marshaling tentatively toward rain. The lights were out in the foyer, and Leonard discerned a pair of shoulders in the dark before he recognized Todd Armitage standing there, framed by the open office door behind him.

"Assuming you heard?" Todd said, a battered copy of the *Register* in his hand.

"Heard what?" Leonard snatched the paper, the business section already facing out.

His staff photo, years old, graced the page under a portentous headline: "The Minister of Nonsense." Sundermeyer had come through with his hit piece. Leonard's legs felt weak as he unfurled the paper, and a montage of memories played out in his head, a highlight reel of every shortcoming, the cosmic joke that had been his life thus far, aggregated in this monument to his failures he held in his hands.

"It's a hatchet job," Armitage said as he followed the men into Leonard's office. "We got completely slated, and we just opened."

"Give me a minute," Leonard said. "Let me read the damn thing."

Leonard sat on the edge of his desk. The article began with a sort of bingo game of sycophantic clichés: "man of mystery," "visionary," etcetera, before a quote provided by Frazer Rae—"Leonard Lundell is a goddamn liar"—set the clock for the rest of the narrative. What followed was a three-thousand-word screed that resembled a cheap morality play, beginning with a semi-accurate summary of Leonard's early life—raised in a small Ohio town, a university dropout who'd somehow weaseled his way into PR—which segued into a rambling account of his tenure at Gurney and anecdotal reviews of his work for various clients, the details of which the author had taken glib liberty in reporting. The article concluded with a reductive description of the Appetite Factory and an echo chamber from Mad Ave luminaries who dogpiled mockery onto Leonard's brainchild concept, essentially claiming his latest venture was indicative of a new era of hucksterism that signaled a nadir for the industry.

The checklist of quotables was extensive. Rae was featured prominently, probably owing less to his esteemed rank than to the sheer amount of opprobrium he supplied, at one point even likening Leonard to Joseph Goebbels. An anonymous source provided a breakdown of how crisis strategies were developed at Gurney. This had Todd Beveridge's handiwork all over it. Thankfully, the Appetite Factory's clients weren't mentioned, leading Leonard to believe none of Sundermeyer's sources had tabs on his current venture. He also noticed Patty hadn't supplied any quotes. Whether Sundermeyer had merely forgotten about her or if she'd refused comment, there was no way to be sure.

His eyes grew restless as he skimmed paragraphs. It was clumsy, turgid writing; besides being grossly editorialized, the article exhibited a tireless commitment to cliché, was bruised with idiotic bromides and inscrutably ponderous descriptive passages that lacked any discernible storytelling authority. Still, he found himself rereading the more hurtful sentences, analyzing their words over and over until they began resembling nonsense.

"Well, this venture was short-lived," Armitage said and pantomimed an exhale. "I guess our ship has hit sand. That article is going to be uploaded, linked, and reposted in the Madison Avenue claptrap for months. The entire PR community is going to have a field day."

"It's pretty bad," Leonard said.

"Does this mean I don't have a job?" Beau said.

"We've got to put out a statement," Armitage said. "If we don't address this, we're not just digging a hole, we're asking for a bigger shovel. We could sue that reporter, you know."

"I doubt it," Leonard said.

"What kills me is it's the goddamn *Register*," Armitage said. "Where were their ad hominems when Bush and his Goldman Sachs lackey Paulson bailed out the banks?"

"All right, Todd."

"You're being awfully cavalier about this." Armitage was pacing now. In the main room, the phone began to ring. "Is it true what the article said? That you never worked in PR before, that you, like, basically lied your way into the industry?"

"It doesn't matter now," Leonard said.

"See, I think it does," Armitage said. "What are we going to tell our clients?"

"You mean the clients who've hired us to come up with imaginary scandals so the public will pay attention to them?"

"I left a job that was paying eighty grand a year," Armitage said. "We're in the midst of the worst recession since the Great Depression. How am I supposed to find work?"

Leonard thought about what to do. For one, he was going to call Sundermeyer and tell him off. There were other scores to settle: with Frazer, the Todds. A revenge narrative had a particular allure to it, but he realized there was a perceptible difference between doing something that made him feel better and doing something that actually improved their footing. Given the opposition stacked against them, the latter seemed like a tall order. Armitage was right: They were doomed.

Beau rapped on the doorframe. "That was Bernie Feinblum at Pinnacle. Said the CEO wants to have a word at our old office."

"What the hell for?" Leonard said.

"Didn't say," Beau said. "What should I tell him?"

"Tell him to go shit in his hat."

"I guess there's a silver lining," Armitage said as the phone in the main room began ringing again. "The article failed to mention that we're located inside a whorehouse. Maybe I'll scoop them on that scandal in our press statement."

"That was Trotwood this time, top dog himself," Beau said from the doorway. "He really wants to talk."

LEONARD WALKED TO MADISON AVENUE THE FOLLOWING AFTERNOON, entered his old building, and took the elevator to the sixth floor. The office was unrecognizable now, everything white and made of modular particleboard. A frosted-glass partition separated the foyer from the main room, and carpet the color of television static stretched the length of the floor, anchored by a large communal workstation that had replaced the cubicles. He was relieved he hadn't bumped into anyone he knew. In fact, the place appeared empty; only a few employees quietly milled about, and their movements seemed forced and stage-managed, a museum exhibit of office life.

He stepped into the research facility, the room that had been Jack's office, and stared at the control room window on its west wall, now an opaque mirror.

"How does it feel to be back?" Graydon Trotwood said behind him, elbow propped in the doorway. "Do you miss it?"

"Miss the clowns, don't miss the circus," Leonard said. "Why's it so quiet?"

Trotwood's superficial charm was still intact. He appeared fresh-faced, absurdly tanned for October, and looked Leonard over with tungsten eyes, a smile people spend entire lives practicing. Then he approached him and sniffed his shoulder.

"What cologne is that?"

"I'm not wearing cologne," Leonard said.

"Well, you smell nice. How's business?"

"I assume you read the papers."

"Hell of a write-up in the *Register* yesterday. You were excoriated, if you don't mind my saying."

"I'm not the first person to be attacked by the press. We're handling it."

"The Appetite Factory is groundbreaking, just the kind of subversive voice this industry needs," Trotwood said. "Admittedly, there's a P. T. Barnum sensibility to it, but you know what the best thing about the whole concept is? It appeals to tribalism. Public shaming is a ritual as old as civilization. What we're seeing with the internet and our entertainment-based news cycle is just another manifestation of our timeless love of the drama. And this puts communicators, our advertising, marketing, and public relations industries, in a fine position. It's what we do. We tell stories. What did Napoleon say, something about history being a fable agreed upon?"

"A fair point, I suppose," Leonard said.

"Advertising is dead," Trotwood said. "Marketing has become so ingrained in our discourse, consumers understand how brands are engaging with them. How do we have a conversation with a public that knows how the sausage gets made? The philosophical implications are vast and far-reaching, Leonard, and the answer, of course, is earned media. Content creation. That's why the Appetite Factory checks all the boxes. It's market disruption; it exploits flaws in the system. I don't care that you lied about your background. I don't care that you're from some jerkwater town in Ohio. I'm a Michigan native myself, did Jack ever tell you?"

Trotwood's expression changed. "I want to show you something." He strode across the room, flipped a switch, and gesticulated to the control room mirror, which began to fade transparent. In the boardroom on the other side of the wall, Patty sat at a large banquet table, fingers walking through a plate of nachos. A rubber tarp was tied around her neck like a bib, and a massive spread was laid out before her. She was flanked by Roger Lawton to her right, who wore a butcher's apron and held a wooden ladle, Wanda Markowski to her left, who gripped a clipboard to her chest. A nervous-looking man wearing a chef's hat huddled in the corner.

"Meet our new tastemaker," Trotwood said. "What you're seeing is an informal culture jam session, just a few of our best talent kicking around some speculative ideas."

Leonard could only characterize Patty's obesity as enthusiastic. She was enormous, billowing. Corpulent. Bombastically fat, like an enlarged photocopy of a person. She appeared engorged, bulging, swollen to the point it seemed she was sinking inside herself. She exemplified fat, was the walking shape of fat; she'd gained several new chins, and her mouth, now permanently agape, drew in air with slow piggish snores. Her skin was blistered, she sweated profusely and seemed delirious, was blinking irregularly as though she'd fallen down a flight of stairs.

Wanda's voice broke through the speaker as she read from the clipboard. "A professional tennis star is caught having sex with a female fan. The woman goes public and sells her story to a network with plans to produce a made-for-TV movie. Despite the star's repeated denials, a dozen other women follow suit regarding dalliances they'd also had with him."

"That's easy," Patty said. Her voice sounded obstructed by her tongue. "Hold a press conference and have the guy say he's seeking counseling for sex addiction. Then hire a celebrity therapist and produce a reality TV show that airs before the made-for-TV movie."

Roger took the ladle and offered a disgusted expression as he shoveled mashed potatoes into Patty's mouth. Leonard appraised the buffet on the table, spotted coins of Massachusetts littlenecks in cucumber mignonette, fillets of sturgeon on beds of endive, hanger steaks in a syrupy jus crowned with potatoes and caramelized asparagus, pickled escargot dusted with bacon and parsley. There were crocks of tapas, ingot-shaped tins of caviar, croquettes stuffed with pink deckles of beef. A plate of pasta resembling a twisted cacophony of musical notes.

"One of our creatives recently developed a new branding strategy we're rolling out in the coming weeks. I believe you know her?" Trotwood said. "A controversy narrative is created for brands as a means of engaging the media. Sound familiar?"

"Creative? She's a file clerk," Leonard said.

"More gravy!" Patty yelled from the boardroom.

"She told us everything, Leonard," Trotwood said. "She told us all about how she came up with the Appetite Factory concept months ago and shared it with you. You stole the idea from her, and us, by proxy. Funny how circumstance can bring people together."

"What else did she tell you?"

"Every PR agency in town is going to have an outrage practice by next year. I'm not letting the ball roll through my legs this time. We've since offered her an elevated position in the company where we can nurture her vision together, in exchange for exclusive use of her flagship concept."

"Trust me, you don't know what you've gotten yourself into with this one."

"The terms of how she wanted to amortize this arrangement are . . . unorthodox. I'll be honest, it's costing us a fucking fortune. But the idea, the concept, is ours. You ripped it off one of our associates, quit your job the following day, and started your own venture to put her ideas into action. You're a thief, and I hasten to conclude the *Register*'s bruising indictment of your behavior was spot-on. You should be ashamed."

"Nice try, but I wasn't born yesterday. You only decided to add an outrage practice to your toolkit once the *Register* article landed on your desk. I started this. My company, the concept, belongs to me."

"You have no idea how far ahead we are. We're hiring an army of content producers to publish fake news reports and mindless top-ten lists across a series of web verticals we've recently purchased. We've outsourced a troll farm to write hoax social media content to antagonize the masses on everything from celebrity gossip to the state of the economy. We're going to supply branded copy for the clickbait sites to run the morning after every awards show, every season finale, the passage of every bill in Congress. Everyone wins here: Consumers who spend their lives staring at screens get to feign indignation gawking at the follies of people more successful than they are, and the media gets a nonstop supply of incendiary content to lure in audiences who lower the bounce rate by arguing in the comments section. This is going to make serious money."

"You sure you want to be telling me this? Being competitors and all?"

"We've got other ideas as well," Trotwood said. "Who do you think is going to win the election?"

"McCain's in trouble, but it's anyone's game."

"We're currently pitching a certain presidential candidate on a media campaign concept, where we push the story that Black Panthers are planning to attack white people at polling sites across the country. We could sway this race."

"This is ridiculous," Leonard said. "Your delusion borders on parody."

"This isn't a free lunch," Wanda said from over the speaker. "The meat industry has come under fire for its adoption of the term 'pink slime.' What's our strategy?"

"Geez, lady, cool your tits," Patty said.

"This is embarrassing," Leonard said. "She can't write copy worth a damn, and you know it. You want to be competitors, great, but your new practice is a joke. I'll look for your cease-and-desist in the mail."

"You don't understand, Leonard. I don't want to put you out of business. We're gutting Gurney PR and dedicating our resources, our full attention, to our outrage unit. I've laid off the entire crisis team, and I'm replacing them with your operation. I'm going to hire you and integrate your agency into our own."

"Oh?"

"It's the courteous thing to do. The alternative is to sue your ass off for stealing our concept. This is a great opportunity, Lundell. You'll have access to our brand-messaging department, our multimedia division, social media managers. Our R&D facility staffs fucking data scientists, for Christ's sake. You'll have the support of key stakeholders, millions at your disposal. You're moving up, Leonard. You're finally getting your seat at the boardroom table."

"I'm convinced you're one of the most ridiculous people I've ever met,"

Leonard said. "Why does everything have to be a zero-sum game with you? Why can't we both own companies that do the same thing and compete for clients like every other business on the planet? Hell, why don't you hire Frazer back? He seems to have an opinion on how this kind of operation should be run."

"Frazer retired. You ruined his career, remember?"

"This isn't how reality operates. You can't threaten people to get what you want."

Trotwood straightened a lapel. "Why not?"

"For one, because places like this ruin everything. What I do, it can't be done at a big agency."

"We can be edgy."

"No, you can't. You could buy my shop for a hundred million, and you wouldn't know what to do with it. You'll offer the same shopworn strategies, you'll overpromise and under-deliver to your clients, you'll water down the campaigns for legal reasons, you'll hire employees who are alienated from the work, and you'll establish a childish reinforcement system of quotas that threatens them for underperforming. Places like this are allergic to creativity. No, thanks."

"Let me ask you something. What's your firm's operating profit benchmark for the year?"

"No idea," Leonard said.

Trotwood laughed. "You don't know how to run a business. You've got an entrepreneurial spirit, but we're results-driven. So, let's be civilized. I'll bet we've got better lawyers." At this, without warning, Trotwood approached him and sniffed again.

"Why do you keep doing that?" Leonard said.

"I'll take you behind the curtain, Lundell. It's an old management trick, used to assert dominance against a competitor."

"It's not working. You're just being weird and making me uncomfortable."

"Fine," Trotwood whispered. "But can you do me this favor and walk out with me? I can't be in here alone when you leave. Senior management will take it as a sign that our deal didn't go through."

"Sorry, I have to get back to work."

The sky had darkened by the time Leonard left the office, the tops of the buildings dissolved behind a pall of fog as he wandered west. He fumbled for his phone and dialed Patty. She didn't pick up, which made sense, as she was probably still stuffing herself in the boardroom. He crossed the street and realized he was standing outside the watering hole frequented by his former colleagues, palmed the glass, and saw the Todds hunched over their favorite booth. He wedged through the crowd, passed doughy men discussing sports or the jobs they'd left for the day. Their ties loosened, the group sat in silence, holding dispirited, clenched faces.

"The Minister of Nonsense," Todd Shillenburg said and sniffed. "What the hell do you want?"

"I want to talk," Leonard said. "I want to apologize."

"For what?" Todd Colton said. "The new bucket shop you and that fruit Armitage opened?"

"What I want to know is how you're going to get any business after getting skewered like that," Todd Beveridge said. "You should be curled up with a bottle somewhere."

"How'd you do it, anyway?" Todd Colton said. "How do you convince clients to lie to the media for clicks?"

"I came up with a concept and put it to work."

"Trolling the entire country, you call that a concept?" Todd Beveridge said. "They're going to have to dig trenches to lower the new bar you've set for the industry."

"I don't care what you think of my business," Leonard said. "Incidentally, I know you're the anonymous source who spoke to that reporter about our client meetings."

"What if I did?" Todd Beveridge said. "They can't fire me for divulging confidential information now."

"We just got laid off, all of us," Todd Colton said. "Apropos of nothing."

"Got the word from Wanda an hour ago," Todd Shillenburg said. "No official announcement yet, but apparently the ax falls for half of the practices on Friday, as well as the media services department and copywriting. Two weeks' severance, resignation letter and nondisclosure agreement pending, of course."

"Did everyone get eighty-sixed?"

"Wanda, Roger, and some of the other top talent were poached," Todd Shillenburg said. "They're moving up to Pinnacle, the big house."

"Swallowed by an ad conglomerate," Todd Colton said. "Turns out Beau was right."

"That's what I wanted to apologize for," Leonard said. "Trotwood called me to the office about a job. He wants to acquire my shop and integrate it into whatever's left under the Gurney banner. He's restructuring the entire crisis unit to focus on outrage services."

"Son of a bitch," Todd Shillenburg muttered.

Todd Beveridge began negotiating with a waitress. Leonard watched Todd Shillenburg slap Todd Colton's thigh. Colton opened his palm and Shillenburg pinched a thimble-sized Ziploc bag into it, and Colton stood and retrieved his house keys from his jacket.

"Bathroom break," Todd Colton said. "Back soon."

"Let's ride the straight-talk express, Lundell," Todd Shillenburg said. "What did Trotwood offer you?"

"It doesn't matter. I'm not taking the gig."

"It makes sense," Todd Beveridge said. "Pinnacle has a war chest, but it's never had an ear to the ground. So, Trotwood offers Leonard a fresh start so they can be on the cutting edge. Thanks, asshole, you cost us our jobs."

"Nostradamus, that's what I just said," Leonard said. "Hence the apology."

"See, but he's not telling us everything," Todd Shillenburg said. "I'm not going to give this any more oxygen, but Gurney was broke. Pinnacle is going to cast some accounting wizardry and sweep its own debt into Gurney, then shutter the whole operation in exchange for a clean balance sheet. This entire company, a forty-year history, is just one giant goddamn tax write-off."

"Got any proof for that?" Leonard said.

"It's the same song and dance the banks pulled to create the housing bubble, so why not?"

"Any chance we could collectively agree to drop the bubble metaphor?" Leonard said. "I can't understand how blowing bubbles is an accurate way of describing a scenario in which the banks wrecked the economy and forced us to clean it up."

"You've got no idea the kinds of wackadoo campaigns Pinnacle's been running out of the old boardroom at our agency," Todd Shillenburg said. "Just the other day I saw Roger and Bernie with that sow from the elevator accident. Remember her? Apparently, they've got her working on some sort of secret project."

"What kind of secret project?" Leonard said.

"I don't know the details, but they're sending her to these hush-hush dinner parties all over town. Mystery chefs, underground culinary societies. Creepy shit—"

"You some kind of hog-pounder, Lundell?" Todd Beveridge said. "I swear your face went white just now."

Todd Colton returned from the bathroom. "I've got an idea," he said and sniffed. "For a new crisis agency, I mean. Hear me out. What if we launch this program where we place ad copy at crime scenes? Like, we put paramedics, EMTs on the payroll. They arrive before the cops, right? We set them up with designs, maybe stickers or banners, or we could pay them to spray-paint brand slogans on the walls, whatever. Anyway, they throw up the copy and go about their business, and then the news teams get there and start filming, and boom, millions are seeing client messages on one of the most coveted media slots in the country."

"That is singularly the most idiotic idea I've ever heard," Leonard said.

"Shut up, Leonard," Todd Shillenburg said. "It's a good idea, Todd."

"Powerful stuff, Todd," Todd Beveridge said. "Get lost, Leonard."

"It's clear I'm anathema around here," Leonard said and stood. "You three enjoy redirecting your shortcomings."

"Leonard doesn't realize it, but he's a bellwether for where things are going in this country," Todd Beveridge said. "And the three of us, we're victims of circumstance."

"How do you figure?" Leonard said.

"The feds have taken over Fannie Mae, Freddie Mac, and AIG. Our government has now begun brokering the sale of investment banks. You see a pattern here?"

"Not really."

"Our economy collapsed because millions of people had no business getting a mortgage in the first place. And now, this clown who might become president wants to roll out some kind of universal coverage for welfare recipients, even though we have the best healthcare system in the world. We've entered the age of entitlement. People have no sense of personal responsibility anymore. Everyone gets a participation trophy. Mark my words: Responsible, hardworking men like us are becoming an endangered species."

"And how do I fit in with this?" Leonard said.

"You didn't even graduate college," Todd Shillenburg said. "You never should've been running things, that's what chaps my ass. Beveridge was right. You're a fraud."

"What other secrets are you hiding?" Todd Beveridge said. "Anything else you'd like to share before we sign off?"

The table grew quiet. Leonard realized that no matter what he said, he lacked the resources to assuage them and didn't care anyway.

"I like to eat things," Leonard said. "Soap, pencils, carpet, you name it. Then someone discovered my secret and threatened—"

"Oh, fuck you, Leonard," Todd Shillenburg said and sprung up from the booth, shoulders squared. "You want to punch down, now that you cost us our jobs? Why don't you stay in your lane?"

Shillenburg shoved Leonard in the sternum with such force he tipped over in the aisle. He grabbed for the table on the way down, taking several glasses with him, and by the time he regained his footing, disoriented and soaked, the Todds had him by his limbs and were dragging him through the bar. Outside, he assumed a turtle position on the sidewalk before a flash of pale hands battered him to a soundtrack of insults, and then they were gone and there were just the arrhythmic sounds of the street, the soft, inconsolable light from traffic as aches gathered in his ribs and around his right eye.

BY THE TIME LEONARD DRAGGED HIMSELF BACK TO THE OFFICE, HIS EYE had nearly swollen shut. In the foyer, he dug out his cellphone and began searching for Patty's number. She hadn't bothered him once since he'd left his job; considering he'd spent the better part of six months trying to rid himself of her, the irony wasn't lost on him that he was now seeking her out. He just wanted to know what the hell she'd been doing pitching copy in that boardroom, and why the agency had allegedly put her on the street as some kind of influencer scout, and what sort of Herculean con she'd pulled to make this happen. There was something either maddeningly complex or utterly stupid about the contradictory interior life of a person, the irrational impulses that underwrote our motivations and constantly sought to subvert our declared intentions. Yet he continued to act on them anyway, even now, as he considered how much he hated her while the phone rang, acknowledging the childish pangs of envy he felt over the fact that she was the agency's resident fabulist, out there gaming the system without him. He thought about this as he waited there in the dark. No answer.

"What happened to you?" Todd Armitage said. He was getting a can of something out of the new mini-fridge when Leonard finally limped into the office.

"The Todds. Seems they were just laid off, along with almost everyone else at Gurney, and it was kind of my fault. Oh, and Pinnacle wants to buy us out."

"What?"

"I don't want to talk about it," Leonard said and gripped his ribs. "Just let me lie down for a bit."

Leonard staggered across the room, passing Beau, who was manning the phones, stumbled to his office, and collapsed into his chair. Somewhere in this room, hidden under the desk or in a filing cabinet, was a shampoo bottle he'd neglected to purge. He was sure of it, and its mystery proximity was enough to leave him aching with hunger.

"You can't just leave me hanging with news like that," Armitage said from the doorway, Beau peering in over his shoulder. "What happened?"

"I suppose we should close up early," Leonard said. He reached for his cellphone and dialed Patty's number again. "No point staying open if we're not signing any new accounts."

"You want to tell him, or should I?" Armitage said.

Beau shrugged his shoulders. "Believe it or not, the phone's been ringing all afternoon."

Chapter 17

L eonard called Patty's cellphone several times that night, to no avail. When he awoke the following morning, her number had been disconnected. He rode the train to Midtown and sprinted to the Pinnacle building, shuttled up and down on the elevators until he found accounts receivable on the ninth floor, a windowless branch of the building with low ceilings and bare pistachio walls. He interrogated a receptionist who had a tattoo of a tampon with angel wings on her forearm. She rolled her eyes each time Leonard asked a question.

"I told you, she's not here. Hasn't been in all week."

"And you have no idea when she'll be back?" Leonard said.

"Management took her off the floor." She huffed, tapping press-on nails against the counter. "I think she was promoted. Which is hilarious because she was written up three times in the last two months."

"Any idea where she went?"

"Sure, we meet for Stove Top chicken Thursdays. I got the rundown on her horoscope—" She wasn't finished, but Leonard was already down the hall, making his way back to the elevator.

IN THE OFFICE, HE MADE A FEEBLE ATTEMPT AT WORK, SPOKE WITH SEVeral prospective clients, and sketched out ideas. Outside his door, the phone lines continued clamoring away. As the *Register*'s jeremiad against Leonard continued to circulate within the corporate world, a curious thing had happened: Companies, driven either by morbid curiosity or a desperate attempt to boost business, were contacting the office and making inquiries regarding

303

the ins and outs of deliberately sabotaging their reputations in exchange for media exposure. This development had invigorated Todd Armitage, who poked his head into Leonard's office throughout the day to keep him apprised of who he'd just spoken to on the phone. Leonard read over some of the notes he'd compiled during his calls that day. A Republican state legislator had hatched an asinine plan to deliberately smear himself with a rumor of a romantic encounter with a gay prostitute in order to discredit the very real rumors surrounding his extramarital affair. A South American country that was the site of a bloody military coup decades prior and had since transitioned into a flourishing neoliberal market economy wanted to position itself in the United States as a travel destination, even though an ongoing penchant for despotism, mass disappearances, and media silencing had continued to sully its image. There was something about his clients' lack of commitment to reality, the sense of entitlement they exhibited in presuming they were special or that their brands somehow deserved a cultish following, that made his work a kind of receipt for our moral failings as a society. His phone began to ring. Leonard picked up the receiver, hung up the call with his thumb, then laid the receiver on the desk.

An idea struck him. He opened his desk drawer and rummaged around, then slipped to the closet, still crammed with the books he hadn't yet constructed shelves to hold, and began picking through boxes. He uncovered Moleskine notebooks, mystery adapters for electronics, old business cards, a wrinkled tube of toothpaste, expired antacids. Finally, in a coffee mug stuffed with binder clips and rubber bands, he found the wadded slip of dot matrix paper containing Patty's address that Griffin Cruz had given him the month before. He pushed the paper into his pocket and ran outside.

Leonard took the train to Queens. The avenues and cross streets had similar numbers, which confused him, so he wandered the neighborhood circuitously for several minutes until he chanced upon the address, an unassuming mid-rise garden apartment identical to every other building in the area. He entered the foyer, perused the intercom panel, and found a tenant, "Pachis, S" on the second floor. He waited. Several minutes later, an elderly woman with a pushcart unlocked the door, and Leonard glided inside, crossed a Carrara marble lobby, and stole for the stairs. He knocked on the door and heard sluggish movements inside, grew impatient, and began pounding at the buzzer, which sounded like the margin bell of a typewriter. The door opened, at first, it seemed, to no one, until Leonard looked down and noticed a middle-aged man in a wheelchair.

"Is Patty in?"

The man looked Leonard over pensively before settling into a smile. "You're Leonard Lundell."

Leonard stepped past him, over hardwood floors balding of varnish. It wasn't unlike his mother's home, if slightly more habitable, the living room crammed with mismatched furniture and nests of magazines, everything swimming in a flurry of dust. A box fan was lodged in an open window, and the air was fouled with mothballs and cat urine. He noticed several litter boxes. Not a cat in sight.

"Panagiota isn't here," the man said. Leonard's first thought was he looked like someone who masturbates on the subway. He had a shock of silver hair and a face that appeared to be slipping off, the cheeks blotched with rosacea, wore a bathrobe and flannel shirt, both stained with sweat. He smelled like onions and ointment.

"And you are?" Leonard said.

"Her father. You can call me Spiros."

"Any idea where she's at?"

"Work, I'd imagine."

"I was just there. They told me she hasn't been in all week."

"That's odd. Did you try calling her?"

"Her number's disconnected." Leonard examined a wall of impressively stocked, if terribly disorganized, bookshelves. "When was the last time you saw her?"

"Maybe last night? She keeps strange hours. Would you like a glass of water?"

Leonard drifted to a desk claiming twin computer monitors. It was littered with mail and random paperstuffs: disability checks, a Weight Watchers monthly pass, a menu for a dessert/mystery theater production company called Dial M for Mascarpone. A half-eaten Mexican chocolate bar called Entonces, resting on a recent edition of Frazer Rae's *Public Relations Fundamentals*.

The man wheeled up behind him. "What happened to your eye? I hope Patty wasn't involved."

"Actually, I haven't seen her in a while." Leonard turned to the monitors on the desk and noticed both had internet browsers open to Craigslist personals forums. "Looks like you've been reading up on the industry?" Leonard said as he held up Rae's tome.

"Oh, that's not mine. But I know a little about your line of work. I taught a psychology course at SUNY for twenty years. Did you know Edward Bernays was Sigmund Freud's nephew? Fascinating."

"Actually, I'll take that glass of water," Leonard said. "If you don't mind."

The man wheeled into the kitchen, and Leonard analyzed one of the screens.

Crib dweller needs playmate.

Toilet bear pain slut seeks cub for good times and bad decisions. Specialties: nub play, shin fluffing, baby plate.

Spiros turns men into dolls.

"Helping your daughter with another scheme?" Leonard said. In separate browser tabs, several unpublished comment fields were open. "Or looking for a date?"

The old man howled with laughter as he returned to the room, his body shaking as he thrust his hands in violent, disjointed movements, swording at the air as though he was quartering a chicken. "Just working on some research. A sort of social experiment."

Leonard settled his eyes on the second monitor.

```
Young cuckold seeks dom.
```

```
Chastity sissy sub in search of cbt master for debt
                    bondage agreement.
```

```
Come juice this fruit.
```

"I suppose you find this entertaining," Leonard said.

"Oh, yes," the man wheezed. "I find some real wackos on there."

"You're as nuts as she is," Leonard said and made his way to the door.

"She's quite fond of you," Spiros said.

"She has a funny way of showing it. She was blackmailing me."

"She's a troubled girl. She's suicidal, you know."

"So she said. She's full of it," Leonard said. "I've never met anyone so hopelessly filled with joie de vivre. Do me a favor: Don't tell her I came here."

"I suppose I could do that. But it dawned on me why you didn't see her at the office. She's been doing a lot of work late nights—"

"If I could loosen your memory," Leonard said and fumbled with his wallet. "I'd appreciate it."

"She told me they gave her some kind of big promotion. Aside from all these new responsibilities she has, you may have been visiting the wrong building. It seems they transferred her to your former agency. In fact, she told me they'd set her up in your old office."

HE WAS BACK IN THE CITY JUST BEFORE FIVE O'CLOCK AND STOOD OUTside the Gurney building, monitoring the brimming crowds, the scrum of employees who gathered on the sidewalk discussing happy hour. It was cold now, the air brittle with hints of frost as he checked the time on his cellphone, paced. Soon he heard a familiar voice and saw Griffin Cruz swaying with laughter beside him. He'd dressed like he was en route to a golf tournament, wore a puce polo and tight-fitting tapered slacks, his face gleaming with an oleaginous luster.

"Ahoy, Lundell," Cruz said. "Trouble in paradise? How'd you get the shiner?"

"Long story."

"Funny seeing you here. Begging for your old job back?"

"Just waiting for someone."

"Not one of the members of your think tank, I presume?"

"A semantic distinction. They're not my problem anymore."

"Ours either. I'm sure they'll find new jobs."

"There aren't too many going around nowadays," Leonard said. "I saw them last night. They seem to see themselves as victims of circumstance."

"O Fortuna, the dulcet sounds of sour grapes being turned into whine," Cruz said. "I think the real problem is our world is falling apart faster than your former yes-men can lower their standards."

"I'm assuming you didn't get a pink slip?"

"Me? Oh no. Gurney is keeping its travel division. In fact, we're expanding."

"See, I find that strange. You'd think tourism would be the first casualty in a recession."

"No way. Travel is crisis with a cocktail umbrella. It doesn't matter if you're going to Paris or Paducah, tourism is the illusion that you can escape the life you've chosen. I've been directing travel campaigns for years now, and let me tell you, vacations are fantasies of being someone else."

"And you're not bothered working for an ad conglomerate?"

"Pinnacle's run some great campaigns. Remember Marriott's 'Give Mom a Break for Christmas'?"

"Nope."

"Who could forget Johnson & Johnson's 'Your Baby, His Future'?"

"I guess I did."

"Well, it's nice work if you can get it," Cruz said. "We influence how Americans get their information, Lundell. That's a lot of responsibility."

"If I begin resorting to sarcasm, it's only to accentuate your overweening sincerity."

Just then Leonard caught Patty shuffling out of the building. She was hard to miss: her elephantine frame was girdled with a pink coat that resembled a toilet rug. She dug into her bag for something, slipped, and righted herself on the curb, and continued down the sidewalk into the boil of the five o'clock crowd.

"I have to go," Leonard said.

He mixed in with a knot of suits and followed, walked within the margin of the sidewalk, huddling close to the buildings, deliberately maintaining a distance. Seeing her walk was like watching a penguin try to jump rope; she was slow-moving and carried herself cautiously, as though she'd tip over at any moment. She stepped into the crush of traffic, and Leonard stole after her, where he was reprimanded by a bray of horns. He fell back, temporarily taking refuge behind a rickshaw carting tourists, and when the crosswalk flashed and the crowd shuttled forward, he lurched into the street until he was skipping behind her, tracing wide, waddling steps against the tide of traffic until she descended into a subway station.

From the mouth of the stairwell, he could hear the southbound train screaming onto the platform. The doors were closing as he crossed the turnstile spokes, but he managed to throw himself into the nearest car at the expense of several tourists he bulldogged through. He inched past a thicket of limbs, pawing for the grab rail as the train lurched through the tunnel until he reached the emergency exit. Shuffling into the adjoining car, which was even more crowded than the first, he stood on his toes, peered over a shiver of passengers, and retracted when he spotted her, arms locked around a pole, eyes flitting on as she consulted her cellphone, her hair rising and falling with the moving train, so close he could touch her if he reached out.

Without warning, she stepped off the train two stops later and disappeared in the morass, prompting Leonard to once again push his way through until he breached the exit, where oppressive crowds splayed out over the sidewalks. He stumbled up the next block and networked in and out of the surge, and a panic welled inside him until he caught a glimpse of her wheezing on the corner as she made furtive attempts at hailing a cab. Leonard scrambled into the street again, flailing his arms for a vehicle as Patty's taxi jounced into traffic and he found himself bounding up the street on foot, giving chase as it negotiated and converged with the rush-hour crawl. The taxi continued west as Leonard sprinted a block lined with pollarded trees before it turned left at Seventh Avenue and tacked south. Thankfully, it came to a stop before a court of shops several blocks later, where Patty entered a nondescript restaurant.

Leonard waited several minutes and went inside, bypassed the hostess, and canvassed a button-up crowd before making his way to the bar. He ordered a glass of wine and buried his face in a menu, periodically peeking out. Patty sat at a small table near the window with an older man. Despite her appearance, she seemed invigorated now, smiling and clapping hands as she scanned the menu. Appetizers arrived and then a main course, and, like always, she ate ravenously. Her dinner companion had a despairing quality about him, a weasel of a man with a red face and bleary eyes who looked like he did a lot of drinking on boats. As Leonard watched the familiar scene, he realized there was something self-canceling about them, the invocation of someone else in the role he'd played for months. Sometime shortly after dessert was ordered, Patty stood and staggered to the restroom.

"I need you to listen carefully," Leonard said as he approached the table. "We don't have much time—"

"Are you with the agency?" The man spoke with a slight stutter, his eyes darting nervously around the restaurant.

"When you're finished, I want you to get rid of her," Leonard said. "Go home."

"My shift is almost over. She's going someplace uptown," the man whispered. His eyes settled on Patty's half-eaten plate, the tooth imprint on a hamburger bun. "Strange stuff. I wasn't invited—"

Then the restroom door faltered open, and Leonard darted for the exit.

"They've had me on the job only two days," the man called after him. "You've got to tell me. What's wrong with her?"

TWENTY MINUTES LATER, FROM THE BACK SEAT OF A TAXI ON THE FAR side of the street, Leonard watched as Patty and her companion exited the restaurant. They seemed to be negotiating something, and signs of an argument ensued. Then a livery cab pulled up to the curb and Patty climbed inside as the man stamped off in the opposite direction.

"Follow that car," Leonard said.

"Twenty-six years I've been waiting for that line, mister," the driver said.

They headed north, inched across town in the snarl of traffic before merging onto the FDR and continuing on Harlem River Drive, where once again they found themselves wedged into impossible congestion, vehicles stopping and jerking forward like cogs in some sputtering machine. Eventually, they exited the roadway near a cluster of low-slung buildings beside the Triborough Bridge and, after a few blocks, entered a campus of high-rise housing projects.

"How long are we playing this game, boss?" the driver said.

Patty's car came to a stop below a stark concrete tower, its bands of windows lined with steel bars. Leonard exited the cab, raced down the sidewalk, and followed Patty across a wasted lawn foxed with orange light from the streetlamps. He passed a dismantled playground cordoned off with rusted chain link, a courtyard lit by floodlights. A statuary cluster of young men gathered near the tower's entrance paid Patty no mind as she breached the building through a single stainless-steel door swinging open in the breeze, the apparent result of a busted hinge. Leonard shielded himself behind the door, peered through a window reinforced with crosshatches of wire, and watched as she entered an access code before bypassing a second steel door into a deserted lobby. As soon as she crossed the threshold, he was inside and rushing after her, catching the door with his foot inches before it closed. He waited a beat on his knees, then passed an elevator bank that had been taken out of service and entered a green-tiled stairwell that stank of mildew and piss.

Leonard pounded up the stairs, slowing his pace once he discerned the slaps of heavy footsteps as Patty ambled across the landing above him. She was wheezing by the third floor, and having a hacking fit by the fourth, where the stairwell's lights began to flicker intermittently. By the fifth floor the lights were out entirely, and, gripping desperately onto the handrail, Leonard heard the sound of footfalls beside him, caught a whiff of after-shave, and swore he could make out the silhouetted outline of an overweight man in a suit lumbering past him in the dark, moving southbound on the stairs. From the landing above, the thunderclap of a steel door slamming shut. He disembarked on the sixth floor, walked a dim, narrow cinder-brick hall reverberating with the seashell sounds of tenant clatter. A latch clicked somewhere around the corner, and Leonard caught a repository of dinner smells, followed his nose, and came upon an apartment door with a taped, handwritten sign that read "hot plate." A cuticle of red light bordered the doorframe. He pressed his ear to the door and felt the vibrations of social activity emanating behind it.

A hulking man in a burgundy velvet dinner jacket filled the hallway inside, demanded a fifty-dollar entrance fee before escorting Leonard into the living room. It was dark and took several minutes for his eyes to adjust, but even then the geometry of the room remained difficult to parse, un-ornamented and featureless, a dungeonesque space of black brick splashed with conical crimson lighting from a single track of red bulbs. All of the furniture had been cleared save for several wooden pews in the back of the room and a rubber tarp islanded in the middle of the floor. A whiff of spices, tamarind and cardamom, lingered in the air, piped from behind a curtain where he discerned a clattering of pans. A boy wearing a suit several sizes too large picked through the crowd with a serving tray bearing wine.

Soon, an elderly woman the color of burnt copper exited the curtain and distributed appetizers, small plates of sweating sausages and finger bowls of prawns in a yellowish broth. Shapes manifested in the dark. Leonard inched into the farthest corner of the room and appraised the men shifting around him—clumsy-looking figures with restless feet and eyes filled with bad intentions. Their features writhed and distorted in the half-light, and there was a horrible quality about their faces now so that they looked like aristocratic fops, grotesque, hungry, licking their lips in anticipation. Soon he recognized Patty's unmistakable contours, her face planted in an appetizer plate. He crept forward, the floors sticky with something, and the void between them grew less defined with each step until their shoulders were almost touching. He held his breath, waited, and the impractical quiet of this gathering accrued weight, accentuated the dynamo of bad vibes he felt in his gut, some primordial foreboding synched to a mysterious, malicious quality in the men's breathing, the nonstop fidgeting of feet.

"They say she can't feel anything," a man whispered to another. "Some sort of birth defect."

Soon the curtain parted, a plank of pale light fell across the room, and the crowd tightened as a young woman stepped out of the kitchen in a woolen robe patterned in arabesque circles. She was the color of raw ginger and had wide expressionless eyes that resembled the moon, hair tightly coiled in a chignon and garlanded with fruit. Behind her, two robed men followed like pallbearers, walking an oblong steel trough that gave off hot offal smells. A burst of chatter shuddered through the dark, and the crowd quivered with excitement as she disrobed, her curvaceous naked figure mottled with welts and weals, burrs of scar tissue, entire sections of her back and buttocks knotted like the base of a melted candle. In the blood-colored light, her face appeared disembodied, hovering there above the crowd with the faded, ghostlike quality of a daguerreotype as the kitchen staff laid down the trough, oblivious or just indifferent to the leering conference of men. The room grew hot and agitated, and, as the assistants lifted and slipped her into a steaming chutney of blackened vegetables and chicken livers, a pungent barnyard stink of stew and human sweat hung in the air and spasms began rippling through the crowd, the mass swelling and stirring around the woman, one of the men getting on all fours and shoveling into the trough with his hands before an assistant kicked him in the ribs. The doorman rushed in, jaw set, arms folded as his eyes tracked the room; but as he stepped between the trough and the crowd he slipped on some drippings on the tarp, his head striking the metal tray on the way down, and then the crowd broke apart and there was a riot of feet and sharp elbows and hands at Leonard's back and batlike shadows rose up the walls as the men swarmed in a fray of flesh on the steaming woman and a foul gravy of gizzards and entrails sloshed to the floor in curling brumes of steam that scudded across the room. Patty crumpled in the stampede as the doorman and the assistants pulled recumbent figures away from the woman, who was curled up in the trough and screaming now as some of the men circled around her in dizzy, narcotized movements, half-naked, their faces spackled with pink meat and one of them leaning into the trough, biting her arm, another straddling the curtains and masturbating with his back to the crowd.

"We have to go," Leonard said as he grabbed Patty's arm.

"What the hell are you doing here?" she said.

It took all his strength to get her to her feet and required nearly as much to shove her through an occlusion in the crowd. By the time they'd reached the hallway and Leonard groped for the door, a full-scale brawl was exploding behind them. They fled into the stairwell to the sounds of screaming, and soon Leonard heard feet rushing at their backs, the howls of a man being beaten somewhere in the dark below.

"The roof," Leonard said. "It's not safe downstairs."

They pushed up the stairs, Leonard periodically stopping to wait as Patty trundled up behind him. She labored for breaths, crabbed her way up the final steps as she hefted her weight on the railing as though she were pulling luggage. Eventually they breached the roof and plodded along the length of the building, its weather-beaten silver surface stippled with water. It was dark, and a cold rain began to slap at them as they crouched behind a low concrete wall. Patty was panting, appeared peaked and sick, had panic written across her face.

Leonard walked over to the parapet edge of the roof and examined a tree line of rooftop water tanks, buildings bejeweled with lights. A bawl of sirens from several avenues away was closing the distance.

"I'd call the police, but it sounds like they'll be here soon enough," Leonard said. "What did you expect would happen down there, coming to a place like this, with those people?"

"I'm just doing my job," she said. She sharpened her gaze, seemed to possess a newfound awareness of her surroundings. "Believe it or not, I'm up to big things these days."

"I know all about your promotion. I saw you pitching account strategies for Pinnacle yesterday. And then I found you at a restaurant earlier this evening. Looks like you've got a solid meal ticket."

It was a crapshoot rhetorical strategy, showing his cards so early, but it provided the illusory cover he needed to retain some modicum of control.

"I know a few things too," she said. "Trotwood told me he offered you a job after the *Register* wrote that story about your new company. Thanks for stealing my idea, by the way."

"I didn't steal it," Leonard said. "I was just inspired by what you said and devised a better concept."

"You're a bastard. You haven't changed a bit. I'm glad that newspaper burned you. It's what you deserve, and now the entire world knows what a liar you are."

"I met your father yesterday," Leonard said. "Looks like the apple didn't fall far from the tree. He's a deranged pervert."

The rain grew harder, and rushing winds came over them. She slumped against the concrete barrier, made a pained expression as she rubbed her ankle. "Leave my father alone."

"As far as your idea goes, how would I know you'd do anything with it?" Leonard said. "I took it for passing conversation. You've never worked toward a goal in your life."

"I told you I wanted to make it in this business. And now I have a job I like, a career! I kept my end of the deal. I didn't tell anyone about your lies or all the crazy things you stuff in your mouth. I haven't bothered you in a month, and here you are, trying to ruin everything."

"Please," Leonard said. "Wake up, Patty. This whole thing is a ruse. Pinnacle is keeping you around because you own the concept, but you and I know they won't put you in a boardroom. They have teams upon teams for that sort of thing. Why do you think they sent you here? They're placating you, making you believe you're part of something. They're using you."

Her face swelled. "Pinnacle's going to sue you."

"I've been thinking about that. I'm guessing I would've been served with papers if that was the case. Then it dawned on me that court documents make Pinnacle's outrage practice public, which is the last thing they want, considering what that kind of publicity did for me."

"That article was about the fact that you're a phony, and that you lied to get a job you didn't deserve."

"An exaggeration. All I did was stretch the truth when my old boss interviewed me."

"And what'd you stretch the truth about?"

"Everything. I'd never worked in PR before. And I never graduated from college. I just kicked around for a few years, working odd jobs in Ohio, and eventually came here thinking I could plant a flag, maybe make some money to help my mom. So, I compiled a bunch of fake résumés and bull-shitted my way into interviews for gigs I wasn't qualified for."

"Color me shocked," Patty said.

"I guess they smelled it a mile away, because I never got a foot in the door. I ended up signing on with a temp agency in Midtown that pimped me out for low-level jobs all over the city. Office work, sales, you name it. Things hit a new low when I was hired to hand out promotional materials for a PR firm to tourists in the Theater District. One day after work, I got picked to carry the residuals back to the client, and I overheard the HR department discussing their schedule for some account executive job they were trying to fill. So, that night I did some research, typed up a résumé, and went back the next morning with this prepared spiel about the call I'd received for an interview. Turns out the South Tower had been struck by a hijacked plane about ten minutes prior, so no one else showed up for the interview, and just about everyone at the office had left to be with family or search for loved ones. Jack looked at my résumé for all of two seconds before giving me the job."

"That's it?"

"The work should've been a pretty good indication that I was out of my element, but as it turned out, I was good at it. They had me sit at a desk and write these press releases all day. I didn't know what I was doing, so I just glued together every cynical retread of what I assumed a media pitch sounded like. The more familiar and overworn the words were, the more my superiors praised my work. It was the easiest job in the world."

"You hitched your dishonesty to an industry that thrives on bullshit," Patty said.

"I was named an Account Supervisor a year later, then Account Director, and ultimately ended up becoming Managing Director when they opened the crisis practice several years ago. I had a career. I became somebody. But I didn't deserve any of it."

"I'm surprised you're telling me this."

"I actually feel like a weight's been taken off my shoulders. You read the article; what good would hiding it do at this point? Incidentally, if you were so angry with me, why didn't you tell your bosses I was the one who leaked those merger documents to a journalist? Why didn't you show them the video you took of me eating pencils?"

"Because it's not relevant," she said. "It never was. As it turns out, your Achilles' heel isn't the fact that you eat inanimate objects. You're a fraud, and none of your ideas are your own."

"To be honest, this isn't the life I wanted."

"Me neither," Patty said. "Out of curiosity, what did you want?"

"To be successful."

"And how do you define that?"

"I don't know yet," Leonard said. He walked back to the ledge, looked to the traffic lights below. White men in suits were rushing across the yard now, away from the scene. "Listen, we need to put our shoulder to the wheel. I have a plan."

"Another plan." She sighed. "Spit it out, Leonard. It's cold, and I'm getting hungry."

"So, Trotwood wants us to work together so he can keep your idea and drive me out of business. How about we beat him at his own game? How about you come work for me?"

She looked him over, as though waiting for an appending clause. "Why?"

"Because you're a disaster. You ruin everything you touch. For a business focused on destroying clients' reputations, you're lightning in a bottle."

"Always with the flattery," she said. "Nice try. You only want me to join your company so you can have ownership of my concept."

"Fine," he said. "But what would you prefer, being a cog in the machine, or working someplace where you can do whatever you want? Wait until you meet the team I've put together."

She was quiet again, and Leonard knew she was processing the idea, that now was the time to swing for the fences. "It'll be just like before, as many meals as you want, wherever you want. I'll show you the ropes, and when you're ready we'll work together, as a team."

"Everyone will hate us," Patty said.

"What else is new? We'll burn those bridges when we get to them. You know what they say: Do what you love, and you'll never work a day in your life."

"They never tell you the flipside," she said, "that doing what you love makes it work."

"So, what do you say?"

"What would my title be?"

"I don't know. Some leadership position. Your choice."

"Co-owner," she said.

Leonard's mouth drew tight, and he gritted his teeth. He had the feeling he was being guided back into familiar waters. "Let's not get ahead of ourselves," he said as he wrested his face into a smile.

"And I want an apology."

At this, he turned away and faced the lights of traffic again. "For what?"

"Forget it," she said. "People like you don't change. Why the hell would I work with you, anyway? You're an entitled child who just wants to make sure your piece of the pie is bigger than everyone else's. The only thing you or Trotwood are good at is manipulating people. As if that's some special talent. If there's anything remarkable about you, it's your awe-inspiring inability to change."

"Keep going," he said. "Call me whatever names you want."

"You're all the same. That's why I'm going to make some money, and then I'm out. I don't want to have anything to do with you careerists anymore. None of you care about me or anyone else. You only want to use me."

"Then I guess we're even," he said. When he turned around, fat tears were rolling down her cheeks, which surprised him. Patty stood and began cantering her way across the roof, back toward the stairwell.

"Look, I get it. Take some time and think it over. No rush," he said and followed after her. "The way I see it, we've already got a toehold in the market, so what do we have to lose? I want to work with you. Believe it or not, I actually had some good times back then. I'm just not very good in social situations. It's a horse I didn't choose to ride on, you know? Hey, I'm sorry I stole your idea. Apology accepted? Hopefully you'll change your mind in a few weeks, and we can bury the hatchet. Hope springs eternal, right? Am I just pitching to the wind here? True story: Henry Kissinger once said, 'There can't be a crisis next week. My schedule is already full.'"

She shuffled to the stair hatch and braced herself against it. She paused for a moment, then began swaying on her feet as she gripped her shoulder.

"You all right?" Leonard said.

A web of muscles gathered at her neck. She made a pained expression, vomited, and collapsed, where she turned on her side and began to claw at her chest.

"What happened? What can I do?" Leonard said.

"It hurts," Patty said. "It hurts."

Chapter 18

The Mount Sinai waiting room faced an outstretched tile hallway. It was broad, paneled with buffed aluminum tables and unfolded with arrows in antacid pastels guiding visitors to various departments. Leonard scrutinized a spread of coffee-table entertainment monthlies, then checked his cellphone and read a text message Todd Armitage had left him. Several nurses commiserated in a nearby corner. A technician pushed a rolling computer cart studded with dents. Leonard leafed through a magazine and debated looking for a vending machine, just to have something to do.

It was an hour before a doctor introduced himself and provided an abstruse medical rundown of Patty's condition using words Leonard didn't understand. He appeared several days unshaven and had a sardonic, downturned mouth that barely moved when he spoke.

"Guess I didn't realize someone her age could have a heart attack," Leonard said, half-listening.

The doctor stared at him quizzically. "She didn't have a heart attack. Her stomach ruptured. Personally, I've never treated anyone with this particular condition. But it can happen."

Leonard blinked several times as he absorbed the words, exhaled as though something heavy had lain over his chest. A numbness came over him, and he found himself scanning the hallway, vacant.

The doctor offered the standard deferential treatment, crossed his hands, and held his head low. "We were able to make a prompt diagnosis based on a physical exam and X-rays," he said. "She has stomach perforations, the result of ulcers, which no doubt contributed to the rupture. We're taking her into emergency surgery now."

"And how is she doing?"

"She's not responsive."

Leonard closed his eyes for some time. His fingers found a frayed thread on his cuff and, without thinking about it, placed it in his mouth.

"I'll be forthcoming," the doctor said. "Even with surgical treatment, prognosis isn't good. She got to us late. She could die from the hemorrhage before the operation is complete. There could be surgical complications. She could get an infection and die from sepsis after the fact. You should understand the gravity of the situation and have realistic expectations."

"Okay."

"I encourage you to remain present until after surgery," he continued. "We have a separate waiting area. In the meantime, we'll need you to go to registration and help us with some information."

"I'm not a family member," Leonard said. "She has a father. I don't have his phone number. I have an address . . ." He trailed off.

After speaking with the clerical staff, Leonard took the elevator to the floor where Patty had been admitted and found a waiting area outfitted with rows of plastic shell chairs. On the far side of the room, an elderly man sat with his shoulders drawn forward, fingers bookmarking the pages of a novel he wasn't reading. Leonard shifted in his chair but couldn't get comfortable. A perceptible silence governed the room.

Time in hospitals bore strange dimensions, a casino-like quality. The fluorescent tube lights above him were migraine-inducingly bright and gave everyone sickly skin tones, and the constant odor of gauze and disinfectant and the chairs that doubled as implements of nagging discomfort underscored an appreciable irony to him: that society's first line of defense against death had occasioned the most joyless place imaginable. A raucous noise came from the street below, and soon there were rioting chants, the war footing of a political demonstration making its way past the building. The elderly man rushed from his seat, propped his elbows on the windowsill, and clutched himself there, transfixed.

"Wonder what they're protesting," the man said.

"Does it matter?" Leonard said.

"Guess not," he said. "They're young. They have everything."

Hours passed. Eventually Leonard closed his eyes and after some time began drifting through the doorway of sleep, but anxiety kept him from fully unmooring from consciousness. Time felt suspended, and, though he remained cognizant of his surroundings, he realized he must have fallen asleep at some point, because now the doctor was standing over him, and Leonard was perched on the edge of the chair, wondering how he'd gotten there.

"She's been out of surgery for an hour," he said. "She's in the ICU and heavily sedated. You can see her if you'd like, briefly."

Leonard was escorted to a gray room that hummed with the drone of medical equipment. He parted a curtain that was drawn around the bed, where racks of chromium machines purred and lilted as Patty slept. She wore a cornflower gown, and a band of sweat collected along her forehead. Her skin appeared chapped and drained of blood, her nose covered with a yellowed nasal mask, and her right forearm, cradled over a pillow, was blackened like an overripe banana and stitched with an intravenous line that ran from a peripheral vein to an IV bag. He stood bedside in the soft-focus light, lost insofar as what to do, listening to the ventilator's ocean sounds, the gentle whispering of the machines as Patty mumbled in her sleep. Then her mouth was moving, jaw opening and clasping as her index finger, clamped with an oxygen-saturation monitor that resembled a small sandwich, began scratching the bed rail.

"I can't believe you're awake," he said.

She lurched herself upright, wincing from the pain. She opened her eyes, and her jaw clasped again, and he realized she was trying to say something. He leaned closer as she peeled off the strip of medical tape that held the mask in place.

"Food." The word dribbled out of her mouth. "Bring food."

"I don't think that's a good idea."

"Bring food."

Several minutes later, Leonard stepped out of the room and took a brief but calculated inventory of the floor layout, the ceiling-mounted camera in the corner, the alcove down the hall where two nurses congregated, before nodding to the doctor, who turned off the lights. A thin rain was falling, and a bank of fog had settled over the street as he walked several blocks until he found a bodega. He ordered the first rank-and-file sandwich that came to mind—chicken parmesan—and returned through the fog to the hospital, passed the waiting area and a vacant information desk on Patty's floor, and waited by the double doors of the ICU ward. A janitor wearing headphones wheeled a mop bucket into a supply closet. Several minutes later, a pair of nurses exited the ward and he scuttled past them and navigated empty, labyrinthine halls.

He fed her in the dark room by the green light of the machines. She opened her mouth, bit, and withdrew, commenced chewing carefully. She didn't actually eat any of it; each bite tumbled out of her mouth and gathered in clumps on her gown, and then her eyes watered and after a while the aperture of her pupils began to turn, bloodshot corneas dilating into a milk-white void. She chewed a few more times and closed her eyes.

"I have just one request," he said.

"What, what is it?" she whispered.

"That video. The video you took of me eating those pencils."

"Ah, that old chestnut."

"Destroy it."

She managed a stifled laugh. "I can't," she said after a prolonged moment.

"Why?"

"There was no video," she said. "You threw the memory card out the window, remember? I never had time to back it up."

He stood there with the words for a moment, feeling the blood rush to his head. He wanted to scream, break something, but as his thoughts cohered and he began to realize what this new information meant, his anger was quieted by ineffable waves of relief.

"Believe it or not, I've quit eating things," he stuttered. "Cold turkey, nearly a month—"

She'd fallen asleep. Leonard gathered the remains of the sandwich, threw it in the trash, and slipped out of the room. With the door closing, he couldn't help but notice the Styrofoam cup on the counter, the message it bore in bleeding orange ink: "When I am empty, please dispose of me properly."

He navigated the halls again, where the lights were doing funny things, were variegated with pulses of wild color, everything fuzzy in his peripheral vision. The boundaries of the floor and walls began to blur like the edges of a watercolor, and as he backtracked to the corner in search of the elevator, it occurred to him that something about the choreography here was all wrong, that he couldn't account for several essential details of the last hour, like how he'd found Patty's room, or how he'd even gotten outside, considering he couldn't remember taking the elevator in the first place. He squinted because he had trouble seeing where he was going, and his feet felt heavy, and he had tremendous difficulty walking, and now voices were fading in and out as the fog of sleep burned away before he opened his eyes to the glint of dawn breaking the soft purple void of night outside the waiting-room window.

THE SUN WAS UP BY THE TIME HE RETURNED TO HIS APARTMENT. LEONard noticed the flashing light on the telephone, the two missed calls registered by the caller ID: one from Todd Armitage, the other from the real estate agent in Ohio. He deleted both messages, then picked up the receiver and dialed his agent.

"About that offer," the woman yawned. "I want you to keep in mind—"

"We got an offer? How much?"

"Seventy-nine five. Didn't you get my message?"

"We said eighty-five," Leonard said. "It's unacceptable."

"We're in a recession, Leonard. These are qualified buyers. They're pre-approved. They have great credit, solid references."

"The house was appraised for less than it's worth, and now we're low-balling the appraisal. If they're qualified, they can afford what we're selling."

"They wrote a letter. It's very moving. I can read it over the phone if you'd like. I went ahead and put a copy in the mail yesterday."

"I don't care. These aren't the terms we agreed to."

"In this market, it's amazing we got an offer at all."

"We got an offer because you're giving the place away. The answer is no."

Leonard hung up, stripped off his clothes, and staggered to the bedroom. He lay down furious, but in minutes found himself gliding over fields of sedum. Then the phone began to ring again. He barreled into the kitchen, angry all over, where the caller ID had registered an unknown number.

"This is Mount Sinai Hospital," a woman's voice said, and Leonard went slack.

PATTY'S VIEWING WAS THREE DAYS LATER, A WEDNESDAY. THE SKY WAS hedged with silver clouds that morning as Leonard's cab crossed the Queensborough Bridge, and a foghorn sounded as a rust-colored flotilla pushed up the river below. Soon the outline of warehouses came into view, the entire borough resembling hundreds of miniature tombstones in the smoke. The funeral home was located on Northern Boulevard between an off-track betting parlor and a Blockbuster Video, cheerless as funeral homes typically go, a modest, drab chapel adorned with sage wallpaper and dull gray natural light. Elderly women with weak chins stood over the casket as Leonard walked in, and several old-timers occupied rows of folding chairs. Patty's father had parked his wheelchair in the front row. He appeared dazed, racked with exhaustion, his eyes staring into space and blinking furtively. Besides that, there was a sparse crowd; from what Leonard could tell, none of her coworkers were in attendance. He scanned the room, then inched back into the foyer and watched everything from a vantage point as removed as possible. Todd Armitage texted him; it was the second text he'd received from him that morning. *Seriously, where the hell are you? I've got a blue-chip client seeking services, and you're MIA. I can't do everything by myself over here.* Leonard deleted the message and turned off his phone.

He hadn't been to work in three days. He'd stayed in bed for the first two, getting up only for the bathroom, where he spent hours in a scalding tub. Slamming doors in the hallway, footsteps from the apartment above, the telephone made his heart thrum. The world had gone gray, was drained of color, and the prospect of venturing outside seemed akin to groping around in a blinding fog. On the afternoon of the third day, he boarded a train and traveled aimlessly between the boroughs, transferred lines until he found himself standing inexplicably in the Financial District, staring at the hole in the ground where the Trade Center had been. It was unnervingly quiet, as though he was watching the city with the volume turned off. Several men on Church Street were selling commemorative memorabilia of the attacks, giving credence to the notion that while the terrorists had wounded us, they hadn't crushed our indefatigable will to capitalize on even our most sacred grievances. Standing there, he'd felt a lot like how he felt now in the funeral home, that he was in a place filled with intimate secrets he wasn't sure he had a right to witness. He'd never rehearsed for anything like this and felt exposed and naked, unsure of what social protocols were expected. Occasionally, eyes looked him over from the chapel, and it occurred to him he should probably introduce himself, at the very least offer his condolences to Patty's father, but he couldn't bring himself to see the casket up close, so he hung back in the foyer and pretended to check his phone. Even looking in the casket's general direction, glimpsing the rictus that peered out over the ledge, brought him palpable discomfort. A low hiss was coming from a radiator in the chapel now, and he occupied himself with the superficial observation of how inappropriately intrusive this was.

The door behind him gaped open, and a cold wind rushed in as Graydon Trotwood crossed the lobby with an excessively ornamental arrangement of flowers cradled in his arms. He cut Leonard a breezy half-smile before making a cavalier promenade up the aisle, where he placed the flowers at the head of Patty's casket. After the adequate show of solemnity was made, he went to Patty's father and took a knee, where he offered sympathy-card condolences, each word limned with false gravity, calculated for maximum effect.

Leonard made for the door, unable to watch the spectacle any longer. He passed a gray strip of bodegas and discount stores as he searched for the subway. He wanted to eat something, hole up in his apartment and gorge himself into delirium. Gales of wind swept across the street and a flurry of dead leaves stirred around him like bonfire ashes.

"She was a visionary," Trotwood said as he galloped up behind.

Leonard quickened his pace. "Get away from me, you asshole."

"I'm surprised you're here. I thought you two were adversaries. Perhaps you're rethinking our talk from the other day?"

"I couldn't be clearer. This borders on stalking."

"Time isn't on our side. My offer, my willingness to come to an agreement on a partnership has its limits. Both of us know no agency in town would hire you."

"You don't have anything without her. I'll admit it, okay? I stole the idea, the entire concept from her. Go ahead and sue me."

"As it turns out, some of our senior management don't want to give you a seat at the table. They think you're too combative, not a team player. I disagree. In fact, I assured them you could be quite agreeable."

Trotwood slipped in front of Leonard and removed a banker's check from his breast pocket. "This isn't my first rodeo, Leonard. The devil knows his own. After all, what is communication if it isn't the art of compromise?"

Admittedly, the check captivated him. He couldn't help it; he'd never seen that many zeros next to his name before. It now occurred to Leonard how much stamina it required for someone like Trotwood to be who he was, to remain in high seduction mode all the time, the reckless arrogance to take whatever he wanted regardless of the cost. This was why he was successful, Leonard concluded: He undertook responsibilities most would find abhorrent; his tolerance for risk and appetite for reward placed him in confrontational circumstances with a regularity that would seem demoralizing for any sane, rational adult. Leonard had followed in the footsteps of men like this most of his adult life, and though he hadn't overlooked their entitled overreach nearly insomuch as he'd tried to see past it, it'd never occurred to him that we allowed these people to assume leadership positions because they exhibited the very traits we'd be loath to possess ourselves.

"Welcome to the deep end of the pool, Leonard. You can do anything you want with it. Buy property. Do you like boats? I have several." He paused. "Admittedly, I'm being a bit impetuous. We'll still need our lawyers to draft an agreement, and there are documents of sale we'll have to sign, of course. And you can't have the check now. It's all pretty much just for show, a way of kicking the tires—"

"Go to hell," Leonard said and continued walking.

"It appears you're having difficulty grasping the reality of the situation. We're going to get you sooner or later. You realize that, right? I could hire one of my patent troll lawyers to file a strike suit against you just to tie this up in the courts for years. This hill isn't worth dying on."

"Why are you doing this?" Leonard said.

"An existential search for clarity and purpose to distract me from imminent death. Is that what you're looking for?"

"I'm serious. You run one of the largest advertising conglomerates in the world. Why do you care about my business?"

A cawing laugh tumbled out of him. "Because I have to," he stammered. "What, you think this is about me? You have a gift, Leonard, but you fail to see the way the world works. I have an obligation to deliver maximum return to our shareholders, and my industry, like all others, is threatened by the possibility that something better will come along and render it obsolete. We need to grow, move forward. I'm faced with immense daily pressure to ensure that we remain relevant."

Several cars wandered through the intersection. The wind kicked up again, jolting him with cold, and he caught a whiff of Trotwood's cologne, a clean, heady musk that reminded him of linseed oil and orange peel, a solvent used to polish antique furniture.

"Let's say we're spiders," Trotwood said, "and I build a web on my branch that catches all the bugs. And then you come along and build your web on the same branch. Not a very nice story for me, is it?"

"I'm having difficulty with the anthropomorphism here. Maybe you could better explain things using puppets?"

"Perhaps I could even survive in these conditions, carve out a nice life for myself. But how could I sleep at night knowing you're just out of reach, stealing from my children, my legacy? That wouldn't make me a very successful person, would it? It wouldn't make much sense for me to tolerate something like that, you understand?"

"Sure."

"You see, then: it's nothing personal. These are the terms human existence has operated on since its inception. It's an essential feature of this machine you've willfully served all these years. The only way we succeed at anything is to make something bigger than what existed before. Our culture confuses expediency for progress, and that's why we're routinely pressured to do what's best for profits, even when it means what's worst for our employees and the public. It sounds insane, but this horse trading is what's expected of us. We're rewarded for this volatility, Leonard. What just happened to our economy proves it. A bubble rises somewhere, and investors race to feed it with massive amounts of borrowed capital until the shares become woefully overvalued. Then there's a massive sell-off, and the markets plummet, and the entire system bottoms out under its own weight. So, the banks start hoarding money, and people like me have to clean up the balance sheet and lay off a bunch of employees, which causes the government to prime the pump with buyouts and bailouts and lines of liquidity and stimulus programs so we'll keep hiring and investors keep borrowing and people keep buying or betting against the market the next time it becomes volatile. And then, what do you know, the markets rally, the engine builds steam, and everyone's happy to be playing the game all over again. We've been down this road a hundred times. I don't like it any more than you do. But I understand the rules. We all have to make a living. We have to protect what's ours. Aside from dying, it's the only thing expected of us. It's how our species survives. What we call free will, it's just a term we use when we assume acting out our nature is some kind of choice."

At some point, Leonard continued walking. Apparently, Trotwood lacked the requisite self-awareness to realize it when no one was listening, because he continued going on, talking to the wind after Leonard was long up the block. He accelerated his pace when he picked up on the patter of footsteps behind him, made to cross the street and erred in his footing, rolling his ankle in a divot in the pavement between the curb and the storm drain, where he went down hard, driving his shoulder into a puddle under the headlights of a taxi already over him, ineffectually throwing up his hands as the tires screamed to a halt several inches from his face. He picked himself up to the howls of children who stood watching dumbstruck from the corner and then promptly fled the scene.

HE RODE THE TRAIN STANDING ALL THE WAY TO MIDTOWN, WHERE HE wandered the streets and navigated meat-grinder traffic. If you had seen him there, stunned by the cold and staggering through the parade of tourists in his muddied coat, you might have assumed he was a vagrant, arms flailing, shouting insults into the void as he limped his way through the weltering mass like a busted marionette. He pushed east, combed through the undulating crowd that moiled around a busy intersection, and soon found himself drifting under Times Square's casino of lights. He intermingled with a mammoth herd of thick, slow-moving men and women who carried expedition-sized shopping bags or pulled hamster-shaped children, all looking skyward as though in a trance, captivated by the carousels of billboards and lights and logos, many watching the spectacle behind camcorders or cellphones, capturing a record of their pilgrimage. Then the crowd grew thicker, their agitated, untrammeled movements pushing him at the shoulders. He pressed forward but shifted his weight onto his bad leg and lost his footing, and a throb of fear went through him as he stumbled and went down on the sidewalk under pistoning feet. He grabbed for something, a fanny pack, a pajama-sized T-shirt, but soon found himself crab-racing on all fours until he reached a clearing at the end of the block, where he sank exhausted onto a worn nub of curb.

When he caught his disheveled reflection in a hotel window, his first impulse was to feel sorry for himself. It took him a moment to recognize the building's trademark dihedral exterior; it was the same hotel where his former coworker Gibby Goodfriend had killed himself last year, the place where he'd counseled the disgraced social media mogul all those months ago, just before this mess began. He breached the revolving glass doors, crossed the atrium lobby and the massive concrete trusses that held the structure in place, and limped to a glass elevator tree. He took the elevator to the top floor and strolled the hallway until he was sure no one was looking, then edged up to the railing and surveyed the ascending spiral gallery of doors that girded the walls, the roaring atrium twenty-four stories below. He wondered what Goodfriend had stumbled onto, what secrets melancholia manifested in those dark moments before he climbed over and stepped into the void. He clasped the railing with both hands. It was battleship gray, oddly warm, and dangerously low, barely belting his navel. He hoisted himself up and leaned forward onto his hip, just to get a feel for it, to be as close to the edge as possible without going over, then craned his neck until his shoulders canted over the edge and peered over the lip of the chasm into the vertiginous lungs of the building, where he watched the rind of tangerine light from the street glow at the lobby doors. An arresting thought occurred to him as he marveled at what little effort it required to send himself over, the fold of an elbow, the slightest bend at the waist. He held himself steady there as a mineshaft of wind tousled his tie, listened to the mosaic of sounds from the lobby reverberate into a meaningless echo by the time it reached his ear, an oddly melodious sound. Eventually he stepped down from the ledge and stumbled back to the elevator.

IT WAS DARK BY THE TIME HE RETURNED HOME. HE STRIPPED OFF HIS muddied clothes, collapsed onto the chaise longue, and flipped on the television, where a lifestyle report offered tips on how to host a woodland-creature-themed baby shower. He stared into the fish tank, the water now a sickly green, and watched as several fish cycled the murk in slow, dispirited laps. He wondered if the patterns offered them a false sense of purpose, if structuring the space they orbited day after day cast their conditions in a more tolerable light or provided the delusion that they were somehow in control of their environment. He checked his email and read a press release about an agency that had launched a "Communications ER" department that could dispatch a team of PR "first responders" at any hour in the advent of a crisis. Eventually, he attended to the neglected pile of mail strewn over his kitchen counter and opened the envelope his real estate agent had sent him, unfolded a slip of eggshell stationery, where a second folded sheet of cardstock floated to the floor.

Dear homeowner,

We are first-time homebuyers from Circleville who have made plans to move to Lanchester with the hopes of raising our family. The layout, amenities, size, and location of your home are exactly what we're looking for.

We have spent a great deal of time in Lanchester and love its sense of community. We are looking for a home in which we will stay long-term, a place where we can watch our family grow. Your house felt like that home to us.

Your agent has received a copy of our financials, pay stubs, and taxes. We have impeccable credit and assets, as well as loan approval and solid references, and are prepared to meet with you and move forward in this matter professionally and expeditiously. We appreciate your consideration.

Finally, our four-year-old son drew a picture based on our visit to the house last week. We would like to share it with you.

Sincerely,

Bill and Debbie Baughman

He'd read more inspired refrigerator poetry. Leonard wadded the letter and threw it in the trash, and, after a beat, picked up the folded piece of cardstock that had fallen to the floor. It was a child's crayon rendering of Leonard's home, typical insofar as kids' scribblings go, the family standing on the lawn police lineup-style, a trio of neckless stick figures with asymmetric limbs and crooked, ghoulish smiles. What the drawing lacked in realism it made up for in symbolic verisimilitude. Several details struck Leonard as strikingly apropos, if only by sheer accident. A tilting house on the verge of giving up, quick scattered strokes of an unkempt yard. A sun that hung low above it all, as though the home had been built at the center of everything.

Leonard looked over the drawing a second time. He felt seized by something. The sensation was raw and new, and he wanted to bury it somewhere, but a low moan rose from his throat, and he began to sob inconsolably. He gripped the chair and swayed like a tree being freed from the earth in a violent storm. His head felt empty now, there was a tingling in his fingers, a stabbing pain in the marrow of his breastbone, and he found he could hardly breathe, that he was seeing the world from the other side of the glass. After a while he picked up the phone and called his agent.

"Seventy-nine five," Leonard said. "I'll take it."

Then he called his brother.

Chapter 19

That Thursday, the morning he was scheduled to leave for Ohio, snow began to fall over the city, granular pellets that, despite a relative lack of cold, demonstrated remarkable resilience on pavement. By the time Leonard's cab approached LaGuardia, whirling eddies were drifting over the expressway. He checked in and, after being groped, wanded, and stage-managed through airport security, arrived at his gate with an hour to spare. He read a newspaper, then stared at the bay of televisions that paneled the walls. The news reported the financial crisis had U.S. consumers spending less on food than they had in sixty years. The winner of a recent million-a-year-for-life lottery was an investment banker who was already a millionaire. A hash of red text began flashing on a nearby monitor as flights were either delayed or canceled. Leonard's chest tightened as he waited, eyes tracking the screen, periodically surveying the fleet of grounded planes on the tarmac outside, wings under cakes of accumulating snow.

A crowd gathered around the jet bridge doorway ten minutes before departure, and a chorus of groans shuddered through the area as their flight acquired delayed status on the monitor. An agent asked passengers to remain at the gate. Leonard paced. On the television, a trade group representing the retail sector claimed the economy would hurt holiday sales figures for brick-and-mortar stores. Thirty minutes later, the Columbus flight was delayed again. Fifteen minutes after that, it was canceled. As the gate cleared out, Leonard considered his options, consulted the monitors, and noticed flights to Cincinnati and Cleveland had also been canceled. He crossed the terminal and returned to the airline desk, where mobs of displaced passengers were rallying their indignation. Speaking with an agent, he determined he could catch an Indianapolis-bound flight that was scheduled to board in an hour, rent a car, and drive the distance. He transferred his ticket, passed through security once again, and killed time in a food court, a bookstore, and an oddly prolific clothing outlet. As he eyed the clusters of doleful-looking travelers now camped out over the terminal's terrazzo floor, it occurred to him this airport managed to wed the worst parts of a shopping mall with the charms of a bus terminal. He bought another newspaper and walked to his new gate, and when he got there discovered the Indianapolis flight had been canceled as well.

IT WAS NEARING DUSK BY THE TIME HE HAILED A CAB AND MADE HIS WAY back to the city. Using his phone, he discovered a car-rental outpost in Murray Hill that still had vehicles available. He signed some paperwork and was on the road within twenty minutes. He drove cautiously through the snow, eliciting outrage from the vehicles around him; anytime he got behind the wheel in this town, he felt like he was negotiating with the criminally insane, and inclement weather accentuated his paranoia. He finally crossed the Lincoln Tunnel, where the freedom of a naked road funneled out before him. An hour later, he was winding through shallow Pennsylvania foothills, feeling the curves and tension of the highway, where the topography relaxed into empty stretches through dark wilds of country.

His mind wandered as he drove through the night, staring at the lacuna of moonlike terrain where the salt-stained pavement met oblivion. He passed vacant weighing outposts, roadside rest plazas the size of shopping malls, mile after mile of sleeping blue country. The highway was desolate, and for hours his only visitors were the shivering emerald lights of overpasses and the steady spindrift of snow. He navigated rambling cerulean hills bearded with smoke, palls of fog that clung to the cliffs that draped the highway, drove until his eyelids were heavy, and found a motor lodge somewhere on the outskirts of Wheeling, where he managed a restless sleep and dreamed of things crawling over him.

He was back on the road at sunrise, armed with, to his estimation, three hours of sleep. The horizon stretched out like a vast ocean in the gray light of morning as he crossed the Ohio border, fumes breaking in waves over pavement as though commemorating his arrival. Then the interstate narrowed to two-lane blacktop and the familiar signposts began to appear: cross-gabled farmhouses, abandoned grain elevators, vacant service stations littered with tire casings and pallet racks. He approached Lanchester's city limits and passed the usual procession of used car lots, rent-to-own appliance stores, guns-and-ammo shops, payday-loan outlets inhabiting former fast-food restaurants, and by nine-thirty made it to Norman's apartment, which occupied the top floor of a three-story quad overlooking the highway. His brother wore a suit that looked like it'd been purchased at a thrift store, sleeves hanging off his arms, slacks pulled up to the navel. By the grace of God, he'd trimmed the mustache, the tendrils of a faint cookie duster the only remaining evidence of the monstrosity that had haunted his lip a month before.

For whatever reason, Norman deemed it appropriate to give Leonard an impromptu tour of the apartment, which thankfully took all of thirty seconds. Growing up with someone always granted a privileged, almost suffocating access to that person, and from early on, even when they were very young, Leonard had known his brother was odd. He slept with the lights on and preferred shaving without lather, habits that didn't speak to outright masochism per se, but suggested he inhabited a bizarre behavioral spectrum whose occupants enjoyed mild acts of discomfort. Looking around the apartment confirmed Leonard's diagnosis hewed close enough to reality for him to continue believing it. The place resembled a showroom unit, a home waiting for the family to move in. It was as clean as Leonard's apartment and had an ascetic quality, minimally furnished, the walls bare and stripped of adornment. As usual, the bedroom was the activity center of the home. A TV and several video-game consoles occupied a particleboard entertainment center beside the bed, which was actually an unfolded futon. Video games and pizza boxes and clothes were scattered across the carpet.

This, Leonard remembered, was why he'd called his brother "Grandma" growing up: he always kept himself shut in the bedroom.

"I'm going back to school in the spring, taking a few engineering courses at OU's Lanchester branch," Norman said as he followed Leonard into the kitchen. "Maybe next year I'll transfer to your alma mater and make the commute to Columbus several times a week."

Leonard's eyes were sensitive to the light, and he saw strobes when he rubbed his temples, realized he was mildly hallucinating.

"You look tired," Norman said. "Whoever heard of a snowstorm in October, anyway?"

"I just want to get this over with. Do you have any coffee?"

"Don't touch the stuff. You want juice or something?" Norman adjusted his tie. "So, what are your thoughts about the meeting? I mean, what's our strategy?"

"It's not that kind of meeting, Grandma. Everything's already been agreed upon. We sign some paperwork and hand over the keys. It's that simple. Where's Mom, anyway?"

"Still at home. I called, but she didn't pick up."

"We need to get going. What in God's name is that smell?"

"Cologne," Norman said. "Do you like it?" He inched uncomfortably close to his brother and thrust his Adam's apple under Leonard's nose.

"You smell like you were molested by a boat mechanic."

They crossed town to their mother's condo. Leonard was too exhausted to deal with Norman's native energy, and, as fate had it, his brother didn't refrain from speaking for as much as a second throughout the drive. It was as though a puppeteer's hand was moving his mouth, assailing Leonard with superficial assessments of neighbors and coworkers he'd never met. Rumor had it Norman's boss at the glass factory had been spiking his orange juice with vodka. Norman wanted to enroll in a German class when he returned to college, because it sounded interesting and fulfilled a humanities requirement, but the only class available was at eight o'clock in the morning, and sorry, that was too early for him. He still saw Herb and Corey, his best friends from high school, on weekends for euchre. Oh, and he'd gone on several dates with a girl he'd met at church, and things were going well. Admittedly, this detail piqued Leonard's curiosity, only because he found it so improbable. His brother had the heat cranked, and Leonard could feel it drying him into a husk, so he lowered the window as Memorial Drive rolled by. The lack of sleep gave everything an attenuated lightness, as though there were a lagging connection between his senses and surroundings. He realized now that he envied his brother in a way he found difficult to articulate. Norman's wants and goals coexisted harmoniously with what a low-stakes environment offered, which was the very sort of provincial indifference that'd always left Leonard's sympathies relatively bounded for the people in this town, the idea that it was enough to simply let life happen while others were out there making things happen. But he realized Norman's contentment spoke to an obscure truth regarding the quotidian smallness of life he'd thought about but had never been able to put into words. How many millions upon millions of one-of-a-kind experiences were occurring at any given second in the world? And how many did a person get to witness in one lifetime? He pondered this for a moment, tried to get the edges of the idea shaped out, but his train of thought was broken at a stoplight, when Norman reached between his legs and ripped a crude square from a pizza delivery menu, proceeded to fold it several times and then commenced squeezing and turning it over in his palm.

"Quit doing that," Leonard said and rolled up the window.

"What?" Norman said.

"That nervous energy thing with the paper. The crinkling."

"Crinkling?"

"Just watch the road."

LEONARD RANG THE CONDOMINIUM DOORBELL AND HUNG BACK ON THE porch. After an uncomfortable beat of silence, he dialed his mother's cellphone. "You called her already?" he said as he keyed in the number a second time.

"Twice," Norman said.

"When was the last time you were here?"

"Guess it's been a few weeks."

"Goddamn it, Grandma."

Leonard yanked the wad of keys from his pocket. Turning the knob, he felt a familiar resistance against the door. His nerves flared as he squeezed through the doorway, and a horrible feeling stole upon him as his eyes adjusted to the appalling sight from the foyer: office chairs, computer monitors, animal carriers, garden tools, luggage sets, coolers, oven mitts, sneakers still in their boxes. A half-dozen wholesale pallets of soda and bottled water. As he took inventory of the salvage yard before them, it occurred to him how stupid he'd been to presume things could've been any different.

"Mom?"

He crossed the living room crabwise, made out the edges of the couch protruding through a hill of debris. The television was on, and a news program listed food-brand mascots some find racially insensitive.

"Mom?"

"Where is she?" Norman said as they clambered through the ruins.

Leonard heard a muffled cry. He was ankle-deep in packages of tube socks when he caught a foot wiggling under a tangle of Christmas lights in the kitchen.

"Give me a hand," Leonard said.

"I'm sorry," she said as they lifted their mother out of the pile. Her limbs were trussed with wires and her face was greasy with whatever she'd put on it the night before. "I'm sorry," she repeated, and she began to cry.

AN HOUR LATER, THE FAMILY DROVE TO THE REAL ESTATE OFFICE, WHICH occupied an unassuming storefront in a strip mall on the northern edge of town. Leonard and Norman left their mother in the back seat, dashed inside, and found the party in a conference room. The group huddled conspiratorially as the brothers entered, looking them over in tentative relief. The table was bookended by both agents, and the buyers, a young, skittish-looking couple, sat between them. The husband wore a tweed jacket and had a strained, constipated expression. The wife had hair that looked like burned rotini and wore a sweater with an embroidered jack-o'-lantern. A child bounced on her knee. Leonard noticed an unopened box of cupcakes in the center of the table, presumably brought to celebrate the occasion.

"Sorry we're so late," Leonard said.

"We've been waiting an hour," the husband stammered.

"I know, it's just—" Leonard found himself looking away from the group. For what he was about to say, it helped to pretend he was alone. "There's been a change of plans."

"What do you mean?" his agent said.

The room fell silent, and Leonard's eyes settled on a piece of craft outlet decor mounted to the wall, a trio of lumpish pumpkins inscribed with some nonsense about faith, friends, and family.

"The house," Leonard said. "We're not selling it."

IT WAS A LONG DAY. BY NOON THEY HAD SECURED A U-HAUL. THEY DROVE to the storage unit, where they crammed the truck with as much stuff as they could. Then Norman went to rally help while Leonard drove to the old house and waited. Within an hour, a fleet of pickups arrived, and a beeline of workers from the glass factory began running furniture up the driveway and onto the porch. Leonard unlocked the front door, ambled through the foyer and living room, noticed the bare walls still tattooed with dust out-lines where the things had been. He meditated on the mausoleum silence of the place, the familiar chest of smells, stale air and aged wood, citrine bars of light diffused by the leaves, spindling shadows from a thin copse of trees just outside the window. What lived on in here, after the people, all the things had been moved out? A house that sweated out the memories, every ambient detail warmed with the past. Obscure moments that lingered like the taste of blood in his mouth, acute, brilliant in their cruelty, suspended in fleeting, single-frame images, time trapped in glass. Somehow, he'd held them in his body all these years, a child's glimpses of the world before he'd known its terrible limitations.

They worked into the evening. Leonard put his old bedroom back together, arranged furniture in the living room and dining room, and vacuumed the carpets. He was taking bags of trash to the curb when he heard laughter and noticed the long shadows of kids bounding their way door to door in the lingering light. He'd completely forgotten: it was Halloween! Inside, he casually mentioned this to Norman, who rushed off to the nearest gas station. Unfortunately, he returned with a contender for the worst excuse for treats of all time, some peanut-butter-cookie holdover from the Cold War. Worse, his brother had lacked the foresight to wrap the cookies individually, simply planted their mother by the door and instructed her to drop them into trick-or-treaters' bags, contaminating their plunder with crumbs. An hour later, a mob of kids returned to vandalize the house, where they threw eggs at the windows and hung toilet paper in the trees and even busted the stone figurine they'd placed on the porch that afternoon.

Exhausted and soaked with sweat, Leonard stepped onto the back porch and drew in the familiar musk of wood smoke and frost, his skin tingling in the cool air as he surveyed simple lawns strewn with dead leaves, the jaundiced light of the moon that spilled over the bare tree line, exposed veins against the night sky. A dog was barking somewhere, and he caught the laughter of the last kids trick-or-treating their way through the neighborhood. It was home, whatever that meant.

"Amazing job today," Norman said as he came out and stood beside Leonard on the porch, set an apprehensive hand on his brother's shoulder. "You did a good thing."

The work continued through the weekend. On Saturday, Leonard and Norman donated furniture from the storage facility to the Salvation Army, snuck items from the closets and garage and gave them away to glass factory employees. In the evenings, Leonard played chess with his brother or watched television in the den as their mother showed off some of the items she'd purchased from infomercials or the Home Shopping Network: There was the "Ab Shocker," which sent electronic diode signals into the abdomen and allegedly induced muscle growth; "Burger Magic," an oval griddle that promised to remove fat from beef patties; and "Pound Poker," a diet card game wherein players consumed only the items listed on the cards they picked that day.

"I cheat sometimes," she said.

At one point he debated driving up to Columbus, maybe visit one of the coffee shops on High Street or catch a movie at the theater he used to frequent in college, but he decided against the idea. On Saturday night, they ventured to a restaurant in town where everyone knew one another. Their eyes flickering in the low light, his brother and mother battered him with a fusillade of questions regarding the new venture he'd talked so much about over the phone several weeks before. He remained mum, aside from the basics: Things were going well, everything running according to plan, business as usual. After a while, they recognized his reluctance to discuss the issue. Thing was, a part of him wanted to tell them everything, about Patty and all the other crazy things that had happened to him in these past six months. It had occurred to him that he probably should talk about it, because he'd feel better if he did, but he didn't know how to explain the few details he wouldn't mind them knowing about. And where to begin, anyway? How about that time he'd ruined the largest corporate merger in marketing history? Or when he'd nearly died and spent the better part of a week in the hospital? Or how his company had been sold from under him, or how a journalist had sabotaged his career but he'd pretty much deserved it anyway, or how the boss who'd taught him the ropes and had basically been like a father to him now couldn't remember his name? Everything sounded so outlandish, it was hard to find the tragedy in it. He wasn't looking for sympathy because sympathy made him uncomfortable, and besides, being in the apology business, he knew that when people said "sorry" it was just a word they used to change the subject. What he wanted was a commiserating voice, and the only person he'd known who'd resembled one had literally just died on him, which had easily been the most traumatic thing he'd ever experienced, and he was still trying to get that all worked out, but he realized now he didn't have the tools to even begin figuring out how to do it, because the unremitting loss wasn't something he could measure, which made it difficult for him to analyze, and he didn't know whether he was processing everything correctly or what adequate public showing of grief was expected of him, and that seemed unfair, the social pressures we put on ourselves when we're suffering. He worried that if others learned what he'd experienced, they'd mistake the taciturnity for indifference and they'd judge him for things they didn't understand, so he figured it was better to go on not talking about it and accept the interminable punishments of defeat in this department too, just like everything else he'd tried his hand at. At one point, his mother brought him hurling back to shallow waters and asked if he planned to come home for Thanksgiving. Maybe, he said. If work wasn't too busy.

Leonard woke early on Sunday morning, packed the rental car with his suitcase and a box of simple childhood mementos he'd salvaged from his bedroom, showered, and got dressed while the coffee brewed. He supposed waking his mother would be the right thing to do, that she'd appreciate the effort of a formal goodbye, but he hated the forced sentimentality of moments like that, those maudlin epilogues demanded by mothers who needed their lives to simulate some made-for-TV movie whose plot required a redemption component before the final commercial break. He supposed there would always be some distance between them and realized he could probably do something about this, but it was just easier to keep things the way they were right now, and besides, he really wanted to get on the road, so he left a Post-it note on the television telling her he'd try to make it home in a few weeks for Thanksgiving. And then he was off, traversing rust-colored countryside and mile after mile of flat, fallow farmland, and when the highway opened up to four-lane blacktop, an acrid, heavy air filled his lungs and brought a thrilling sense of clarity to his mind. He drove all day, into West Virginia and beyond, over lazy, sinuous stretches of river crusted over with

ice and into the mouths of tunnels bored into mountains, through glaci-
ated valleys where rocky outcrops and sandstone crags leered over the road
and past blue ranges of sharp, sunlit hills whose shadows slid and wilted
eastward. The smells changed as the hours passed, from the pines of the
Pennsylvania turnpike to the brackish yeasts of the Chesapeake Watershed.
Sometime just before nightfall, serpents of smoke curled above low-lying
factories lining russet-colored cliffs, and the city came glistening into view,
its skyline resembling the jagged ridges of a key in the alpenglow of dusk,
canopied by a yellow haze that spanned the river with gas-flame wisps of
red and gold where the sun's failing light met an endless, shuddering valley
of ocean.

He found a service station on a trash-strewn strip of Jersey turnpike, pulled
over, and turned on his phone for the first time in four days, which reported
nine missed calls and three voicemails from Todd Armitage. In his final voicemail, Todd said he was quitting, which made sense. It took him a while to work
up the nerve, but he didn't like returning to the city with unfinished business,
so Leonard called Todd and told him everything, even the bits he'd intended
to leave out. Working, having a job, implied that you accepted a certain base-
line of frustration. How else could you describe spending your days performing
tasks you wouldn't do in your free time? But he'd never realized it could be as
mortifying as it was during the rundown of intimate details he relayed during
that phone call. Todd was more diplomatic than Leonard had anticipated, and,
thankfully, offered a good-faith reading of Leonard's naiveté regarding how foolproof he'd thought their venture would be. Stranger yet, he didn't say anything
in response to Leonard's admissions that he'd been managing a crisis of his own
the entire time. Whether Todd had met others who'd struggled with an addiction to munching on inanimate objects, or if he simply didn't believe him,
Leonard couldn't be sure. He said only that things hadn't worked out, and he
was going to Pollard PR and begging for his job back, and he hoped Leonard
understood. Yes, of course he did. Todd then said that starting a new company
was an ambitious undertaking and always carried some attendant risk. Leonard
had never seen things that way; the singularity of purpose that had driven him

never left much room to imagine a scenario in which his dream to open a crisis shop would be reduced to just another orphaned plan. And he definitely hadn't taken into consideration the possibility that his inability to run a business, or the fact that his talents were marginally capable at best, would be what ultimately unhorsed him. It just wasn't how things were supposed to be. Todd listened to all this charitably. Then he wished Leonard good luck and hung up.

HE SPENT THE EVENING ALONE IN HIS APARTMENT, SPRAWLED OUT ON the sofa in sweatpants. The news claimed predictive modeling projections showed Obama leading McCain by wide margins. A report found that many grocery stores now sold optimal shelf placement. The living room was empty and colorless, save for the pale glow from the TV. He changed channels, fed his fish, paced a while. There was one more task he promised himself he'd carry out before he went to bed, and he'd put it off all day because the speculative terror that accompanied this chess move left him frozen in equivocation. The drudgery of office life, the prospect of working for people he hated, seemed infinitely more tolerable when it involved doing something he actually liked, and the possibility of going back to such a spiritually profitless environment, of being trapped all over again, bore an unshakable cruelty, especially considering he'd already broken those chains several months ago. He'd always held the expectation that some combination of fate and hard work would shuttle him into a better life, and he'd spent years doing everything he was supposed to do to make that happen. He now realized this was tantamount to sabotaging himself in order to stay free. But he was all out of ambition and too tired to want much else aside from being able to make a living, and a life sentence among the cubicles or wallowing in penury with his dignity intact were the two levers available to him at this point. Why did it always seem like these were the only accessible paths forward? It was getting late, but he finally picked up the phone and, heart hiccuping in his chest, dialed Trotwood.

"Fine. I'll do it," Leonard said. "But I have some stipulations."

He was starving. Once he got off the phone, Leonard found a package of instant noodles in the cupboard, which he boiled over the stove and seasoned with powdered detergent. He brought out a roll of toilet paper and soaked wads of it in hand soap, then sat on the sofa and began stuffing everything into his mouth, eyes rolling back as he settled in, delirious and drooling in the relief of a long-spurned indulgence, the inbound thrill of climbing back in the saddle. Envisioning a proper dining experience, he returned to the kitchen and went to work, whipping up an extravagant bill of fare. He made a fingerling potato salad out of couch-cushion foam and a relish of French milled soap crumbs and sweet pickles, a quivering flan of microwaved dishwasher pods dripping with a hazelnut chocolate spread, artisanal cheeses doused in air freshener, a dryer sheet to sop up the juices. He ate until he was sick and ate some more, determined not to deny himself the buzz, the high, the white bang from which he'd abstained for so long, which returned to him now not unlike an old friend, familiar and natural as the lines etched in his palm. His stomach began to hurt, and in the moments during and after coating his bathroom in vomit, it occurred to him that he could probably kill himself this way if he wanted to, add drain cleaner or the old standby of antifreeze to the menu, but he ignored this impulse and continued to dine uninterrupted, and as he nibbled on chair legs and licked the surface area of his apartment clean, a sedative property in something had him drifting and disengaging from reality, and in the seconds before passing out, as sounds from the television drifted into the bathroom, a confusing medley of headlines danced in his head. Six tips on how to eat ethnic food without screaming racial epithets. Ten ways white people are being offensive when they say happy birthday. Eight hardships that will make others take you more seriously. Recipes for meatloaf—

He awoke in the harsh light of morning to the sounds of a waking city, blares of traffic from the street below. When his eyes settled on vomit-encrusted floors, the latticed bars of light that drew in from the window, his shame was eclipsed by an ineludible sensation of disappointment. He was still alive, and it felt terrible.

ON TUESDAY, HE RODE THE TRAIN TO GRAND CENTRAL, TREKKED TO Madison, and retraced the familiar route to his old office. In the foyer, former coworkers came out to welcome him back. After making the requisite acknowledgement and address of a happy return, he strolled across the floor where the aisles of cubicles had been and down the hallway, then scrutinized the makeshift sign taped to the door, a temporary substitute for his forthcoming nameplate, which he was assured would arrive sometime next week: "Leonard Lundell, Partner, the Appetite Factory, a division of Gurney Public Relations, a Pinnacle company."

It wasn't an entirely ideal situation. His salary was slightly below market, and he didn't get the office he'd wanted: A new creative director had taken the corner suite, Wanda's old space; and his former office was now being used as a sort of ad hoc storage facility for the holiday decorations. Instead, they'd put him in a small room at the end of the hall, which was drafty and cramped and had walls patched with colonies of black spots he suspected were mold. But he had a Partner title now, which sounded much better than Senior VP, and he got to keep the Appetite Factory name, and, as a bonus, they'd also agreed to hire Beau as his assistant. So, in a way, it all worked out.

The procedure for handling client campaigns was different from what he was accustomed to. Where Leonard used to simply flap concepts with his team, Pinnacle mandated a more stepwise process, including a systemized discussion procedure called "ideation sessions," where he was forced to sit in a boardroom with middle-aged jowl-shakers and jog through a pre-written forensic of tactics and principles while everyone listened with all the enthusiasm of someone waiting for a late-night train. The strategy was then sent to lawyers for approval, as well as to the various ancillary services departments, who evaluated the campaign under consideration to make sure it squared with everything from research analysis to social media solutions to turnaround time. Leonard was told each campaign would then be revisited once a month to monitor short-term and long-term benchmarks. While he didn't understand this process, he wasn't surprised by any of it. Impressions took precedence over impact; campaigns were decided by sophisticated algorithms based on millions of data points. Everything was beholden to conversion rates and billing. The work exhibited an obscurantism that invariably occurred when ideas were crafted for executive approval as opposed to public interest. Anything remotely original, let alone provocative, was a dispensable casualty. They'd paid a small fortune to buy his brand because they thought it offered something new, but the production process rendered his efforts so toothless, it ended up resembling what was being done by every agency in town.

The day crawled by. He took calls and attended meetings, concocted phony crises and diversionary strategies for start-ups and established brands. Clients came and went—executives, B-list celebrities, Silicon Valley technologists who uttered the word "disruption" twenty times in every sentence—and Leonard listened to their windy platitudes and marketplace grievances before offering whatever glib bromide he thought might assuage them and senior management. Outside the office, the waiting room filled like a leper colony awaiting the succor of a faith healer, and by noon a line snaked from Leonard's door through the office and into the foyer. Beau organized the crowd, coordinated appointments, and arranged billing and supplied clients with coffee before ushering them into Leonard's office. Waiting executives flipped through newspapers or played on cellphones, exchanged rumors they'd heard about the Appetite Factory and its enigmatic founder, the Minister of Nonsense or the High Priest of Bullshit or whatever moniker the trades were calling him this week. In between meetings, coworkers stopped by to welcome him back. They repeated variations of the same stories they'd told him months before. He nodded and laughed and looked them in the eyes and pretended it was the first time he'd heard them, amazed at people's ability to have an entire conversation without producing anything resembling actual communication.

He had a real job. He was a Partner now, a success by any contemporary measure. Everything was planned, laid out; he knew how tomorrow would be and the day after. And yet, seeing the years, the decades uncoil before him left him panicked, riddled with existential dread. By mid-afternoon, he swore the walls had lost several inches. He found himself staring at the clock that hung above his filing cabinet. Its second hand moved at an impossibly slow pace. He was just like everyone else now, on the same turning wheel for the rest of his life.

At seven o'clock, just as he was shutting down his computer for the night, his phone rang. A prized client's brand manager said he needed three new concepts by the end of the week or he'd lose his PR budget for the year. Leonard made several harried calls to coworkers, but no one picked up, so he fired up his computer and commenced outlining ideas. He stared at the screen for a moment before writing a sentence, then rewrote several variations of it. He wrote another sentence, scrolled down and back up, copied and pasted that sentence into the previous sentence, then deleted the document. Frustrated, as lights began to shutter outside his office, he decided it could wait until tomorrow. He gathered his things, locked the door, and walked empty halls, which smelled curiously like new shoes. In an alcove just before the photocopy machines, he found Beau on his knees, jamming a plastic paper tray into an uncooperative printer.

"Don't stay too late," Leonard said.

"That's a luxury I don't have," Beau said. "These jobsworth pricks rat-packed me into putting together promotional materials for some campaign they want to roll out before Thanksgiving." He set the tray on the carpet and unfolded a pocketknife, which he used to twist and manipulate the tray's underbelly of springs and levers. "You know, I can't help but feel a little ripped-off. I went from being an account executive to basically becoming a glorified secretary. Growth opportunity, my ass."

"I know you didn't have a burning desire to come back," Leonard said. "The economy being what it is, we didn't have much choice. At least having a job makes this situation somewhat better than mulling over our grievances from an unemployment line."

"Better, hell. True story: This morning someone from the art department asks if I have a spare USB cord. I say sure, you want a three-foot cable or the six-foot? She says, 'What's the difference?' These are the types we're dealing with here. Being paid to work with these lunatics is like putting mustard on a shit sandwich."

Beau tried to shove the tray into the printer, but it didn't budge. Frustrated, he kicked it down the hall. Then he settled back on his haunches and let the notion stew inside him.

"I was in a dark place about this shit for a minute," Beau said. "I'd been dumb enough to think I could escape the person I was by leaving where I came from. All I found was another place I don't belong. But I figure the worst thing you can do is spend your life peddling some fake version of yourself, just like how you can't change something just by using different words to describe it. At least being at a job that constantly lets me know how small I am is a daily reminder I'm not what I do for a living. It takes some people their entire lives to figure that out, so I guess I'm the one-eyed resident in blind country in that regard. Truth is, I don't need to be rich. I'm still young. I'll keep a job to pay the bills while I spend the rest of my time focusing on my passions."

"What are your passions?" Leonard said.

"Shit if I know. I'm just glad it's not work."

A battalion of vacuums was making its way through the halls as Leonard continued across the floor and into the foyer. As he exited the office and waved to the janitor, the reality of what he'd done began to sink in. He'd made sacrifices and risked everything and stuck obstinately to his principles, yet he'd still wound up back where he'd started. His greatest success had been, by any traditional metric, a failure. All he had left was the consoling myth that his life held some greater purpose through the same small victories that crowded out everyone else's thoughts in the squirrel cage. Better living through lower expectations. On her best day, Patty couldn't have contrived a worse fate for him. He pondered this as he walked the hall, where he found Griffin Cruz waiting by the elevator bay.

"Funny how they put the travel division next to crisis," Cruz said as they boarded the elevator. "Guess we both send a lot of people to Belize, am I right?"

"You and that stupid joke," Leonard said.

They exited the building and headed west on Fortieth while Cruz brought Leonard up to speed on office gossip. Pinnacle had hired a new Gurney creative director who held early-morning staff meetings and took everyone to the woodshed. The entire office hated him. Ron Viola from finance and Karen Clinkenbeard from tech were having an affair. They were keeping things hush-hush, which was ridiculous, because even the janitors knew about it. The incoming account execs were young and partied hard. Oh, and Pinnacle had rented the Marriott Marquis for the holiday bash this year, and it was sure to be a bacchanal.

A warm front had moved in, and the snow from last week's storm had melted, lending a preternatural balminess to the November air that roused people from the indoors, the streets mobbed and airy now and buzzing with tourist laughter. At Seventh Avenue, they headed north and made their way under Times Square's arcade of lights, where wonder-struck crowds gathered to gawk at the city's neon nerves. Here the ritual of consumption resembled something like a clumsy ballet: Phones raised, they paraded under the panorama of jumbotrons and pulsing billboards, hypnotized by the images of Broadway shows and financial news crawls and hundreds of flashing spectaculars promoting soda brands and new-model-year cars and erectile dysfunction cures, palimpsests of electro-kinetic text that appeared as though they'd been projected onto the sky. These beamish visitors had come from every corner of the globe, traveled like moths to an electric lamp to witness this simple spectacle, this sculpture park of advertisements. What did this grotesque fantasia offer them? Presumably, it promised something greater than the quiet disappointments of their inner lives, as it had for him the first time he'd laid eyes on this fabled parcel of skyline all those years ago, some pernicious myth about their dreams they'd overheard in a TV commercial, a contestants' row of elusive freedoms always manifested in the same language of fortune cookie clichés. They'd spent years chasing them as though they were extensions of their own shadow, enculturated lifetimes to this endless pursuit of becoming some kind of anything, but here they were, at the world's crossroads, standing in the doorway of those grand futures where they'd shed the lives they'd inherited for the fictions they deserved, head-on toward some distant outpost just beyond the lights of the TGI Fridays.

"Took me two hours to vote this morning," Cruz said. "I hear the polls are seeing record-high turnouts."

"I'll be honest," Leonard said. "I completely forgot."

"You want to get a drink or something? Maybe find a bar and watch the election?"

"I don't know," Leonard said. "I have some things to do."

"No, you don't," Cruz said. "Let's get a drink."

It occurred to him that getting drunk somewhere and commiserating with a coworker on the incommensurable torments of office life wasn't an entirely bad idea. And so they pushed through the crowd, and when they breached a clearing on Forty-Fifth, gales of applause broke through the street as the first election results came in over the rows of screens above them, now accompanied by live news footage of crowds beginning to gather in Chicago's Grant Park. He'd heard somewhere that only tourists looked up in this town, which was funny, because that was all he ever did, and as they kept walking west toward Hell's Kitchen, the night sky pulsed with a vermilion afterglow as the clouds roiled with the thrum of the city before rippling out above the river and the orange fingers of light that trembled along cliffs of Jersey shoreline, already gaining size as they approached Ninth Avenue. Then they turned right and pressed north and headed toward no place in particular.

Thank you!

First, I'd like to express my gratitude to Stephanie Beard and Todd Bottorff for taking a chance with this novel and for recognizing its potential, and for allowing me to share this story with the world without compromising my voice or vision. Your enthusiasm, encouragement, support, and guidance throughout this process have been invaluable. Thank you, Stephanie and Todd.

Thanks to Phil Gaskill, Ryan Smernoff, and Ashley Strosnider for their deft and careful edits, their suggestions, and for giving these pages the attention they deserve. Thank you, editors.

I really like the cover design! Thank you, William Ruoto.

Thanks to these friends who saw early drafts of this novel and whose thoughtful input, criticism, and impressively close reading of the material helped me shape it into the work it became: Ellen Finegold Bregman, Cailin Barrett-Bressack, Norman Danzig, Oliver Edsforth, Pierre Hauser, Peter Kapp, Patricia Kruger, Jeff Loeb, Leslie Margolis, Mia McNiece, Matthew Riordan, Chandler Klang Smith, and Zak Van Buren. Thank you, friends.

There were a few scenes in this novel that required medical expertise. For these scenes, I relied on the input and advice of Rebecca J. Allred, MD. Thank you, Dr. Allred.

Thanks to these great teachers who taught me just about everything I know about writing: Jonathan Dee, James Lasdun, Dale Peck, Helen Schulman, Jackson Taylor, and Stephen Wright. Thank you, teachers.

Thanks to my colleagues at the Gotham Writers Workshop. Particular thanks to Dean of Faculty Kelly Caldwell and President Alex Steele. Good bosses are a rare and cherished find. Thank you, bosses.

Thanks to everyone at the J.R. O'Dwyer Co.: Steve Barnes, Jane Landers, Kevin McCauley, Christine O'Dwyer, John O'Dwyer, and Melissa Werbell. Thanks to Jack O'Dwyer, who may be gone, but will never be forgotten.

Thanks to my family and friends—for everything.

Above all, special thanks are in order to Stephen Wright, without whom this novel would never have been completed.

ABOUT THE AUTHOR

JON GINGERICH is a fiction instructor at the Gotham Writers' Workshop in New York. Since 2006, he's served as the editor of *O'Dwyer's* magazine. His short stories have been published in *The Saturday Evening Post*, *The Malahat Review*, *Pleiades*, *Grist*, *Stand*, *Oyez Review*, *The Helix*, and others. Jon's freelance writing regularly appears in trade and consumer magazines, as well as web outlets dedicated to politics, culture, and writing craft. He's a graduate of The New School's creative writing MFA program. He lives in New York City.